ONLY  HUMMINGBIRDS FLY BACKWARDS

ROSIE PARKER

The Book Guild Ltd

First published in Great Britain in 2022 by
The Book Guild Ltd
Unit E2, Airfield Business Park
Harrison Road
Market Harborough
Leicestershire, LE16 7UL
Freephone: 0800 999 2982
www.bookguild.co.uk
Email: info@bookguild.co.uk
Twitter: @bookguild

Typeset in 11pt Minion Pro

Printed and bound by CPI Group (UK) Ltd, Croydon, CR0 4YY

ISBN 978 1914471 117

British Library Cataloguing in Publication Data.
A catalogue record for this book is available from the British Library.

Dedicated to my brother

'Fiction is a lie that tells us true things, over and over.'

NEIL GAIMAN

'either you take to believing in miracles or you stand still like the hummingbird.'

HENRY MILLER

Prologue

*I*t's a glorious sunny day in April 1989, when Jake Johnson comes haring along a Cambridgeshire country road on his friend's motorcycle. He is already late for a rugby match: he's playing on the right wing.

Riding along, Jake goes – Whoops – as the bike's back wheel skitters beneath him when he takes a corner at speed. Tricky fucker, he thinks as he accelerates out of it, correcting his course and holding on tight to the handlebars as if to the reins of a bucking horse. Pig of a bike's still not handling well. He's been working on it for Mike.

Being a Japanese bike, it's lighter than his British Beesa and rides higher in the saddle. Still, the road's dry and fast, the weather light and bright, the fields green and fit to burst with a promise of spring. Ahh. Life is good.

He thinks of his wife Angie, at home, preparing their Sunday lunch, of the lads up ahead at the rugby pitch, of the pint which will be waiting on the clubhouse bar for him after they've played – its head topped with froth, the side of the glass cold, the tug on his throat of that first draught. He can almost taste it. He's not going to think of the row he had earlier with his mother. She can be a right cow. Going on about Ronnie like that.

Stopping at the crossroads, he looks right, then left; it's all clear, and he opens up the throttle as up ahead is a straight stretch with nothing on the road. He's just changed up a gear, when a pheasant darts out from the side and stands stock still right in the middle of the road. On hearing Jake's roaring approach, the stupid fucker doesn't move, just slowly swivels its head to watch as Jake executes an easy swerve around it and up onto the grass verge, gripping the handlebars and easing up on the gas as he travels thundering and juddering along as if the verge was the cobblestones outside The Old Duke pub on Bristol's harbourside; those same cobblestones along which he rode, as a kid, with a piece of card pegged to the spokes of his pushbike so it made a put-put-put sound like a small moped.

That's got it, he thinks, as he grapples the Yamaha more under *his control: and now his heart isn't pounding so fast, and he allows himself to feel some relief, as overhead a beneficent sun peeks out from behind a cloud, reaching forth its long finger of warmth to caress his cheek. He remembers how the other day, when he and Angie had been chopping vegetables together, Mike had come by to ask him to have a look at this Yamaha because it wasn't running properly, how the bike's kickstand kept coming down and scratching along the surface of the road, creating sparks like the top of the prong on the back of a dodgem car.*

Jake eases back some more – Phew, that was close *– getting his feet ready to help slow the fucker right down, when the wheel appears to get stuck in some sort of rut along the verge, and he isn't sure he'll be able to get it off the grass – maybe he should stop it here on the verge. Angie is in his mind, turning to smile at him she says, 'I expect you can fix it,' and it's like he can reach down to touch the top of his small daughter Sarah's head which is warm from the sunshine – if only he can wrestle this bike to a standstill – and Sarah has that smile she gets when she looks up at him, and it's then, right then, that the kickstand flicks down, catches in the soft ground, or a tree root, and he's being flipped off – soaring through the air.*

This is going to hurt, he thinks, as he hits the tarmac – Oof!

– tuck and roll, tuck and roll. His bike training kicking in: if you come off a bike, go shoulder first and tuck and roll.

Fuck it, his helmet is wrenched off – that smarts – and bam bam bounce bounce – the motorbike, not falling over on to its side, not bouncing or skidding along on its own trajectory is – and what are the chances of this? – bouncing along behind him, following the same course – would you believe it? – the same line, hurtling towards him like some asteroid on a collision course with the Earth.

The human brain contains one hundred billion neurones, which is roughly the number of stars in the Milky Way or the number of trees in the Amazon Rainforest.

He raises his arm in a reflexive defensive movement – the brain is capable of voluntary and involuntary actions – *as the bike on its final bounce falls out of the sky heading straight for the globe of his head – reminding him of that moment in* The Hitchhiker's Guide to the Galaxy *where the whale hurtles inexorably towards planet Earth.*

'Luckily it's about to land on his head,' says Dad. As – splat – brain cells explode like supernovas as worlds within worlds collide in a blinding flash.

'Stay where you are, mate. Don't get up. Has somebody called for an ambulance? You, go, go, run to that house. I'll stay with him. Oh, Christ. I can see his brains or something.'

Your brain weighs about 3lbs and has the texture of blancmange. It is bathed in cerebrospinal fluid to stop it bumping about on the sides of your skull. In the case of a forceful blow to the head, the impact can send the brain crashing against the opposite wall of the cranium, much like a boxer thrown against the ropes. This is called a contrecoup injury, which can result in being what is known as "punch drunk", or far, far worse.

Ding ding. And he's trying to get up on to his feet, but someone has exchanged his legs for rubbery ones. He feels like he might giggle. This is all so ludicrously hilarious.

'Stay still, mate.'

Must get home. I'll be fine… must…

He topples over.

A snatch of the band Them's "Here Comes the night" plays in his head – how weird.

Ron. Veronica.

Oh, fuck!

…then starry, starry nights and black.

ONE

Friday in Bristol, July 1990

To look at me, I probably appear your everyday, run-of-the-mill new mother. Going about my business. Smiling, blowing raspberries into the delicious-smelling neck of my baby daughter, taking her to the park – where I throw her up in the air to hang for a nanosecond, before she starts her fall, and I catch her.

You may even think I have it all: new wife, new mother, lawyer husband attractive enough to draw admiring glances from other women. Nice house. Good income (on paper). I wouldn't blame you if you did think so; I'm sure you wouldn't be the first – or the last. But the truth?

There are days when I'm merely going through the motions. Trying not to scare others by having the screaming ab dabs.

'What is it you're hoping for?' asks Carol, my therapist.

'The impossible,' I say.

I have never believed in God, and yet there was a time – soon afterwards – when I prayed in earnest, knelt on harsh floors inside chilly stone churches with high-vaulted stained-glass windows and fervently tried to magic up the impossible. Once we believed in magic – my twin brother Jake and me. When we were children, we'd collect plants, petals, insects, all to stir together in a battered saucepan full of water. We'd chant our incantations and homemade spells, and I made myself believe – even if it was a very faint hope – that if I wished hard enough, if I sent out enough positive energy, repeated affirmations over and over, asked guardian angels, believed in this, bought into that... then maybe, just maybe, I could conjure up a miracle...

It's all bollocks, of course. The magic never arrived – either with a fanfare or in a small, whispering way. The universe remained deaf dumb and blind like those three brass monkeys which used to sit on our parents' mantelpiece.

Still, I'm getting ahead of things.

Let me introduce myself. I'm Veronica – or Ronnie – and that geeky, good-looking-if-you-like-that-sort-of-thing man giving me a lift to my therapist is Gerry. We're not long married – I forget the exact date...

Tomorrow we're off on holiday to France. I can't recall whose bright idea that was. Probably Jake's wife Angie's. Even though it's only fifteen months since his motorbike accident (I can tell you the exact number of weeks, days, hours since – but I won't bore you). Angie's way of coping is to employ Optimism (with a capital 'O') and the adoption of cheery catchphrases: "Everything will be all right" being her current favourite. As for me... I've become adept at the whole "Acting As If". Some days I even pass for human.

'To help you over this period, Veronica, the trick is to act "As If"', Carol, my therapist, explained, using those annoying double-air quotes.

'As if what?'

'As if you're happy. As if you're a good mother, as if you can mix socially – and before you know it, all this will be true.'

So now I'm getting pretty good at it. Having had lots of practice.

I stare out of the car window as the world rushes by while Gerry drives with his usual disregard for other traffic on the road. These days I can't summon up the energy to tut. I'm worried about our finances too, finding it hard to fathom why he agreed (without consulting me) to this madness (said holiday), when we are so overstretched with the mortgage on our sweet little house on the edge of Clifton's Downs – a house which is now in negative equity, meaning we can't afford to move or increase our loan; and we've an overdraft so large the bank manager has warned that if we don't get our affairs "in order" we could well be declared bankrupt. We've borrowed from his dad – we're barely keeping afloat now we don't have my money coming in. And there's no way I can work. Not for now. 'Let's worry about the money later,' Gerry had said. 'You need a holiday, and Angie could do with a break.' (*What, another one?* I'd thought rather unkindly – because we'd been popping up and down to Cambridgeshire to "give her a break" for some months now.) 'It'll be fine,' he said.

I wasn't sure then, and I'm not sure now.

Anyway, so here he is, dropping me off.

Once settled in Carol's consulting room, she comes straight out with her killer question. 'Where do you see yourself in five years' time?'

I stare at her as if she's asked an impossible-to-solve conundrum, my brain refusing to conjure up any imagined future for me at all. Even with my daughter. I am suitably appalled, but still nothing comes. We sit with her water feature doing its bubbling away thing and I think of how ghosts, flashes, images seep into my consciousness, often seeming more real than my every day. Time has not been behaving itself: time has been dislocated, disintegrated, discombobulated.

And words feel inadequate to the task. Several minutes,

maybe ten, maybe two, pass. (Time, see? Not behaving.) I have been known to sit for the whole hour of our session without saying a word.

'I... I...' I try, and then cease.

Carol does that steepling thing with her hands which comedy television priests like Derek Nimmo do. 'Why not try writing down how you feel?'

'I wouldn't know where to begin.'

A pause – not so much pregnant as expecting twins. 'How about writing letters to your twin brother Jake...'

Twin, it's close to twinge, isn't it, is all that comes through, that and the feel of the invisible indefatigable cord which links Jake and me being twanged. Twin, twinge, twang.

'...you don't have to actually send the letters.' She smiles her encouraging smile. I'm now familiar with her whole repertoire. The more common being oh-come-on-we-don't-really-think-that-do-we smile, through to the I'm-doing-my-best-to-empathise-with-you smile, and to this one.

'The physical act of writing down what you are feeling or what you might want to say to Jake, can help. Enormously.' She pushes her box of tissues towards me. I had no idea I was leaking tears.

'There's something else you may want to focus on.' She waits as I do my utmost to compose myself. 'Why not try and see this holiday as a positive? A chance to get your own marriage back on track. Find a way to look to the future, hm?'

'I guess.' I blow my nose, and then go on to say how I feel there's too much riding on this trip.

'And how are things between you and Gerry?'

My gaze drops down to my lap. 'I don't know,' I say as I listen to the babbling water and then begin to babble myself (perhaps that's what it's there for: to get the babbling going?). Lifting my eyes to briefly meet hers, I say, 'He's been wonderful, I guess.

Taking Finty off to give me a rest when I can't bear it all. But it's like he's tip-toeing around me and that can't be good, can it? I know we've discussed this before, but I still doubt we would have got married if I hadn't become pregnant, and then... there's what happened to Jake. Me and Gerry haven't had much chance to be properly on our own, you know, not since... what with all the worry. So I don't feel we've bedded in as parents, do you see? Everything went to shit so soon after Finty was born.'

'It sounds as if Gerry cares for you very much. My question to you is, do you love him?' she asks, softly.

'Honestly? I don't know. I suppose I must do.'

'Going away can put extreme pressure on any relationship, and that's without the added stress of spending twenty-four/seven with Jake and his family.' She gives me a rather watery smile. 'Promise yourself that you won't make any rash decisions when you're away. Especially as we've already established, haven't we, that you've a tendency to run away from relationships if the going gets tough.' (I can't help that burst of song in my head – "When the going gets tough, the tough get going".) 'Of course,' she continues, 'in the past you had your twin to steady you, or to help pick up the pieces.'

She pauses as if for effect.

'My advice to you, is to take one day at a time,' she says. (Being a wise and warm woman, she's prone to the odd platitude.) 'How is his wife getting along? Angie, isn't it?'

As if she doesn't know. Angie has, after all, featured large in our sessions.

Carol sits back in her mud-brown easy chair – not looking terribly at ease – and then leans forwards ever so slightly. The air is expectant. Clearly this is my turn to speak.

'Angie's in denial,' I say. 'Yes, I've been thinking it over and it's true. I have suggested counselling to her, but she's dead set against it. As far as she's concerned Jake's recovery is their business and nobody else's, and if Jake works hard enough he'll keep on getting better until he's all fixed.' I close my eyes. 'Fat chance.' I sigh and open my eyes to see Carol hasn't moved a muscle. 'Angie's taking a New Age approach to his head injury,' I say, looking down at my hands, which are oddly still and flat in my lap as if waiting for something. 'She's got him on a special diet which seems to involve the soaking of this horrendous big mushroom in some filthy concoction...' My voice tails off as I think of all the potions and flummery out there, and how I might well have taken that route myself had I not been a physiotherapist and known what's what. Knowledge having disproved the adage that it equals power. It's done nothing but render me powerless.

'The thing is,' I say, this time looking Carol straight in the eye, 'I *know*, you see. Being a physiotherapist, I just know that he will *never* be himself again. Because the vast majority of his brain damage is irreversible – and that's a fact.'

This is when she asks me, 'What are you hoping for, from this trip?' And this is when those two words clang around the small room, bouncing off the walls to land in my lap like a solid black ball.

'The impossible,' I reply.

Our one-hour sessions are held in her home, once a week. It's a tiny terrace in Greenbank facing the graveyard opposite the now-derelict Elizabeth Shaw chocolate factory. 'Death by chocolate desserts,' I once quipped. Carol says any return of my sense of humour is a good sign, and it's imperative that I practise not feeling guilty. But I do. Feel guilty, that is. Each time I laugh, each time a sizzle of happiness threatens to fizz, each time I forget. Mind you, it's hard to forget when you have that feeling – how to describe it... is it a pain? It's more than that.

It can make you gasp, catch you unawares as if a hole has been ripped out of your middle and you're disembowelled like

John Lennon's character in *Oh! What A Lovely War* (have you seen it?). On such occasions the pain is so bad it's an effort not to clutch at my innards to stop them spilling out – splat! – all hot and steamy onto the pavement.

Other times pain snarls and growls like a wolf in the forest gnawing away at a carcass.

'That's good,' says Carol. 'Write it down. Keep a diary. Write poetry.'

But that would be self-indulgent, wouldn't it? As if something positive could ever be gained from any of this. I can't read a book, watch television, go to the cinema: any entertainment – any moments of joy are a betrayal.

Except for the chuckles, the plump, gorgeous squidginess of my baby girl, a child full of smiles and sunbeams, born only three weeks before The Accident.

What I have been learning from Carol is that the brain is an amazing organ. It protects us by shutting off/shutting down. I voice a hope that this holiday might help.

'That's the spirit,' she says.

We search for the positives.

Dear Jake,

I'm supposed to write you letters as part of my therapy. So here goes. Carol said that if I got stuck, I could begin with "I remember". Okay, so here goes. I remember, I remember, I remember – ahhh... here's one – we're at our old house in Bristol. It's the end of that long, hot summer of 1976 – when you got your first motorbike.

Do you remember? I can see us now – the two of us – in Dad's workshop, which is also his garage. We're nut brown from days spent sunbathing, swimming at Portishead Lido, and hanging out on College Green. That day, we'd just returned from a day trip to Weston-super-

Mud in Dad's new Zephyr Zodiac. Huge, monster of a car. Once we used to go to Brean all the time, didn't we? Where sand dunes shift and change to bury their secrets – Mum and Dad don't like going there any more after... well... you know...

Back then I had long, dyed blonde hair. You used to call me a right poseur. D'you remember? I was probably swishing it back – all stiff from the salt of the sea. We both turn as one when a sudden wind rattles the doors as if trying to come inside. But we're safe and warm. Together. At the far end of the garage squats Dad's tool bench – his pride and joy – equipped with an oiled stone for sharpening chisels, and those two brutish vices – one for woodworking and one for bigger stuff (I can't remember what).

If I close my eyes, I can almost taste those workshop aromas: they are male, mixed in with wood shavings, a leftover whiff of Dad's pipe tobacco and the cloying smell of that glue which comes in a tin. Pwah! Had a right whiff, didn't it? Dad would heat it up in a saucepan of water over his primus stove.

This particular day I seem to recall you tinkering with this second-hand bike which you bought cheap from Trade It: having a go at customising the thing.

'Did you know, Ron,' you say, 'that consciousness is more than the sum total of brain cells in your head?'

I probably say something like, 'Fascinating,' not bothering to keep a sarky tone out of my voice, as I don't want to hear about Zen and the bloody Art of bloody Motorcycle Maintenance again (and again). How you loved that book.

You probably wore a pair of cut-off Levi 501s, with me worrying that Mum will go mental once she sees those greasy oil marks. I can see us now – you throwing an oily rag at my head, me ducking just in time. 'I hate that wanky Zen rubbish,' I say, wandering behind you to flick your ear, and then returning to my perch on the workbench with the full insouciance of an eighteen-year-old girl who's pretty and knows it.

'Shut up and pass me one of those,' you say. Or might not have. You know what tricks memory can play.

I fastidiously pass over some spanner or other, careful not to get muck on my new pink halter neck top. You like to think and talk whilst doing things. Or rather, did. I don't know if you still do. Suppose not.

You and your motorbikes... You're extending the forks on this one, hoping that once you're finished it'll be like Peter Fonda's Harley Davidson in Easy Rider. You've got it gleaming all spick and span, with its polished chrome and shiny red paint.

This motorbike is what will prove to be the first of many. I never did like them. Too scarily unprotected. I'm not a daredevil like you.

'You're a long time dead, sis,' you liked to say.

I know people say we're like two peas in a pod, but sometimes, you can be really annoying; sometimes you got right on my tits. Sometime later you'll say it's that sense of freedom which motorbikes give you, which you love. The thrill of almost flying: like when you're a kid and you run really fast, your feet slapping the pavement harder and harder, each step a little higher and longer, until both feet are right off the ground and for whole moments at a time, you're flying.

You used to like running, and jumping, and climbing, and swinging from trees. Then it was sport, painting and singing in bands, pot-holing. Anything new.

But I know exactly where those little scars are on

your head. Scars from coming a cropper in one scrape or another: cracking your head open – falling off walls, tripping over kerbs, stumbling into sharp corners.

'It's lucky he's got such a tough nut,' Dad would say.

'It's a blinkin' wonder he's got any brains left at all,' Mum says.

Back on that day I expect your too-long hair hides those tiny bald patches as it curls over your collar, like a right proper greaser's.

Your leather jacket with the Stars and Stripes, is slung across the workbench on which I'm swinging my legs backwards and forwards, watching you twiddle and fiddle with nuts and bolts and bits and pieces of bike, which I can't believe will ever go back to where they came from.

Steppenwolf's "Born to Be Wild" probably blares out from our Dansette record player. Sounds clichéd, but I'll bet you were playing that song. Those days being pre-punk: you into prog rock bands like Black Sabbath, Pink Floyd, Led Zepplin, 10CC; me more Roxy Music, T Rex, funk and disco.

I've decided university isn't for me – what with all those smelly hippies – instead I can't wait to get out into the real world and earn some money.

'So, sis,' you say, standing up tall (Here we go, I think). 'What if Planet Earth is the equivalent of an atom, and our universe of planets and suns all make up a larger organism? You know, in the same way that we – our bodies – are made up of all these molecules and atoms. Think about it.'

I'm giving you a quizzical look.

'Just because we can't see or know it from our own perspective, doesn't mean it isn't so.'

'Right. What you're saying is that we're teensy-weensy

people living on some molecule – our planet – which in turn is part of a bigger whole. Hm…'

Those were the sorts of questions which exercised the young minds of you and me, back when our childhood was informed by C.S. Lewis's Narnia, Dennis Wheatley's The Ka of Gifford Hilary, black and white movies like The Incredible Shrinking Man… Star Trek.

Back then, I suppose I believed the soul was like a mini me living deep within a larger external me. And that once you die, this soul is freed from the body and released to a different plane, to one of the worlds within worlds within worlds.

That was then. When we were kids. I know different now.

'So,' I seem to remember saying, probably trying to sound bright and breezy, 'you're off to Bognor Regis next week?' (I mean, Bognor. Whoever goes to a teacher's training college in Bognor?) It'll be our first real separation, and fear flutters my chest.

I'll miss you, I say, without speaking.

You look up and wink. 'Don't worry, sis. I'll be back.'

That's what you promised: that you'd be back. You probably don't remember all this. You haven't kept your promise, though, have you? You git.

TTFN Ron xxx

TWO

Saturday and We're on Our Way to France

Finally, we're at Gatwick airport.

'Cutting it a bit fine, aren't we?' says the check-in girl, stating the bleeding obvious, as is their wont. She beams a heavily-made-up-plasticky smile which they all seem to possess. 'Better get a wiggle on.'

'No shit, Sherlock,' I mutter. I don't mean to be bad-tempered, but it's been one of those mornings in a whole string of mornings.

At the security point, the airport X-ray scanner displays the innards of my bag: camera, cotton wool, creams, pencils, paper and other objects which don't look like anything I packed or even possess. Finty's little rucksack reveals her toys in varying positions of surprise: Winnie-the-Pooh standing on his head, one arm in the ear of Clown, who appears to have Duplo stuck up his nose.

We're almost at Departures, and Finty is wriggling away like mad, kicking her heels against my side and grizzling, so I lower her to the ground.

'Gerry, can you?'

'What?'

'Finty.'

He hoists her onto his hip, while up ahead I can see Jake sitting in one of the airport seats. (Of course, this will be the first time you'll have met him since The Accident. Prepare yourself for a bit of a shock.)

I make to walk towards him – he's about twenty feet away – when Angie steps in front of me: arms crossed. 'Where the bloody hell have you been?' she hisses. Gerry is busy wiping Finty's nose.

'Angie, look, I'm sorry,' I say, trying to see Jake over her shoulder.

My twin – who has clearly spotted me – half waves and then sets about getting out of his chair in that awkward way of people with partial paralysis, as he lurches to the left, pushing up in a kind of a slow reversal of a wonky backflip.

Angie has now turned to Gerry. 'Hello, Gerry, you all right?'

He smiles at her. 'You're here then,' he says.

'Clearly.'

Gerry is dusting something off Finty's dress, and I'm watching Jake, who's making his way towards us, leaning to the right and swinging his left leg to clear the ground. As he laboriously bobs and weaves – like hapless Bob Hope's Painless Potter in the gunfight scene of *Paleface* – I can't help but grin. (*He shoots to the left, so lean to the right. The wind's in the East so turn to the West...*) We used to love that movie.

C'mon, Jake, I encourage in my head. *That's it. Keep going. Good man...*

'We were worried you weren't going to make it,' Angie continues as she fiddles in her bag for a packet of Polos, pops one in her mouth without offering me one.

'I truly am sorry we're late,' I try again. 'But Gerry had to nip to the Law Centre on the way. You know how he likes to think the whole place will fall apart without him.'

'Thanks a lot,' he says, pushing his glasses back up his nose.

'Fine. But we could do without the extra hassle,' says Angie. 'It's not good for Jake's chakra.'

Mentally, I roll my eyes.

Lauren, their youngest, has toddled over to greet Finty. There's a mere four weeks between the two of them, and they look so alike they too could be twins. 'Hello, sweet pea,' I say, and she rewards me with a toothy grin. 'Say hello to Lauren, Finty,' giving my daughter a gentle push towards her cousin. The two girls shyly regard each other for a moment then reach out to hold hands and waddle across to the airport seats. Together.

'Play nicely, now,' I call after them.

'Jake was so worried,' continues Angie. 'I had to administer Rescue Remedy.' Angie's into alternative remedies big time. Like a born again. She's also oblivious to the fact that Jake has now arrived and is hovering behind her.

''Lo, Ron,' he says, awkwardly negotiating his way around Angie, whilst I grin from ear to ear.

'Jake! Jakie, Jakie!' I envelop him in a hug, almost knocking him off balance.

'Careful,' he half-slurs, half-slurps.

'Good to see you, bruv,' I answer, clapping him on the back, while Angie still looks cross.

'How you doing, Jake?' says Gerry – all full of bonhomie as he reaches to shake Jake's right hand, remembers and goes for the left. 'How are things, okay?'

Jake nods, clearly delighted.

'Right.' Angie frowns up at the board. 'Best get a move on, everybody.'

'Wait!' Gerry gestures for everyone to stop. 'Aren't we forgetting somebody?'

As one, we turn to stare at him. 'Who?'

'Where's that lovely Sarah?'

He pretend casts about for Angie and Jake's eldest girl. A charade, as he knows perfectly well that seven-year-old Sarah is being all shy and hiding behind her mother's legs. 'Ah, there she is! Pretty as a picture. Come and give your Uncle Gerry a hug.'

Sarah gives him a supercilious look and then turns to Angie instead. 'Is it time to go, Mum?'

'Yes, darling.' Angie considers her watch. 'It's time.'

'Don't you just love holidays,' says Gerry, as he gets our bags up together.

'I'd better fetch Finty,' I say, looking around and discovering her standing next to one of the small tables concentrating hard on having a poo in her nappy.

*

Our airplane bumps and grinds along the tarmac, and soon buildings start to angle away. A collective yet silent sigh of "we've made it" emanates from fellow passengers.

Planes are weird, aren't they?

Down below, Sussex's green downs frilled with a lacy edge of white chalk pass beneath, as if – instead of the plane moving forwards – the Earth is being pulled backwards. I used to think the same with the car when staring out of its window on long childhood trips through the Somerset countryside. As if we were stationary while the whole world whooshed past.

Finty sits on my lap. Ruffling her hair, I kiss the top of her head and she stretches up her little chubby hands to pat my cheeks.

Across the aisle Sarah sits, fidgeting, next to Jake. 'Mum?' she says, and sicks up all over her dress. 'Mummeeee!'

'In a minute, Sarah...' Angie is busy with Lauren. 'Is it your ears, darling? Do they hurt? It's all right. Here, suck one of these... Jake?' She tries to catch his attention, motioning him to help their daughter, who's sitting staring at the sick pooling in her dress.

Unbuckling my seat belt, I pass Finty over to Gerry. 'No worries, I've got it,' I say, while Jake sits perfectly still like he's playing statues as I do my best to wipe Sarah's dress with paper towels.

'Thanks.' Angie nods in Jake's direction, her normal smiley composure all but gone. 'See?' she says as she jiggles Lauren up and down on her lap. 'See what it's like?' She looks into my face. 'He's no help at all. No help with the packing, with the getting ready, no bloody help with anything. It's like bringing three kids on holiday, not two!'

There's not much I can say, so I continue wiping at Sarah's dress – 'There there, soon be better' – while Jake munches a sandwich, not noticing the dribble trickling down his chin.

*

Homeopathic pills and potions have been administered by Angie to her family (we have declined).

She is training to be a homeopath – has talked of some sort of "proving" (I'm not sure what that entails) of stone from the Easter Island statues, for a new remedy she hopes might help Jake. The theory being something along the lines of, if you take the teensiest weensiest amount of what's causing the problem (in Jake's case he's almost turned to stone – do you see?) and then dilute it in water over and over again so that only the memory remains... like a drop in the ocean... I don't understand this part... and then it's somehow turned into pills. Angie once told me how someone caught a thunderstorm to prove a remedy for finding one's own true love. It all sounds nice... but...

'What do you believe in?' she once asked me.

'Honestly? I don't know.'

Can water have memory? Can a road? A tree? Air? What does the road, tree, air know that we don't? And if we can somehow capture it how can that possibly reverse the effects of Jake's accident? There again, some days I feel as if the curtain has been whipped back and the magic and wizardry of the Wizard of Oz has been revealed as a conjuror's trick, all held together by a wish and a prayer. Bit like this plane. I mean, how can a metal tube weighing three hundred tons or so, remain airborne?

'Ron? Ron?'

'Hm?'

'I hate it when you zone out like that,' Gerry says.

*

Now we're sitting comfortably. Finty sandwiched between me and her father: our seats over the wing and close to the emergency exits. I never used to be nervous of flying, but now I like my escape route nearby. All around, fellow passengers gaze out of their small windows, close their eyes, chatter: some appear nervous, some shoot me sympathetic grins and some appear to be in silent prayer. Perhaps all that keeps a plane airborne is a collective act of faith. What was that bump? (Try harder, people.)

'Whoops,' says the stewardess as she stumbles near my seat. 'Bit of turbulence, madam. Would you care for a drink?'

I'm glad for the interruption. 'Gin and tonic, please.'

'Think I'll join you,' says Gerry.

Finty's busy with a carton of juice as I stroke her rounded head. Outside, the wind flicks along the plane's wing. From the inside looking out, the wing is as flimsy as a piece of Meccano. Do airplane wings twang along their length? Do they make wobble-board type music together? Do planes signal each other, like huge whales lumbering through vast oceans of sky? Truly, Ron. Get a grip.

'Did you know,' Jake once said, 'that the Earth spins on its own axis at speeds of just over a thousand miles an hour, and at the same time it revolves around the Sun at 67,000 miles per hour.'

'And?' I'm trying not to sound impressed.

'And – thicko – it's only centrifugal force which is keeping us on the planet.'

'Don't call me thicko, Mr Smarty Pants. So, go on then – what would happen if the Earth was to stop spinning? Just stopped altogether?'

'Then we'd go hurtling off into outer space, wouldn't we? Like we'd been fired from some massive catapult. Puh-ding!' Jake says, making a catapult motion. (He's good at catapult – likes to shoot tin cans lined along the garden wall.)

'Shut up!' I say.

THREE

We Arrive in France

The coach journey to our destination is terrifying, what with the driver hurtling along at breakneck speed, jumping traffic lights, swinging around junctions and lurching as he slaloms hairpin bends. Very bad cover music doesn't help as it blares its mediocrity from the coach sound system: "Michelle", "Yesterday" and other Beatles hits covered by unknowns. Some of the passengers half-heartedly join in. Not me.

Not only is this holiday meant to help Jake and Angie have as "normal" a time away with the girls as possible, but also for Gerry and me to spend quality time together. It's fair to say that lately things have not been fine and hunky-dory between us. I'd even go as far as saying there are times when I truly don't think I want to be with him anymore.

Gerry and I had only been seeing each other for ten months when I announced I was pregnant. I'd called him round to my flat and was all calm having worked my game plan out in advance. 'You'd better sit down,' I told him.

'It's fine,' I said once I'd finished letting him know. 'Don't look so shocked. I've worked it all out. You are under no obligation whatsoever. After all, we didn't plan on my getting pregnant. I suppose something must have gone wrong with the pill, or whatever, but I consider it my responsibility. And so...' I'd taken a deep breath – I can see him now, sitting on my Habitat sofa. 'I've decided I'm going to keep the baby and you don't have to worry about a thing.' (We weren't living together at the time. Truth be told, I thought he was cooling off.) So I was prepared for going it alone. But then he surprised me by jumping up to hug me and then bursting into tears, begging me to stay with him and insisting he wanted us to be together. Maybe get married, even... 'But,' I said, 'neither of us is up for that sort of commitment. We haven't known each other for long enough.'

No, no, he insisted. He wanted us to be a family – him, me, baby makes three...

I suggested in that case we ought to receive couple's counselling, to help us definitely decide if we wanted to be a couple. So we started seeing Carol. Then a couple of months before the birth, we bought a house and started living together – to see if we could make it work – and we stopped seeing Carol. She'd helped us over our major blip, we were hopeful, and then what happened happened and here we are again. Me back in therapy but this time solo as Gerry insists he doesn't want or need any, and in any case our marriage is sound.

I'm not sure I've totally forgotten let alone forgiven what happened at that conference he attended.

'Pass over my rucksack, Ron,' he says, interrupting my thoughts. 'I'm sure there's a bottle of water in there.'

'On your right is the vineyard which you can visit later on in the week,' announces a young woman in uniform, who stands at the front, bracing herself against the swaying of the coach.

Villa Bagatelle is right where it's supposed to be – according to the brochure – on the main street of Plouer Meillele, standing in its own grounds, shutters on every window and looking very French.

As we collect our bags and round up the children, Jake stays where he's been placed – on the pavement, not moving a muscle – as we try and sort things with the holiday rep. Well, I say we, but…

'What d'you mean, there are no travel cots?' demands Angie. 'We've got two toddlers *and* we placed an order. So you'd better fetch them right away. Come on, kids, let's go inside. Jake?'

I touch Jake on the shoulder. With slow and studied deliberation, he part-drags, part-lifts his bad leg to the fore, and then sets off on his jerky walk: leaning, swinging and dipping.

'You okay?' says Gerry, giving me a nudge as he beams at his surroundings. 'Brilliant, isn't it? Gotta love France. Smell that clean air.'

Right then a clapped-out *Citroen 2CV* splutters past. 'See what you mean,' I say, unable to resist a sarky cough.

'C'mon.' He's rubbing his hands together. 'We're going to have a terrific time.' He bends down to our small daughter. 'Aren't we, Chipmunk?'

Of course, I worry it's too soon after the accident; I'm bound to, being a physio and knowing that head-injured people take at least two years to plateau. Maybe after then might have been more sensible. But Angie insisted – Angie in her I'm-in-charge mode. Everyone too afraid to say no.

'Right then! Gather round.' She actually claps her hands together. 'We'd better sort out the money first,' she announces in that Mary Poppins manner she's adopted of late, but without the nanny uniform. Instead, she's wearing a loose pair of jeans which I suspect may well be her maternity ones, plus a long-sleeved blue T-shirt with a rather washed-out Bognor College logo across the front.

'Now, you and Gerry don't have cash on you – yes?'

'Yes,' I mumbled. 'I mean, no we don't.'

'So why don't I pay for all the outings and cots when the holiday rep returns, and then you can give me your share in travellers cheques?'

'Um, Angie?' I say, and she turns to me with that same look on her face which I've seen her give Jake. Exasperated meets long-suffering.

'Yes?'

'I hate to ask, but can you possibly lend us two hundred francs cash until tomorrow? That would be a big help, wouldn't it, Gerry?' But he's not paying attention and instead is play horsey-horsey with the little ones. 'Gerry?'

'Hm?'

'Money.'

'Ah.' He stands up, brushing imaginary dust from the front of his shorts.

Angie nods and reaches for her purse. 'Of course.' She holds the notes out. 'You sure that's going to be enough?'

'Yes, that's great, great,' I say, taking the proffered money. I hate asking, but as I've already explained to her, Gerry didn't have time to withdraw any – what with his last-minute office-dash. 'Is it okay if we decide on a kitty and all that tomorrow? I'm sure we're all worn out from the journey.' Gerry places his arm around my waist, giving me a pointed look – we've agreed to not bother Angie with our money woes. She has quite enough on her plate.

Just then a huge wasp or hornet comes buzzing in through the open window, causing Sarah to scream and swat at it, but when it makes a pass of Jake – who's still standing stock still – he reaches out and catches the insect mid-air. Jerkily he walks a few steps to the window with the wasp thing angrily buzzing away in his closed fist, then he chucks it out as Angie closes the window behind it.

'There, all done,' she says as she turns over his palm to check he hasn't been stung. 'He doesn't like to kill them,' she adds. 'He tries to be a Buddhist.' (As if that's news to me, his twin sister.)

She collects up one of their smaller cases and hands it to Sarah, who's still agog (as are we). 'Come along, Sarah. Anyone would think you haven't seen a hornet before,' and promptly leads the way out of the kitchen, dragging a suitcase in her wake. Jake stands and watches until Lauren moves to slip her small hand into his and pull him towards, and through, the kitchen door.

'Righty-oh,' says Gerry, to me and Finty as if nothing has happened. 'Good time to go and explore.'

'Yes, but did you see that?'

'Ssh, not now.'

'No, but did you see it? He used to do that before, you know. Catch them midair. Flies. Bees. Wasps. Says it's Zen.'

'Of course I saw it, but let it go.' He regards me over the top of his glasses in that way of his – like he's Miss Marple or something.

'Fine, but the size of that thing! It practically had a face on it,' I hiss. 'I had no idea Jake could move that fast. After. You know.'

'Probably a fluke, or some sort of learned reflex, or perhaps you don't know as much as you think you do... He may surprise you yet.' Before I can get in a comeback, he's hauling Finty onto his shoulders, conversation closed.

'Do cheer up, and let's at least try to have a stress-free holiday, shall we?' He has to duck under the door's lintel as father with daughter exit the kitchen. 'Let's go explore!'

'Yay!' Finty answers, mid-squeal, as he jiggles both of them up and down and gallops down the corridor.

'Hold up!' I say, and they both grin as they turn and wait for me.

All the rooms are big and airy (and mercifully hornet-free), with wallpaper that curiously starts halfway up the walls, runs across the ceiling, then over to halfway down the other side: maroon, blue and green patterns with small white flowers. Except for in the kitchen where it's tiled, all the other floors are thick boards of oak weathered by generations of feet: jumping, running, clacking, springing until they now smile a beaten sheen.

Determined to be more chipper (Acting As If. See, Carol? You'd be proud), I find I rather like the villa's otherness with its big differently carved old furniture, the quirky wallpaper; I even like the novelty of the cheap modern pieces – the glass-top coffee table and the cottage-style sofa with its squiggly design, resembling a black and white television on the blink.

We determine who is to have which bedroom. (Or rather, Angie allocates them.) Gerry and I are to have the old-fashioned one facing the front. It's in between the bigger bedroom which Sarah and Lauren claim, and the small box room-cum-dressing-room adjacent to ours is an obvious choice for Finty. Angie bags the bedroom facing out back as it's further along the corridor, past the bathroom and away from the children. 'Jake and I need this room for extra peace and quiet,' she informs us.

Dumping our bags in our room, I fling open the wooden-slatted shutters on the window to survey our very own French street scene. Turning to Gerry I ask, 'Where's Finty?'

'Next door with the girls, I expect.' He's trying out the bed – testing its bounce – when a series of loud bumps start a split second before my legs pound into action. Finty! Stairs! She's no good on stairs.

As I reach the top of them, the bumping noise has ceased while Finty sits firmly – little legs jutting straight out in front of her – at the end of a long curve. Gazing up at me with a "What happened?" look on her face, I almost burst out laughing. But she's only been catching her breath for that first ear-splitting wail. 'Mummeeee!'

'I'm coming.' Running down, I gather her into my arms. 'There, there. Sssh. Mummy's got you.' Finding a tissue up my sleeve, I wipe her little button nose and brush a tousled ginger curl out of her eyes, as I surreptitiously check her over to make sure nothing's broken. 'It's okay, everybody,' I call to the small crowd clustered on the top landing. 'She's more frightened than hurt.'

'You'll need to keep a closer eye on her. Especially at that age,' says Angie as she leads Sarah and Lauren away.

'There there, darling,' I murmur to my child, rocking her backwards and forwards, trying not to mind Angie's barbed comment.

'You sure you two are okay?' asks Gerry, who has now joined us. 'Good. Good. No harm done, then.'

'No. But – as Angie reminded me – we do need to watch her at all times.'

'Oh, she's fine, aren't you, poppet?' he insists as he carries on down the stairs. 'There's no need to make such a song and dance about things.'

'Moron,' I mutter at his back.

It's fair to say that Gerry's parenting style is more laid back than mine.

Still miffed, I carry our girl downstairs into the villa's confidently large and welcoming kitchen, where a late-afternoon sun shines through the expansive picture window, cheering up the white cupboards and red quarry tiles, no end.

'Right!' Gerry claps his hands together like an out-of-uniform Redcoat. 'Let's see what's what, shall we? Leave this to me.'

Taking the opportunity to sit in an ancient rocking chair, Finty dozing on my shoulder, he searches the cupboards and drawers, revealing strange utensils – and a coffee pot. 'No kettle,' he announces, pulling out a saucepan. 'This should do the job.' He fills it with water, places it on the hob, lighting the gas underneath with a match. 'Tea bags?' he asks.

'Um… In that box on the table, I seem to recall.'

Between half-closed lids, Finty's eyeballs flutter up into her head. 'Gerry?' I whisper. 'Do you think it'll be all right? Seriously? What with all of us cramped in here, all together? Only Angie does seem pissed off and it's only our first day.'

'Be fair,' he says, pulling tea bags from the Intasun hospitality pack. 'Who wouldn't be angsty after that journey? What with two kids and your brother?'

I stroke Finty's cheek.

'Come here,' he says as pulls me in close, and the three of us stand staring out of the open kitchen window into the fading light. A breeze, soft as a hush, whispers my hair as the smell of pine trees fill spaces in my head.

'Buddhists love the sound of wind in trees,' says Gerry, and even though this is some of his quasi-Buddhist shit, I feel more confident we might get through this, might even enjoy our holiday, if we can stick together and provide a united front.

Behind us, there's a clattering. As one we turn to see Jake lifting the saucepan off the cooker with one hand and setting out two cups with a tea bag in each, with the other.

'Tea?' he says, then sucks at the corner of his mouth.

'Yes, please. For me and Gerry, thanks,' I say, passing Gerry the still-sleeping Finty.

Jake frowns, his dirty blond hair sticks out at all different angles – looking as if it's been cut with a knife and fork (as our mum would say). 'The girl…' he starts, 'her, here…' mumble, mumble…

'What's that, Jake? Does Angie want one?'

Finty is now grizzling in Gerry's arms.

'No. This girl.' He gestures towards me. 'You… Want da flippy flup?' He looks confused, as if he knows he's got the wrong words.

'Yes, I'll have milk with mine,' I answer, then glance across at

Gerry, who's busy wiping our daughter's face with a damp cloth. 'There's some in the hospitality pack. Hang on, I'll get it.'

Gerry smiles across at me and Jake. 'I'm going to take this little lady upstairs for her nap. C'mon, Fints.' He leaves the kitchen, slapping Jake on his shoulder as he passes.

My brother returns to his tea-making ritual; his whole being concentrated over the cooker. Suddenly weary, I lower myself back into the rocking chair and watch him as he goes about his task, sensing how his thoughts and feelings flit about like goldfish – all tricky and slippery.

Sad thing is, I can't do our twin telepathy thing anymore. I let out a sigh, and Jake turns, gives me what might be a wink – although it's hard to tell as now he has a bit of a squint.

'Could die of thirst here! Whose bloody turn is it to pour the tea?' asks Jake, looking around from the stove, where a large aluminium pot blows bubbles through whatever-is-cooking-inside.

'It's Veronica's!' his three housemates all chorus, pointing at me.

'Thanks a lot,' I pretend to moan. I've arrived at their shared student house in Bognor for the weekend. At home with Jake are his housemates Mike and Tony. I pour from a large brown earthenware teapot and then hand around the teas, together with milk bottle and sugar bowl.

'Hey, watch where you're stepping!' calls out Jake, as I'd nearly trodden on his twelve-string guitar.

'All right, keep your hair on,' I say. 'You should put it somewhere safe.'

Taking it from me, he places his guitar on a proper guitar stand. Sometimes he plays at local pub folk nights: Ralph McTell or James Taylor covers. He's completely self-taught and very good – and don't we all know about it!

Mike sits in a chair which looks as if it's slowly devouring him, bottom first, as the cushion sinks through broken elastic slats. Bits of motorbike are strewn around, adding authenticity to his biker look of greasy hair, one silver cross earring and a moth-eaten brown jumper. He wipes bike grease onto already smeared jeans. 'Ta,' he says. Clearly a man of few words.

Tony, with the brown curly hair which bounces as he ducks past Jake, picks up a wooden spoon and tastes whatever's cooking. 'Mmm. Nice one.'

'Sugar, Tony?' I ask. He gives me a shy smile and moves to sit near Jake. He likes to stay close, I've noticed. Clearly got some kind of crush/hero worship going on. I've seen it before in those around my brother.

And there in the corner, cradling a mug of herbal tea, is Angie. I've only met her twice yet it looks as if she's moved in. Bit quiet, this one, but better than the last, who was into tarot cards and made macramé covers for anything which stayed still for long enough. Jake gives Angie a thumbs-up and she visibly relaxes as if she's been waiting for a cue to sip her tea.

Wandering over to the kitchen window I can see that outside lies a rusting motorbike over on its side in the tall, unkempt grass of the back lawn, forming an imprint like courting lovers. While further down the garden, unpicked runner beans wave from their tall stakes of bamboo. Mm. Deliciously hanging over the kitchen is a yummy pall of beef, paprika, tomato, loads of garlic and something else. My tiredness starts to lift. It was a long drive from Bristol to Bognor. Mm, oh yes, smells like one of Jake's goulashes. Classic.

'That food not ready yet?' asks Mike as he looks up from rolling a joint on a Pink Floyd album cover.

Jake flicks a tea towel at him. 'Clear the table first, then, you old tart!'

''Bout time,' Mike good-naturedly grunts as he stomps across in his Frankenstein's monster-style biker boots. Tony's shoving books, pens, rizla papers, tobacco tins, pot plants and other miscellanea to one side, then passes round forks and spoons as the food is dolloped into large clay bowls.

I've come to visit for a reason. 'Jake?' I say, and he turns with his spoon midway. 'Is it okay if we go for a walk later?' I'm aware how all have stopped to listen to me. 'Only I need to talk to you about this physiotherapy course I'm thinking of doing, yeah?'

Angie gives Jake a possessive glance, then gets up and puts a record on the stereo.

'Yeah, sure,' says Jake. 'Anything for my sis.' He looks across at Angie. 'Wanna come too, babe?'

I try not to mind as she nods her head. 'Great,' I say, trying to smile like I mean it as the stereo blasts out Meatloaf's "Bat Out of Hell" and Jake jumps up, abandoning his food, when it comes to his favourite bit where he dances around their kitchen/diner doing air guitar, singing away...

Outside, the night's darkness gathers around.

*

Mike came to visit Jake in hospital once. He didn't come again. Said he couldn't bear to see him like that. As if any of us could.

FOUR

Still Saturday

Angie and I decide on a stroll to find the shop we saw on the journey in and buy food to cook for tonight. She's changed into shorts and sensible brown Birkenstock sandals, while I've remained in my now-crumpled sundress. The two of us crunch up the white gravel of the driveway at the side of our villa which squats solidly on a main road. Everywhere is as sharp and as glary as a bright postcard. At the gates we pause to get our bearings as French cars whizz past. 'Down here.' Angie points and we turn left, doing our best to stick to the narrow pavement.

Houses are different here, in Brittany, aren't they? I'm thinking. What with the light brighter and reflective in a different way, the plants greener and more colourful – geraniums in pots adding splashes of red: sights, sounds, smells – all different. Foreign. And not solely in a French way, either. I sigh. These days, little feels familiar and safe, as if all has shifted on its axis.

The Earth's axis tilts at 23.5 degrees giving rise to the seasons on Earth – nothing to do with bloody hippies and celebrating the Equinox, sis.

Maybe not. But I'm still off down to Stonehenge.

Sometimes it can wobble on its axis, like a top, you know.
Fancy that. Moron!

Shielding my eyes with my hand against the sun angled low in the sky, I wish I'd brought my sunglasses with me. God, I'm tired. We all are. Food. That's what is needed.

We try some small talk: 'Lovely, isn't it?' 'Look at that?' 'What shall we buy?' 'Beautiful village.' etc., etc.

The tangles in my hair are thick and sticky with dust as if I've sprinkled talc on them. The colour of my hair is close to the poppies on my frock, whereas Jake managed to completely avoid the ginger gene (from Dad's side). Typical. When Jake was a child at first his hair was white-blond and then a riot (yes, that's right, a riot) of golden curls. He teaches (used to teach) agriculture at a local comprehensive – complete with a small farm and in the summer (*when the tilt of the Earth… yeah, yeah, I know*) and when it's particularly sunny his hair is burnished bronze. His youngest Lauren's hair will go the same way, no doubt – it being white-blonde at present; Sarah's is the dun-brown of Angie's. Before she was born I hoped Finty would have wavy orange Disney's *Little Mermaid* hair, with eyes as jade-green as my mother's: but instead of green her eyes are bright blue, and her hair somewhere between orange and blonde. Gerry and I call it "blorange" – which used to make us laugh. We don't laugh much these days.

Angie's a little way ahead of me, so I lengthen my stride to catch up. 'How are your girls?'

'Great. All fine,' she answers, with a voice which brokers no invitation to discuss how they're coping with their father, post-accident, which I thought might be a good thing to talk about. Especially now that we're alone and… Oh, well. Dare say there'll be plenty of time to have a heart-to-heart soon.

On reaching it, the corner shop is nothing like an English one. But they why would it be, stupid?

Ding! goes the old-fashioned bell. Excellent. Everything screams 1950s and French. Angie has a go at ordering in her schoolgirl French, as *"combien?"* is about all I can manage. Thanks to some champion pointing and mouthing, we come away with carrier bags full of baguettes, spaghetti, tomatoes, mushrooms, and other bits and pieces for a sauce. On our return Gerry is minding all three children single-handedly, as Jake has parked himself outside on a garden chair beneath a lemon tree in the middle of the scrubby garden. I give him a wave, but he doesn't notice, seemingly engrossed in his beer and the muddle of his mind. I find myself – as I too often do – wondering what he's thinking, or whether he thinks at all these days, and...

'Oi, you,' calls Gerry. 'Don't stand around daydreaming. Come and give Angie some help with the cooking.' Angie is about to demur, but he waves away any objections with the bottle of beer he's about to open. 'Chop chop, Ron,' he says. 'Chop chop.'

After supper, Sarah helps clear away. 'Thanks, love,' says Angie, then she turns to us. 'I think we should discuss how we're going to sort the money,' she starts. 'We'd best decide on a kitty, don't you agree? Sort who pays for what?'

'Right, yes.' I pour a drop more wine into Jake's glass. He's been quiet throughout the meal.

'Jake's pretty exhausted.' Angie gives him a weary smile.

'What do you suggest, then, about the kitty?' I start.

'As there's four of us,' she says, looking across at Jake, 'we ought to put more money in for food and electricity.' She nods her head as if it's decided, then opens her tobacco tin and starts to roll a cigarette while Sarah helps Lauren and Finty off their chairs. They run to the sofa, where there are colouring-in books on the coffee table.

'No, no. I won't hear of you paying more money,' says Gerry. 'It's not like Sarah eats all that much! We'll go fifty/fifty. Split it down the middle.'

I bite my tongue. Aware of what little money we have, I'd be happier if we made our own arrangements and spent as frugally as possible, but now's not the time to mention this.

'Fair's fair,' says Angie as she lights her rollie, and opens the back door. 'We insist.' She leans with one leg bent against the doorframe, inhales deeply, blowing a long stream of smoke out into the early evening air. It's kind of sexy, and I can't help noticing Gerry noticing too.

'Don't you agree we should pay more, Jake?'

But Jake's lost – picking at a piece of bread with his good hand.

'Christ's sake, Jake,' she says, stamping her foot to get his attention. 'Will you leave it alone? Sit up straight to the table, okay? You remember what the physiotherapist said?'

'Angie's right,' I say, adding weight to her suggestion. 'It'll help with your balance.' I'm more than happy to lend my support, especially as I know how much she worries that Jake will think her a nag. 'If you're not using your right hand,' I add, 'then you ought to place it on the table.'

He raises his blank gaze to me and next lifts his right shoulder up to his ear as his face contorts with the effort. Slowly, his right hand rises as if lifted by a crane, and he plops it onto the tabletop with his "good" hand. 'That's better,' I say, smiling encouragement, especially as I know how hard that move is for him; how – whereas it's almost an unconscious movement for "normal" people – it's akin to mind over matter for him; having to will the right nerve impulses for the task. 'Next time,' I can't help adding, 'do make sure you lift from your elbow, yeah?'

'Give the poor bloke a break,' says Gerry as he takes a large swig from his beer.

Angie leans over to stub out her cigarette in the ashtray, touching him ever so slightly on his shoulder.

'I've got an excellent idea,' I say. 'Why don't I help with Jake's physiotherapy exercises? Give you a break, Angie, hm?'

She wipes her hands on a tea towel. 'No, thank you. We can manage perfectly well on our own.'

'Yes. Yes, of course. That's fine. But the offer's still there should you change your mind—'

She places the towel on the chairback. 'Tell you what, then. Why don't we take it in turns to babysit the girls so the others can go out for the evening on their own?'

'Sounds like a good idea,' declares Gerry.

'Very well,' says Angie. 'I propose you have first go.'

I'm sure she means to be kind, but a niggly part of me would like to have been involved in this decision.

'Good-oh,' is all I say.

FIVE

Saturday Night

In our room, getting ready for our night out, I'm pulling my red silk dress over my head, allowing the slinky fabric to come to rest over my curves. *Not bad*, I think, turning this way and that to better view my reflection in the long mirror. *Not bad at all.* I've lost all of my baby weight – and a little extra – although I do have a tiny bit of a belly. Grabbing a pink hibiscus hair clip, I pin my hair up to the side, apply a slick of lipstick, slip my feet into silver strappy sandals and – 'Eek!' – startle as Gerry touches my shoulder.

'Sorry. Didn't mean to sneak up on you.' He drops a soft kiss on my neck, then lifts my skirt and kisses the tattoo on my hip just above my knickers. He says he loves it now, but he wasn't too thrilled when I came home with it that day. I still don't fully know why I did it – although, it does feature in some of my therapy sessions.

It's a tattoo of a hummingbird. I got it done the day after Jake came round enough from his coma for the doctors to reckon he was going to wake up. Not that he was fully awake, but nearly there as if struggling up through passages and labyrinths like Orpheus who must not look back else his wife is turned to stone. You could tell it was exhausting for him.

But it was a good sign. And so, wanting to mark it, I found

myself walking into a tattoo parlour on Park Street, sure that what I was about to do was an appropriate response to good news.

I remember joking to the tattooist – when it was underway and those little needles were jabbing their tiny beaks – feeling more like a woodpecker than a hummingbird.

'You want me to change it to a woodpecker?'

'No, no. Just joking. It's fine. Carry on with the hummingbird.'

Because this had been one of those promises I'd made to myself, at Jake's hospital bedside. Get better/wake up/show me a sign. I was in a state myself when he slightly turned his head to me and mumbled what could have been "bird".

You see, we'd joked before about tattoos. I said I'd have a hummingbird as they've long fascinated me, and Jake said his would be a spider because he loves that film *Whistle Down the Wind*, with the kitten called Spider, and a man in a coma – no, hang on, he's not in a coma, is he? He's asleep – the man they think is Jesus.

Can having a tattoo be like sending out a silent prayer? I don't know – but just in case...

Gerry was angry at first. 'You've finally gone nuts!'

I cried, he apologised, then later he said he thought it was sweet, and beautiful, and kind of sexy. Sexy is the furthest from how I felt – then or now. He thinks I hide the tattoo to keep it private for him. But truth is, I don't want Angie to see it and think I've done something frivolous while Jake is...

'You look scrumptious,' says Gerry.

'Thanks,' I say, smiling at him in the mirror. 'You don't look so bad yourself.' And he does look handsome in his slightly crumpled cream linen jacket, pale blue shirt, 501 jeans and brown leather sandals.

Tonight is not only our first holiday night out, but our first night out at all since The Accident. We've arrived at the bar of the Café

L'Escale; a darkly lit place, full of young French people. Even if we weren't in France you could tell they're French because they all have dark Gallic hair, with skin toning to match. And they're all speaking French. Dead giveaway. (Shut up, Ron.)

Rock music dances around the bar then out through open doors and into the street. It's loud, but not so loud we won't be able to talk. If we want to. Gerry signals to the barman. '*Deux beers, s'il vous plait,*' he orders, then we both swivel round on our bar stools to get a better view of things.

God, will you look at them? They're gorgeous, aren't they? All these young people, so dazzlingly beautiful. They make me feel so old.

Drawing deeply on my beer, I catch my own reflection in the mirror behind the bar. Luckily the light is kind and – d'you know what – I don't look so bad. Buoyed up, I give Gerry what I hope is a seductive smile (I'm out of practice).

He squeezes my hand. 'It'll be okay, you'll see. We'll have a grand holiday.'

'I do hope so.'

'Let's dance.'

'Oh, you are joking.' He starts pulling me to my feet. 'But you can't dance.'

'Who cares? We're on holiday, and no-one we know will see what a numpty I am on the dancefloor.'

He leads me to the small space where we hold each other and sway, feeling shy and tender. I'm experiencing a definite tingle as he stares at me and I turn my head away, afraid to meet his eyes. Feeling guilty again, aren't you?

'Stuff and nonsense,' I can hear Carol say in my head. 'You are allowed to have sexual feelings.' I often want to giggle when she says stuff like that – if I'm not close to tears, that is.

'You like to call yourself Ron?' she says. 'Isn't it a boy's name? Did you ever wish you were a boy, like Jake?'

Gerry holds me close to his chest. There's some slow French music playing, and other couples are smooching on the dancefloor.

'What's with all the debt?' had been another of Carol's questions.

Gerry took unpaid leave to look after me when I... well, when I had to leave work after I couldn't cope with a new baby and... you know. Our savings gone, we can't sell or remortgage the house, and the bank is turning ugly – threatening bankruptcy. We're only just holding them off. We're paying for this holiday on our credit cards... Who knew that a baby – now toddler – and all the stuff you need for her could be so expensive on top of wanting to be there, pay for things, following... It's fair to say we took our eye off the ball.

'Money,' says Carol, 'can define a relationship. You control it, or it controls you. Don't you think you should make it more of a priority?'

What I'm learning about Gerry is he has a student mentality where money's concerned, and I... well, I've let it slide. Got reckless. And now this has to stop. We have a child now.

'Give him a chance,' Carol had said. 'He's a little immature, but he'll catch up.'

'Yeah, well... I'm a mother now and I don't have the luxury of being immature, do I? Someone has to be the grownup.'

'But see how he's looking after you? Taking care of you both. Give him a chance.'

I wish he would hurry up and mature, I'm thinking, now.

The music plays on.

Angie and Jake are okay-ish – money-wise, that is. They're both teachers: she's taken some sort of paid leave, and he has his pension from teaching. We thought there might be, but there's no compensation following his type of accident. We've become quite the experts on this. Unlike the US, the UK does not allow for no-fault compensation. Which means that if it's caused by an "act of God" or a fluke then you're more or less buggered. There was hope for a while – hope (a dreadful thing to hope for) – that it may have been a hit-and-run. But then the private accident investigator Gerry and I paid for, disproved that theory. He pieced together a lot of what must have occurred and declared it not to be a hit-and-run. You so want it to be someone else's fault. Random feels wrong and totally against the laws of the universe. Dad remains convinced of another scenario entirely: Jake has this a small defensive wound on his wrist (probably putting his hand up before his own bike struck him), and to Dad, this is evidence that someone... 'Hear me out on this,' he'd said when he mooted his idea. 'I think someone must have fired a ball-bearing at him. With a catapult or something. Think about it. Makes sense.' Mad, see? We've all gone a bit mad.

Gerry's kissing my cheek now where tears are trickling. 'Hey, come on,' he says. 'Let's boogie.' The DJ is spinning "Boogie Wonderland". We start to dance – apart.

I need to stop going over and over everything. What is it again: give me the serenity to accept the things I cannot change, to change the things I can and the wisdom to know the difference? Yeah, well, easier said than done. Maybe a good fucking could give me a break from my thoughts. A good old-fashioned banging. Most of these kids in here look like they'll be getting some tonight.

Gerry's good at fucking – our mutual friend Freddie had been right about that. Look at Gerry, now – dancing away in his funny bouncy Morrissey kind of way. But no, we can't. Not when we're sharing a villa with Angie and Jake. That's enough to put the mockers on things. Even worse than staying with your parents.

Grace Jones' "Pull Up to the Bumper" comes on, and we both grind away. Opposite and close.

The first time we did it we couldn't get enough. We did it six times that night – the first night we met. I was in the mood for a guy-slut. To be fair, it had been a while. So yes, he'd been good at fucking; the loving part came later.

Of course, it was all Freddie's fault we met in the first place. Dear Freddie.

Ah, here comes Freddie now. I spot his legs first. Even descending the stairs his walk is unmistakable. As is Freddie. With intricate waves of his hands and loud use of his voice, he shepherds his group of three – a couple I don't know and his new girlfriend Razia – into the downstairs bar of the Mall in Clifton.

'My dears,' I hear him say. 'No-one would be seen dead in the upstairs bar.'

I wave from my table near the back of the room. Freddie flourishes back.

'This way. This way.' He herds his group over to me. 'Veronica. Come here.' He kisses me on both cheeks. Tres chic. Freddie is as camp as a row of tents and – as he likes to tell all and sundry – bisexual.

'What, no hat?' I say. Disappointed. Because the wearing of hats is Freddie's latest craze.

'So last week's news, darling. Not quite in keeping with my new image of butch chic. In any case,' he whispers in a theatrical aside which anybody can hear, 'Razia doesn't like them.'

I glance across at Razia, who looks stern in her substantial glasses and efficient curly hair. 'Hi, Veronica,' she says, plonking her black briefcase on the floor and taking the seat next to me. (We've met before.)

'Ron, let me introduce you to David and Helen.' Freddie gestures at the other two. 'Both of them work in housing benefit – aren't they sweet? Absolutely made for each other.' He gives them a proprietorial smile.

'Freddie, you are a terrible matchmaker. You don't change, do you?'

'I sincerely hope not, sweet pea,' he says, then lowers his voice. 'Otherwise I wouldn't be able to share my latest treat with you, now would I?'

What on Earth is he up to now?

'Have you seen our lovely Gerard yet? But, of course. How silly of me. You don't know what he looks like, do you? He's our latest crush. Bit of a dish, isn't he, Raz?'

Razia huffs at him.

I know the story, according to Freddie. Apparently both Raz and Freddie had designs on Gerry – a housing solicitor in a law centre – and both made unsuccessful and separate (more like desperate) passes at him. Razia being the most miffed because she'd invited him to dinner, had prepared her best dishes and put on her most posh sari, only for Gerry to eat her food and dash off to meet another woman.

Now Freddie has hold of Razia's hand in an affectionate clasp. He's trying out heterosexuality again, is what he told me. Having had enough of cock, or so he says.

I've been celibate for a whole year now, ever since Dr Ross Chambers. We'd been seeing each other on and off – on the QT – for nearly six months. I thought I was in love with him. Had started dreaming of him leaving his anaesthetist wife, of him declaring his love for me, of a house in the country with rosy-cheeked children and a black Labrador. I'd even started to believe he could well be the love of my life.

How stupid can you get? Married doctor – hello? Then one day – yes, you've guessed it – he announced in front of the whole ward team (hadn't even had the guts to tell me in private) – that his wife was pregnant. So much for their not sleeping together anymore. What a cliché.

So, I'm not up for getting that involved, that vulnerable or *that hurt again. And Freddie's Gerry sounds interesting. Perhaps a fling? Just sex? Because I enjoy sex. Always have – always will. Yes, this fix-up could well fit the bill; besides which, I'm feeling horny.*

'There he is. Over there!' Freddie points to a far corner.

He's sitting alone with an almost-empty pint glass in front of him, reading from a fat book held high enough so the cover is plain to see. Some historical tome about Stalin.

'Gerry!' Freddie shouts, beckoning him to come join us. 'Over here.'

He lowers his book and acknowledges Freddie with a quick smile and a slight lifting of his hand. I find it hard to believe he didn't hear Freddie's entrance. Poseur, I decide, as he navigates a couple of tables on his way over. Must say, I'm a tad disappointed. He's not my normal type. Which is roguish good-looking bastard. No. Gerry's a bit of a nerd. I'd been hoping he'd turn out to be the hottie at the bar – the one with dark curly hair and stubble whose long legs I'd been admiring. God, I'm so shallow.

The trouble with being a twin is, not only do other people compare you both, but you start doing it yourself. Now, Jake is strong and forthright and secure in himself – and even though he's a bit Marmite, more love than hate him. Me? Well, I too am strong and forthright – I'm his twin, after all. But I'm a girl. And men – the nice ones – are scared of strong girls. This makes me less secure about myself; I guess this is partly why I'm a feminist – I can't bear the unfairness and Jake is a reminder of gender politics. I have both the silver and gold Anne Dickson women's assertiveness books, I hate Thatcher, I supported the miners' strike, and often wear – with pride – my Coal Not Dole badge. Luckily, I also like to Party with a capital "P" and view lovers as recreational. Motherhood's not for me, I've always thought. I'm a woman, and I have choices. Jake and I have many heated gender discussions.

Looking at Gerry I wonder if I might eat him for breakfast. Hmm. He has a Number 1 cut – used to call them crewcuts when I was a kid. He sports a red lumberjack shirt and vintage Levi 501s. Bet you anything he likes The Smiths.

'See you shop at Uncle Sam's,' I chip in once Freddie has done the introductions. Uncle Sam's, on Park Street, sells second-hand vintage American clothes. And then he turns his extraordinary gaze my way and I get the full blast of his twinkly eyes, big and smiley behind thick-rimmed glasses. A flicker of interest passes between us.

'Pleased to meet you, Gerry,' I say, offering my hand. When we touch, a zing licks through me – or maybe it's static electricity from the Mall's overly fussy carpet. 'Freddie's told me lots about you,' I add.

'That's nice,' he says, holding on a moment longer than he should. 'He's told me nowhere near enough about you.' He wears a highly amused look as if these cheesy lines are making him close to cracking up.

'Get a room, you two,' says Freddie, causing me to flush. Gerry drops his hold and flashes a rather knowing grin at me – cheeky bugger.

'You have brought the tickets with you, though, haven't you, Ger?' says Freddie. 'Do tell me you didn't forget.'

'Hm?' he says, pulling a stool over to sit beside me. 'Tickets?'

'Don't mess about, Gerard. Tickets? To see George Melly at the Green Room?'

'Of course I have them.' He reaches into the back pocket of his jeans to retrieve his wallet. As he roots out the tickets, I notice what good hands he has. Long, tapering fingers...

'Here they are.' He places them on the table, then gets to his feet and offers me his hand. 'I expect you'll be able to sell our tickets at the door, Freddie. Me and Ronnie here are off to the Dug Out. Aren't we?' He stares his challenge at me. I'm well up for it. A good bop versus boring jazz?

'Sure are.' I take his hand and knock back my cocktail.

*'Very well. Have fun, children,' says Freddie with a dismissive
wave. 'My job is done.'*

I kiss Freddie on the cheek and gather my things.

'Do everything I would do,' he calls after us.

'Phew, I'm knackered. Shall we get a drink?' Gerry leads me
back to the bar, and soon we have two lovely cold beers in front
of us.

'Cheers.' We both chink our glasses. Gerry half turns to view
the antics on the floor while I notice the way his neck curves to
meet the soft fuzz of hair underneath his haircut, vulnerable as
an adolescent's. I want to lean forwards to kiss that place.

'It's very smoky in here,' he says as he swivels round to face
me.

'God, yes, isn't it?' I agree. Seems like everyone around us
is smoking, strong in their convictions of immortality. You'd be
hard pushed to find anybody not smoking. Me? I gave up when
I was pregnant. Yet here, all around the bar packets of Camel,
Gauloises, Gitanes are being flashed as matching Zippos flip
into action and first drags are lit.

I'd love a cigarette, but I mustn't – I've been very good. At a
nearby table a boy flicks one up into the air and catches it in his
mouth. The girls are impressed. They laugh, throwing back their
heads and exposing their necks. One more step up the sexual
ladder for him. I'll bet he scores tonight – ahhh, to be young and
have nothing awful happen in your life.

The smoke is threatening to bring on my asthma, so I
rummage in my bag for my inhaler.

'Want to move outside?' asks Gerry, as I puff and then inhale.
'Why don't we drink up and go?' he adds. 'It'll be nice to walk
back through town.'

As we're leaving, a man dressed in brown leather jacket and
black jeans holds the door open for us, as I pass him I catch a

whiff of his delicious aftershave and risk a glance at him and his glorious dark gallic locks, when I see he's giving me a rather naughty smile. Moving on down the road I risk a look behind, only to find he's watching as we walk down the road. *Yep, still got it*, I think. *Must tell...* and then remember how I can't share these little confidences with my twin, anymore.

The sky is clear and the air clean in that way it has in summer seaside towns. The sounds of cafes and bars, Renaults and Citroens, hang and dance about us as we head back to the villa. A warm promise for tomorrow tantalises our nostrils, mingling with crisp green, red, purple, and pink garden and hedgerow smells. Crickets sing. We used to catch grasshoppers in the long grass at the back of our house, didn't we, Jake? Kept them in matchboxes – England's Glory or Swan Vesta, I can't remember which. Breathing holes punched in the top with our school compasses. When I was you, and you were me. Oh dear. Placing my head on my husband's shoulder, I hug his solid arm.

'Hey,' he protests.

'I do love you.'

'That's nice,' he says.

S I X

Saturday, Later

The others are in bed when we return to the villa, and Gerry and I sit companionably at the kitchen table. 'I do think Jake's speech is getting better, don't you?'

'Yes, I do,' he says, running his fingers through his spiky hair – a habit he has when he's nervous.

'Seems clearer in his head too,' I say.

'Hm. Yes, I suppose you're right.'

The room has that empty echoey feel they get at night, and peering at my watch I can see it's gone midnight. We really ought to be going to bed, but having a night out is such a rare occasion I want it to last for longer.

'Of course, it's still early days,' I say, because I need to say something about it. Lately, and before this trip, we'd mostly avoided discussing it too much. Worn out from going over and over what happened in the first days, weeks, months, after Jake came tumbling down. 'I'm sure the exercise regime which Angie's devised will really help his brain – and his walking, too.'

'I guess so.' Gerry opens a beer. 'Want one?'

I shake my head.

'It's going to be a long haul,' I finally say – as if Gerry's not heard this before. 'Fifteen months is no time in the scheme of things. From my experience as a physio, the best we can hope for is he won't be as bad as they initially thought. Perhaps we could find him something to do, to take part in, something tangible which would remind him of what he is, what he used to do.'

'Something tangible... Like what?'

'I don't know. But the brain is much like a labyrinth and since his accident it's like many of the pathways through are blocked by scar tissue.'

I've scant knowledge of Greek myths, bar the Ray Harryhausen movie of *Jason and the Argonauts*, which both Jake and I love – oh, and that book on the myths which I read as a child but so long ago I can't remember details.

'I know the physical aspects of a head injury,' I tell Gerry, 'but the brain is also the metaphorical, the myths, the memories, the stories we tell each other.'

'Who would you be?' Jake asks.

'I'd be Medusa and turn men to stone.'

'Sorry,' says Gerry, 'are you saying you want to be the Medusa?'

'Oh, sorry, never mind, but what I'm thinking is perhaps if we give him tasks to do—'

'What? Like those of Hercules?'

'Oh, ha ha – no, but if we could do something tangible, something he can do which reminds him of back when, then that might help. Can you think of anything? Anything at all?'

'Yes, I think you're going more than a bit bonkers, and you'd better not let Angie catch you spouting your mad theory.'

I'm feeling rather crestfallen by his lacklustre approach, and he must have seen because he relents. 'I'm not promising anything, but I'll give it some thought, it's just that right now I'm dog-tired. Why don't we go upstairs?'

Gerry turns the light off in the en-suite and joins me on the oak four-poster, where he sets about caressing my thigh, moving upwards.

'Gerry,' I say, putting down my book, 'I'm worried about our money too.'

'Don't be,' he says, his eyes all misty.

'Thing is,' I say, as he starts to cup my breasts, 'all that business with the kitty and travellers' cheques… Somehow we appear to be fifty quid down while they're twenty quid up.'

'Don't fuss,' he says, tweaking my nipple, but I bat him away. 'Does it really matter if they have more money than us?'

'But we're broke, remember? And very nearly bankrupt.'

'I know what'll take your mind off things.' He starts to move in, eyes fixed on what he calls my "business end". 'Don't suppose you fancy…?'

'No, I don't.' My earlier mood is forgotten as I tug my T-shirt back down. 'Sorry, but I'm too wound up. Can't we read for a while, instead?'

He rolls onto his back. 'Suppose I can always take a photograph of your bottom and not trouble you anymore.'

'I'm sorry. But you know how it is.'

'It's fine, Ron. Honestly.'

Angie and I sit side by side. It's quite a nice room, really. Daffodils in a white vase cheer up the right-hand corner of the consultant's desk, and his name plate reads Mr McPherson. Angie asked me to come with her and so here we are. Both uncertain. I stifle an urge to giggle. Nerves, I know.

'How bad is he, Doctor?' asks Angie.

'Hard to tell. But not good. The prognosis is not very good at all, I'm afraid.' The doctor looks earnest.

'Oh.' From me.

The doctor sits back in his black and padded leather chair.

'Your husband has something called anomic dysphasia. Amongst his other problems,' he's saying. 'Memory loss, cognitive difficulties, motor... um. I am afraid he'll have some spasticity. Walking and fine motor movements will be a problem. It's like he's had a stroke on both sides, you see—'

'This anomic dysphasia,' says Angie, picking on the one new thing to try and understand. 'What is that?'

'Well.' He glances at me, but I sit frozen. Stunned, I guess. 'It means,' the doctor continues, 'that he will experience difficulty in recalling nouns. Naming things. This will be a problem for his incoming as well as outgoing messages, so to speak.'

Hello, is there anybody out there? Bleep. I'm sorry, you have dialled the wrong number. Beam me up, Scotty. I can tell my face is inappropriately going for a smile. Why? Concentrate, Ron.

Mr McPherson frowns. 'Your husband will not always understand what you say, Mrs Johnson. And in turn, he will find it difficult to explain himself.'

Doesn't he talk nice? I'm thinking. That's what a good education will do for you.

He continues. 'Jacob' (how weird to hear anyone call him Jacob) 'will also experience difficulties with concepts. Um, let me try to explain...' and here he twiddles his Parker gold-plated fountain pen. 'He will experience difficulties with thoughts. Ideas. Abstracts. That sort of thing.' Doc leans forward. 'I'm sorry to have to tell you this, Angela – may I call you Angela?' She nods. 'But you did say you want to know everything.'

One of the flowers in the vase is bent over at an angle, its stem broken. I fight an urge to try and straighten it up.

'It's his brain, you see,' the doctor says. Doctor knows best. 'All these different areas have been affected. As well as what we call the speech centre. I am so very sorry.'

'Yes,' comes from me. I place my hand over Angie's. 'Thank you, Doctor.'

'Yes, thank you,' says Angie as she stares at my fingers.

'Things might improve slightly,' says the doctor as we prepare to leave. 'But I wouldn't hold out much hope.' He sits and waits as we stand to leave.

Angie turns back at the door. 'You don't know him like I do. He's a fighter. We'll beat this. Together. Won't we, Ronnie?'

'You go on,' I say, closing the door behind her. Then I turn to the doctor. 'It's bad, isn't it?'

He sighs, his shoulders relaxing as he indicates for me to sit back down. 'Well, Miss Johnson—'

'Mrs O'Keefe.'

'You're his twin, I hear.'

'Yes.'

'And a physiotherapist, too, so you will understand when I say how amazed we are that he's even alive. Can I be frank?' I nod. 'He left a fair amount of his brains back on the road. I'm sure you realise the implications... and what this means.'

Dread spreads like a slick of mercury spilled on the ground.

'Maybe it would have been best if... well... I sometimes wonder if heroic life-saving is always the best option.' He gets to his feet to see me out. 'I guess his family will be relying somewhat on you now.' He pats my shoulder and gives me a rueful smile. 'Good luck with it all,' are his closing words. Blunt. But I'm grateful for his candour.

As I close his door behind me, his phone starts ringing.

Ring ring. Ring ring. 'Hello, Ronnie?' comes the voice on the other end.

'Christ, Jake. What fuckin' time is it?'

'You not up yet, you lazy cow? It's nearly lunchtime.'

'Yeah, well. You know what newborns are like. Not all sleep through like yours, you know. Finty was up nearly all night, so Gerry's letting me have a lie-in.'

'Oops, sorry.'

'S'okay. I'm awake now. So what is it, bro? What d'you want?'

'Nothing. I don't know why I'm calling you, really. Just wanted to give my favourite twin a ring – that's all right, isn't it?'

'Yes, of course. But why?'

'Who knows? Because it's a fabulous day. The sun is shining. It's spring. It's April. And life is great. I might even ring Mum.'

'Are you drunk?'

'Don't be daft, it's way too early in the day. I guess it suddenly struck me how lucky I am. I live in a great part of the country. Have a beautiful wife. Two lovely girls. Oh yeah, and a clever sister who has just had the most amazing baby girl. Life is fuckin' great. Touch wood.'

'Piss off, you soft tart.'

'Love you too, you old slag.'

'Bye then.'

'Bye.'

Bye

Bye

Bye

Bye

Bye

That was only the day before Jake fell down and broke his crown – but unlike the nursery rhyme, he couldn't be mended with vinegar and brown paper…

SEVEN

Sunday

When I wake I'm in a sweaty, disorientated state, not knowing for a moment or two exactly where I am. Then I remember – Brittany. Our big family holiday in Brittany. Gerry's gently snoring, and when I poke my head inside, I can see Finty lying on her front, in her travel cot, fast asleep. Gently I tiptoe in and turn her on her back; she grizzles a little in her sleep but still doesn't wake when I ease back out the room.

Taking care not to disturb anyone else, I pad down to the kitchen to fetch a glass of water, only to discover my brother sitting on his own at the table.

'Jake?'

He turns his poor hurt head towards me – the scars still livid where they tried to put him back together again. 'Yeah?' he slurs.

'How're you feeling?' I rub my fist on my chest. 'Deep down inside, I mean.' Taking the seat opposite him, leaning in. 'You can tell your sister anything, you do know that, don't you? Anything at all.'

'Well,' he says as he noisily sucks at some spittle in the corner of his mouth. 'The chemical potassium is my problem.' He frowns at me in a most earnest way. 'Its compound formula has a distance for me.'

And then he shakes his head.

'Um, Ronnie,' begins Angie. It's later in the day and we're clearing away the breakfast things. 'I, um, hope you don't mind...'

'Mind what?' I take the plate she passes me to wipe.

'But I think it would be a good idea if we go our separate ways. Probably just for today – I'm not sure.'

'Oh, I see, okay.' The plate clatters as I set it down.

'We're going to set off for the Plage des Dunes,' she quickly adds. 'And who knows, if we should meet up with you lot later, then I'm sure it'll be fine. I mean, we won't be ignoring you or anything.' She returns to the washing-up bowl and I can't see her face.

'Good idea,' I say, trying to sound chipper, but inside I'm thinking, *Well, if that's the way you want it then it's fine by me.*

She squeezes past – ''Scuse me' – to place a homeopathic remedy underneath Jake's tongue. 'It's just...' She wipes both hands on her shorts as she straightens up. 'Please don't be cross or anything but... this is all proving harder than I thought.'

'Oh?'

'Seeing you and Gerry with Finty, I mean.' She rubs her forehead.

'Ah.' I twiddle with the tea towel.

'Because, you see, you remind me of how we used to be. You know. Me and Jake. When we were together with just Sarah. When she was Finty's age – and before – you know.'

'Yes, of course. I understand what you're saying, and I'm sorry I didn't pick up on that before.'

'Gerry is so good with Finty, you see. Like Jake used to be with ours – but nowadays he hardly takes any notice of Lauren. Or Sarah.'

'I hadn't realised. But it's not yet been two years, and you know how the doctors and physios said there should be improvement during that time. It'll get better, I'm sure,' I say, aware this is a pretty rubbish platitude.

Angie vigorously wipes a plate. 'All the same.'

'Yes, I can see this is a good idea,' I say, keeping my tone bright. 'We don't need to do everything together, do we?'

We vocally circle each other like a right pair of dysfunctional passive-aggressives. (See, Carol? Am learning the terminology...)

Give me a stand-up row any day. Like with me and Jake. Frequently.

Didn't

Fuck off

No, you fuck off.

Right!

(Scream – chase around the furniture.)

Stop it, you two!

(Hitting each other with cushions until we collapse, laughing. Or arm wrestling – I'm stronger than I look.)

Wuss

Butch cow

Naff off

Aaargh, that hurts...

You don't know this, Jake, I'm thinking as I watch him outside in the garden, *but I got a tattoo of a hummingbird done. I'll show it to you one day.*

He is sitting outside, freeze framed in his own world: the sun caressing his stillness, his shoulders hunched forwards as if he's curling in on himself. I wish I knew what he was thinking; I wish I could place my head in his lap, feel his hand on my head and hear him say that everything will be all right.

'Jake?' I say, walking through the back door of his home in Cambridgeshire. It had been a tiring journey driving up on a Friday during rush hour. Sunlight shafts through to glint the gold

in his hair as he looks up from where he's peeling potatoes in the sink. Bob Marley's "Three Little Birds" plays on the radio as he smiles his smile.

'You got here all right then?'

'No, I'm a mirage.'

He flicks water at me.

'This is Gerry,' I say, presenting my new boyfriend for inspection.

Jake dries his hands on a tea towel and moves across to greet us. He's young and fit and at ease in his body. A natural athlete, they said at school, where I was more the academic one.

'So, you're the bloke she's been telling us about.'

'Jake!' I say, mortified. 'Do behave.'

'Don't I always?' he says with a mischievous look. 'The model of decorum, me.'

Gerry shoves his glasses further up his nose then shakes Jake's hand.

'Come on in, Gerry,' I say, giving my brother a thump on the arm – 'Ouch!' – 'Come and meet the rest of my brother's family.' I pull Jake aside and whisper, 'Be gentle with him.'

'Hullo?' Angie is calling out from the dining room. 'Is that them? Have they arrived?'

'Yes.' Jake ushers us into their sitting room. 'Da-da! My big sister and her toy boy.' Gerry's only four years younger than me! I give Jake another punch on the arm. 'Ow – did she tell you she was this vicious? Here – where are my manners? Let me take your coat.'

Gerry shrugs out of his full-length Crombie under which he wears white tee and soft blue plaid shirt ala Morrissey.

'Welcome to our humble abode,' says Angie as she arrives in a bustle of country-red cheeks, jeans and tight long-sleeved t-shirt. She's small-boobed and bra-less and looks about twelve. 'Come on in where it's warm. Shut the back door, Jake.' We follow her to the lounge.

Through the cottage window we can see snow has pitched on their lawn – there wasn't any when we set off from Bristol. Decidedly more chilly up here in Cambridgeshire – in more ways than one, as it's clear to me that an argument hangs in the air between my brother and his wife.

'Well,' says Jake, as we gather on our various chairs, around a roaring fire in the hearth which Jake built. 'So you're the new boyfriend?' I shoot him a warning look. 'I hope you like them batty, cos my sis is as batty as they come.'

'Thanks a lot, bruv,' I say, stomping on his foot. He grabs me in a wrestling hold and we pretend wrestle for a while – whacking each other with cushions.

'Oi, watch out!' Angie grabs hold of Sarah, who looks on – a little scared and a little excited. Jake lets go then kisses Sarah on her chubby cheeks, taking his place next to Angie on the sofa. 'Put the kettle on, sis,' he orders as he gives Gerry a wink.

The weekend expands in the countryside. Away from our city lives, we unwind on long walks where we trudge across crunchy snow and muck in with household chores – Jake and Angie like to set their guests to work. 'Take us as you find us, and be prepared to get stuck in,' Jake likes to say.

Sarah plays with us (I dare say we're a novelty as there are no small children living near the cottage). She likes to show off the wooden playhouse which "Daddy built" in the garden.

'Better than much of the housing around Barton Hill,' says Gerry, who's clearly impressed. 'Your brother's a bit of a handyman, isn't he?'

'Isn't he just.'

In the evenings we sit listening to music, talking, playing silly games involving some kind of guessing element – which I'm rubbish at! For one there are four bits of paper on the floor and someone has to point to one and say something – I forget what as I'm pretty far gone by now, having drunk most of the red wine single-handed. I seem to spend most of the game going, 'What? What? I don't get it!' Whereas Gerry's in his element. (Well, he likes to play chess – collects cuttings of chess moves which he keeps in a little box... I know, right!)

After Sarah's safely tucked up in bed we smoke joints from the cannabis Jake grows, concealed – he hopes – in his greenhouse. 'Growbags are best for bringing on a good crop,' he tells Gerry, who asks polite questions about Jake's job teaching agriculture at the local comp, whilst I regale everyone with hospital stories as a physiotherapist, adding in as many gruesome bits as I can, and then bask in the laughter and the soft looks Gerry throws my way.

When I pass Angie and Jake doing the washing up together, I overhear Angie say, 'So come on then, whadda you reckon? Has this one passed the test of meeting her twin brother?'

EIGHT

Still Sunday

After lunch, the others remain behind at the villa while we take ourselves off to the beach. Following the path from the main drag, we pick our way down a steep incline as it windingly wends its way around the contours of a hill and down to the sands. The walk isn't easy, particularly as between us we carry Finty, buggy, nappy changing bag, beach umbrella, miscellaneous paraphernalia, beach mats, rucksack.

'Christ, you sure we need all this?' Gerry grunts as he hoists Finty further up his side – from where she clings on like a little monkey.

Gingerly, we make our way down wooden steps which descend through the dunes, taking care to negotiate the twisty cypress tree roots half-submerged in sand. Rounding the last bend is our first proper glimpse of the sea. 'Wow. Will you look at that!'

Beyond the sand dunes the beach lies spread before us, resembling a crisp white tablecloth held down either side by rocky outcrops. Soft sands gently slope down to a sea which tamely licks at paddling children, while crashing through – flicking and spraying – young men chase balls and squealing girls into the waves.

'Nearly there,' says Gerry, as he collects up one of my bags.

We scramble down the final steps onto warm and yielding sand where I pause to fill my lungs with the sea's tangy breath.

'It's gorgeous.'

'Isn't it?'

Gerry picks out a spot. 'This'll do,' he says, dumping our stuff and lowering Finty onto her feet.

Soon we're unpacked, and Gerry and I stripped down to our swimming costumes. 'C'mon on, you,' he says as he sets about removing Finty's clothes. She waits, patiently naked, as he instructs her to step into her swimsuit then pulls it up. She tries to jiggle away. 'Not so fast,' I say, grabbing hold of her and lathering what I can reach with Factor 30 suncream.

'Anyone for a swim?' Gerry says, looking at me.

'Not now, love. You go, and we'll stay here.'

I'm rubbing Hawaiian Tropic on myself while squinting up at him. He really does have a surprisingly fit body – yes, underneath that mild man exterior is a bit of a hunk. Very Clark Kent/Superman, I think, suddenly proud he's mine. Taking off his specs, he blinks at me, myopically. On second thoughts… more Penfold…

'Back in a tick.' He places a kiss on my lips before setting off at a lope towards the sea, in his swimming shorts and Nike trainers.

Finty points gives out a little bleat.

'Daddy'll be back soon,' I tell her.

Shading my eyes I can pick him out, messing around in the shallows, a little way beyond the incoming waves. And now he's performing handstands. Bonkers. I can tell it's him because he's the only man English enough to wear trainers in the sea. *Weirdo*, I think, rather affectionately as he shoots up out of the ocean, shakes water from his hair and then peers shorewards and waves.

'Look, Finty, over there.' I wave back. 'Look, darling, there's Daddy.' I point to where he's turned onto his back and is swimming – head barely visible as he ploughs through the water backwards, parallel to the shore, his trainers breaking the surface every now and then as they propel him along.

Trying to rub more suncream into the Michelin-type folds of Finty's tubby body and any bits I missed first time around, she's wriggling away, twisting and turning, so that I miss Gerry's return until I'm hit by a rush of wet and kicked sand as he flops down with all the grace of a seal.

'Gerry!' I protest.

'Chuck us that towel, will you?' He sets about rubbing his hair. 'How's the tan coming along?'

'What tan? Fat chance I'll get a chance to sunbathe with this little madam.'

'Then why don't I take Chipmunk here for a walk? Leave you in peace to work on your tan? You can even have a snooze if you like. Hm?'

I sit up. 'Now that really would be lovely. Are you sure you don't mind?'

'What? Mind having the chance to spend some quality time with my lovely little daughter?' he says as he turns to Finty, who is exploring the inside of her nostril with her finger. 'What do you say, Chip? Shall we go and explore?' He wipes her hands and snotty nose.

'Des!' she says, with a definite nod of her head.

'Righty-oh. We'll see you later, alligator.' And off they trot, him carrying Finty on his shoulders as I lie back, staking myself out in the July sun.

Once I've closed my eyes, I allow myself to sink deeper inside of me. The sounds around me fade: laughter and conversation drift away until all I can hear is my own breathing. In and out. Its rhythm passing through me – in, and out. Breathing in, and out – the dark expanding to merge with a light breeze coming in off the sea. And behind my eyelids it's all dark and cosy... then sunbursts spangle and red blobs across, transmogrifying into black and back again. Stoned by the sun's stroking of my brain waves. As daytime holds its breath, I concentrate on the internal respiration between capillaries and tissue.

It's warm... a warm summer's day...

'Howzat!' cries Dad, not bothering to keep a note of triumph out of his voice.

'Aw,' says Jake, as he drops the cricket bat.

'Not fair. You should have bowled underarm,' I shout at Dad. But the wind carries my voice up and away, just as it had sailed the ball plop into Dad's hand.

'What?' he calls out.

'Oh. Never mind.'

I glance over to where the cars are parked at the edge of the dunes. Brean Sands is long and flat, the beach damp and hard from drizzle and high tides, allowing cars to be driven onto its sands to park up.

When you swim in the sea, you get covered in brown stuff. We're never too sure if it's silt from the Bristol Channel Estuary or sewage from neighbouring Weston Super Mare. I wonder if Mum is getting out the sandwiches yet? There's no sign of her.

Beryl waves from her deckchair which is parked next to their Hillman Minx. Both her and stupid Marilyn (her and Slimy Bob's weed of a daughter) are wrapped in blankets on their chairs. I've been round to play with Marilyn. They moved in, three doors down, last spring. Marilyn has some sort of illness which means she goes to hospital sometimes. Her skin is a paler version of the strawberry Nesquik she makes for me in her wooden Wendy house; we drink the milkshakes through straws. I would have preferred a chocolate flavour one. She has dolls and teddies suffocating in clear plastic bags at the bottom of her wardrobe. Weird. Her bedroom is an explosion of pink and white and lace and satin, and – you know – girlie stuff. Yuk. As sweet as those chemical milkshakes she likes to show off making. I'd rather be off playing boys' games with Jake, but Mum insisted I play with Marilyn. 'Be nice to her,' she said. 'She's not well.'

I thought it would be like Heidi with me tending the sickly Marilyn, but she didn't appreciate my sacrifice. Instead, she made me sit on the floor of her bedroom, follow her orders as she laid out the tea things – 'Don't touch' – and then watch as she scolded and nagged first one doll, then another, then another. I stopped going in the end. Even though she has an unhealthy sickly sheen like a sick child is supposed to have. Being Heidi is much overrated.

Beryl, her mother's all right. She reminds me of one of those Beatrix Potter animal characters – plump and mumsy – fussing about with food and housewifey stuff. Not like my mum at all. I don't much like her husband. He wears sharp suits whatever the occasion. His face is always shiny and smells of aftershave. Mum says he's handsome – in a Lawrence Harvey kind of way – but he has no hair, and Jake and I call him Slimy Bob when no-one else is around. He's an estate agent, and Mum says he's fun. They're always having parties round at their house – even with a supposedly sick child. Wonder where he's got to an' all.

'Come on, Veronica,' calls Dad, beckoning to me with large gestures. 'Look lively. It's Jake's turn to bowl.'

I'm still fielding.

Jake runs up to the crease Dad has made in the sand with his bat, and bowls – overarm – and wide.

'Bad luck, lad. Try again,' shouts Dad, as I fetch the ball then throw it to Jake, who rubs it on his groin – like real cricketers do. He's up on his toes, getting ready, then pounds up to the crease, bowls and this time Dad hits it. High, high up into the sky only to disappear into the dunes.

'Six!' shouts Dad. Showing off as usual, *I think, as I half run, half walk to fetch the ball, my brown Clarks sandals plodding on the sand. Dad is a member of Clifton Cricket Club: Jake and I are only ten. Which tells you all you need to know about Dad's competitiveness.*

The wind off the sea is quite strong, but I can hear a soft laugh from behind the next dune.

With a bit of an effort, and despite the blinding light from the Brittany sun, I sit up and reach for the bottle of Perrier water. *That's quite enough daydreaming*, I think, shaking my head and then giving a quick glance around the beach. I don't want to recall that day again – we did it to death in my therapy sessions.

Stretching out my legs and checking they're not too red, I reach inside my bag for the latest Jilly Cooper, thinking that'll do nicely.

NINE

Gerry

Gerry has schlepped further along the beach than he thought he would, certain he must come across something like an ice cream van. Surely. *Although when you think about it*, he reasons, *why would there be a van? It's not like we're at Weston or anything.*

Finty starts to feel heavy so he lets her walk alongside him, slowing his pace to hers. 'Let's try up here,' he suggests.

'Ice bolly,' she insists.

'Soon, Chipmunk. Soon.' He hopes he does find somewhere soon, or she'll get a right grizzle on. He ought to have brought her sunhat, he realises, as he feels her hot head. She looks up and gives him a gappy grin.

Ah. Up ahead is a path which he's sure will take them back to the main road, very close to their villa. Yep. Halting on the thoroughfare – cars whizzing by – he gets his bearings. Good. There's the shop. Surely they'll have ice cream. 'C'mon, Fints,' he says, hoisting his daughter back onto his hip. 'Cor, you weigh a ton.' He hopes the holiday will help cheer up Ron. At the very least it's taking him out of the office and away from Hilary.

He's going to have to put her straight, even though she is his boss, in effect, being the Law Centre director. He shouldn't have allowed himself to get drunk when he knew she had designs on him. He knows it was only a kiss, and he'd managed to untangle himself, but she's been trying to engineer their being alone ever since. Which is awkward. And his being drunk is no excuse, but he was feeling vulnerable – and more than a little unloved, because Ron couldn't bear to have him anywhere near her. Yes, he knew that was no excuse. But Hilary had practically pounced on him.

He continues to stride purposefully along. *You need to man up, Gerry,* he told himself. *This is all your fault. You're the married man. You're the one who should never have gone there. Full stop. Especially when you suspected she fancied you.*

A quick image of Hilary on that night flashes through his mind. He'd stayed late at the office: a client had left a bottle of Scotch for him to enjoy after the case went their way. A finding which now meant a man and his two children didn't have to leave their home after all. It was good when he won an eviction case. Truth be told, it always made him feel a bit horny – winning in court. Normally he'd go home to Ronnie, celebrate and have sex – if he was lucky... But Ron wasn't interested these days and he... well, he was flattered when Hilary made her move. Looking back, he can see how she did most of the running. Not that this excused him... Oh God. He can see her now. Blonde hair mussed up, lipstick smudged from the glasses of Scotch they'd downed, her neat hand lingering a little too long on his arm. Her step towards him, that tilt of her head, the white of her neck, the taste of her lip gloss when he responded and everything became a blur of wanting and pulling and undoing, and... he'd only managed to stop in time.

Yes, it had been thrilling – losing himself to sensation. But then he felt cheap and annoyed at how he could let Ronnie down so badly – again. Hilary hinted that if he said anything – complained – then who would believe him? And in any case, she could say that it was him who had sexually harassed her! And who would they believe? He was in a tricky spot, and no mistake. And since she'd been pursuing him with her sly looks, her brushing her hand against his, her engineering things so she was in the same lift as him, calling him into her office because they need to go over a contract… and now with a conference coming up in a couple of months, she'd made it very clear what was on offer… No, he'd have to have another go at setting her straight.

He wonders if he ought to tell Ron. But she's got enough on her plate. He'll have to handle this himself before it gets out of control. It was bad enough when he had his fling with Fran – an old flame from his law student days. He'd lost his head at a law conference – scared by Ron being pregnant, feeling trapped is what Carol thought it probably was, when he and Ronnie went for couple's counselling. What a stupid mistake Fran was. Somehow, they'd managed to get back on track. And now, Hilary hassling him was the last thing he wants or needs.

It's Ron he wants to be with, stay with. Him, Finty and Ron, one team together. Facing everything and anything together. Yes, they'd been well on the road to happy after the counselling and then Finty being born, and he couldn't imagine leaving either of them, not ever. But then Jake got on that stupid motorbike, which wasn't even his… Ever since, their marriage has suffered under the unbearable strain of trying to manage Ron's grief and guilt, together with giving Angie as much practical and emotional support as humanly possible. He shakes his head. This holiday could prove to be a make or break for him and Ron, and he's determined it isn't going to be the latter.

He stops in the middle of the pavement and looks down at Finty, who looks back up at him. 'Why is life so complicated, Chips?' Her face is all eager as if she would help if she could, with whatever it is.

'Ice cweem?' she finally says.

'Ice cream it is!' He takes her hot little hand as they step into Madame's shop, the cool of the interior hitting him like a sigh as he casts about for a freezer unit.

He spies a small courtyard out back with a few tables and chairs dotted about, and he sees Angie sitting there alone – apart from Lauren, strapped in her buggy and sucking an ice lolly. Should he turn and leave Angie to her own devices? She looks so lost, so young, like a fresh-faced kid.

Perhaps she senses him standing there, dithering, because she glances up and beckons him over when Lauren calls out, 'Binty,' and paddles her feet on the buggy's footrest.

'Fancy seeing you here,' says Gerry as he approaches and places a soft kiss on Angie's cheek – she smells of Pears soap. 'Mind if we join you?' Finty already has her chubby arms around Lauren's neck as she half falls on top of, half embraces her.

'Please do.' Angie offers a welcoming smile as he sits opposite, pulling Finty onto on his lap. 'Ow!' His daughter gives him a kick. He nods over at Lauren in her buggy. 'Wish I'd brought our buggy along,' he says. 'It's only when you end up having to carry them that you realise how heavy they are.'

'Tell me about it,' says Angie.

Finty clearly wants to play with Lauren, so Angie undoes Lauren's buggy straps, and the two adults watch as the girls toddle about a bit.

'Ron's still at the beach.' He shrugs – semi-apologetically. 'Having a nap – thought I'd leave her to it.'

'Lucky her.' Angie grabs Lauren, giving her face the once-over with a wet wipe and giving Gerry a side glance from under her eyelashes. 'I'm sorry. I suppose that sounded rude.'

'Nah. You're all right.'

'It's just… well…' she starts. 'This holiday isn't turning out to be the break I hoped it would be.'

'Are they ever a break, though – you know – with kids?'

'Try it with Jake too.'

A waitress appears. 'Coffee?' he asks Angie, who shakes her head.

'I've already had one. In any case, we shall need to make a move in five minutes.'

'Good that you don't have to go yet, I mean.' He orders an ice lolly for each of the girls – because if Finty's having one, then Lauren insists she must too.

'That's them sorted for a while. So, where are the other two?' Gerry asks. 'Jake and Sarah?'

'I left them at the villa with Jake minding Sarah.' She clocks the look on his face. 'I know what you're thinking. You think Jake can't look after her. But she's very sensible and anyway... I had to get out. Plus,' she lifts her head defiantly, 'he has to pick up the reins at some time. You and Ronnie... You have no idea...' He waits for her to continue. 'I do love him and everything, of course I do – but he's changed so much...'

'I get that it can't be plain sailing.' He encloses his hand over hers. She has such a small hand, not at all like Veronica's, which are nearly the size of his. All due to her Viking build, she insists. 'We've got big bones,' she likes to say. He doesn't know if he believes this, but Angie – well, the bones in her hands are small, almost like those of a tiny bird... or a titchy mouse... Next she's staring open-mouthed at the doorway, and as Gerry follows her gaze, there, standing at a cock-eyed angle, is Jake.

Gerry scrambles to his feet, signalling to a chair. 'Jake, mate. Come and join us – here, take a seat.'

But Angie's standing, casting anxiously around him. 'Where is she? Where's Sarah? Jake. Listen to me – where is Sarah?' She takes a step towards her husband. 'Christ, Jake. Where is she? Don't tell me you left Sarah all on her own.'

Jake sucks in some spittle. 'I. She...' he starts, then shrugs and gives up.

Hurriedly, Angie gathers up her stuff up, hastily straps Lauren back into the buggy, all intent on returning to the villa. But then Gerry makes a snap decision. 'Don't you worry,' he says, grabbing Finty. 'You take your time and we'll dash on ahead.' To both of them he adds, 'I'm sure she'll be fine.'

Angie shoots him a look of relief and for a moment she reminds him again of Hilary. Also, he can't help noticing – as she leans over – how her blouse gapes just enough so he can see the pink areola of her nipple.

He gives himself a mental shake: *Fuck's sake, Ger.* Then to Jake, 'Don't you worry, I'll go find her. I'm on it.'

Outside, Gerry's glad for the activity, for the feel of his feet pounding on the pavement and his daughter jiggling on his shoulders as he runs along the street. *Bloody unreal,* he allows himself to think. *Takes only the sight of some flesh and I've got a semi. Wonder if it's true that your balls will explode if you don't get laid.* His are aching right now.

TEN

Back at the Beach

I'm still enjoying my sunbathe when I'm rudely disturbed by Finty landing – *Oof* – on my bare stomach.

'Oi!' Sitting up, I blink against the blinding sunlight – 'You little monster' – and start to tickle her until she's squirming about like a captive lion cub.

Gerry takes his place beside us. 'Sorry we took so long.' He flops back onto his elbows. 'Spot of bother back at the ranch,' he adds, crossing his feet at the ankles.

'Oh?'

He fills me in on what happened.

'Christ. Was Sarah okay?'

'Yes, she was fine. Just fine.' Gerry reaches for the bag containing our packed lunch as Finty – now lying on top of me – places her little face alongside mine and paddles my chest with her pudgy hands.

'I dashed into the villa. Half-expecting all sorts, and there she was, as calm as you like, colouring in one of her books. She looks up at me and says, "I'm fine looking after Daddy on my own, you know." Just like that. I swear that girl is too old for her years.' He pushes his glasses further up his nose. 'Want one of these?' He passes over a sandwich: some sort of ham.

'I know what you mean about Sarah,' I say, opening a packet of crisps for Finty. 'I sometimes wonder if Angie relies too much on her. Whether she forgets she's only seven.'

Gerry gives an audible sigh. 'Well… It's tough for her.'

'It's tough for us all.'

Gerry takes a handful of crisps and places them inside his sandwich. 'This all we got to eat?' he says, peering into our bag of food.

'Afraid so.'

Gerry munches his ham and crisp sandwich. 'Never mind. Guess we'll buy more grub on the way back?'

I sigh. 'We can't. Don't you remember? Most of the kitty money went on ice creams and croissants for them this morning.'

Overhead a few wisps of cloud flicker across the sky, and a seagull lands with a small thud very close to Finty, its beady eye sweeping the beach for any stray scraps of food. Gerry kicks sand at it – 'Shoo' – but the gull merely hops a few strides away, watching side on for it's moment to seize its chance.

'Bloody seagulls,' says Gerry.

'Bubby eegulls,' says our delighted daughter.

'I'll cash some travellers cheques at the Hotel Bretagne. Okay? Look, it's no big deal.'

'Yes, well.'

'I might as well ring the office while I'm in there. They're bound to have a public phone.'

I busy myself trying to get Finty's sunhat on her head. Every time I put it on, she pulls it off again.

'There's this tricky case, which I need to keep an eye on. Hilary's been ringing me, putting pressure on because the other solicitor is unsure what to do. I've told her to wait until I get back, but you know how they are.'

I do? He's been mentioning this Hilary quite a lot, lately; perhaps there's more to her than work. But he seems innocent enough, and

I decide I'm being paranoid; still, who could blame me, after that thing with his ex Fran? Seemed like the minute I discovered I was pregnant he hooked up with her at a conference for a shag. After he confessed, he was the one to suggest we consult Carol for couple's counselling, especially as I was all for finishing with him. Because you can never trust a cheater, everyone knows that.

'Can you not?' Carol said. 'Don't you think that could become a self-fulfilling prophecy?' *Next she'll be making out it was all my fault,* I'd thought, rather ungraciously.

She insisted on Gerry writing me a letter telling me how he felt about me, about our relationship and about the baby. In the end, he wrote a heartfelt letter, pledging it would never happen again, and he seemed suitably repentant. And now we seem to have got past it. If anything our sessions and his panic have resolved a lot of stuff for both of us. He'd clearly freaked out about my surprise pregnancy, had a wobble, and when he returned from conference and I'd sensed something had happened… well, it didn't prove hard to get it out of him. I think he was dying to confess and get it off his chest. In the past I've been a champion bolter, so my first instinct was to end things and run for the hills. 'Not so fast,' Carol had said.

Still, here we are. Back with my same antennae twitching. How I wish I could speak to Carol, but she insisted on no contact for this holiday week.

I watch him wiping Finty's mouth and grubby mitts, remembering how I once thought he wouldn't be long-term. More a bit of a fling. He's on the geeky side and not my usual good-looking, commitment-phobic-bastards, but he's grown on me, and there's something most attractive about a man who doesn't appear to know how attractive he is. Clearly, he has some allure going on, as other women seem drawn to him. Once it used to amuse me how women would flirt with him while he remained oblivious – but that was before Finty, and before the stakes got so high. Perhaps we should discuss him wearing a wedding ring, to show he's off-limits?

I frown, thinking how we don't have much of a solid footing, do we? Two unattached, uncommitted young people, not even cohabiting when I discover I'm pregnant, then there's the moving in together weeks before the birth, Jake's accident and our quick, low-key marriage (as we didn't think it was right to celebrate or have a joyful occasion – Gerry accepting what I had to say on that score). Perhaps too much depends on Finty being the glue which holds us together? But it shouldn't be like that, should it?

He's sitting and smiling over at me, and I hold his gaze perhaps a second too long before looking away and thinking how he does lift my heart. Especially when he's being "good Dad". Maybe he's right, and this holiday is exactly what we need.

'Penny for them?' he says.

'Pass me one of those ham sandwiches?'

I'm distracted by Finty squeezing her sandwich to pulp, then deliberately opening her fingers to let it drop on the sand: giving that waiting seagull its chance. With a few hops and a spear of its beak, it has the sandwich away, flapping off with its big flappy wings so close to Finty they almost knock her over.

'Gaaa!' shouts the gull.

'Mummee!'

'Never mind, darling. Sssh.'

Gerry chases the gull, shooing it away.

'Now this time, young lady,' I say as I place half of my own sandwich in her paw. 'You hold on tight.'

Her sobs have subsided into hiccups. 'Bab bird!'

Gerry trails back to us. 'My hero!' He takes a bow, then pulls me to my feet, scoops up Finty and, enfolding us both in a hug, says, 'You're gorgeous, you are, Veronica.' He gives me a short snog, causing Finty to slap a hand to her face and a neighbouring couple to shake their heads then return to their books.

'Gerroff!' I say to my husband.

All of a sudden I want to run. 'Won't be long,' I say, my head up.

'What do you mean, you won't be long? Where are you going?'

'Wait here!' I shout as I take off – Gerry's face a picture of "what the?" – but I'm on my toes, running and running for the sheer hell, the sheer joy of being alive! Talk about runaway bride!

My bare feet are pounding the sand as somewhere behind me Gerry's voice calls out, 'Ron! Ron!' But I'm faster, faster, veering to the left and skirting the edge of the sea – the great unknowable sea which I could run into if I so desire – but no, I hurtle along the stretch of sands, salt air whipping my hair, and I'm in my body, inside my body; I'm sharp, defined and I won't feel guilty anymore. I'm going to run and run and run as if I could fly, as if I'm about to take wing and soar above the ground; I even start to do aeroplane wings, turning, swerving in a big swoop, past holidaymakers, jumping effortlessly now over sandcastles in various stages of construction, castles which will never make it into the sky, weaving around picnics, past startled happy families: running, my lungs bursting, as I now finally have my own family back in my sights. Will I veer off or head towards them?

Finty stands waiting with her father, and as I run towards them he lets go his hold and she takes a few toddler steps, arms outstretched to me, her mummy, arrived to scoop her up, swing her around and around, but instead I slow to a walk, sides aching with the start of a stitch, lungs gulping in sweet fresh air. Once I reach them, I bend forwards, arms on thighs, to catch my breath, while Finty jumps up and down around me until finally I kiss my daughter and take my place alongside my husband.

Still catching my breath, I feel more "me" than I have done for a long while. 'That was brilliant,' I manage to get out.

'But what was it in aid of? Your running about like that?'

'I just needed to run.'

'Bonkers. Still, you know what they say, don't you?'

'No, what do they say?'

'Da doo run, Ron Ron. Da doo run, Ron.'

'Oh, very funny.' And we all three laugh, together.

It's the end of the afternoon as we clamber back up the hill, the going tougher than on the way down. Stopping for a breather near the brow, my attention rests on a cypress tree which stands sentinel against darkening clouds scudding across what could easily be a Hollywood-lit backdrop. It reminds me of the scene in *Gone with the Wind*, when Scarlett O'Hara makes her pledge that she and her family will never go hungry again. I half-expect the whole frame to be scorched by lightning, as elemental forces gather. *Don't be so melodramatic*, I tell myself, as I bow my head and carry on. There's a bit of a wind up, though, that's for sure.

ELEVEN

Angie

I'll go mental if I don't get out and away, thinks Angie, as she looks right and then left before attempting to cross the road. There's a moment before she judges a gap in the dashing-about-chugging-and-beeping French traffic when she nearly makes the move which could end it all. If she were to only step out – a small step is all it would take – in front of this lorry, say. In that flash she wonders whether it would hurt, whether she'd feel anything except for blissful quiet. Would there be a bird singing on high as she slipped into oblivion? Oh, how she longs for it. Then the face of Sarah is before her, asking if she's going to be long – an extra anxiety on those tiny little features. Sarah. And Lauren. An image of Jake standing like a raggedy scarecrow in a doorway flashes through her mind. No, she can't do it. Judging the speeds and distances, she successfully crosses to the Hotel Bretagne. Ostensibly to get some cash. But she doesn't think for one moment she fooled Sarah. Or Ronnie, either. 'You go,' she'd said – as if bestowing permission on her to get away and try to have a break, a smidgeon of peace and quiet.

Safe on the other side, Angie lifts her chin and strides into the foyer. There's Gerry – over in the corner – on the payphone. He looks engrossed. If she creeps forward a little she won't disturb him but can wait until he's done. Perhaps they can have a coffee – or even a drink – together. Merely so she can stretch out this precious time.

She slots in behind a pillar. A little too close, perhaps, as she can hear Gerry's side of the conversation.

'…No… look, Hilary, I've told you. It was a mistake. Well, I'm sorry you feel like that…'

He leans his hand against the wall above the telephone. '… You and I know it was nothing…' Voice softens. 'Yes, I am sorry. Don't be daft… I have a wife, a family…' Runs hand through his hair. 'That's blackmail… fine… you go ahead and do that… I'm going to tell Ron in any case… This is ridiculous. You're making this out to be more than it ever was. It was only a kiss, and nothing more… Fine, you go ahead and do your worst, Hilary.' He hangs up and stands staring at the phone as if it's betrayed him.

Angie flattens herself against the pillar as Gerry strides past but doesn't notice her. From the look of him, he wouldn't notice if his own mother or a crowd of booing people were here. Watching. Listening. *Perhaps there's trouble in paradise after all*, she thinks, not sure if she should enjoy the idea quite so much.

TWELVE

Sunday Evening

Tonight it's the turn of the others as Jake, Angie and their girls all troop out to the Hotel Bretagne for the Intasun Summer Barbeque. Music, laughter and shouting soon dance across on the balmy evening air (the threatened storm never did happen). Earlier, Gerry returned from his telephone call to the office all stressed and tight-lipped. I decided not to quiz him as I'm sure he'll tell me when he's good and ready. I'm just glad he's brought back cash, a bottle of wine and a six-pack of beer for our own indulgence.

I nod towards the open window. 'Sounds like they're having a good time over there, doesn't it?' I dish up our meal of leftovers and decant the last of our wine into glasses.

'Did you want to go with them?' asks Gerry as I place a dish of potatoes in front of him.

'God no. Nah.'

'It'll be full of Darrens and Kylies. You wouldn't like that at all. They'll be pissed by now, playing pass the matchbox on their noses.'

'Don't be such a snob,' I say, chucking a wet cloth at him. 'It might have been fun.'

'If it's fun you're after,' says Gerry, straightening Finty in her chair, 'then why don't we go to this party on the Quayside Thursday night? It sounds like a right good craic.'

'I'm not sure.'

'Doesn't cost much,' he says, in his most cajoling voice. 'We are here on holiday and we should make the most of what's on offer.'

'Ah, go on then. But if it's rubbish then it'll be all down to you.'

'That's the spirit.'

Outside the evening spreads its dark across the backyard as chill creeps in through an open window and over the sill, like some invisible crawling hand. Giving a small shiver, I pull on Gerry's sweatshirt for warmth – it smells of him.

'Mm,' he's murmuring as he finishes off a last morsel of potatoes and ratatouille, and then pats his belly. 'That was great.' Pushing his plate away, he says, 'Fancy a beer?' and gets to his feet.

'No, thanks,' I say, shaking my head. 'Crikey, is that the Macarena song I can hear?'

Dancing around the kitchen, beer in hand, and much to Finty's delight, Gerry starts to sing "I'm a Little Teapot", complete with teapot actions, as Finty jumps up and down, clapping away as Gerry dances out of the door, muttering, 'Loo.'

'Your daddy's barmy,' I say, wiping at the chocolate yoghurt she's managed to get all around her mouth.

'Dink,' she demands.

'Hang on...'

I turn as the back door clangs open. 'Is there a beer in the house?' hails Angie as she bustles in, clattering an empty buggy behind her. Her face is rather grim, despite her cheery call. 'Could bloody well do with one.'

'Did you have a good time?'

'Don't ask.'

'Where's Jake?'

'What? Oh, he's coming – behind us somewhere. Now, where's that beer?' She helps herself to one from Gerry's six-pack, as Sarah skips about holding a jauntily jerking balloon. 'It was great, wasn't it, Mummy?'

Angie gives a strained smile as she deftly folds the buggy. 'Hurry up, you two.' She's clearly calling out to Jake and Lauren. 'Where are you?'

Lauren's the first in the back door with Jake half-pulled along behind her. 'Hullo,' he says, giving me a broad grin – I say broad, but one side of his face lifts more than the other. 'Anyone want tea?' He's making a beeline for the cooker to set about his laborious task of picking up the matchbox, turning the knob on the cooker, opening the matchbox with his good hand, striking a match with some pretty nifty one-handed dexterity, filling the newly bought kettle and then placing it on the top of the burner. All one-handed.

Lauren watches, her adoring face shining up at him. Once he's finished, he beams his lopsided beam at her.

'Where's Gerry, then?' says Angie as I free Finty from her chair.

'Just popped to the loo.'

She leans across and says, close to my ear, 'You know what? Times like this I want to scream.' She sits down on a chair, legs out in front of her. 'Because every bloody fucking thing Jake does is so fucking slow!'

Sarah tugs at her mother's sleeve and Angie turns to her with a smile (am I the only one who notices it's fake?). 'What is it, darling?'

'We played games – didn't we, Mum?' says Sarah, all eager. 'And there was this man, Auntie Ron… And he, he fell over. He looked so funny… didn't he, Mum? And we played the one… Oh, what was it, Mum?'

Angie gives out a groan. 'God, yes, that god-awful one where you pass the orange along. Chin to chin. Trouble was that the woman next to me had no chin to speak of. At all.'

'Yeah,' says Sarah, waving to gain her father's attention. 'It was funny, wasn't it, Dad?'

But Jake's not paying any mind; instead, he's watching water boil. Literally.

Angie closes her eyes.

'Mum?' Sarah's not excitedly hopping about any longer. 'Is it all right if I go and play with Lauren and Finty? Until bedtime?' Poor thing has probably had enough of us grownups.

'Okay, okay.' Wearily she opens her eyes once more. I notice the deep shadows around them. 'But take the girls into the other room, yes? And don't forget – crayons on the table, please.'

The girls run helter-skelter from the room, Jake waiting for them to pass as he holds a tray carrying four cups of milky tea – very carefully – his tongue sticking out with the effort as he distributes them to each of us.

'Thanks,' says Angie, without meeting his eyes.

I wrap my hands around the cup Jake gives me, grateful for its warmth. 'Truly, though, Angie. How was the Intasun Barbecue?'

'As you'd expect, I suppose.' She lets out a long sigh. 'People either don't talk to us because they're too embarrassed, or they look away. Or, they come over and ask what's happened to Jake, isn't it a shame – blah blah. All the usual crap.' She leans her elbows on the table. 'The thing is,' she continues, 'and I never thought I'd ever think this – but I'm starting to envy these people. Normal people. Anyone, frankly.'

'How so?' I look across at Jake, who's slurping his tea, seemingly not following our conversation but lost in a world of his own.

'Their "normal" little families. And you know the worst thing of all?' (I'll bet she's about to tell me.) 'The top, number one, very worst thing? Most of them are a bunch of prannies who I never ever would have envied before. I'm sorry, but they are.'

'Not all of them, surely.'

'I'll bet not one of them have what we did before the bloody accident. And now...' She runs her fingers through her hair. 'They're the ones who seem to have it all – and I'd give anything to be them. Isn't that fucking hilarious! I'd give anything to be boring old them. Instead I have to endure their pity, or their thinking that Jake is a retard, or subhuman. No, don't give me that look. It's *exactly* what they think.' She's shaking her head. 'And I have to smile politely and take it. Take their looks and their fuckin' awful pity.' The music and noise outside has stopped. The party is over.

'So,' she says with a bitter laugh, 'it's not only you two I envy. Or did...' She flickers a glance at me. 'I envy them all. Their banal talk. Even their arguing. At least they've got something resembling a normal life going on.' Jake finally looks up from his tea.

'You still have something too.' I reach across the table, but she snatches her hand away.

'Easy for you to say.'

Oh, it really isn't, Angie.

'I even find myself listening to what they're talking about,' continues Angie. 'Eavesdropping, you know? Thinking how lucky they are to be talking about stuff. Discussing their kids. What they're going to buy at the supermarket.' For the first time, I notice she has grey snaking through her brown hair like straggly brambles.

'Hallo!' calls out Gerry as he bursts into the kitchen with another six-pack of beer in a carrier bag. 'Did you miss me?' He cheerfully closes the door behind him and then looks unsure as he clocks the atmosphere in the kitchen. 'I popped to the shop. Good idea or what?' he says, looking first at Angie and then at me. 'What is it? Did I miss something?'

'Nothing much,' I say.

'Should I be worried? Were my ears burning?' He places the beers in the fridge.

'Should they be?' says Angie in an arch kind of way which causes both Gerry and I give to her a queer look. 'I saw you earlier, you see. On the phone in the Bretagne,' she says, while he looks rather furtive. 'You seemed engrossed, so I didn't want to interrupt.'

I'm not sure what's going on but decide I'd better change the subject. 'You don't want to take any notice of what other people say or think. They have no idea whatsoever what it's like.' I'm looking at my brother, who blankly stares back. 'No-one but Jake would've got this far. He's a fucking hero, that's what he is. You do know that, don't you, Jake?' He seems rather bewildered at the turn the conversation has taken.

Angie's face softens as she goes to Jake's side. 'Do you remember what I told you, about the accident, Jake? How we don't fully know what happened? And how long you were in hospital, and what you were like?'

Does he? I certainly do.

The day we get the call is a sunny April day with no hint of what is to come. We're strangely calm as the three of us - me, Gerry, and our new baby Finty - load up the car then set off up the M4 to the National Neurological Hospital. On reaching the outskirts of London we pass people shopping, dogs barking, families playing in parks enjoying the sunshine. Everywhere talking and laughing like nothing has happened. But I... I feel catapulted into limbo. I can't tell you much about that journey, apart from Gerry was doing the driving.

When we arrive, there is nothing dramatic about the hospital scene. No flashy machines surround the bed. No handsome young doctors with adoring nurses stand around talking in hushed asides. It looks like an ordinary ward. Patients sit up in bed. Cards, flowers and visitors all around them. Nurses walk up and down, hailing patients, telling them off. Even cracking jokes. Reality isn't behaving itself. Critical, they said on the phone. Come right away. He's very poorly. But it can't be that bad, can it? This doesn't look like an intensive care ward.

I miss the bleeping machine at first. Tracing your heartbeat. It sits unobtrusively above your bed. Angie is there. Half crouched over you. I assume it's you – you look such a mess that Angie is my main clue.

She gets up. 'I'm so glad you're here,' she says, kissing me on the cheek. But I'm staring down at the body lying beached on the bed. It looks like yours. Tubes snake in and out of a face which is so bruised, cut, disfigured and horrendously swollen that it looks nothing like you at all. I stifle the urge to laugh – they say that can happen, don't they, that when faced with something this dreadful all that comes out is a laugh.

'He has a hole in his head, and his right ear has been sewn back on,' Angie says, bizarrely sounding matter-of-fact. But I'm thinking, how can anyone's head and neck swell to three times their normal size, and live? A bandage struggles to keep your brain, and bits in place.

Perhaps it isn't you? Perhaps there's been some mistake.

It's your hands which finally clinch it. When I finally look down, I recognise those knuckles thickened by hard knocks at rugby and volleyball. Those are the hands which held my new baby a mere week ago. These hands can tickle a tune out of any guitar. I'd recognise them anywhere.

'Only one or two visitors at a time,' says a nurse. I want to stay, but Angie's turned back excludes me.

'Come on,' Gerry says gently, as I let him lead me away.

In the ward dayroom, the family is gathered. Mum has set

up camp in a corner with suitcase and holdall. Dad tells me how they're staying at the hospital with Angie, for the duration. Mum drinks tea from a thermos and blows smoke out of an open window as she chain smokes Benson & Hedges, trying to blend in with the chipped paint on the wall. She looks as old and tired as the room which has long brown plastic seats lining two facing walls and a public telephone on another. Dad returns to pacing, keeping vigil by the door.

Carefully, I place my new baby Finty in her carrycot on one of the seats, as we wait our turn at Jake's bedside.

A doctor enters. He's tall with dark hair and glasses, and he wears authority and a white coat as we listen to what he has to say. 'I'm glad you're all here,' he starts. 'Jake is very lucky to be alive. But I'm sorry to have to tell you that if he does survive, he'll be severely disabled. Both physically and mentally.' Just words. No-one can take them in. Except, perhaps, me.

'It's lucky you have a physio in the family,' he says, smiling across at me as if we're co-conspirators.

Then it's my turn to sit by your bed.

'Heavily sedated, you know,' says the male nurse, fussing about with the tubes. 'It helps with the pain,' he says by way of explanation. 'It also helps to keep him nice and quiet.' (I can't be bothered to say how I know all this.)

I'm holding your right hand. Underneath the hospital bedsheet you are naked, apparently without a mark on your body, nor on your paralysed arms and legs.

'Just going to make you cough, Jake,' says a male nurse who's arrived to pass a suction tube down the hole in your throat while a machine vacuums out the secretions. 'He's got two children, I hear,' the nurse says. 'I've got five myself. We live in Hitchin – which is a bit of a way to travel for work.'

He prattles on, making me feel irritated. You should not talk over him, I long to say. People in comas can often hear what's being *said around them. Do you not know that? Don't treat him like a non-person. But I know the male nurse is doing his best. He leaves me to it, so I pull up a chair and begin talking to you, telling you about Finty, about my life with Gerry, when the index finger on your left hand slowly rises. It quivers and points to out of the ward. As if outside is where you want to go. Then it flutters down to rest on the bed like a bird making a failed attempt to fly.*

And as I sit here, I can sense you – with my twin spider-brain. I can feel your vitality, and images of you surround me with good feelings. Free spirit, do you remember? We used to say we were free spirits, you and I, didn't we? But Mum used to say you were forever tempting fate, what with your getting into physical scrapes.

Why motorbikes? Why did you always have to have some sort of motorbike? Who do you think you are? Evel Knievel? You and your bloody, bloody motorbikes.

'Jake,' I say, getting down low, so I can whisper in your ear without anyone else hearing. 'Concentrate. Concentrate hard on keeping your heart going. Come back to me.' I peer up at the machine, which bleeps strongly.

'C'mon, Jake. You can do it. Concentrate on getting your brain better.' I place my hands gently over the bandage wrapping your head and try to beam my life force into you.

Then I'm sobbing. Begging. 'I don't give a monkey's about anything else, Jake. Don't you go die on me. Don't you dare fucking die and leave me here. Alone.'

Because once we used to float together. Side by side we kept company, shifting and turning until our time had come.

I am bursting for a wee, and there's no en-suite in our holiday villa. But when I get to the bathroom it's full. Angie has her back to the door as she kneels next to the enamel bath where Sarah and Lauren are happily splashing – their naked pot bellies glistening with shower gel – grinning away. Jake slowly arrives to stand and watch them from the doorway. Then they stop, mid-splash, on noticing him there, causing Angie to turn round.

'Fuck's sake, Jake! Will you stop sneaking up on us like that! I can't stand it! Why don't you ever help me with the girls? Do something? Don't just stand there!'

But Jake stands. Still.

'They're your children as well,' she says, sitting back on her heels. 'Christ almighty.' She's on her feet now, facing him full on. 'Just look at you. You're like some fuckin' zombie!' She turns to me. 'See? It's like living with one of the Living Dead!'

Jake slowly moves away, his hands hang loosely by his side, his face slack, and for that moment I can see what she means.

With a set jaw, she returns to the girls. 'It's all right,' she murmurs, as their faces begin to screw up into threatened tears. 'It's all right.'

'I'll wait until you're done,' I say as I retreat, one step at a time.

Back in our room, Gerry lifts the covers for me to climb in next to him.

'Look, Ron,' he says as I plump the pillows, all ready to sit up and listen to what is to come. There's a bad vibe swirling around this room which I'm so highly attuned to, I can almost see it.

'I need to talk to you,' he says.

'Yes?'

'It's about Hilary.'

Later, after he's told me, and I've assured him I really do believe his version of a drunken snog, I wonder if he would have said anything at all had it not been for Angie overhearing his conversation in the hotel? I'm suddenly weary of it all. Can I be bothered to use this as an opportunity to re-examine our marriage and get it back on track? Is this even what I want?

All I know is I don't have energy enough to care. That might sound awful, but it seems such a small crime in the big scheme of things, doesn't it? A snog. Somebody giving in to what sounds like a mild attraction. What does a small betrayal count for? What does it matter? It's not as if it's going to rip the heavens open. It's not like anyone has shot poor cock robin, is it? No. Because he's already dead.

That night I dream of rainforests, of impossibly beautiful butterflies swirling round and around until they form a tornado which scoots across the oceans to reach our shores, where it blows a little jolly robin redbreast out of its nest. Makes a change from a hummingbird, I suppose.

All the birds of the air were a-sighing and a-sobbing,
When they heard the bell toll for poor Cock Robin.
When they heard of the death of poor Cock Robin.

THIRTEEN

Monday

'Open wide, now, Jake,' says Angie as she pops a few drops of tincture under his tongue. 'Gingko biloba,' she says, as she next hands him his Omega 3 capsule, which he swallows with water, followed by juice with protein and acetyl-choline mixed in. His early-morning supplement regime – worked out by Angie and her homeopath. ('Homeopathic doctor, actually.') I know the routine – in twenty minutes' time she'll be slipping Jake a tiny homeopathic pill.

Gerry's making a bit of a song and dance about clearing away the breakfast things, as if he expects a round of applause, when a small elderly woman dressed in black, save for a white collar and apron, appears at the kitchen window.

'*Bonjour*,' she greets us.

We gather around, as she talks in French. She is Madame, who owns our Villa Bagatelle and the general shop along the road, explains Angie, who then does most of the talking. I don't understand a word but nod and smile encouragingly, and decide I like Madame's characterful, lined face.

Madame nods in the direction of Jake, I add my '*au revoir*' to the chorus and she is gone.

'I can say *bonjour*,' pipes up Sarah, who has her bucket and spade ready for the beach.

'That's lovely, darling,' says Angie as she ruffles her eldest daughter's hair.

'So come on, then, what did Madame have to say?' I ask.

'She wishes us a good holiday and when I told her about the leaking tap in the sink she said she'd send her son Xavier over to fix it,' says Angie. 'And then, she said, "your husband, he looks tired," was he well? So I told her he'd had an accident.' She points to her head. 'In the head.' Angie bends over to kiss Jake on the top of his. 'Apparently, her husband had a stroke and speech problems, and she looked after him until he died last year.'

'Oh.'

'Anyhoo,' she adds, hugging Jake around the neck as he grins away. 'She said we can pop round for coffee anytime. Especially you, Jake. I do believe she's taken quite a shine to you.'

He looks up. 'That's absent,' he says.

I bump into Angie in the corridor; she's about to squeeze past. 'Gerry thinks you may have overheard a conversation he had on the telephone? At the hotel?'

'Oh yes, that. Yes, I did overhear him, and I must say, Ron, he'd clearly gone to the hotel so that nobody would overhear. Sadly for him, though, I was there.' She pulls herself up straight.

'You needn't worry about anything you heard, because he's told me all about it. He's being hassled at work by his boss – some Hilary woman. She's got a bit of a crush on him, and he's in a difficult position as she's the director and has threatened that if he says anything she'll sue him for sexual harassment.'

Angie remained purse-lipped.

'Gerry doesn't like to upset people, but it's got to the point where she keeps on phoning him and imagines there's something special between them, so he's trying to set her straight without it all being awkward at work. And that's all there is to it.'

'Good, I'm glad he told you. Because it doesn't pay to have secrets, does it?' She's got that judgemental look all over her face. 'Just look at what happened between Jake and your mother. How they fell out and weren't speaking before his accident. And all because you'd been keeping a secret you should have shared with him long before.'

'That's different and you know it is. We were children, and I was trying to protect him.'

'They always come out, though, don't they? These secrets.' With that passing comment she pushed herself off the wall and walked off.

Ah, bugger.

Once the others are out, I allow myself a good old sob. Suddenly everything is all my fault. I'm full on having a pity party of my own when there's a gentle knocking at the door.

Looking up, I see a tall man hovering in the doorway – it's the bloke from the café. Has he been stalking me? Wiping at my eyes with a tissue, I scramble to my feet.

'Erm… Hello?'

'*Excuse moi*,' he says in a voice which sounds husky from Gauloises and Remy Martin. Now I see him closer up and without any beer goggles, he's even more attractive than I'd first thought. He has the look of a gallic Gabriel Byrne – twinkly-eyed, older than me (but not by too much), strong stubby hands, dark dishevelled curls – just my type – well, used to be, before Gerry, of course. '*Mon mere*, I mean, my mother. She tell me to come.'

Hurriedly I wipe at my eyes and softly blow my nose (or try to, but it comes out more like the trumpeting call of a lonely elephant).

'Of course. Yes. Sorry. You must be Xavier.'

He smiles. 'Ah yes, I must be.' He has a chip in his front

tooth, his teeth slightly stained from – oh, heck – from espresso coffee, small cheroots… kissing women…

'*Maman*, she say—'

'Oh, of course, of course.' I wonder if I have mascara smudged under my eyes. Would it be awful if I checked myself in the mirror? Is my hair sticking up where I've been lying prostate, and crying, across the table? 'Sorry about…' I rather feebly gesture to my face, then change course and indicate towards the sink. 'It's, um, it's over there… ah, the um… Sink. Yes, of course. Silly me. You know where the kitchen sink is.'

'*Mais oui.*' As he walks past, his presence seems to fill the room, sucking out all the air so that I feel quite dizzy, and I can smell his delicious faint tobacco, slightly unwashed male smell mixed with cologne. He's wearing shorts which display strong calves and thighs, and as he reaches for the handle of the sink cupboard door, I'm transfixed by his hands – they're large and tender like those of a sculptor's. *I'll bet they're rough to the touch*, I'm thinking as he catches my gaze and meets it with a challenge in his eyes. A thrill shoots through me. I almost laugh at myself. Still turned on by a bad boy, Ron. You are such a ridiculous cliché. And, you're behaving like a schoolgirl.

Swiftly looking the other way, I manage a, 'Do carry on.'

Yes, carry on, stepping towards me, with a hard look in your eye… placing down your spanner… walking slowly and deliberately towards me – God, now I've gone all *Confessions of a French Handyman.*

Taking a swig of my now-cold tea, I try and collect myself. Stop being so pathetic. Any minute now you'll start rubbing against him like a cat on heat.

But, oh, how I'm enjoying the sensation of being alive. Even if it is mere fantasy I'm relishing that spark spluttering to life. I'd always prided myself on having a healthy libido. But of late, since the you-know-what – nothing. And I can't fake it if I don't feel it.

There's no Acting As If, far as sex is concerned. No matter how much Gerry wishes I would. We've tried since then, of course we have – last time, a few weeks ago: empty sex, like trying to eat a chocolate éclair with no filling. But what's the point of that? And now my mind is thinking of an eclair, of the crunch of chocolate and the texture, the taste of cream oozing on the tip of my tongue as I bite and lick a deliciously chocolatey sexy éclair...

'Why are you smiling?' says Xavier as he puts down his wrench. 'I could not help but notice.'

'It's nothing,' I say, brushing non-existent crumbs from my shorts.

'You should smile more often, and not cry. There. That is better. You are very pretty when you smile.'

And then who comes in but Angie, of course.

'I'd best get a move on,' I say, getting to my feet and giving Xavier a non-sexy nod. 'Nice to meet you.'

'Likewise,' he says, as he wipes those long grubby strong fingers on a dirty rag.

I stay upstairs until I'm sure Xavier has gone and it's safe for me to go downstairs without embarrassing myself. Through our bedroom window I can see the sun climbing into what promises to be another glorious day.

'Yoo hoo!' calls Gerry from down below. He's hand in hand with Finty, waving his wallet in the air, both of them grinning. 'Got the dosh.' He glances around.

'Where are the others, I say?'

'You've missed them, they've gone ahead to the beach.' He hoists Finty onto his hip. 'Shake a leg, then. We're in the money, and the day is ours.'

'Righty-oh.'

He's fine, we're fine, everything is all tip top, fine and dandy. In the end we decide to explore the town first. As we walk, we breathe in luscious green smells of ivy cloaking walls, of big oaks spreading leaves and all around, thick hedges hugging houses snuggled in warm gardens. I think of how much these leafy lanes remind me of England. My part of England, that is, the West Country. The houses here being rather like those posh ones glimpsed on strolls through Blaise Castle Estate. Over the small footbridge – grandly called "The Iron Bridge" – and on into the fairytale Dark Wood which borders Kingsweston Down – where once Jane Austen's Catherine Moorland galloped across in a horse-drawn carriage with romance with a dark stranger on her mind and then across to the other side and on down to the dingly dell of Coombe Dingle.

Of course, this is different. I'm not totally daft. Here, pink and cerise hydrangeas, red geraniums and fuchsias, brightly wave from earthenware pots or window boxes or flower beds. Shutters painted white, green, open and close windows, and gravel paths crunch their dissonance. Still…

'Don't you love France?' says Gerry, striding ahead with Finty in her buggy. 'Look.' He points to a small hotel. 'They've got three flags – French, Breton and European. God, I love it. I'm definitely European.'

I walk on to a bridge spanning a small stream, where I stop and peer down at its green weed, its dappled pebbles and its darting fish. Lots of tiny tiddler fishes: minnows and sticklebacks. The water clear and shallow as it busily chatters over stones and rocks.

'Race you to the bottom!' yells Jake. 'Woo hoo!'

I chase after him. Down the sloping green field to the trees and stream of the Dingle. Jake's grey knee socks are falling down round his ankles, and my navy duffle bag bounces away on my back. I'm wearing a pair of Jake's short trousers and one of his white shirts. Mum was too "tired" to notice. My hair is cut short, and we look even more alike. 'Two peas in a pod, that's you,' says Mrs Lyons, the lady at the corner shop, when we stop there to buy our sweets. Black jacks, and sherbet fountains, and those red liquorice firemen's hoses. On the way back we'll buy a Tip Top each. Or I might have a cider ice lolly. We took the money from Mum's purse while she slept on the sofa. We'll have to eat them all before we get home because Mum doesn't allow sweets.

'I won!' Jake gasps, all breathless as he plonks himself on a big rock beside the stream, which is an end trickle of the River Trym. His voice sounds very loud down here in the dingly dell, where trees rustle and water bustles, and sounds like birdsong – even whispering – are hushed yet sharp. Whenever we track something or follow birds to their nests we have to shush. Today, though, we're after sticklebacks to take home in the jamjar which I'm carrying by its string handle. Jake has a net he made from one of Mum's nylons cut off, knotted and then threaded through a wire frame pushed down the middle of a bamboo stick. Easy peasy lemon squeezy.

The long afternoon stretches before us and it's to be one of the last afternoons of our summer holidays. Yesterday, Mum received the letters saying we've both passed our eleven-plus, meaning I'll be off to an all-girls' grammar school, while Jake goes to an all-boys'.

'You can't stay together, and that's that!' Mum said. But how will Jake do his homework without my help? Who will stand up for me? There'll be no more secret signals. No more rushing to the playground to swap stories. No more the Johnson Twins. Instead, we'll only be brother and sister Jake and Veronica.

The sun mottles leaves here, making pools of light there. It's warm even in this hollow as we cross the stream on stepping stones. We chat and laugh. We tell funny stories about friends, school chums, about our neighbours, and argue about who has the best pets. My slow-worms or his white mice. In the end, we decide *our shared guinea pigs are tops. Then we set about catching the sticklebacks we'll be taking home to the tin bath aquarium we've made up in our back garden to join our other captives – those miniature dinosaurs – palmar and great crested newts.*

White froth collects around stones jutting above the water. Mum says the froth is caused by detergents – like washing powder – but I think she's wrong. Opening my duffle bag, I lay out our lunch on a rock: corned beef and tomato sauce sandwiches, one Bowyers pork pie cut in half, and four Jammie Dodgers. We drink from the stream, cupping our hands. It coldly tastes of iron and makes our teeth ache. A water vole flashes by and we search for its home in the riverbank.

'Look,' I say, signalling him to be quiet as slowly I point to the bright kingfisher which darts almost quicker than the eye can see from branch to water and back again. A speared tiddler wriggles on the end of its beak.

Jake looks up to the sky. 'We'd better head back,' he says, pointing to our shadows which are long, signalling it's later than we think.

'Time to go,' one of us says as we gather up our things and head for home, carrying our prizes and sporting grazed knees and muddy faces.

'What shall we make for tea?'

'Beans on toast?'

We let ourselves in with our own back door key. Mum lies crashed out on the sofa, and Dad will be late home from work.

Gerry joins me on the bridge. I don't look up as he approaches but continue staring at the water below. 'It's sad how Finty won't enjoy the things we did,' I say.

'Hm? Things like what?' He leans on the parapet, next to me.

'Oh, you know. Fishing for sticklebacks. Birds' nests. That sort of thing.'

'I didn't do any outdoorsy stuff in any case – and I turned out all right.'

'Even if you didn't.' I fling a twig into the water. 'That's not the point, you could have if you'd wanted to.'

'I liked chess,' he says.

'Did you know that there are hardly any newts left?'

'Erm. No – I'm not sure I'd recognise a newt even if it bit me.'

'They can't bite you. France is so beautiful,' I say, leaning my body over the parapet, letting my feet swing free. 'It's so much cleaner than back home.' I look down at the river again. 'It's not polluted – I don't know, it makes me feel alive. Is that wrong?' On impulse, I turn to him. 'Maybe we should move to France.'

'Now there's an idea,' he says, his face showing that he is giving it some consideration. 'Perhaps we ought to consider it.' He swishes a stick against the wall. 'Property is cheaper, Finty could be bilingual and we'd definitely be European... If you want we can weigh up our options. Although, quite what we'd do for money is another thing. I guess we could invest in a *gite* or something...'

'It was an idle thought, Gerry,' I said, sure that dreams don't come true. 'No need to go overboard.'

'Wait, it might be good to have a total change of direction. Perhaps it would prove to be just the thing for us. A fresh start.'

'What? Away from Jake? Away from Angie, who still needs our support? And what about your job? You wouldn't get a job here as a solicitor, would you? No. I thought not.' I storm off, not sure why I'm so cross apart from his really getting on my nerves. 'You just don't think, that's your problem!' I fling at him.

He catches up with me. 'Meaning what?' he says, pushing Finty in her buggy before him. Luckily, she hasn't woken up.

'Nothing.'

'No, you don't get to do this whole pushing me away again. I think I know what this is all about.'

'Oh, you do, do you?' I say, stopping in my tracks and causing him to a couple of strides further on. 'Let's see.' I begin that awful counting on the fingers. 'Getting into debt for one. Then there's sleeping with your colleague for another.' I hate myself as soon as the words are out of my mouth – but I can't stop.

'You mean Fran? But we've gone through this, had couple's counselling and everything, and I thought you were... that we were cool with it all, and we'd figured out it was me being a total prick about you being pregnant.'

'Unreal. You really thought I was cool with it?' I shook my head. 'And it's not only her, is it?'

'You can't mean this Hilary thing, haven't we already been over this? I thought you understood. *She's* the one who's been doing all the chasing, not me, and I did not sleep with her. All this fuss over one drunken kiss. Okay, I'm sorry, I know it's not nothing – but it can't still be bothering you, can it? I thought we discussed this yesterday and cleared the air. You told me you were fine about it. Look, I really need you on my side, Ron, because she could get all nasty and put in a claim of sexual harassment against me!'

'Maybe I wasn't fine with it after all. Maybe I can't be bothered to get all het up about it.'

'That's exactly what you're doing. Well, I'm sorry I'm not as perfect as your brother Jake!'

'I'm sorry too!'

We walk on in silence with Finty fast asleep in her buggy. She's heard it all before.

FOURTEEN

At the Beach, Monday

'Over here!' Angie waves as we trudge through the sand to join them, me all determined to shake off my bad mood.

'Oof!' I grunt as I plonk myself next to Jake. 'How's it going, everybody? You all having fun?'

'Great.' Jake grins. 'The girl – her there – pinch an airband for the whatsy so.'

'Right.' I spread our towels out and strip down to my bikini. 'Blimey, Jake.' It's then that I notice he's wearing a pair of black socks with his sandals. 'What on Earth are you wearing?'

'What?'

'Never did have good taste in clothes, did you?' I look across at Angie. 'Did he, Ange? Hm? Remember those clogs.'

'God yes,' she says, raising her eyebrows. 'He wore them until they disintegrated. I can assure you those socks are definitely *his* choice, not mine.'

But Jake is not following our gentle ribbing and instead is watching Sarah, who sits only a few feet from where waves cut intermittent curves onto the shore.

'Sarah?' calls Angie. 'Come and have a sandwich.'

But she's taking no notice as she inches closer to a family of four – mother, father and two small children. Next she stretches her long brown limbs and tosses back her tumbling hair in the self-conscious manner of the very young and beautiful. She's feigning a lack of interest in the neighbouring family, with all the hamminess of a seven-year-old. And when the father gets to his feet and runs with his two children into the waves, Sarah too stands up, kicks some sand with her right foot and trails along behind them.

Angie moves over to sit alongside me. 'Did you see that?' she says.

'What? You mean, Sarah?'

She nods. 'She does it quite a lot, you know. Hangs around other fathers with their families. It can be quite embarrassing at times. I know it's because she misses her own father, but she doesn't want to talk about it.'

Pulling on my sunglasses I watch Sarah at the water's edge, where she collects a ball from the waves and throws it to the father. He throws it over to one of his own children, and then Sarah mooches around a bit before settling down on the fringe of the sea to paddle the water with her feet.

'How is she with Jake, these days?' I ask.

'She ignores him most of the time,' says Angie as she grasps her hands beneath her knees. 'Mind you, it's wasted on him. Either that, or he doesn't mind. When I think of how much they adored each other...' She glances across at Jake, but he's not listening. He has no attention to spare as he's engrossed in the intricate and laborious process of moving from his back, over on to his front.

Angie calls Lauren over, then the two of them make their way to the seashore to join Sarah.

Jake is watching them. It's taken me a while to realise his gaze is following them, or that he's humming a Rolling Stones song. Of course, it's "Angie". Now, clearly having decided to follow them, he begins his move by pushing off the sand so he can slowly position his legs as he next crosses left leg over right, plants his foot on the ground and, with a final heave, is up on both his feet, steadying himself before setting off after them.

He runs into the waves, laughing and splashing Angie, who shrieks with delight. Grabbing hold of her, together they roll in the shallow water. A bright sun beams down on them as they kiss. Angie runs towards their baby – Sarah – who sits digging sand with her spade. But Jake is there first as he lifts Sarah into his arms and up into the sky, like Kunta Kinte in Alex Haley's TV show Roots, *giving thanks for his first-born. Then he hugs his daughter close and reaches out to Angie as the three of them stand at the shore's edge.*

I watch as Jake wends his uncertain way towards the sea, where he stands at the lapping waves, staring out to where Angie and Lauren are jumping and squealing whenever a small breaker hits them. Overhead a gull cries its lament, and I can hardly bear to watch.

'Gerry?' I say, trying to inject some cheerfulness into my voice. 'Do us a favour, will you? Rub some of that suntan lotion on my back, there's an angel.' And bless him, he stops digging in the sand with Finty and prepares to do what I ask as I fashion two small hollows in the sand for my breasts and lower myself onto my front.

'Oo, cold!' I say as he squirts suncream on my skin. And, as Gerry starts to work on my back, pleasure pings up and down my spinal column as he shifts skin and tissue over muscle and bone. It's calming. It's arousing, even. *Small wonder he's good at making bread*, pops into my mind as he kneads away.

'That's enough for now,' he says, slapping me on the bottom.

'I enjoyed that,' I almost purr. I know he's been hoping this holiday would be full of sea, sand and sex, but, I don't know, even with the massage I still don't feel in the mood.

'How about a kiss,' he says. 'No? Thought not. Fine. I can't get anything right, can I?'

'Gerry?'

But he's already got a hold of Finty, and together they run to the sea, passing Jake and splashing out into the shallows, making a beeline for where Angie, Sarah and Lauren are paddling about.

Angie shrieks when she spots him splashing towards her and attempts to run away, but – placing Finty on her feet next to Sarah – he gives chase, then rugby tackles her so that they both fall laughing and spluttering into the small waves. All three girls come charging around them.

'Aargh! Get off! Save me!' he shouts as the girls hoot with laughter, and a smiling Angie shakes water off her arms.

FIFTEEN

Monday Evening

The time is early evening, the kids are in bed, Gerry is cooking us grownups our meal, and Angie and I have moved to the dining room, where she spreads out sheets of A4 on the big oak table while Jake sits, waiting.

'So,' she commences, 'this is the programme of exercises we've been doing at home.' She points to a couple of pages then smiles at me uncertainly. 'I thought you might like to cast your expert physiotherapist eye over them and let me know what you reckon.'

'Of course.'

'Yes, I've realised I was being silly – wanting to do everything on my own. And so I'm happy to take up your offer of help from before, if that's still fine by you.'

'Yes, yes it is.'

'I'm sorry about before – guess I was being overly protective.'

Jake nods encouragingly at the two of us, as we hug, then I turn to him and say, 'Both hands on the table. Might as well start as we mean to go on.'

As I give the exercises the once-over, I can't deny that I'm impressed. The programme is very full, and not with homeopathy and affirmations and whatnot, but with real practical stuff.

'How about walking practice? Are you managing to get some of that in?'

'Yes, we do it every single day – at home I've made our spare bedroom into a sort of gym. Sarah's even made a sign saying Daddy's Gym.'

Aw, that's so sweet.

'Sometimes Jake even practises on his own, don't you, darling?'

He nods.

'And you are sure that you're making Jake practise his walking in front of a mirror?'

Angie gives a little sigh. 'Of course. I haven't forgotten what you said.'

I busy myself with looking through another sheet. I know I shouldn't mind how Angie hasn't wanted my full input until now – she likes to do things for herself, after all – but I won't lie, it smarts that I've not been asked for more. (*They're asking you now, Ron. Don't be a twat.*)

'I worked these out from what he's been doing in OT, physio and speech therapy,' Angie is saying as I regard her with new respect. She really has gone the extra mile and then some. 'See,' she continues, 'how we even get in lip and tongue exercises? I've become quite the expert. Have had to be now we're on our own with no physio or OT from the hospital.'

I fold the exercise sheets over. 'Honestly, this is amazing. Seriously, you've done a brilliant job. Just look at it all. I can't see anything you've missed. Have you tried getting Jake to do something more practical, more tangible, like his woodworking? Remind him of who he used to be? Because he always loved his woodwork, didn't you, Jake?' He used to like making things like their tree house, a rocking horse, cupboards, toys.

'Yes, of course I have. Don't you think I'd already considered that? But he isn't interested. I took him to his workshop where he was working on a table – before. It was an old Victorian one which came apart when it was dipped. It's an easy job to glue it back together, and it should have been a doddle for him, even with his bad hand. But when I returned two hours later, he was still where I left him, fiddling with wood shavings and not doing any work on the table at all. He'd looked at me and said, "Go now?", like he was a child who wanted to go back home.'

'Right. Sorry.'

'Anyway, we've quite enough to be going on with as it is.'

'Perhaps Gerry or I can come up with something he can do while we're here?'

'Be my guest.'

I look across to where Jake is waiting and showing no interest in what we have to say. Instead, he's pulling at a piece of loose skin on his thumb. I decide that if something presents itself, then fine, and if not then I'm not going to knock myself out trying to think of something.

'Shall we get back to the exercises?' Angie pulls out a high-backed chair to sit at the table. 'If you could run through some of his exercises for me, check that we're doing things all right then I'd be grateful.' She motions for me to go ahead.

I survey the room – this time with an expert eye. Plenty big enough for what I have in mind. If we move back the sofa and chairs, take up the rug, it'll do nicely. I can't wait to get my physio hands on him.

'Have you managed any of his exercises since we've been here?'

'Not really. And before you have a go, I can assure you it's been a deliberate choice. Jake needed a rest when we first arrived, and so did I. It's been rehabilitation this, exercise that, care meetings, social workers – I just want us to be as close to a normal family as we can get – even if it is for a couple of days. Do you understand?' The end of her sentence reverberates around the room.

'Fair enough. But it is vital you keep things ticking along.'

Angie rolls her eyes. 'Fuck's sake, Ron. Everyone needs a break or they get stale. Tell you what. Whatever. You can think what you like. Now, do you want to help or not?' She pulls out a Marlborough cigarette and lights it. 'And don't say anything about the fuckin' cigarette, ok?' She squints against the smoke. 'You could do with a rest an' all. A rest from being so bloody judgemental and' – she waves her cigarette at me – 'bloody accusing.'

'I'm not—' I begin.

'Yeah, yeah.' She stubs out her ciggie. 'Let's get on with it, I don't want to argue.' Then she softens. 'I don't mean to come across as a bitch, you know, but I've no patience left for niceties. Not with what we've been through as a family, okay? So please, try not to take any notice – chill out, yeah?' She gives me a steady look. 'And now will you kindly do us the honour of taking your twin Jake through his exercises and letting us know how he's doing.'

My shoulders relax. 'Fair enough. Oh, and for the record, I think you're right. I do need to chill and not get wound up about Jake's progress.' I reach towards her pack of Marlborough's. 'Mind if I have one of these?'

'Help Yourself'

'Okay – bossy teacher!'

'Physio nutjob.'

'Fuck off.'

'No, you fuck off.'

For a moment we stare at each other, and then together we burst out laughing until our sides hurt. Truth be told, I've missed her. Things haven't been the same, since...

Once upon a time the two of us got on well, so well I began to hope that on their marriage, I'd be gaining a sister. I'd always wanted a sister. Looking at her now, it's amazing how on the surface and two children later, she hasn't changed much at all since the day they got married. Which must have been eight – no, nine years ago…

There's a little Norman church in their village which is dressed with pretty stained-glass windows and stands self-importantly on top of a hill. Inside, solid pews face the aisle side on, so that we all have to crane our necks to witness Jake and Angie take their vows. Tears stream down my face. Not because I'm the type to cry at weddings. No. It's because loss has snuck up and caught me unawares, leaving me with puffy eyes and an aching absence in my stomach. Naughty loss! You pathetic twerp, Ron.

"*All things bright and beautiful*

All creatures great and small…"

Angela's mother – call me Sylvia – sings at the top of her voice. Sitting opposite me, she's delicately dabbing at her eyes with an embroidered handkerchief as she gives me a sympathetic smile. Clearly she thinks she understands why I'm crying, so I smile back at her. I'm nothing if not polite.

"*All things wise and wonderful*

The Lord God made us all…"

I'm wondering if Jake really is married, because for some reason we twins aren't baptised. Mum said she wanted us to be able to make up our own minds when we were old enough. Personally, I think she couldn't be bothered.

Would Jake not being baptised make this church wedding illegal? Should I have stood up at the "Does anyone know any legal impediment" Apparently Jake told the vicar he has been baptised. He doesn't consider it matters if he lies because we don't believe in God anyway. We think Life is one big cosmic joke.

"*The little flowers that open*

The little birds that sing…"

Mum passes me a tissue from her bag. She looks like an old-

fashioned movie star – not unlike Sofia Loren – what with her new peach suit and matching hat, which complement her striking looks. Dad sits on her right next to his brothers – all eight of them. They love any excuse for a get-together do the Johnsons, and at each family occasion I'm struck by how alike they look. Each with full heads of golden or ginger hair, each with matching dimples and each with the same soft Bristolian burr to their voices.

"He made their glowing colours

He made their tiny wings…"

Trust Jake to pick this hymn. It was our favourite.

The happy couple walk slowly back down the aisle, Angie's simple cream wedding gown swishing with each step. A garland of flowers sits atop her hair, setting off her freshly scrubbed and glowing face. Jake looks very handsome and grown up in his new suit. As they pass my pew, he winks at me.

We all loiter outside, waiting to be organised for the wedding photographs. I stand near a traditional yew tree which drops its poisonous berries one by one, onto the gravestones of those who'd hoped they'd been good enough for heaven.

'All the family gather over here for a group photograph,' announces the photographer.

In between my call-ups I stand alone, not feeling sociable and in some ways wishing I hadn't split up with Richard, because at least I'd have had a plus one for today instead of standing here like a right lemon.

Oh, Christ. Here comes Mum. Weaving in and out of the crowd, coming from the direction of the car park. Surely she can't be tipsy. Ah yes, silly me. The car. It's where she keeps her emergency supply of ready-mixed gin and tonic. I stroll across to try and head her off before she embarrasses herself, but I mistime things and she veers to stand smack bang in the middle of Aunt Mary, Uncle Arthur and their son, the GP – Doctor David Johnson. All of them smile proudly at David, who is saying something which I don't quite catch. Quite the Adonis, isn't he? *I think, as I peer up at him. Must be all of six foot six, with the Johnson curly blond hair and the kind of physique which could block any rugby tackle. I've heard he plays regularly for Bristol, his chiselled face unmarred by broken nose or cauliflower ear. I've not seen him since he was a small boy, but look at him now. He's gorgeous. Such a shame he's my cousin... Uh-oh.*

'I wish I was twenty years younger,' slurs Mum as she prods David in the chest, her face all flushed. Aunt Mary giggles nervously.

'Here,' Mum adds, pulling me over. 'Our Veronica's still footloose and fancy free, aren't you, dear?'

I'm mortified. 'Mum,' *I hiss.* 'Cousins...' *I look for Jake and then remember he won't be around to rescue me, anymore.*

David has a fixed – almost rictus – smile on his face as Mum, impervious to our discomfort, elbows me in the ribs. 'I'd give you a run for your money, my girl, if I was younger.' She nods towards David, who's trying to act nonchalant. 'I definitely would – you know.'

You do have form, Mother, *is what I'm thinking but don't say. To divert her, I ask,* 'Where's Dad?', *trying to keep my voice bright and breezy, and thinking how he always conveniently disappears whenever Mum gets tricky.*

Uncle Arthur – *perhaps sensing my discomfort* – steps in and takes Mum's arm. 'Now then, Lily. You're embarrassing the boy.'

'There, there,' says Mum, tweaking David's cheek. (*Actually tweaking his cheek!*) 'You do know I'm kidding, don't you? Just a little bit of fun.'

'Of course, Aunt Lily,' he says. 'It's always a pleasure to see you.' *The smile on his face doesn't quite reach his eyes. I wonder if he's the same with his patients – tolerant but oh-so-slightly disdainful. They probably love him, though, don't they – everybody loves a handsome doctor.*

'Now my Veronica, here,' continues Mum, while I consider it's way past the time somebody should be leading her away. 'She takes after my side of the family—'

'Mum.'

She shrugs me off. 'Right looker is Veronica, but a bit of a worrier. Takes after my mother in that respect. And she was a right miserable cow.'

At the top of the yew tree, a jackdaw caws then flaps away.

'Can we have the mothers over here with the happy couple?' pipes up the photographer – saved by the bell, or photographer.

'Oo. That's my cue,' says Mum, as she trips off like a girl.

Making sure she's suitably occupied with photographer, posing, and the other women, I go in search of Dad and find him round the back of the church with two of his brothers, having a sneaky cigarette. Quickly he stubs his out with his foot.

'Veronica.'

'It's all right, you don't have to hide your smoking. But you will have to come with me. Now,' I say, pulling him to one side. 'It's Mum. She's been at the gin again.'

'Oh.' He turns to his brothers. 'I'll see you at the reception.' They nod, unsurprised at my interruption.

Dad matches me stride for stride as we make our way to the front of the church. 'She's not doing any harm, though, is she?' he asks, searching my face.

'No, but—'

'Well then. You leave her to me.' With that, he waves to Mum and goes across to join her.

Shaking my head, I wander off on the closely cropped lawn – all springy and green in its summer best. Half-heartedly I scrutinise the gravestones: some stand to attention, whilst others lean at an angle as if their occupants, down below, are shifting about.

I'm in between jobs and staying at home for a while. But I'll have to leave soon, especially as things are rather fraught between

Mum and Jake. They're having one of their regular spats. I'll tell Mum and Dad next weekend that I'm going to house share with Julie and some of the other girls on our physiotherapy course. Julie's a right laugh.

Angie approaches: holding her stiff white wedding shoes in her hand, she strides towards me. 'I'm so glad you're here,' she says as she affectionately squeezes my arm. 'I do hope we're going to be close, don't you? I've always wanted a sister.'

'You have?' I squeeze her back. 'Me too,' I say, surprising myself by actually meaning it.

Jake waves as he lopes across with a big cat-got-the-cream look on his face.

'There you are,' he says as he kisses both of us on the cheek. 'My two most favourite girls in the whole wide world.'

*

I phoned our parents to let them know about the holiday. Mum answered.

'You'll do what you want to do, Veronica. You always did like sticking your oar in.'

There wasn't much point in telling her the holiday was Angie's idea, and besides, Mum was already hanging up.

SIXTEEN

Monday at the Pizza Parlour

We're all off for a pizza, walking along the main street of town, which isn't too bustling with tourists, even though it is high season. Some of the shops haven't opened yet and instead hide behind grilles, flaunting their window displays of tiny bikinis, Breton shirts and jaunty sailor caps. They tantalise, like the laughter which dances back from Gerry and Angie, who are walking ahead with Sarah. I can't hear what they're saying, but they're laughing and at ease, and almost touching.

We decided on pizza because no-one much fancied doing any cooking. I'm several yards behind Gerry and Angie, pushing Finty in her buggy and keeping Jake company. He's holding Lauren's hand as he walks jerkily along, like some clockwork toy winding down – I wish he could walk faster, as I'd love to know what those other two are gabbing about.

It's a bit of a squash on the narrow pavement, meaning that sometimes I have to pull even further back when we reach a narrow part, or when other people approach. Of course, Jake carries straight on. Regardless. Like a man on a mission. His pace is so slow it matches little Lauren's, who's struggling herself with this new-fangled thing of walking. Fleetingly I wonder if she might be enjoying not being hurried up for once. But it's

Angie and Gerry I wish I could hear. Up ahead. Whispering and laughing together.

On arrival at the pizza parlour, Angie and I are doing our best to keep a hold of the girls to stop them rushing ahead, as Jake navigates the front step and a bored waitress waits to one side. Gerry sets about folding up the buggy, and Jake reaches out to help, I'm supposing, when he stumbles into a plant pot on a stand. I manage to catch Jake before he falls, keeping him upright as the pot crashes with a loud smash, depositing broken pot pieces, soil and plant on the ground. 'Gotcha!' I say to Jake, casting around as if expecting the fellow diners to break into unlikely applause. But instead, they are staring. Each and every one of them. Gerry is edging his way inside when Angie, who has now burst into tears, rushes out of the restaurant door. The waitress is still standing, looking bored. 'Aren't you going to tidy that up?' I say, and am rewarded with a shrug as a waiter appears with requisite dustpan and brush. (Turns out Jake wasn't going to help Gerry fold the buggy after all but instead had been reaching to help himself to one of the mints by the till – which he now pops into his mouth, grinning at us all, as he begins chomping.)

Gerry parks the buggy by the coats and grabs hold of my elbow. 'Can you take over here?' he's saying. I give him a "Where?" face.

'I'm going to go after Angie,' he continues. 'Check she's all right.' Before I can object, although of course I won't as clearly someone needs to see if she's okay, I follow the waitress to a long table, somehow managing to usher Jake and the girls along to where a version of musical chairs without the music begins. 'Lauren, over here… no, stop… Finty, come back… Sarah, grab hold of Lauren, will you…' Jake pulls out a chair and sits as I manage to get the booster seats plus girls onto their chairs. I feel like I've been doing the human equivalent of keeping plates spinning.

Gerry returns. 'Everything okay?' he says. 'Are you girls fine? Ready to order?' Nods all around. Gerry leans across to whisper in my ear, 'She'll join us in a minute. She's finishing off her cigarette.'

'What was that all about?' I whisper back – mind you, we needn't have bothered, as Jake was now picking apart a paper napkin.

'Tell you later,' he says. 'Ah, here she is.'

Angie makes her way over to our table. 'Sorry about flouncing out,' she says, painting a smile on her face as fake as Bob Monkhouse in *The Golden Shot*. 'I'm back now.'

She kisses each of her girls on the head and sits next to Jake. Sarah peers up at her and asks, 'Are we all right, Mum?'

'Don't be silly, of course we are. Now, have you ordered yet? I'm starving.' I catch her mouthing "thank you" to Gerry.

Inside the restaurant, its decor is pretty much like any other pizza place, anywhere else in the world, I'd imagine. On each table, freesias slump in glass vases. Young waiters and waitresses gather around the bar, looking in our direction every now and then – it's not hard to guess what the topic of their conversation is.

Our table is in the farthest corner. I wonder if this is intentional, whether we've been placed here on purpose. According to what Angie has said before, it wouldn't be the first time.

'You know what you're going to order?' asks Gerry.

'Think so. Give me a minute.'

The menu is in English first, then French, then German and then in picture form for the internationally illiterate. 'Good, then you go ahead and order for us lot.'

'Why?'

'I've got to call the office and check there have been no hiccups with this new case. Sorry, I won't be long, only I spotted a phone box when we came in.'

'Christ's sake. Surely, they can do without you during this week, can't they? Nobody's indispensable – not even you.'

'That's what they'd like me to think.'

'But you haven't enough money for an international call,' I half-whisper.

'Yes, I have.' He waves his wallet at me as he heads for the door. 'I've been saving those big ten-franc pieces.' He indicates to the waitress that he'd like to use the phone while I try not to mind.

'You'd better not be calling you-know-who.'

'It's not.'

'Even so...'

Once the waitress is ready, Angie takes charge of their order and then it's my turn. 'We'll have one large Spicy American and one medium Vegetarian pizza, thank you.'

'Is that all you're ordering?' says Angie.

'Yes. We like to share.' But not share with her the real reason, which is that it's all we can afford if we're going to last the week without resorting to our credit card. Turning to the waitress I ask whether we can have more bread – seeing as Jake's polished off the five pieces in the breadbasket. The waitress heads back to the kitchen, returning with a full basket. '*Merci*,' I say, nabbing bread for myself and Gerry.

Our food order is quick to arrive and just in time to distract the children from spearing paper napkins or tattooing the table with forks. Finty blinks in disbelief at the pizza on her plate and shakes her head; Lauren starts giggling and joining in with the head shaking.

'Me no like! No like!'

'Ssh, come on, darling, it's lovely – do eat up. There, see? Sarah's eating hers.'

But Sarah is prodding hers as if expecting a woodlouse to crawl out.

'Stop being silly, girls,' orders Angie. 'You must not play with your food.'

Gerry has returned to our table.

'Everything okay?'

He squeezes my shoulder then takes his seat. 'This all looks yummy,' he announces, rubbing his hands together. 'We sharing, are we?' I give him a meaningful look and he cottons on. 'Right you are,' and he reaches for a piece of bread.

'Is everything okay with the case? Because you are meant to be on holiday.'

'Yes, yes, all sorted. Now who's for ketchup!'

It's an attractive feature of Gerry's that he cares about his clients and tries his hardest. I guess my family's problems have taken away his focus of late.

On the table there's the usual friendly kerfuffle as kids' pizzas are cut up, pepper is ground and Jake shakily passes Gerry a ramekin of mayonnaise.

'Mummeee!' Finty cranes her neck to peer forlornly at the floor – to where her pizza slice has slid.

'Got it!' calls Gerry giving it a blow and a wipe with his napkin before placing it back by the side of her plate. 'What?'

'If she gets salmonella it'll be all your fault. Why couldn't you notice she'd dropped her food on the floor? Honestly, I'm fed up with doing the lion's share of the childcare.'

'Now, that's not fair. Who gave you the chance to sunbathe today when—'

'Stop it!' Angie slams her napkin on the table. 'Will you two stop your bickering for one bloody second!'

I stop, open-mouthed, while the kids freeze mid-pizza and Gerry looks first to Angie and then to me.

'I think that's a bit strong,' I start. 'I'd say we weren't so much bickering—'

She cuts me off. 'I don't care, and I don't want to hear about it. Can't you do us all a big favour and sort yourselves out!' Angie attends to her children and wipes at Lauren's mouth a little too harshly.

To ease the embarrassed silence, Gerry volunteers to get the children to play "I spy".

'Who's going first? I know, I'll start, shall I? I spy, with my little eye… something beginning with "p",' he begins.

'Prat,' I mumble.

'Pizza,' says Sarah in a bored fashion.

'Yay! Your go next…'

Jake has got up out of his seat to head for the toilets, and just as he lopes past one of the tables, I can hear a mother say to her child, 'Don't stare,' as one by one the rest of the customers turn their heads to watch his progress. I feel for Angie because even I'm getting weary at the effrontery of others. I decide to glare at as many as I can when I stop mid-glaring because I Spy something beginning with "X" – Xavier – who's striding past the café window in a rather dashing fedora which he doffs to me (and the others – don't forget the others, Ron) in a little salute.

'That's Madame's son,' Angie says, as if I didn't know.

Back at the villa and thinking the others are safely upstairs, I get Gerry on his own. 'What is the point in trying to keep our spending down if you go and offer to pay halves for the whole meal? You know they eat loads; I don't know where they put it all. Their grocery bill at home must be astronomical.'

'Um… Ron?' says Gerry, pointedly nodding his head in the direction of where Angie has entered the kitchen with Jake.

'Thanks for that insight into what you're really thinking,' says Angie. 'What do you want? You want us to eat less, do you?'

'Look, I'm sorry. It's just that…' I take a step towards her.

'Oh, don't bother. If you want to have petty squabbles about money, then go ahead, but don't bring me or my family into it.' She goes outside – ostensibly for a cigarette.

'Nice one, Ron,' says Gerry.

Jake taps me on the shoulder. 'Where's the button head?'

'The what?' I look to where he's pointing and pass him the broom. He sets about sweeping the floor as Angie comes back in. 'You know what?' she says, flinging her bag on the table and then taking out her purse. 'Here you go – here! Go on. Take the money – take as much as you need!' Then she bundles it back into her bag. 'On second thoughts – you can sod off!'

'You've gone too far this time,' says Gerry.

'You can sod off too, Gerry. I didn't expect that of you, I really didn't.'

Stunned, I flop in a chair, feeling like crap.

Later, after we've all said our sorries, Angie collects the dishes and things for washing up, and stands at the sink, and froths the water with suds, as Sarah stands next to her, gazing up at her face.

Jake and I come hurtling in through the back door of our family's typical suburban 1960s kitchen. Out of breath, I run up to Mum and hug her around the waist.

'Not now,' she says.

She fills the washing-up bowl with water frothed from a single squirt of Fairy Liquid and pulls on a pair of Marigold gloves. Clearly, she doesn't believe that jingle on telly – you know the one, about hands that do dishes feel as soft as your face.

I offer up a bunch of wildflowers which I picked especially for her. Just like the golden girl in the advert does for her mum. The sun angles through our kitchen window onto my eager upturned face as I wait for her to bend down, just like the Fairy Liquid mum, and smile and give me a hug as bright as the sunlight dancing off those squeaky-clean plates.

Mum inspects the flowers.

'They're weeds,' she decides. 'Fancy picking me weeds.' She walks over to the yellow and white bin, steps on the pedal, and shoves the flowers headfirst into its gaping maw.

'Should have got me real flowers instead of those. Now real flowers would have been nice.'

'Sorry,' I mumble. I only get a shilling pocket money and we can't afford real ones.

'Never mind.' She sighs as she unties her apron. 'Now then, what have you two monkeys been up to?' She gives us one of her full-on dazzle smiles, and soon I'm forgetting my disappointment as Jake and I dance around her, trying to outdo each other with tales of our morning's adventures in the woods.

'We saw a nut hatch hop into a hollow in a tree,' I say, still touched by the wonder of it all.

'Yeah, and we found its nest,' proudly asserts Jake.

'Don't say "yeah", Jake,' Mum interrupts as she carries on washing and stacking the dishes onto a white plastic drying rack.

He prods at some imaginary thing with his foot while I take over. 'We found lots and lots of bluebells.'

Both quiet now, we stand either side of Mum and stare at her lovely face. As beautiful as the face of one of those starlets in a black and white film on telly – Hedy Lamarr, or Maureen O'Hara, or... or... Joan Crawford.

'You're the best mommy in the whole world,' says Jake in his best imitation of an American accent. It's what loveable Dennis in that American sitcom says to his mum. We like to say it to ours too. Usually it makes her laugh.

'Yes,' I join in. 'The best mommy in the who-o-ole world.'

'Go on,' she says. 'I know you'll grow up one day, get married and leave me.'

'No!' we both chorus. 'We won't! Not ever!'

'I'm going to live in the same street as you,' says Jake, moving in closer to her skirts.

'I'm going to live next door,' I say.

She crouches down and gathers us to her. 'My little chickens,' she says, and my heart overflows because her voice is silky and kind. 'But you won't want me when I'm old and infirm.'

'Yes, we will,' we protest. Both together. Panic flutters my chest like a bird trying to escape.

'Stuff and nonsense,' she says as she straightens up. 'I'll go into an old people's home, that's what I'll do. I wouldn't want to be a burden to anybody.'

'No! No!' we chorus. 'We'll stay with you always,' we say. 'You can live with us.'

'Ssh,' she says. 'We'll see.'

For some reason I'm really upset now.

I haven't seen my mother in person since that visit to the neurological hospital when we were all there together. That was the time when she told me it was all my fault. My fault she'd fallen out with Jake, my fault they hadn't been speaking and my fault for telling him the secret I'd promised not to tell and then been whispering on the phone about her. Ipso facto – my fault.

I now know, with the help of Carol, that it's nobody's fault. Not even my mother's. I've admitted she's an alcoholic. If only to Carol and Gerry, but it's a start. Oh, I know she's not a falling down in the middle of the road kind of drunk – but a middle class behind net curtains, drinking sherry, vodka and gin drunk; and it's her illness which feeds her paranoia. The thing is, though, we *were* whispering about her. Jake was fed up how whenever they visited, she seemed to prefer sitting in her conservatory drinking gin and tonic rather than spending time with her grandchildren. And then he'd declared he was fed up with her paranoid accusations. I was trying to placate him – on the day when they fell out. Trying to remind him that she is our mother. Our only mother. He'd cried and said, no, this was the last straw and that he was not going to speak to her ever again. Me? I'm sure he would have come round. But it's too late now.

Carol says that at this stage in my recovery I cannot see my mother in person. Not yet, because she's too toxic and I'm not strong enough.

There are times when I miss my mum. When all I want is a motherly hug and a kiss, plus the enveloping aroma of L'air Du Temps – with its floral and cedar wood base notes – as worn by Hollywood bombshell Lana Turner, or so Mum said.

'You can't forgive her until you are able to forgive yourself,' Carol says.

Easy for her to say. Easy for her to say don't see your mother. But what if something was to happen to Mum? Something out of the blue? The flap of a wing, a disturbance in time? She may be a rubbish mum, but she's my rubbish mum.

Once upon a time she was fun, they'd have friends' round and late-night parties, with Dad presiding over the drinks cabinet like some ringmaster at a drinks circus.

Roll up, roll up, as he lifts the lid and a glass shelf ascends from the depths of the highly polished cabinet, like a Wurlitzer cinema organ playing the tune of a fairground ride: inside its mirrored display are bottles and an assortment of glasses, ranging from tumblers with a man in a red coat striding across the name of Johnnie Walker, to a prancing Bambi blinking at popping bubbles on Babycham glasses. The stage lighting is provided by strategically placed bulbs around a backdrop of mirrors with flowers and scrolls etched around the edges. Yes, it is your typical retro cocktail cabinet.

SEVENTEEN

Tuesday

I'm slowly turning on an inflatable sunbed adrift on a sparkling California pool embraced by a warm sun, enjoying a break from having to know who or where I am. I do know that I'm somewhere between asleep and awake, but I want to stay here... floating... floating... wishing I could stay, that I could drift away for ever... drift far, far away... far, far, far away...

And now I'm awake with tears tickling down the side of my nose, even though I can't remember why I'm crying.

The room is dark because it has shutters, which are doing a grand job of being shut. Gerry shifts next to me, and I can sense he's opened his eyes – my senses attuned in the early morning. Or I think it's early morning.

'Ron? Whatever is the matter?' Gerry asks as a strip of light peeps through a crack. Light is dawning in more ways than one.

'It's Jake,' I say. 'You know each morning when I first wake up it's like everything is normal. It's like I've forgotten and am ready to face a day where I could phone Jake, even get to see him if I wanted to – and then it... it hits me all over again.'

'I know,' says Gerry, reaching out for me.

'It's like there's a sliver of not knowing, and then I remember, and the force of what's happened hits me – kapow! Every fricking morning, I must face the fact that he's gone. Gone but still here.' I turn to face Gerry. 'And it's not getting easier.'

'Ssssh. Give it time.'

'Give it time, give it time! That's all everyone says. But he's gone and he's never ever coming back. Even though he promised me he always would. My twin has left me and is never coming back.'

'I know you miss him – more than most brothers and sisters. But ssh. Come on, come here.' Gerry holds on to me as big, juddering sobs wrack my body.

'If it wasn't for Finty, I swear I'm not sure I could carry on without him.'

'You mustn't say that.'

'It's true. I wish it was me who'd died, instead of him.'

'But he isn't dead. You have to hold on to that.' Gently, he wipes my nose with a piece of scrunched-up tissue.

'Oh, I know I should be glad he's still alive, I know I should. And I am. Really I am. But you see, he's no longer *my* Jake. My twin, Jake – do you get it? The best way I can describe it is he's not *in here*,' I say, thumping my chest. 'He's not here inside me. I don't feel him anymore. Oh, you don't understand, no-one can who doesn't have a twin. You don't even have a brother or a sister.'

Gerry tries to shift from underneath me. 'Sorry,' he says. 'But my arm… it's gone to sleep… sorry…' He frees himself then turns onto his side. 'Why don't you cuddle up to me?' he says. 'Do a bit of spooning. That'll be nice.'

I sit upright and hug my knees. 'Oh, never mind, forget I said anything at all.'

'Sometimes,' he says, turning back to face me, 'I swear to God you're the most difficult person I've ever met. You do know that, don't you?'

'Then maybe you ought to be call Hilary back. Or how about Fran? Or any of the others?' I can't stop myself saying.

'Now you're being ridiculous.'

'We'll leave it at that.' I start getting up out of bed. 'I can hear Finty moving about. Better go to her,' I lie.

He grabs hold of my shoulders and in the morning light I can see the worry etched on his face – his silly face, all blurred and young without his glasses. 'I love you, Ron. In spite of everything. You are the only one I want to be with, although God knows why.'

'Is that supposed to cheer me up?'

He tries a wry smile on me, but I've lost my sense of humour. 'I believe in us.' He grabs my hand. 'In you, me and Finty. But right now my main concern is you. I am worried sick about you.'

'Don't be,' I say, trying to shake him off, but he places his forehead against mine.

'Don't you get it? That's my job to worry about you, and about Finty. It's my job to keep us all safe.'

'It's not always possible to keep your loved ones safe, though, is it?' We both know I'm thinking of Jake.

He pats the pillow beside me. 'Why don't you stay in bed, have a lie-in and I'll get Finty sorted.'

'No, I don't want to stay in bed. It doesn't help while I've got all these morbid thoughts running through my mind. Look, I'm sorry if I scared you, but sometimes... Sometimes it's hard to stay positive. In any case, I want to get up if only because it might stop me thinking.' I let the covers fall from where I've been gripping them tightly. 'I'm sorry for what I said. You're putting up with a lot from me, aren't you?'

'I get it, it's a difficult time for us all.' He slides out of bed, naked, and pads across the floor. Grabbing hold of the shutters he flings them open to the harsh reality of daylight, exposing him to its glare and to any passers-by.

'I've been thinking,' he says, turning to face me, his cock flaccid between his legs.

'Gerry,' I chuck his boxers at him, 'put your pants on – anybody could walk in. Finty, Angie – anyone.' He hops about first on one leg then the other, as he pulls them on.

'No, listen, I've come up with what I'm sure you'll agree is a brilliant idea. Why don't you have a real break today? Go somewhere on your own. Do something different, yes? You could even take a bus ride to Quimper and do a bit of sight-seeing or shopping.' He pulls on a T-shirt. 'I'll be fine staying here keeping the Chipmunk amused while you take yourself off for the whole day. A change of scenery will do you the world of good.'

I won't deny it sounds appealing. 'Are you sure that's what you want? Let me have a think about it.'

Slipping my feet into a pair of flipflops I shuffle to the small box room where Finty is wide awake, sitting upright in her travel cot. She looks up startled and mid-burble with a *Meg and Mog* book in her chubby grasp. 'Mummy!' My heart does a little skip as I lift her out and return with her to our room.

'Well?' says Gerry. 'Have you had time to consider this Quimper trip?'

'Why are you so keen I go? Anybody would think you are trying to get rid of me.'

'Curses! My plot has been uncovered!' He pulls me to sit next to him. 'Seriously. I spent most of the night thinking about things.'

'What, you've been thinking? Again? This could develop into a habit.' But clearly Gerry is in a serious mood.

'You might not like what I have to say.'

'Go on then, I'm all ears,' I answer, cupping my hands behind my ears.

'Here goes… Don't you think you expect too much of Jake?'

'What? What do you mean?' It's not so funny, now.

'Hear me out. It's like you're all expecting him to buck up and slot right back into his old role as father/husband/twin. Small wonder he doesn't know who he is, because he's not had the time and space to work that out. Don't you think this may be why he's switched off? Don't fly off the handle, please,' he says, stopping me getting up and leaving the room. 'Maybe you're all expecting too much of him, wanting him to fulfil the roles of husband and father before he even knows who he is – or who he's become.'

'Is that what you think? That we've been putting too much pressure on him?'

'I've not always thought so. But then last night it struck me that our approach may be doing more harm than good.'

'You cannot be serious. These early months are crucial.'

'Ok, look, hear me out. It's not like you don't all love him and want him to do well – because you do. Of course I see that … But love can be suffocating, too. Take the daily exercises, for instance… to an outsider it could seem like you're expecting him to get fixed if he works hard enough.'

'That's not fair.' The physiotherapist in me wants to object.

'As I see it, both you and Angie are too close to see how far he's come in his recovery. It's like you're both fixated on what he can't do? Whereas I can see that he's switched off.'

'Bully for you,' I mutter.

'Perhaps he's overwhelmed by everybody's expectations.'

I go to protest, but Gerry reaches out, taking my face in his hands. 'All this is not meant as criticism, Ron, just observation.' He lets his hands drop. 'It's easier for me to take a pragmatic view because he's not my brother. Let's face it - us men are simple creatures and all I see is that Jake is this good bloke who just happens to be my wife's brother, who just happened to get himself fucked up, and who may or may not get better. All of which does not take away from the fact that he's a good bloke.'

'I love you,' I say, giving him a quick kiss on the lips. 'You and your blokey philosophy.' I shake my head. 'But I can't possibly go on a day trip, not now that you've told me how you feel,' I begin to cry – not big heaving sobs, but like a child realising she's lost a precious object. 'I don't deserve a break.'

'Stop it. You have to go.' He grabs my shoulders. holding me out at arm's length. 'I mean, just look at yourself, Ron.' He turns me to face the mirror. 'You're worn out and not thinking straight. I'm worried that if you don't take some time out you'll risk another breakdown...' He let go. 'What do you think Carol would say? Wouldn't she say that having time with yourself will be a good thing? Don't you think you need space to get in touch with who you are, never mind Jake. The two of you are lost, like two babes in the woods.'

'We're Hansel and Gretel now, are we?'

'Shut up and listen, will you?' Gently he takes my hand and leads me back to the bedside. 'I have a cunning plan.'

'It's not another of your blokey observations, is it?' I say, trying for light humour. 'We're not going all Blackadder and Baldrick? I hate turnips.'

'Shush, now hear me out. I've decided that while you're off gallivanting in Quimper, I shall make the most of it by coming up with something tangible which Jake can do. Something that won't set him up to fail.' He's animated and excited. 'There must be some activity he used to enjoy before his accident. Something he can do to can gain confidence and be reminded of who he is and what he likes. Yes, the more I think about it, the more I'm convinced it's a brilliantly cunning plan. What do you say?'

'Why not? Anything's worth a try,' I search his eager face – his vulnerable bespectacled face. 'How did you get to be so wise?'

'Maybe I always was, but you never noticed,' he dops down beside me on the divan while I set about playfully prodding him in the ribs.

'You? Wise? Nah!' I try to tickle him, but he just isn't ticklish.

'Gerroff,' he says, followed by - 'Right then!' – and a slapping of his thighs like some pantomime prince. 'We've done quite enough soul searching for one morning.' He pulls down his white t-shirt which has ridden up. 'So it's agreed that I'll take the reins for today, while Finty and I have a grand time. Then when you return you'll be all refreshed and batteries charged.'

He fetches Finty from the other room, and we both watch as she bounces away on our bed without a care in the world. If only I could keep it that way.

'You're absolutely sure you can cope with this little monster?'

'You betcha. We shall engage in our own super dooper father and daughter bonding thing.'

He takes our daughter over to the washstand where I watch him do the whole washing of her face and brushing her teeth.

I'm wavering. 'I don't know ...'

'Well I do. You're going, and that's final. Now go get dressed, have fun, have an adventure, and then return to tell us all about it!'

So here I am, all bright and early with the sun climbing its way up into another glorious summer sky, as I make my way to Madame's shop to get details about buses. Outside the jam-packed-with-stuff shop is shaded by two green and white striped awnings, pulled across like half-closed eyelids. I duck inside to where it's dark and cool, causing me to blink while I get my bearings. The shop is full. I don't think I've ever been in one with shelves so crowded with an eclectic assortment of beach shoes, beach mats, beach umbrellas, clothes and more, all threatening to bustle over onto the floor.

At the counter stands a lady assistant who's not Madame.

'Um...' I start to say, when I spot Madame through an archway leading to a room out back. She's at a small table playing draughts with – well, I never – Jake. Now there's a surprise.

'*Bonjour,*' I say, nodding at the same time to the assistant as I move towards the room which turns out to be a private kitchen and diner.

'*Ah, bonjour, madame.*' The old lady beckons me further inside. Reaching into my pocket for the note which Gerry scribbled down in French – as my comprehension doesn't go beyond O level – I spy Madame's son, Xavier, who's entered the room, and is now lounging against a wall, languidly smoking a French cigarette.

''Allo.' His voice has the texture of a caress – what is it about French accents? Nimbly he steps forwards to lightly grasp my hand in his, and electricity pings from his hand to mine and up through my body. *Ridiculous*, I think, as I catch my breath and Jake winks at me.

'Ah, Jake's sister. *Voici mon fils, Xavier,*' says Madame.

He smiles and half bows in my direction. He says something in French to his mother, then turns to me. 'We 'ave met before. Your name is Veronique, and you are Jake's sister, *non*?' He's flashing me an amused smile. 'Would you care for a coffee?' He gestures to where a pot simmers on the stove, giving off delicious aromas.

'Thank you, that would be lovely.'

He goes about the business of coffee making while I appreciate how handsome he is – in a dark, louche, rather dashing kind of way.

'Milk?' he asks, turning his face, framed by big fat curls. 'I know you English. But I have the espresso.'

'Mm?' I'm worried I might have been staring, so I give a little cough and stand up straight, trying hard not to blush.

'Yes, I mean, no. No milk for me either,' I manage to say. 'I mean, *merci beaucoup.*'

I'm rewarded by a dazzling smile.

'He nice zzh-man,' slurs Jake.

Okay, smarty pants.

I want to hold my brother in a big sisterly hug, but he's returned to his game of draughts. Weird how he can remember the rules of draughts when he's forgotten so much, and can probably no longer say the word "draughts".

As I wait for my coffee, I watch Madame move a counter and then Jake pick up one of his which he jumps over one, two, three, four, five of Madame's. She sits back and mutters something in French, then laughs and pours him a stiff glass of Remy Martin.

'She likes to win,' Xavier says as he passes me a piping-hot espresso.

'You speak very good English,' I say.

'*Bof.*' He raises both palms in a Gallic shrug. 'But of course.'

'Can I ask you for a favour, please? You see, I have the words written down – but it would be easier if you were to ask… Can you please ask your mother if she has a timetable for the buses to Quimper today? I'd be ever so grateful.' I try to ignore the way his eyebrows shoot up in a quizzical yet sexy way (how does he do that?).

'My French is not so good, you see.' (No shit, Sherlock.)

Xavier places a hand on the table and leans towards his mother. As they speak in French, I can't help admiring the way his black shorts strain nicely over his muscular bottom. Good legs too: athletic and deeply tanned. I watch as his head bobs around. Talking. Expressing. I can glimpse a little chest hair at the V-neck of his black short-sleeved shirt, when he glances up and catches me in the act. Our eyes meet and I quickly look away, but not before noticing his eyes are a deep blue. The part of my stomach where chemicals do their swirly thing, is swirling away. Oh, do behave. Honestly… a little attention from a good-looking man, and you go all doolally…

'Maman says you can purchase a timetable from the Office de Tourism, or l'Hotel de Bretagne.'

'Yes, of course, I should have thought of that. Thank you,' I say, gathering up my bag.

'There is one bus every hour,' he says.

'Well, thank you for the coffee.' I drain my tiny cup then place it on the sideboard. 'I'd best be off, then.'

'No, wait.' He reaches but does not quite touch me. 'I have to travel to Quimper now, this morning. May I offer you a lift in my car?'

'Thank you. That would be most kind,' I say speedily before I can change my mind.

'Bo,' says Jake as he gives me a knowing wink. Nothing escapes you, does it, bruv?

EIGHTEEN

Quimper

I don't notice much of the scenery as it zips past on our way to Quimper as I'm already missing my baby girl: her smell, her little chubby legs, her reaching up for her mummy.

Come on, Ron. Isn't it nice to relax back in a vintage car with leather seats being driven by... a virtual stranger! What on Earth were you thinking of? (Oh, come on. Live a little. It's an adventure.)

As we hurtle along the road, I listen as Xavier tells me how he studied English in Paris in the late sixties, early seventies, and how it was there he met Emma from Kent, and how they lived together in Paris and Rennes for ten years. He flicks his indicator on, and we pull onto the highway.

'Now I live and work in Quimper, where I have my own travel company.'

'How about Emma?' I ask shyly, trying to keep a neutral tone to my voice (although it shouldn't matter at all!). 'Does she help with your travel business?'

'We are divorced.' He reaches for his pack of Gauloises which lies between the two front seats. I retrieve it for him, pull out a cigarette and pass it over.

'*Merci*,' he says, lighting the cigarette with a chunky Zippo. He rolls down the car window to blow smoke outside.

'Any children?'

'*Non*. Sadly not. And you? You have a daughter?'

'Yes, only the one daughter. Finty. She's fifteen, almost sixteen months old now.'

He grins with his cigarette clamped between his teeth. 'Ah.' He gives me a quick glance and removes the cigarette from his lips. 'You get your figure back well – *non*?'

'That's very kind of you...' But already his attention is straight ahead, concentrating on the road and the next drag of his smoke.

'It is good not to lose your shape,' he finally says. 'Emma would have been as fat as a pig, I am sure.' He chuckles as if at some private joke.

Thank goodness I bothered to put on makeup and don my fifties-style sundress with the big yellow flowers. I stretch my legs out in the car's footwell, glad to see my tan's coming along nicely.

We park up in one of the side streets. 'Thanks for the lift, it's been most kind of you.' I go for a handshake, but he instead takes my hand in both of his – making me all hot and flustered.

'I have the free time this morning,' he says. 'Let me show you around. I insist.'

Um. Okay – Gerry did say to have an adventure. He may not have meant with Xavier – but where's the harm? It'll be good to have someone local to show me around, even if he is coming on a little strong. And besides, Gerry did have that thing with Hilary boss-woman, even though she did all the running – or so he says. What does it matter in the scheme of things if I spend some time in the company of a dishy man? Maybe have a flirt, even? After all, what's sauce for the goose...

Xavier waits for my answer.

'If you're sure, then how can I say no?'

'Ah, *bien*.'

The bank is the first stop on our whistle-stop tour. The sound of its echoing floors is something between a church and a public lavatory. Xavier takes charge and I'm more than happy to let him get on with it as he speaks in French to the young woman behind the counter and then he signals me across. 'Passport,' he says. I surrender my passport and Mastercard.

'Can you ask for seventy-five pounds' worth of francs, please?'

Xavier nods and takes care of business which, if I'm honest, is a relief. I'm rather enjoying being with a man used to taking charge. There are times when Gerry can verge on the passive, expecting me to sort everything. Still, I mustn't be disloyal – he did suggest this trip.

'*Eh voila!*' Xavier flourishes the money and soon we're outside in the sunshine, where I fumble my francs into my purse, then follow him down the street. Almost skippily, seriously as giggly as a schoolgirl. Not at all like the Ronnie of late. Gerry's right. This is a good idea and from now on (but only for today, and surely taking one day out can cause no harm), I shall pretend that I'm young, single and free with no husband and no broken brother.

We enter what must be the old town. Some of the buildings resemble English Tudor. Which I find strange, as it's – you know – France. They have the same kind of exposed and blackened wooden beams striping and crisscrossing whitewashed walls of townhouses whose floors jut out at different angles, giving that familiar higgledy-piggeldy effect. And everywhere, flowers and flowering plants adorn shop fronts, balconies, verandas, splashing them with red and green and occasional smatterings of yellows and pinks.

Xavier points out historical landmarks as we walk along pavements and pedestrian areas laid with small flagstones –

which are not rounded (like English cobblestones), but more regular. See? Similar yet different. I'm starting to feel like I'm in a parallel universe where whatever happens is fine and won't impinge on when I return to my own world.

Xavier leads me down little streets where his favourite shops are to be found. I am enchanted and don't find it at all strange when he takes my hand in his large, cool one. I feel daring – freed from normal conventions where a married woman wouldn't dream of holding hands with a raffish single man. It's all rather thrilling.

We emerge into a small square in front of the cathedral – still holding hands like schoolchildren or young lovers (I'm feeling rather like Audrey Hepburn in *Roman Holiday* where the young princess defies convention to spend a glorious romantic spree out of time and out of place away from her duties, with the handsomely devilish Gregory Peck). We wait for cars to pass before crossing the street to the market. At first, I'm disappointed to see the stalls here all sell the same kind of acrylic jumper and cheap cotton T-shirts as back home. But then Xavier pulls me deeper into the market, where we find local Breton lace and lace-makers dressed in traditional Breton costume, looking very puritanical in their black dress and white apron topped with complex lace and ribbon bonnets like some towering sugar confectionary. They make me want to giggle.

'They are called *coiffe*, or head-dress,' Xavier tells me. 'This way,' he says, and I follow him up and down aisles, where I buy meat and vegetables and two apples to eat straight away. Juice dribbles down our chins as we bite into the fruit and laugh and talk. I feel light and wonder whether gravity will be able to keep me Earthbound. But I don't care. Even my child feels like she belongs to someone else in a different world, a different time – lovely Finty – I almost start to well up as I conjure up her smell, her sights and sounds. But no, it will be good for me, good for her, good for my marriage, if I can find myself in the company of someone who is not touched by The Accident – the sadness of which has tainted us all. Perhaps this is how I start to find my way back?

Xavier pauses at a stall, where he carefully selects a cream fedora hat and tries it on. It's perfect.

'What do you think?' he says.

'You look dashing,' I say. 'Beautiful.'

He takes the hat off and focuses on my eyes. 'No, it is you who are beautiful.' His voice is softly soothing.

Warmth flushes my chest, and I half turn to try on a hat to my left, sensing that he must have noticed my blushes. I mean, I couldn't have been flashing clearer signals if I'd been a blinking Belisha Beacon. He throws me a quick glance then skips into the shop.

'I bought it! It is mine,' he announces on his return, donning the hat and a broad smile. 'How about we have lunch to celebrate?'

'I don't know.'

'But I insist.'

A bird which may be a starling hops from one branch of a tree to the next.

'Is there something the matter?'

'What? Oh, no. It's nothing. I'm fine.'

He softly touches my face. 'Sometimes you look a little sad, *ma cherie.*'

I turn away. Sometimes I feel as if I am being washed out of time, and I want to hide away. Once there was a cellar which Jake and I carpeted with bits of old cut-offs, where only children – and then only those who knew the secret password – were allowed to enter. Now I have secret places in my head.

'Right,' I say, forcing myself to sound chipper. 'Where's that café?'

He leads me past shops whose wares spill out onto the streets. Cards on turnaround racks. Vases stacked on plastic-coated wire frames. Only forty-nine francs. A real bargain. And over everything looms the huge edifice of Saint-Corentin Cathedral, above and between the buildings – to the right, now to the left and now straight ahead – as we find seats at a pavement cafe. Xavier's chair is red. Mine is yellow. Above us the wind gently lifts the skirt of a large umbrella which advertises "Frigecreme" in pink letters, speared through the table as if impaled to the ground.

As we view the menu, I am aware of the admiring glances of one or two men. Inadvertently, I catch the eye of a tasty one with black Raybans and hair to match; I return his smile. And why not? I'm enjoying my rediscovered allure. A waitress weaves through the diners and Xavier signals for her to come take our order.

'What would you like?' Xavier asks.

I choose a buckwheat pancake and salad. He orders a seafood platter.

'Wine a good idea for you?'

I nod and lean back, lifting my head so that the sun glints my hair and highlights my throat.

'Are you enjoying your vacation?' he says "*vacation*" in a very French way. I watch as he pulls a pack of cigarettes from his shirt pocket.

'Can I have one?' It's like I'm playing hooky with a bad boy from a local school. I take a cigarette from his long fingers, light it, then rearrange my face like a teenager might after much practice in front of her bedroom mirror. Ridiculous, Ronnie – you're as excited as if this is a first date. Get a grip.

'Tell me about yourself,' he says.

And so I do. Over lunch. In between mouthfuls and glasses of wine, the words flow out, tripping over themselves for attention.

I tell him about Jake's accident and Xavier's eyes mist over: he waves to the waitress for more wine.

I tell him about being a mother. How I love Finty to bits. 'But there are times,' I say, 'now, don't get me wrong...'

'Go on.'

'Times when I miss being me. You know. Instead of Finty's mother. I've lost myself somewhere. I don't even feel sexy or attractive anymore.' He gives me a look that implies this isn't so, as I reach for another cigarette.

He orders coffee and liqueurs as I tell him how I don't laugh anymore.

'That is sad,' he says as he touches my hand. I wish he would touch my knee.

I tell him today is the first time I have laughed – properly laughed – in ages. He leans towards me. 'It is good to laugh,' he says.

The waitress appears with the bill and he waves away my money, leaving notes and coins on the saucer.

'Come. Let us depart.' He pulls me from my seat and grabs my shopping as I sling my handbag over my shoulder. 'This way.'

We cross the road, down a street and into a doorway. I'm almost floating as I'm rather tipsy. He pulls his doorkey from his shorts pocket and opens the door. Inside, he envelopes me with a kiss that sucks the breath from my lungs. We lose balance and half-crash against the wall, our bodies straining as sunbursts explode in my head.

Then we are climbing the stairs, panting, to his apartment door, where we burst in, tearing at our clothes. He slams the door shut with his foot and carries me to the bed. *What am I doing?* is my last clear thought as he assaults me with little kisses over my eyes, my cheek, my breasts and stomach; he turns me over, lets out a little gasp as he finds my hummingbird tattoo at the top of my right buttock, and now he's murmuring something in French: kissing it, licking, biting. Before I can even think if this is what I want, he has a condom on and deftly slides two fingers inside me, then rams his hard cock inside. 'Vero, Vero, Vero,' he moans, then stops to stare deep into my eyes. His are round and dark, and he's pushing deeper inside and for once I want to forget myself, to lose myself to sensuous pleasure, to feel wanted by a handsome man who doesn't know me as poor Veronica. *Just this once,* I'm thinking as I hold tight on to his buttocks, pulling him deeper inside me as he thrusts and we're banging and bouncing thoughts out of my head other than I want something else, to feel something else. He's grinding now, and the reality is hitting: *What am I doing?* I try to push him off, but this seems to urge him on.

'No,' I'm murmuring. 'Stop. I'm so sorry – stop.'

'Ah, Vero, Vero.' He's carrying on, and I'm resigned to the fact there's no stopping him now. If anything, he's gaining momentum, the headboard banging away as I try to shift out from under him, but he pins me to the bed. 'No,' I'm saying, but he's placing his hand over my mouth. 'Ah, yes, yes,' he says. 'Yes.' And he's the goat, the goat devil in a satanic rite of Dennis Wheatley – the thought nearly forcing out a moan. 'You like that, eh?' he says. I see my mother in the sand dunes; my mother whose hands are on the shoulders of Slimy Bob – not pulling him in after all but pushing him away. Pushing him away.

And now, with a final guttural grunt, Xavier's done.

I lie still as he rolls over, expertly whips off the condom, wraps it in a tissue to drop it onto the bare wooden floor and flops back onto the pillows. Next, he reaches for his cigarettes, offers me one – which I decline – then he grasps his half-drunk glass of whiskey from the bedside table, takes a slug and lets out a satisfied sigh. I'm half-expecting him to crash the glass against the grate.

I've got to get out of here, is all I'm thinking right now as I quickly scrabble around for my dress and knickers as all the while he watches me – this dishevelled man with stubble darker than it was before we began.

'This has been good for you too, yes?'

I'm too ashamed to say anything. 'Come here.' He beckons. But I'm too busy hopping from one foot to the other as I put on my sandals. 'Ah, *merde!*' he utters, regarding his watch. 'I am so very sorry, Veronique – but I have the appointment.' He stubs out his cigarette in an ashtray. 'Please. Wait here for my return if you would like?'

'No. No, that's fine. I must get back to… Yes. Um. That was…' He's looking at me expectantly. 'Lovely,' is all I can come up with (okay – so I panicked). 'But, um, this can never – ever happen again. Indeed, it shouldn't have… well… and I did try to halt proceedings but – ah…'

'But you wanted it too, yes?' He's giving me a most cheeky look.

'Could you please be so kind, as to tell me if there is a bus? Back to…?'

'Ah, *oui*. The bus to Plouer Meille, it stops on the street outside the apartment. If you are sure you must go. Do you not want to wait for my return?'

'No. I have to get back.'

'Vero. You were enjoying it too – you cannot fake how you were with me. You should not feel bad. I have seen the way you look at your husband. The love has gone, no? Is clear that he gets on your nerves.'

'Yes, well…'

Rising from the bed and slapping me on the bottom, he strides past to head for the bathroom tucked away in a corner of his loft-like apartment. His nakedness causes me to look away. *C'mon, he is rather magnificent*, I think. (Traitor.) Okay, a little part of me was proud that I'd managed to nab such a handsome man. Oh, Veronica, though, what have you done?

Without bothering to shut the door behind him, he places one hand on the wall above the toilet bowl and takes a piss so strong and long, it's like a horse relieving itself.

Clutching my things I call, 'Bye!' and scoot out the door before he's finished.

NINETEEN

On the Way Back from Quimper

I can't believe I have been so stupid, I think, as I shake my head and then laugh out loud. Stupid and yet thinking how I've still got it! Are you mental? You are risking the best thing you've ever had, with Gerry. And for what? A quick bunk-up? Are you really so desperate to sabotage things?

You wanted him to fuck you, though, didn't you? You used him and then tried to get him to stop because you realised what you had to lose. Striding to the bus stop I barely register traffic passing by.

I'm confused, because I don't feel guilty, I feel strong and very much in my body. Perhaps this dalliance is what I need to reconnect with myself and reboot my system, make me remember that I'm a woman, in my own right.

I climb onto the bus and take a seat. Who are you trying to kid, trying to put a positive spin on this? You've only gone and let a total stranger fuck you, whilst your husband is back at the villa taking care of your child. It's nothing to feel proud of.

Slumping in my seat I'm thinking how I don't feel so good now, do I? Oh God, does this mean I have to tell Gerry? After

I've made him promise to not keep secrets from me? Is Xavier right, and it's plain to see that Gerry and I are struggling to get along? Is it really a case of him getting on my nerves, and I'm testing how I feel?

Looking out of the window at the fields and houses rushing by, I see an old woman dressed in black with a baguette tucked into her armpit. She stops to let the bus pass, and in a fleeting moment of what appears to me like recrimination, her eyes meet mine like she's some bleedin' Greek chorus of one, and when I turn to look back – she is gone.

You can't go back, Ron. What's done is done.

'I want my marriage to work, I do,' I say out loud, causing the woman across the aisle with a basket of groceries on her lap, to smile indulgently at me with an "we've all been there" air about her, although she of course doesn't offer any advice but reaches into her bag. I nod and murmur my thanks as she offers me an apple.

Knock knock. I stick my head around the door. 'Jake? I have to talk to you.'

'Okay. Come on in. You don't mind if I carry on, do you?'

Jake stands in his blue overalls, rubbing a wardrobe down with a piece of sandpaper folded over a block. 'No.' I perch on the edge of the dressing table as he stops to gently scrape at the wood with a metal-ended tool.

'It's Gerry,' I begin. 'I have to talk to you about him – because… Well, you know… because you're a man.' I give him a sarcastic look. 'Apparently.'

He raises one eyebrow, then returns to his sanding.

'You know what I mean,' I continue. 'I need to understand. Men are so bloody strange.'

He wipes the golden dust off his hands and onto his overalls. 'So what is it this time?' He grins at me, but I'm not in the mood for his teasing. This is serious, I think as I stroke the reality of the growing bump in my belly.

'It's Gerry. He told me yesterday that he slept with somebody else. Some solicitor he knows from uni. Her name is Fran, and they had sex – at a conference of all places – such a cliche! I'm nearly five months pregnant.' *I'm up on my feet now, voice louder and close to shouting.*

'Steady on.'

'Just great, isn't it?' *I pace the small area between dressing table and window.* 'He tells me all about his grubby shag and expects me to… Oh.' *I turn and pace the other way.* 'It makes me so angry. He's been feeling bad about it, he says. So what does he do? Offloads it onto me, and now I feel like crap. But him? He feels relieved, he says, and is glad he told me. Well, bully for him. He honestly expects me to thank him for making a clean breast of it. Actually expects me to tell him that everything's going to be okay. Well it isn't.' *I stop pacing in front of Jake. He's stopping his sanding and is listening.*

'It's not only the hurt,' *I continue.* 'It's the humiliation. That and the way he doesn't take any responsibility for it himself. Instead, he says it "just happened",' *I say, using air quotes.* 'That usual sort of bollocks.'

Jake returns to his sanding of the wardrobe. 'You'd rather he hadn't told you? Is that it?'

'Yes. No. I don't know.'

I sit back on the dressing table and watch the dust motes dance in the autumn sunlight shafting through the many paned windows of Jake and Angie's cottage. Then it all spills out of me. At first in a slow trickle of telling how, according to Gerry, she was an old girlfriend he hadn't expected to bump into. 'Perfect opportunity for a quick shag, more like,' *I say.* 'Turns out she'd written him a letter and slipped it into his suitcase. Says she never stopped loving him. And you know what? I suspected something had gone on when he* got back from this bloody conference. I did! But at the time he lied to me! Reassured me he'd never do such a thing as be unfaithful. He practically pooh-poohed all my fears and put them down to my hormones. Then last night, he confesses, all of a sudden, in one big rush. Leaving me feeling defeated not only by his betrayal and duplicity, but also by my betrayal of myself. Because I'd denied my own instincts – and all because he told me to.' Jake continues rubbing, sanding, listening. 'In some ways,' I add, 'that's the worst of it all – his managing to convince me that I was in the wrong.'

Jake blows along the contours of the wood.

'So what do you think?' I ask. 'What would you have done if you were Gerry? Would you have told me?'

'Probably not,' he says. 'Not right away – if at all. Because what's the point of confessing if you're only doing it to make you feel better? Because you can't handle the guilt.'

'That's it! That's exactly what I mean. He only told me because he was feeling guilty, and he wanted me to make it all better. Like he expected me to offer some sort of absolution.'

Jake leans against the wardrobe and opens a can of Ruddles beer. 'Want one?'

I shake my head.

'The way I see it,' he says, 'is that people don't talk to each other. Not properly, and not about what they really mean. For instance, a couple might argue over who does the washing up, when really they're worried about money or are angry because they're not having sex. Too many people find it hard or impossible to talk about how they feel, and what they want. Because they risk being exposed, and it's too scary. Huh?'

I give him what I consider to be a wry look.

'Sometimes, sis,' he continues, 'someone will do something daft like sleep with somebody else because they're scared of commitment. Or maybe they're testing how they feel. Or sometimes maybe these things happen, and don't mean anything at all.'

'Okay. But... for fuck's sake, Jay.'

'You know your problem, Vee?'

'Sounds like you're going to tell me, smart arse.'

'It's communication. I've noticed from seeing you two together, and from hearing what you say, that you don't talk. You don't communicate. Maybe if you had talked first about what living together and having a baby meant to you both, then this one-off might never have happened.'

'So it's my fault too, is it?'

'Only you know that, sis. You've got to figure that one out for yourself. And work out what it is that you do want, for yourself and for your baby. Never mind Gerry and what he wants. Your needs are every bit as important, and you need to decide what your own priorities are, and don't go looking to him for solutions.' He takes a swig from his beer. 'If you decide to stay with him, then you'll have to compromise, so you need to know your bottom line. And if you don't want to compromise then... well, then it's best you discover that now.' He pulled me towards him, and the two of us stood next to the window. 'Whatever you decide – you will survive this. Believe me. It's life that's important. Look out there,' he says, pointing outside to their oh-so-perfect garden. 'Birds are singing, trees are growing. Life, sis.' He reaches down and gently pats my belly. 'That's what counts. Life.'

'Fuck off, you knobhead. You'll be bursting into song next.'

'You know what I mean.'

From somewhere below we hear Angie call out my name.

'Yes?' I call back.

Her footsteps come halfway up the stairs. 'Gerry's on the phone.'

'Tell him I don't want to talk to him.'

Jake fixes me with his quizzical eyebrow again.

'Let him stew for a while,' I say.

That was the weekend when Mother's secret had come out, via a slip of the tongue on my part, because I'd forgotten that he didn't know.

There then followed a phone call between Jake and Mum when words were said, and they ended up not on speaking terms and remained that way so when he had his accident, it was the longest time for a rift.

'Your fault,' Mum said at the hospital. 'Your fault that my beautiful boy wasn't speaking to me and now it's too late.' Unfair, I know – but I guess it kind of was.

I fish around in my shopping bag. I know it's here somewhere – ah, there – I bring out a can of Coca-Cola to press against my forehead. Because it's hot in this bus. Cracking the can open, I take a deep drink, enjoying how its bubbles bustle over my teeth as liquid coldness spills down my throat. Not quite washing my sins away.

As we enter the outskirts of town, I'm trying to convince myself this whole adventure with Xavier was merely one of those things. What goes on in Quimper stays in Quimper, etc. There's no need to cry over spilt milk – whoops – coach goes over a bump – or even spilt Coke.

As the bus finally draws up outside the villa, a single – one for sorrow – magpie lands on the wall and cocks its head at me. *And you can fuck off too*, I think, then give him a salute to be on the safe side.

Oh God. I've been a total bitch, haven't I? I see it all now. To Gerry, to Angie – a total bitch. Grief has made bitches of us all.

Is Xavier right? Is it plain to see that Gerry and I are struggling to get along? Is it really a case of him getting on my nerves? Does this mean I have to tell him about today, or not?

Outside our villa, standing on the pavement, I pause to gather my thoughts – even though I'm dying to get inside and have a shower because it's like Xavier is on my clothes, in my sweat – every pore oozing a concoction of cigarettes, garlic and cum. I can smell him on me. In me. So strong (and deliciously naughty) it makes me feel quite nauseous with guilt.

My earlier bravado has deserted me. What have I done? I did try to say no, didn't I? A bit late, it's true. Still, a gentleman would have stopped and not carried on. Oh, come off it, Ron. It's not like you're an innocent abroad. You consented – come on, you were enjoying it – and then you said no too late. You'll just have to live with it.

My head aches and I need a shower, so collecting up my shopping bags I set off down the drive. A wave of nausea coming over me again. Maybe it's something I ate… Pausing, I place a hand against the villa wall and vomit on the gravel. Charming. Once done, I use my foot to try and cover up the mess with gravel, like a cat concealing its poo. Like I said – charming.

I must look a right sight, I think, as I sit on our bed staring at my reflection in the mirror. Was it the same for my mother? Did she too get carried away too and then immediately regret it, all those years ago when she forced me to keep her secret from Jake?

All I know is that I've been acting like Gerry's lucky to have me, when it's the other way around. I've been too wrapped up in Jake, and in his and Angie's marriage, when I should be focusing on mine. Well, this changes now.

'Come on, Veronica,' I tell my reflection. 'Moping around and feeling stupid won't help. What's done is done. Now you have a marriage to save.' I wipe at my mouth and under my eyes with a paper tissue. Gerry might not be perfect, but he's pretty close to perfect for me.

It's time, I'm thinking as I pull the small toilet bag from out of my suitcase. It came with me like its own secret I have to tote around.

Opening the zip lock, I empty out my stash – the stash I've been collecting in case I can no longer stand the pain. Mainly sleeping tablets I easily obtained from the doctor following Jake's accident, plus heavy-duty pain killers from when I said my back was playing up. I have been deliberately hoarded them, just in case – and neither Carol nor Gerry knew anything about them. They give me control over my life; they have been my secret, my comfort, so that if things got really bad I would have an option for a way out. Should I need it.

'Enough,' I whisper as I purposefully walk to the washbasin in the corner of the room. 'I need to face up to what's what.' Standing at the sink I first shake out one bottle then the next, emptying the pills into the bowl, and turning on the tap to wash them all down the wastepipe like the skinny baby who slipped down the plughole in that Music Hall ditty, "A Mother's Lament". How we used to sing and laugh at that song.

Dearest Jake,

Once upon a time you were a baby curled up next to me as tight as a male seahorse loops its tail around its young. Once we thought we'd caught the merest glimpse of alternate universes where we'd run across soft grass. Once you cracked open your head, ending up beached on a white hospital sheet, our invisible cord severed so badly that I've not been sure if I can carry on.

But today I choose life and will do so each day until it's like breathing and not something I intentionally decide over pills.

I miss you, you plonker. Wish me luck.

Your twin sister

Ron xxx

TWENTY

Tuesday, Continued

I've had my shower, scrubbed my skin, washed my hair and changed my clothes. Yep, I've washed that man right out of my hair!

In the kitchen I set about washing up some plates. Outside I can see Jake's in the garden, but Gerry and Finty must still be at the beach.

'You've caught the sun,' says Angie, causing me to turn so quickly I nearly knock a dish over. 'You're all rosy and positively glowing.' She's grinning away at me from the doorframe. 'Enjoy your day out? Don't worry, we can have a quick goss while Gerry and Finty are down at the beach.' She looks around. 'So what was he like, then?'

'Who?' I'm annoyed that I'm starting to blush. (I'll never make a spy.)

'You know perfectly well who I mean. Madame's son, Xavier.' She's giving me a definite squinty eye. 'Come on, do tell. What was he like?'

What was he like? Can she sense what I've been up to? That I have carnal knowledge of Xavier!

'How d'you mean?' I say, going for feigned innocence as I fold a tea towel.

'Your secret's safe with me, only I heard from Jake that

Monsieur Sexy Pants gave you a lift into Quimper. Your trip's certainly put the apples back in your cheeks.'

'Oh. The lift.' Phew. I attend to wiping the cooker's hob rings to give me time to compose myself. 'It was pleasant enough, you know. Xavier dropped me off at the Old Town and then I wandered about a bit. Did some shopping. Usual stuff. Nothing terribly exciting.'

Nothing like ripping each other's clothes off for a quick shag. Oh, heck. Deep breaths – and don't blush!

'Okay. Sounds pretty boring then. What did you buy?' She watches me unpack the bags.

'Some fish, and lamb. Oh, and there's this great market for fruit and veg…' My voice tails off. 'That's about it.'

'Right. Shame. No gossip, then.'

'No.'

She appears to have lost interest, much to my relief. 'For our night, me and Jake have decided to push the boat out. We're going fine-dining at the Hotel Thalamot,' she says.

'That sounds lovely,' I say, not mentioning how it's expensive too. I busy myself trying to make space in the fridge.

Remember what Gerry said? Don't fret about the money, and remember your pledge to stop being a bitch.

'Thought a little extravagance might do us good. You know, cheer ourselves up.' She looks sad. I know she's sad, of course I do. I can't say anything about my own hurt, as her sadness takes priority over mine. I know the score.

It's like there's this hierarchy of pain. In order of importance, it goes: first Angie, then their kids, then Jake's parents, then me down at the bottom. Somehow this seems fair to the rest of the world i.e. my pain being least important, but it doesn't seem fair to me. I know Jake and I aren't identical twins – but we're still twins. Nobody knows him like I do, and nobody gets me like he does. Nobody.

'Shall we crack open this bottle of wine?' I suggest, putting on my well-used (if not well-worn) brave face. 'It's meant to be excellent. It's a recommendation from Xavier.' I know I've said his name, but I'm trying to act as if acknowledging his existence is no big deal.

'Is it now? Go on, why not. Yes. Good idea.' Angie parks her bum on the windowsill, half in and half out. 'Jake?' she calls. 'Do you fancy a glass of wine?'

''Ess,' comes his reply.

'Any idea at all when Gerry and Finty might be back from the beach?'

'Hm?' Angie has her eyes closed, holding her face up to the afternoon breeze. How young she looks. I feel a pang of guilt for having so many mean thoughts about her. It's no excuse, but I'm all over the place, too. Still, remember that you've resolved to change all that.

There's a knock at the back door and Madame enters. '*Bonjour!*'

Angie stands bolt upright like a schoolgirl caught in the act, while I fight the urge to run around like a headless chicken.

'*Ah, bonjour, Monsieur Jake,*' Madame calls, giving him a wave as he smiles back then gets to his feet in an awkward scramble to begin his stiff walk to the window. She nods at me and then says something I don't understand in French. All I seem to be able to do is blush whenever she looks my way.

Angie translates for Madame. 'She says that she hopes her son got you to Quimper all right.'

'*Oui. Merci, Madame,*' I go for, and set about hunting for the corkscrew. Anything to not meet her piercing stare.

I needn't have worried, as Madame and Angie have embarked on a conversation involving much smiling and nodding over at Jake. During the course of all this, Madame passes Angie a white bowl from her basket inside which, nestled in straw, lie six brown eggs. She squeezes Jake's cheek in farewell and departs.

Once sure she's gone I say, 'What was all that about?' and pass both Angie and Jake a glass topped with wine I've somehow managed to open.

'She brought us these eggs, "for your 'usband",' says Angie, mimicking a heavy French accent. '"To build 'im up. 'E is looking tired."'

'She speaks fluent 'Allo 'Allo! French, does she?'

'Shut up, don't be mean.'

'Seriously, it's sweet,' I continue. 'She seems to have taken quite a shine to Jake, doesn't she?'

'She necessary,' chips in Jake as he limps through the back door and into the kitchen, holding his wine aloft.

'Is she now.' I turn to Angie. 'Did you know that I found the two of them playing draughts when I went round earlier?'

Angie nods. 'She told me. Apparently, she says she used to play draughts with her late husband. And continued to do so after his stroke, before he passed away.'

The wine is far better than English supermarket plonk, I think as I take a sip. 'It's funny, isn't it? How she can't speak English, and Jake – well, I guess.' I cast a look Jake's way. 'Sorry, bruv, but you can't speak English at the moment either, can you? Yet they seemed to be chattering away.' (Or were they? Perhaps they weren't.)

'Huh?' The look on his face suggests he's doing his best to follow the conversation.

'Don't you see?' says Angie, all earnest now. 'That's the point. She doesn't notice his speech problems because she's used to it. Her husband lost his speech as part of his stroke. They've been kind of communicating – her and Jake – without talking.'

'You mean by sign or something?'

'More...' Jake is saying. We both stop what we're doing, to give him our full attention. Now he's frowning with concentration.

'Her... play. Not, um... oh, what the compound...' He sucks at the deadened corner of his mouth. 'It's the... she is not unnecessary.'

I think I might know what he's getting at. 'You mean, she doesn't mind?' I offer.

His face brightens. 'Yes. Doesn't mind. Not talking.' He sighs with the effort, takes his glass and returns to the table outside as Angie and I both watch him go, lost in our own thoughts.

'They looked so comfortable together,' I finally say.

'Jake and Madame?' says Angie. 'Yes, I suppose so.'

She pulls out a pack of Camels from her bag. She's smoking a lot these days, I've noticed. 'Sorry for snapping earlier,' she says, then offers me the packet. 'Would you like one?'

'No, thanks. You're all right.'

She closes her eyes and pulls the smoke deep into her lungs, and I change my mind. 'Can I have one after all?' I say, reasoning to myself that it's been a pretty stressful day, one way or the other.

'Help yourself.' She pushes the pack across the table.

'Ta.'

We both move outside to sit on the back step. 'Kids okay?' I ask.

'Yes. They're upstairs, playing. Sarah's very sensible and knows to come get me if they need anything.'

'It's been a lovely afternoon, hasn't it?' I say, more for the sake of having something to say. 'Weather-wise, that is.' I'd rather keep talking, especially as I don't want a moment of weakness to creep up on me in case I spill the beans on exactly what happened with Xavier.

Angie places her arm about my shoulder, and I lean my head against her. I have missed her. But I've also been wary of her, because it's like she's surrounded by a prickly hedge which I've been unable to get through since the accident. She pulls away to take another drag on her ciggie.

'So,' I start, not fully knowing quite what I'm going to say, 'how's it going so far? Would you come away on holiday with us again, do you think?' Pathetically, I realise I want her to say yes.

'Probably not,' is her reply. Well, that shot me down in flames. She stares straight ahead at the pine trees, which stare back. 'Oh, it's not your fault.' Her shoulders droop as if she's suddenly let go of tension in her neck. 'We're not used to sharing, you see.'

I'm not sure I do, but I say nothing.

'I don't like having to rely on you guys so much.' She casts me a glance, then takes a big breath. 'That's part of it. And don't think I haven't noticed your being funny about the money, either. You've made it quite clear that you think we don't contribute enough.'

It's like she's taken a course in mind-reading. I try and explain. 'Gerry's been a bit rubbish with money, you see, and I've not been keeping my eye on things closely enough, and the bank called him in to warn that we could go bankrupt. So there you are. We're both worried, and it looks like I'll have to go back to work soon.'

'Maybe you should go back to work. Oh, I'm sorry, but I don't really care.' She takes a sip of wine. 'All I care about is I'm finding it difficult seeing you and Gerry together when me and Jake... well...' She takes another drag.

'Things aren't exactly rosy between me and Gerry, you know. But I haven't wanted to say anything because you have enough on your plate—'

She holds up her hand like stopping traffic. 'Please. Enough. You're quite right, I don't want to know. I can't care about your problems. Can't you see they're trivial and nothing compared with ours?' *Here we go again*, I think. 'Just look at him!' We both look to where Jake is fiddling with the cord on his duffle bag. She continues, 'It's all I can do to focus on what matters. And what matters is us. Me and Jake and the kids. I'm sorry if that sounds harsh, but that's how it is. My mother's all for putting Jake into some residential care, as she says I can't possibly manage Jake on my own with the children, but I'm having none of it.' She waves her cigarette in the air. 'So don't tell me you're having it bad. You don't know how lucky you are.' She stubs her cigarette out in a saucer. 'You see, I have to believe that everything will be all right, in the end.' She holds her chin high. 'I have to believe that he will recover, that if we keep fighting it, if we have positive mindfulness, then everything will come right. Jake and I are strong so long as we pull together, and I can't waver or change my focus from that.'

'Right,' I say; there's not much else to say. But a residential home? Please tell me that's not on the cards.

Angie clambers to her feet to call upstairs, 'Girls! Come on down! Sarah! Lauren! It's nearly time for food! I'm giving them a short snack before we go out.'

The girls come crashing into the kitchen. 'Goodee,' yells Sarah, bounding over to greet her mother.

Standing by the side of the sink, emptying the final dregs from my glass, I'm unsure what to do next. Lauren and Sarah take their seats at the kitchen table, and Jake enters from the garden, lightly patting me on top of my head as he brushes past.

'Did you know, that in the middle of the Atlantic Ocean is the Sargasso Sea, where eels come together to mate.'

'Cool.'

'And... and... it's where Jules Verne's Captain Nemo did battle with that giant squid. D'you remember?'

'You mean that film Twenty Thousand Leagues Under the Sea? *The one where Kirk Douglas lops off one of its tentacles and James Mason gets eaten?'*

'That's the one.'

'It had those big dinner-plate eyes and that weird mouth like a bird's beak?' Does beak opening and closing motion with his hands.

'Yeah. Shut up. Anyway, that's where the Bermuda Triangle is.'
'No!'
We're both fascinated by tales of the Bermuda Triangle.

'Yes. Dead spooky... where ships and planes disappear, and ghostly galleons still sail, and the death screams of horses are heard all the way down to Davy Jones's locker. They used to chuck live horses overboard when they were becalmed in the doldrums.'

'That's horrible.'

'Yeah. Wooo-ooooo-oooooo-ooooooo!' he says, doing ghost noises and chasing me around the room.

It's hard to forget that when he first came round from his coma he kept calling me Jude, which was the name of his first steady girlfriend.

Jake would play his guitar and sing that Beatles song, "Hey Jude". Most annoying song, I always thought. I hadn't taken much to her, either.

Gerry and Finty are still not back from the beach – I do hope Finty has not been in the sun all this time. Already the events of earlier today with Xavier seem like I must have been under some mad spell.

Flushing the toilet, I take in the view outside of the bathroom window to where I can see the sea. Somewhere along the way this sea becomes the Atlantic Ocean: once Brittany was attached to the west of Britain, but they're now like two separated twins. Pulled apart by fates, elemental forces and tectonic plates. Jake will know about those sorts of things. Or would have.

*

Downstairs Jake sits in the middle of the bustle of the kitchen. If he concentrates, he can tell that something has passed between the two women. Something not good. But it's too difficult to concentrate. Ideas and words flit past and away as if they're tropical fish darting in and out of a coral reef... yes... um... that's it... like those television programmes with people in those black outfit thingie things... go underwater to where they have the... the... big things on their backs for breath and what were those things called again they were what I don't know what that might be and who was and where was and that... she's nice but doesn't... it was different once was it and what's her name was it Jude no that was another one I remember her with long dark hair and a dress it was – oh what was it – hang on it was Laura Ashley that was it and... where did she live it was down the hill somewhere near the whatsit what was it and... oh where's sister she's she's she's Ron that's it Ron and and and...

He can tell that a cup of tea will be nice and that he doesn't have one so better make one. He can do that oh yes he can. He just has to get up with – which leg is it again and damn swing it it's all cronkety crup what's the... oh fuck. 'Tea, anybody?' They seem to... yes... good. Uh oh. Here's comes trouble – oh that not his name... it's...

*

Jake turns and smiles as Gerry enters, carrying a tired Finty on his shoulders. I'm ridiculously happy to see them, and rush to envelop them in a big hug.

'I missed you today,' I say, making him happily surprised as I nuzzle my face into his neck: he smells a heady mixture of sun, sea and ozone.

'Blimey,' he says, clearly chuffed to bits. 'You should go on a day trip more often.' He sniffs my hair. 'Pooh, you've been smoking.' Finty is nodding off to sleep, so he lowers her into her buggy, and stupid me is overwhelmed with emotion. 'What? What is it?' He holds me out at arm's length. 'Are you crying?'

'Of course not, only a little bit. It's just...' Suddenly I am very close to bursting out crying, and suddenly I want all three of us – me, Gerry and Finty – to be out of here, out of Brittany, out of France. Out and away from all that's gone on.

Gerry lowers his voice. 'Has something happened? Only you don't seem yourself. Not anything to do with...' he says, giving a meaningful nod over to where Angie is busying herself at the sink.

'No, it's not that. Not really,' I whisper, as I don't want Angie to hear – but I needn't worry as she has her back to us clattering away at the sink and oblivious. It's then that I start to notice a noise coming from Jake. It's a low mumbling sound which is almost like he's whining.

Mumble, mumble: '...liquid.'

'What?' I say as I turn towards him, straining to understand.

'Liquid,' he insists, holding up his left hand in an expression of lopsided hopelessness. A puddle is spreading at his feet.

'Have you spilt some water?' I say, not getting it – yet.

He looks puzzled, then angry. 'No. All this compound liquid. Here.' He points to the floor. 'It's here.'

I try again. 'Shall I put the kettle on? Is that it?' But Finty has started to grizzle and I lift her out of her buggy.

'No. Oh, it's here,' he says, pointing to where his combat trousers are wet from mid-thigh down. 'I piss myself.' He grimaces apologetically. 'Sorry.'

I'm galvanised into action as Angie stops what she's doing and I beckon Sarah over. 'Can you take Lauren and Finty into the other room to play? There's a good girl.'

Sarah nods. Lauren and Finty stare mutely at the adults as the big girl rounds them up and leads them away while I fetch a cloth from under the sink and Angie slumps into a chair.

'Don't you worry, mate,' says Gerry. 'Hang on a mo.' And he dashes from the room.

'It's all right, nothing to worry about, we'll soon have this all cleaned up,' I say to Jake.

'Sorry,' Jake says to Angie, a hang-dog expression on his face. 'I pissed. On floor. Lots.'

'Well, that's it – we won't be going out for a slap-up meal now.'

Gerry's back at Jake's side, Finty has run in to throw herself onto my leg. 'Gerry, can you take her?' I say as I do my best to finishing mopping the floor as Sarah comes to collect Finty once more. 'Thanks, love,' I say.

Gerry helps Jake step out of his sodden trousers and pants and into a pair of striped pyjama bottoms which he fetched from upstairs, while Angie remains in the chair, an unreadable expression on her face. I'm on the floor, mopping and sitting back on my haunches to wring the cloth out into a bowl, and then look across at Jake and give him a small smile. Time contracts and slows down.

There was that time – I don't say out loud – d'you remember, Jake? When I got insanely pissed at one of my parties? When I sat on the toilet, unable to move until you came and rescued me.

If I concentrate really hard, then the sink might stay in focus. 'Ohhhh.' I don't want to be sick. 'Bleugh!' Luckily, the sink is right next to the bog so I manage to puke right into it. Bright yellow and orange slime and lumps. Why does it always look like you've eaten carrots?

Able to stand a little, I somehow turn on the taps, scoop water into my cupped hand and rub it over my face, wiping the snot from my nose. I've been crying. Why have I been crying? I cannot remember why. I should not have started on those Bacardi and Cokes before the party, either.

Plonking myself back on the loo seat, I think I vaguely remember passing out in the front garden earlier. Before that I'd been thinking what a great party this was. Still is, by the sound of things. Must be at least a hundred people crammed into mine and Shirley's two-bedroomed flat. And then next thing I know, Shirley has asked me to deal with a bunch of gatecrashers out front – and that's where she found me. Flat on my back on the front lawn. Somehow she managed to get me to the downstairs loo. Shirley. My best mate Shirley. I hope she's enjoying herself. It's her twenty-first, you know. Of course I do. Why am I talking to myself? God knows.

Bleugh… Retch.

Feels like my body's possessed by some pissed-as-a-fart, throwing-up demon of The Omen type. 'Bleugh!' Christ, surely (or Shirley, geddit?) there can't be anymore left?

'Now we have a record to play for Veronica – where are you, Ronnie?' Mo is calling out, over his microphone. He's DJ-ing upstairs in our lounge. The neighbours have already complained. 'It's "Stay with Me Baby" by Lorraine Ellison,' he's saying. 'Great party, everyone. So, for Ronnie – wherever you are. Take it away, Lorraine.' And my all-time favourite song starts to swell.

'Heesh a good DJ,' I mutter, as I hang on to the sink, trying not to register the smell. A bloody good DJ with just the right mix of funk, Motown and disco. 'Ohhh.' Self-pity takes over as I roller coaster in and out of focus. Will it ever stop? Better try and get up. But I can't, as my knickers are down around my ankles and they seem an impossible distance away, and – oh, look – my arms won't work.

Rattle, rattle. In slow motion, I turn my head towards the door. Best not move too quickly in case head falls off. Whoah.

'Veronica? Ronnie? Are you in there?' That voice sounds familiar. Now who is it, again? 'Ronnie!'

I try to say yes but only a moan comes out.

'Let me in, Ron. It's Drew.'

Drew? Slowly my brain flicks through its index cards of names. Nope. No Drew here. Bit of a stupid name if you ask me. Unless of course you're Drew Barrymore, which I'm guessing he's not (I start giggling to myself).

'Oh God, Shirley,' *I hear him say.* 'Do something. It's Ronnie, she's locked herself in the lav.'

Oh dear, what can the matter be, three old ladies locked in the lavatory... runs through my head.

'She's in there,' *he continues.* 'Christ knows what state she's in.'

Shirley? Who is this bloke, Drew?

'Why weren't you keeping a better eye on her?' *I can hear Shirley say. Bless Shirley, she does like to be a mother hen.* 'She is your girlfriend, after all!'

I am? Ohhh yes, I remember now. Drew – short for Andrew – although why he doesn't call himself Andy...? But – no. I can't open the door to him. Shirley, we can't open the door to this Drew chap. I don't want him to see me like this – unable to even pull my knickers up. My head almost drops off, it falls forwards so violently. I'm starting to think I might be more comfortable if I can somehow slide down and lie on the floor. The floor is starting to look very inviting...

'Ronnie? It's Shirley, babes. Let me in.'

'Nooo.'

'Come on, Ron. Be a sweetheart, and let your best friend in.'

'No,' *I manage to get out.* 'Jake,' *I slur.* 'Fetch Jake.'

I have to use one of my hands to lift my head – it's getting bored staring at the blue mosaic-patterned lino. Yes. It'll be all right when Jake gets here.

'Ron? It's Jake.'

Jake, I knew you'd come.

'Come on, Jake. Leave your sister to it. She's only a little drunk,' *I can hear Angie say. (I'd forgotten she's here too.)* 'In any case, Shirley and Drew are here. They can handle things.'

'She won't open the door to anyone but Jake!' snaps Shirley.

'But Drew is her boyfriend. He should sort her out,' insists Angie.

'She's my sister,' Jake says. 'She needs me. End of.'

'Right, then. I guess I'll see you later. Perhaps you can come and find me when Veronica has finished with you.'

But Angie, you don't understand. Only Jake will do.

'Come on, Ron. Open the door. Yes... That's it.' With his encouragement I discover I can actually control my fingers. I watch them with proud gratitude as if they are robot fingers which I've just had made and am testing them out for the very first time on Tomorrow's World, or something. They feel dead strange.

'That's it.' Next thing, the door is open and Jake fills the gap, as if he's stepped from a time machine or a parallel world into my little capsule. Jake the Rescuer.

'Look at the state of you, you prize idiot. What a mess,' he says, and – half-amused – he pulls me to my feet. 'Pull her knickers up, Shirl, will you? While I hold her upright.'

'Jake!' I'm crying with relief now. 'I couldn't move,' I sob. 'Didn't want anyone to see. Such a ninny.'

I know, I know – he doesn't need to say. Instead he holds me upright while he wets a towel under the tap and wipes at my face. 'You div,' he says. 'Let's get you to your room. I think you've had quite enough of this party.'

He picks me up and carries me, while I rest my head on his shoulder and give Drew a feeble wave as we walk on past.

'Is she all right?' Drew asks.

Jake nods and carries on. Once inside my room, he gently places me on my bed, undresses me, tucks me in and creeps out. 'Night night,' he says as he quietly closes the door behind him.

I'm here again at the sand dunes in Brean. There's a fog which creeps inland from the Bristol Channel and I can just make out

Jake a little ahead of me. As usual, when I try to run it's like the sand is gripping my feet and ankles while I try to make headway through the shifting sands. He's not far ahead; I know I must reach him. This is when the panic kicks in. Someplace else, I toss and turn on my bed and moan.

Harder, I must try harder, or the fingers of the fog will grab hold of me and I'll be dragged back. Lost and alone.

'Mummy. I want my mummy,' I murmur in the other place.

She's on all fours in the dip of the next dune; she turns her head to look back over her shoulder at me. Above her, marram grass waves at the top of a sandy hillock.

'No!'

Now I'm running and scrambling down the side of a long, long dune. Trying to get away. Run, run. Run away. Long grass tries to tangle around my legs.

There – lying on the ground – is that little boy from our street… the one who was murdered… Somebody came and took him away. I remember… He was found, battered to death, in the woods of Blaise Castle. *He liked to watch Jake tinker with his motorbike*, I'm thinking as the boy opens his eyes – those long dark lashes above two round moons – and I stumble backwards, desperate to get away, scrambling to my feet to run once more, my hair streaming behind me.

'Jake! Jake! Jake, where are you?'

There he is. Up ahead at the entrance to the beach. His back is towards me, so I slow to a walk, holding the stitch in my side. As I approach, I stop right behind him, gulping grateful gasps of air.

'Jake.' I reach forwards to touch his shoulder, but when he turns – he's someone else. His face belongs to somebody else.

'Jake!' I cry out, sitting bolt upright in bed. Momentarily unsure where I am – here/there? Now/then?

'Ron? Ron? Ssssh. It's all right. It's all right,' says Gerry, who's trying to hold on to me.

With loud footfalls, Angie dashes into our room. 'What on Earth's going on?' she demands. 'What's all that shouting for?'

'Sssh. It's Veronica,' says Gerry. 'She's having one of her nightmares.' He tries to rock me in his embrace, but I remain dead still, staring to the left of the open doorway to where Jake stands in the corner of our room like Boo Radley, half in and half out of the shadows.

TWENTY-ONE

Wednesday

I can tell that it's raining, even before I fling back the shutters, by the drop in temperature and that washed metallic smell coming in through the open window.

What a shame – being on holiday should mean that it's sunny each and every day. Everyone knows that. Gerry lies next to me, fast asleep. Without his glasses on he appears so vulnerable, with his arm flung across his face like a young boy in his abandonment. As I sit up in bed, propped by pillows, I watch him breathe.

Dear Jake,

I'm writing this letter to you, in the hope that one day you will come back. Somehow, someway. I do know you're trying to.

You won't remember – because they say that after a head injury you don't remember anything of the accident or the recovery period afterwards – so chances are you won't recall how I sat at your bedside every day for two weeks after you came flying off your motorbike – you silly boy! Who did you think you were? Daredevil motorcyclist Evel Knievel?

Anyway, I was either there by your bed or waiting for

my turn in the hospital's relatives' room. Gerry did most of the baby-minding. Because Finty – well, Finnoula's her real name – Irish, you see, like Gerry's family. It's from the legend of the children of Lir. They all lived in a castle in the woods and their wicked stepmother changed Finnoula and her three brothers into swans. When the spell was broken Finnoula placed her arm about the boys' shoulders and they all died. Weird how I remember that now.

Finty was only a few weeks old when you had your silly accident. I say silly because it was. You big eejit. And there was me, with a new babe all fresh and titchy and needing her mamma. But at the time all I could think of was you. Oh, I know that sounds bad, but it's true – I couldn't concentrate on my own newborn child. I suspect sometime in the future there'll be years of therapy to be paid for, but there we are.

In those first days after your accident, I could feel you. Did you know that? Well, yes, of course you do. You were still in there: thrumming along those invisible lines which connect us. You and me with our twin superpower – which we have even though we're not identical twins. For how could we be, you being a boy and me a girl, but people do ask, sometimes, don't they? Are you identical twins? they say. Duh. No, we're not. Yet – we still feel each other, in that telepathic way that twins are meant to.

Because we'd lain side by side in our mother's womb. Growing together – separate and joined – we'd shift, and spoon, and push and pull in an embrace which grew ever stronger until one day we were expelled with a whoosh, out into the world…

It's still difficult to concentrate on day-to-day stuff when the pull to be with you is so strong. Feeling that you need me. But as Gerry keeps reminding me (now that I'm better), your place is with Angie and mine is with Finty. He's right, I know he is...

Anyway – where was I? Ah. Those first days afterwards – when I could still feel you... Could you feel me? I was doing my old beaming – you know, like we used to when we were kids? Like if one of us was hurt the other would hold their hand over the place and beam our life force; feeling the warmth of our healing powers. Do you remember? We were sure we could be one of the Tomorrow People – like on the television show – and we could have been, couldn't we? Because we could read each other's thoughts, beam how we felt...

You were so strong that day – three days in, after your accident – when I was trying my utmost to pull you back, trying to hold on to that thrumming thread, trying to transmit my energy into you to make you whole again. But then you experienced that big bleed on the brain, and – snap! – just like that, you were gone.

I haven't felt you properly since. Although there are times – times like a memory in an empty house – and I can't tell if I'm imagining it or if...

Did you know, bruv, that a hummingbird hovers in mid-air by rapidly flapping its wings at around eighty beats per second? And it creates a trail of wave vortices. Imagine that. They can fly backwards too, being the only birds which can. And they live in South American rainforests, don't they, with all those butterfly-effect butterflies.

And so, it got me thinking that if the flap of a butterfly's wing can cause a catastrophic event in another part of the world, think of the damage a hummingbird might wreak. Think about it. Perhaps this was the cause of your accident... No, bear with me... Look, if you go by Newton's second law of physics how for every action

there is an opposite and equal reaction, then surely it
would have had to be something as gloriously beautiful as
a hummingbird to cause something so ugly and hideously
catastrophic as what happened to you. See? The opposite.
So perhaps that's what's to blame. A bloody hummingbird.
  Love for ever,
  Your sis xxxxxx

After The Accident I came very close to a nervous breakdown…
Or maybe I did have one… One expects a full-blown carted away
in a straitjacket by men in white coats type scenario, don't you
think? Or at the very least, a stay in a mental institution. Mine
seemed to involve being unable to get dressed, unable to see the
need to have a shower, unable to laugh, to watch television, read
a book, taste food, and even – at times – to place one foot in
front of the other – even though I had a new baby who needed
me. Back then, it was like she was an inconvenience.

What I most recall of those times is days spent at the
neurological hospital alternating with my own counselling
sessions back in Bristol, where I would sit on the same brown
fabric armchair, saying little or nothing until finally it all came
out. Wave upon wave of crying: so much so that I thought I
might drown or be washed away by my own tears. Plus that
feeling that I could plunge my hand in deep into that hole in the
middle of me and pull it out all covered in blood and gore like
Magua from *The Last of the Mohicans* plucking out the heart of a
British soldier… I can't be worrying Angie or anybody else with
it, and that's why I have to pay for someone to listen, see? I'm
only the sister, after all.

On Carol's advice, I began writing these letters. 'Express
your anger. Vent your spleen. And then, because you won't want
to hang on to all that toxic negativity – you must burn your
letters afterwards. (Safely, of course.) Burn your words and send

any bad vibes out into the universe.' Like I said, she's a bit New Age, is Carol.

Still, it does work – after a fashion. I do feel better, and sometimes I do tear them up and burn them in the open air (on our barbeque, if you want to know). I watch the smoke travel upwards and outwards. That's the bit I especially like. And she's right, I do feel lighter, unburdened, cleansed. Watching those heat waves ripple, beating in the wings of the flames. Perhaps one of these events might cause the hatching of a bird... Perhaps a hummingbird. Perhaps things aren't so random after all.

Well, I was a bit mad at the time. But then so was Angie... Her horror so obvious no-one dare say no to her. Carol says we've made our own monster in Angie. By not refusing her anything...

Before the accident, if I phoned home Dad would answer and say, 'I'll put your mother on.' Now, it's Dad who calls me, never Mum. I miss the chats I had with Mum – yes, she may be a rubbish mother, but she's my rubbish mother. And the only one I've got.

With Dad our conversations go along the lines of:

'How are you and Mum?'

'We're fine, Veronica. You?'

'Yes, thanks.'

'How's The Boy?'

Because that's another change in the family dynamic. Dad now refers to Jake as "The Boy". Which is new; as if somehow The Accident has flung Jake back into childhood.

Not that Mum was rubbish all of the time. Before, she was funny, quick-witted, supportive even. My student friends would thrill at her visits armed with parcels of food, large supplies of G&T and girlie chats.

Memory. It's weird what you remember, and how someone else's memory is totally different, isn't it? Take for instance, this short exchange between me and Angie.

Angie: 'I'm tired of trying to make everything all right for you.'

Me (thinking but not saying): What? That's a bit rich. After all we've done trying to make everything all right for *you.* The weekend visits...

Angie: 'Coming to see us most weekends was draining when we needed to be on our own.'

Me (saying nothing, biting my tongue in case I upset her while thinking how me and Gerry had desperately needed to be on our own to bond with our baby).

Angie: 'Having to pussyfoot around and not upset your feelings, Ron.'

Me (thinking): My feelings?

Angie: 'All you do is say how you're hurt about this, you're sad about that or you're cracking up. I've tried to be supportive. But honestly, Ron, you should try and be me.'

Memory, see? Plays tricks. My reality is mine. Yours is yours. Who's right, who's wrong? What's up, what's down?

Danger, Will Robinson, danger.

My head hurts.

The trouble with therapy is you can end up annoyed with everyone. It's like you take this big stick to the hornet's nest of your family – plunge it in, wiggle it about. No, that's not quite it... Let's see... Carol describes it like approaching a forest. (Bear with me here.) As you approach all you can see is a clump of trees up ahead. Then once you're inside, you lose that focus: it's now a tangle of branches which snag at your hair, roots which trip you, brambles which pull at your clothes; and there are dark places and lurking monsters and wolves with shiny yellow eyes, and brief clearings with fairy rings where you take deep breaths before you plunge back in amongst the trees again – trying, trying to find your way through. But once you've made it to the other side, you look back to where you've been, and you can see that it was only a forest. Do you see? It made sense at the time – perhaps it's the way she tells it.

I daren't be angry with Angela, but I have been angry with Mum. I will go and visit her, on our return from this holiday, I decide. Having my own child I can now imagine the sort of pain she must be in about her child Jake. I'd like to try and make up with her, somehow.

Like I said, we were – still are – a bit mad. As for Angie... I'm about to take you back to a scene in the hospital, then you can judge if this is mad or sane...

It's our second or third visit since the accident. Jake remains in a drug-induced coma to give his brain the best chance to heal. I'm opening the door to the grey relatives' room which has become a hangout for our family, where we wait, moving slowly like matching pale grey wraiths which you half-expect to start wailing... Anyway, Gerry and I have arrived from the local B&B where we're effectively camped out. I'm holding Finty, our three – maybe four-week-old baby in my arms. I've not been sleeping and breastfeeding has not been a bloody joy, but an experience akin to having your nipples slashed with tiny razorblades. Finty was born twenty-one days early and as a consequence, she's a little jaundiced – which apparently is why I'm having such trouble getting her to latch on to my breast. My bosoms are enormous – the size of two rugby balls and as hard and as sore as hell; my nipples are cracked and bleeding. It's murder. Torture. But I'm determined to carry on even though it's exhausting – on top of everything else. I know that mother's milk is best, and so each time I struggle with this most basic mother/baby thing and end up feeling a failure. It hardly fits the picture I had of joyous mum and suckling/content baby.

So, here I am; I don't even have the chance to remove my coat, or put down my bag, when Angie rushes up to me, 'Thank Christ you're here,' she says, snatching Finty from me before I have time to react.

'I've had to leave Lauren behind with my mother,' she informs me as she unfastens her top. 'I'm so full of milk that it's absolute agony and I have to relieve it.'

Then, before my startled eyes, startled everything – so startled that I'm incapable of movement, speech, or thought – she takes Finty to a seat and has my daughter successfully latched on to her breast, guzzling away as if she's a wee starving thing who's finally found her mammy.

My shock doesn't appear to register with anyone else save for a nurse who gently leads me from the room, tears streaming down my face. My overriding emotion is one of failure: that it hasn't been Finty's jaundice after all but my failure as a woman with breasts which are unable to suckle her own child; that my darling baby daughter prefers Angie's breast to mine, and that Angie's so bloody much better at being a mother, being a wife, being anything, than me!

To add insult to injury, my breasts balloon even more as they ache for my child – some hormone alerting them to the fact that some place else, my child is suckling.

I'm sobbing now, head in my arms, as the nurse comforts me. 'There, there,' she says, giving me an awkward hug. I suppose she must have seen it all in this hospital. And although my instincts are telling me – adrenaline pumping through me – that I must go and snatch back my child… how can I? Angie mustn't be upset any further. This is the unspoken law.

I give in to the ministrations of the nurse, who suggests that she fetch me hot towels so I can relieve my breasts and, 'See if we can't express some of this milk. Then you'll feel more comfortable, dear.'

It's arduous: I towel and towel and pull and smooth – all to little avail. I doubt I expressed even a teaspoon's worth that *afternoon. It's painful, I cry, the nurse consoles, my nipples crack and bleed...*

On my return to the relatives' room Finty is delivered back to me, fast asleep, and nothing is said. No apology. No acknowledgement of what had happened. Nothing. Instead, we continue to attend to our own thoughts.

Like I said – mad. All of us unhinged.

And now there she is. My child. Mine, mine, mine, mine, mine. Holding her podgy little baby arms out to me while I reach down to pull her out of the cot, then set about kissing and stroking her (much to her wriggly-piggly annoyance), before placing her on the floor along with her cloth picture book of farmyard animals. Who'd have thought I'd make an okay job of being a mum or that I'd get the hang of breastfeeding in the end? Although my breast didn't stop being sore for months.

Leaning back against the dresser I watch her burbling about – having toddler conversations with her book – and think of how I love the back of her head. Right there where her soft hair meets the top of her spinal column; right where I like to snuggle and inhale her smells. My child. I still find it surprising in a – what, me? I have a child? – sort of way. A beautiful and amazing child. How lucky am I? I let out a contented sigh then return to the business of selecting her clothes: a little top and shorts outfit with a watermelon and grapes pattern. I shake out the shorts, turn the inside-out top the right way round, and am ready for the business of wrestling her into her day clothes.

'C'mon, missy,' I say. 'Time to face another day.'

'Bes,' she says, and I'm rewarded with the sunniest of smiles.

While I struggle her hand through an armhole, I decide *not* to tell Gerry about Xavier. *There's no need, after all*, I reason with myself. Besides, it would spoil our holiday, and in any case, what good would it do? No. I'll save it until we get back home and that way I can discuss with Carol how best to tell Gerry. Yes, that's what I'll do. I'll discuss it with Carol, and for the time being I'll merely act as if nothing has happened with Xavier at all. Xavier who? (That's better.)

TWENTY-TWO

Still Wednesday

'I'm not sitting next to her!' announces Sarah as she points at Finty and leaves the breakfast table to move herself and her plate further along.

'Nuh,' adds Lauren, as she too gets down from her chair and crosses over to sit next to Sarah.

'What's going on, girls?' says Angie.

Sarah throws Finty a fierce glare. '*She* keeps hitting Lauren on the head, Mummy.'

'Gosh, I'm so sorry.' I'm mortified. I mean, no-one likes to hear their child might be a bully. I bend down until I'm level with Finty's face. 'Darling, you mustn't hit Lauren.' But my wayward daughter merely grins and tries to take another swipe at the hapless Lauren, who's thankfully out of range.

Then Angie – with all the skill of a magician – deftly places a spoon in Finty's fist and a bowl of Cheerios in front of her. She sploshes milk into the bowl, whereupon Finty, with attention suitably distracted, sets about her breakfast treat. Ta da! Marvellous Angie strikes again.

'Don't worry about it, I'm sure she'll grow out of this hitting stage.' Angie smiles up at me. 'Some children hit at this age.' She wipes Lauren clean with a wet flannel. 'Not that mine ever did.' Her smile is a tad too saccharine for my liking.

'Right,' I say. My voice – I can hear – has a shade of don't-you-dare-say-that-about-my-child edge to it.

'But then, they're all different, aren't they?' Angie adds.

Talk about smug. I set about whacking the top of my boiled egg, then peel shell back from the cracks and stop as it strikes me: poor Humpty Dumpty with his cracked head. Or Mr Bump. With his bandaged bonce. I'm feeling rather queer, so I get to my feet.

'You all right?' Angie is saying, sounding as if she's underwater.

I vaguely wave her away, overwhelmed by memories oozing out like the yolk from a smashed egg, spilling like the blood on a Cambridgeshire road, seeping and spreading like a big stain: leaking memories of sunny days, the joyful holding of babies, crabbing off Clevedon Pier, running through the meadow at Shirehampton Golf Course, marram grass waving from the top of sand dunes. Twins holding hands. Together forever. Then wobbling, with a smash and a leaking away with a sigh… We were told that two men stopped their car to dash to his aid… Wake up, lad. Can you hear me, son? Ambulance sirens, lights flashing. All the king's horses and all the king's men couldn't put Humpty together again… Christ, he looks a goner. Hello? Don't try to get up. Stay where you are. Hold him down. Don't try to…

But he'll never get up, will he? Never walk home to where everything waits?

'Gerry, what's wrong with…?' I can hear Angie say from very far, far away.

'Oh, shit. Hang on.'

Gerry catches me a nanosecond before I hit the ground – like in some trust exercise. And before it goes all black and whooshy as a raven's wing, there's a stab of guilt that I wasn't – couldn't – be there… to catch Jake.

And now, someone's wiping my face with a wet cloth. 'Gerry?'

'Ssh, it's all right, Ron. You fainted, that's all.'

Later I say, 'You've a lot to put up with, haven't you? I'm sorry I'm such a mess.'

'Ssh,' Gerry answers, stroking my hair and smiling down at me. 'Sssh. You're my mess. We're going to get through this, you'll see.'

Forgetting my earlier resolve, I tell him about Xavier. All in a rush, it all spills out. How I did and then didn't want to have sex with him. How I tried to pull out… but… well… yes, I end up telling him about the whole sorry business.

'Right,' he says, once I'm done. 'Right.' He marches from the room, catching me unawares.

'Gerry?' I run after him.

Into the kitchen he goes – me, hot on his heels. 'Keep an eye on the kids, will you?' he says to Angie.

'Why? Where are you going?'

'Family business. Ron?' he says, his face all steely like Clark Kent before he changes into Superman. 'You wait here.' He strides out of the back door.

I take just a beat, then ask Angie if she can look after Finty. 'Sure.'

'Best go check everything's okay,' I say, indicating after Gerry. 'Why—'

'Sorry. Can't stop.' I scurry after my husband, hoping to catch him before he does anything stupid. Ah. There he is, up ahead, purposefully striding along the pavement. His back ramrod-straight, he does a sharp turn into Madame's shop and I'm not far behind.

Xavier looks up from the counter. Sees Gerry, sees me and takes a step to the side. He holds both hands in front of him, but Gerry takes him by surprise, as he steps forward and… Pow!

Bops him straight on the nose, and Xavier goes down.

'You're lucky I don't call the police,' says Gerry, standing over him. 'What sort of a man are you? Taking advantage of a vulnerable woman like that.'

Xavier, on the floor, wipes away a trickle of blood from the corner of his mouth.

Throwing him a look of utter contempt Gerry turns on his heel, grabbing me by the wrist. 'Come on, you,' he says, as he pulls me out of the shop then frogmarches me back to the villa.

'What the…?' begins Angie, but Gerry pulls me past her and into the hallway, where he stops and stands me in front of him.

'Don't look so scared,' he says. 'I'm not going to do anything to you.'

I go to touch his face, but he brushes me away. 'Look, I don't want you to freak out – but I'm going out for a walk.' He glances towards the front door as if he can't wait to escape. 'I need to clear my head. Is that okay?'

I'm hardly in a position to say no. 'Shall I come with you?' I ask quietly.

'No. You stay here.' He's pacing now, like a racehorse keen for the off. 'I need some thinking time.' He nods as if to himself. 'A walk should do it. Yes, that's it. A short brisk walk.'

He seems to half-relent his decision as he places a tender kiss on my mouth. 'We'll be fine. We will. I know that all of this was not your fault. It's mine. Somehow I've failed you—'

'No.' I reach out towards him. 'No. You haven't.'

But he's gazing off into the middle distance. 'I'll be back soon.'

'Right.'

With that, he's gone, leaving me to stare at the space vacated by his walking out the door.

I'm back at the mirror again. 'Hello, mirror,' I say as I peer at the wild-eyed/wild-haired woman in the bevelled one next to the door. 'What have you done?' I ask her.

It's then that I decide whatever happens with Gerry, I'm glad this Xavier thing is out in the open – unlike my mother's secret, which wreaked so much damage.

I'm determined to mend things if I can, and if not… well then, with or without Gerry I shall carry on for Finty – and more importantly for myself.

Angie pokes her head around the kitchen door. 'Are you sure you're feeling okay?'

'Yes, I am. Look, everything is fine with us and Gerry will be back shortly,' I say, more in hope than anything.

*

Gerry strides along the pavement, so deep in thought, and so cross, that he nearly steps out in front of an old-style Citroen van with corrugated sides. Whoops – luckily it isn't going fast. The van peep-peeps its horn and the driver shoots him the finger. 'Sorry,' Gerry calls out in typical English fashion, then idly watches the van pootle off on its way, a plume of black exhaust fumes belching out the back.

We can't carry on pissing about like this, he thinks, as he strides into the Hotel Bretagne. He knows Ron has been making progress with her therapy, and so he doesn't want this Xavier thing to cause a setback. But he's bloody angry. Not with Ron, but with this Xavier bloke who clearly took advantage of her. The scumbag.

He wasn't proud of losing his temper, but he was glad he lamped him.

Gerry rubs his knuckles, still red from the punch, and then lets out a sigh. He can hardly take the moral high ground, though, can he? Snogging his co-worker – and then there was his ex at that weekend conference. He knows he's to blame every bit as much. That he too has contributed to whatever's wrong with their marriage.

He finds himself a table in the back bar of the hotel and orders a café au lait, thinking how he's going to do his damnedest to get his marriage back on track. *This is it*, he decides. *Ground zero. The two of us have to stop faffing about.*

TWENTY-THREE

Wednesday Still

Thank goodness. Gerry's back, bringing lovely smells of shop-bought pain au chocolats.

'Get that oven on,' he announces in a cheery voice as he draws me to him in an embrace and then empties seven pastries from a brown paper bag. 'These babies need warming up.'

Finty comes haring in from the dining room. 'Daddy!' she calls, launching herself at him.

'Chipmunk!' He blows a raspberry in her neck and sets her back down again.

We okay? I mouth.

Yes, he nods.

'Orange,' says Jake. He still has the remnants of toast around his mouth.

My hand hovers over several things on the table, trying to work out what he's after.

'The hard... it's necessary,' he says, sucking at the dribble from his too-slack jaw. As my hand passes over the butter he becomes more animated. 'There,' he says. 'The... oh...'

'You mean the butter?'

'Yes. Butter.'

I pass it over and with his left hand he dips the knife into the butter, and then – by splaying his fingers – manages to spread it on a piece of toast. His face matches the contortions of his hand, and I don't have enough energy or inclination to remind him to use both hands. In any case, he's been doing well, working at his standing and walking.

He nods in Gerry's direction. 'How long, Terry?' he asks.

'You mean Gerry?'

'Yes.'

'Talking about me behind my back, are you?' says Gerry as he light-footedly moves around the kitchen, filling up the cafetière before carrying it to the table. 'Coffee, everyone?'

'Yeah, great.'

'Bring over the sugar.'

'Milk?'

'Don't you remember, Jake,' I begin, 'how I've known Gerry for two and a half years now?'

Jake looks amazed – his left eyebrow shoots up almost to his hairline whilst the right one refuses to be impressed.

Later, Jake and I sit side by side in the backyard. The rain has stopped, and the clouds have picked up their grey skirts to make a run for it before the sun burns them away.

I begin to sing George Harrison's "Here Comes the Sun" and he comes in at the chorus exactly in the right place. Not for the first time I marvel at how he has perfect recall for the lyrics of old records. Whereas conversation – everyday words? They flitter/flutter away.

'Good old Beatles,' I say. 'Remember when we used to sit in the back of our car and sing Beatles tunes?'

'*There*,' sings Jake, hitting the first note of "Here, There, And Everywhere". His voice is as rich and beautiful as it ever was.

We start to sing but can't remember all lyrics properly adding in silly ones like falling off the back of her chair, having no money to spare until we have to stop as we're laughing too much… 'Remember how Dad would say The Beatles were rubbish and he'd try and drown them out with Bing Crosby songs?'

Up above, the sun peeps between two white clouds as the crunching of gravel announces the arrival of Angie. 'Doing our Remember Whens, are we?' she says.

I squint my eyes against the sunlight. 'Just trying to remember songs from when we were kids.'

'Back in Bristol.' I can hear the exasperated sigh in her voice.

'Uh? Can't fix the necessary.' Jake sounds worried.

Angie crouches down next to him. 'You okay?' she asks, and he nods his head.

'We've had a good laugh, though, haven't we?' I say; he looks at me in that trying-to-figure-things-out way of his. 'Trying to remember those songs…'

Sarah comes dashing out of the house, then does a skidding halt in front of us. 'Mum!' she pants, holding her side as if getting a stitch. 'Finty has tooken Lauren's crayons and she's hitting her with them.'

'I'm so sorry,' I say, going to rise out of my chair.

Angie waves for me to sit back down. 'No worries. I'll sort it. You two stay here.' She already has hold of Sarah, the two of them heading back indoors. *Where's Gerry?* I wonder. Jake is on his feet – sort of hovering to one side – as if he's an alien who hasn't got his impersonation of a human being quite right. I have that odd feeling that the real Jake has been carted off by the fairies, or by evil imps, and replaced with a substitute. A changeling. And the real Jake is trapped somewhere, unable to yet trying to get back. Daft, I know.

'Are you sure this is such a good idea?' I hiss as Gerry and I take our seats on Angie's sofa, right in front of the television.

'It helps,' Angie calls from the kitchen, clearly having heard me. Oops. I grimace at Gerry.

Sarah and Lauren are upstairs in bed, and us grownups are trying to relax after a day of visiting Jake in hospital. Quite frankly, I'm dreading this – but Angie has insisted.

Finty lies asleep next to us, in her Moses basket, content and quiet after her last feed. Thank heavens.

Angie returns with three cold beers. 'Here, catch.' She throws one to each of us then settles into one of the squashy armchairs. 'He seemed better today, don't you think?' she asks, slipping a video into the waiting mouth of the VCR, which sucks it in with a whirring slurp.

'Um. Yeah.'

She hits the rewind button and the machine witters for a while, then clicks. Next to Angie, Jake's chair is empty, staring vacantly at the screen.

'I need to watch one of our home videos from time to time,' she says. 'It reminds me of who he is, and what we have to aim for.'

'Hm,' I say, not sure if I'm up to this, or if it's a good idea full stop. Gerry gives my hand a comforting squeeze.

'You see,' continues Angie, 'I don't think I could go on if I didn't think he was in there, somewhere.'

Somewhere else Jake lies beached on his hospital bed, waiting to be turned two-hourly by nurses. Unable to talk. Unable to walk or go to the toilet. His thoughts – jumbled and incoherent – dart about, flashing images he is unable to catch or interpret. And horrifyingly shrunken and pale, his body loiters below a swollen and broken head which sits – one eye now higher than the other – squinting at a cock-eyed world.

In front of us in their cottage, the picture on the television screen scans a room. It's a recording of the very same room we're sitting in. And it's like we're peering through a looking glass into some parallel yet identical universe. This other same room is littered with toys, and there – in the corner – plays a younger Sarah. She turns to smile up at the camera. Prickles run into my hairline as Jake speaks. (Although we can't see him because he's operating the camera.)

'Today's date is Sunday the twentieth of November nineteen eighty-eight,' he says. 'And here's the beautiful Sarah. Wave to the camera, Sarah.' She waves, then returns to her cutting and pasting artwork. The camera zooms in to wobble a bit on the picture she is creating.

'That is lovely.' Then, in an aside, Jake's disembodied voice adds, 'Only four years old and already she's the artistic genius of our family. Takes after her dad, of course.'

'Stop it, Daddy,' she half-protests, half-giggles to the camera.

The picture pans out to the living-room door and on into the dining room, where Mike, who long ago abandoned his biker gear for sensible jackets, is reading The Guardian's education pages.

'Here's Mike. Busily helping out, as you can see,' runs the commentary. Mike flaps his paper in a go-away gesture. 'He only comes here for a rest,' continues Jake. 'Teaching tires him out – poor thing.'

'Piss off,' mouths Mike. Good-naturedly. The camera scans the room, circling to the left and then to the right.

'Now where's my gorgeous Angela?' The camera moves about the room, searching. 'Angie? Where are you?' comes his call. And now we can see Angie through the open kitchen door where, clearly pregnant, she is busy at the cooker.

It's then that the Angie on our side of the screen mutters, 'Over here, Jake. Look! I'm over here!'

Gerry and I say nothing as Angie sits dead still, her whole being fixed straight ahead at the screen as if she can transport herself by power of thought into the other side: through the looking glass and into the past.

The picture steadies. Jake must have placed the camera on

its tripod because there he is, standing in front of us, waving idiotically at the camera and into our room.

'I'm off to fetch my lovely Angie,' he confides. Then moving his face close up to our screen, adds, 'If the mountain won't come to Mohammed...' And through the screen we watch him effortlessly, energetically move to embrace Angie in an exaggerated hug. He places his cheekily grinning face alongside hers so they both are beaming into the camera as he pats her tummy.

The Angie on our side absent-mindedly strokes hers.

'I hope it's another girl,' he's saying to on-screen Angie. 'Just like you.'

I'm struck by how vibrant and active he is. Positively radiating health and happiness. If there was any sound to be heard on our side of the looking glass it might well have been the crack of my heart breaking.

Then the picture tilts alarmingly to the left and there's a loud crash. Jake's legs run towards the screen at an angle, until all we can see are his feet in his brown Doc Marten shoes. Then before the picture flickers, we hear him mutter, 'Bugger it,' and the window closes.

On this side we're all staring at the screen. I feel so weird; it's not even registering in my brain. What is registering is Angie's sobbing.

'Come back,' she's crying, as she slumps forwards in her chair, defeated by the television's blank response. 'Fucking come out from behind that camera, damn you! Damn you!' But her shrieks merely echo in an empty black hole.

I go for a nap, but I can't sleep. Outside and downstairs I can hear the muted noises of the others. Inside my head are chattering voices:

'She's got a lot on her plate, you know.'

Yes, I do know. Who hasn't?

'She's terribly brave. Amazing, really,' says another.

I know. I know.

'*Such a handsome boy...*'

That you, Mum? My head starts to buzz.

'*...Had everything going for him.*'

'*Got two children, hasn't he? Such a shame...*'

Who's this now? Anyone? No-one? I turn over, trying to get more comfortable. But these voices are unrelenting.

'*Lad's trying hard, isn't he? If he tries harder, no doubt he'll get better. I know he will.*'

If only it worked like that, Dad. It is you, Dad, isn't it?

'*Aye. He's come a long way.*'

Dad, I'm so alone. Tell me everything will be all right, Dad.

'*Hm? Now, where's Angie? I must go find Angie. I expect she'll be needing me to do something.*'

Dad, don't leave... Don't go...

'*Must be a comfort to your parents. Your being in the medical profession, so to speak. Expect they rely on you...*'

No. They don't. They don't listen to me. Don't take me seriously...

'*Must be hard for his wife. Don't suppose he'll ever be the same again.*'

I sit up, reaching for the glass I brought upstairs with me, and take a large gulp of wine, not much caring that it's gone off. If anything, its rancid tang is fitting, as if that's all I deserve.

'*Still, at least you've got Gerry.*'

Gerry? Oh, you really don't understand. I shake my head then rest it in my hands.

'*...he must be a comfort to you. Poor Angie.*'

I lift my head. I miss Jake too, you know.

'*Of course you do, but you are only his sister.*'

'*Imagine what Angie is going through.*'

I can. I do. But what about me? Don't my feelings count? Gerry comes into the bedroom and softly closes the door.

'I can't bear it,' I say, before he has the chance to open his mouth. 'How I've lost all our Remember Whens. Mine and Jake's, you see. And,' I continue, with a catch in my throat, 'I don't know who I am anymore.'

Gerry's been leaning against the door, regarding me thoughtfully. He moves towards me. 'We'll have to make our own Remember Whens, won't we?' he says.

I turn my head, not wanting him to see that they won't be the same.

It's later and I've returned downstairs, where Angie has returned from a walk in the fresh air. It's plain to see that she's been crying, and crying so hard that her nose is red and the skin around her eyes is puffy. Plonking herself at the kitchen table, she lights up a cigarette.

'Have a good walk?' I ask.

She shrugs and then shakes her head. 'It's the arguing I miss,' she says. 'No matter what I say, he simply takes it. It doesn't matter how horrible I am, or how cross or unreasonable – he takes it, like some whipped dog.' She reaches for my new glass of wine to down it in one. 'I can't stand it, you see,' she continues, while I fetch another glass to pour us both fresh wine. 'It drives me mental, it really does. If only he'd tell me to piss off. Get angry – something! I can't help trying to provoke and get a reaction from him, and I hate myself for it.'

'Angie... I...'

'There's not much else to say.' She flicks cigarette ash into a saucer with a little tea left in the bottom, and the ash spreads like a Rorschach ink blot.

First she fixes me with a piercing stare, and then she looks away. 'It's all right for you,' she says. 'Because you've got Gerry.' The pattern spreads slowly, as if tentatively seeking out how far it can go. 'Who have I got? Jake's so bloody quiet these days.' She draws on her cigarette. 'Before the accident he couldn't sit still for more than two minutes without saying something, doing something. You know that. But now? Now he can sit for hours and hours without saying a bloody word.'

'Give him time, it's still early days.'

She gives me a sardonic grimace. 'But how much time? When does it stop being early days?'

It's then that Gerry breezes in. 'Okay, you mums? The kids are all washed and ready for their bedtime kisses. What?' His look darts back and forth between me and Angie like an actor who's come on stage before his cue.

'I'd better go and see to my lot,' says Angie as she gets to her feet then grinds her cigarette into the saucer.

'Did I interrupt anything?' asks Gerry as she squeezes past him. 'You two weren't talking about me, were you?' I know he's trying to lighten the room, but Angie's had a sense of humour by-pass.

'As if!' she retorts. 'Not everything's about you!' And she leaves the room.

'That told me,' he says as he fetches himself a glass. 'Why don't we take this wine outside? It's a lovely evening sky, and besides, you could cut the atmosphere in this kitchen with a knife!'

Together we saunter into the backyard, where we gaze up at a moon which stares blankly back. I'm feeling dog-tired so lean my head against Gerry.

'Pwah,' he says, flapping the air in front of his nose. 'How many cigarettes have you smoked tonight?'

'I don't know – does it matter? Four? Maybe five?'

'You're becoming a right fag ash Lil.' His face comes into sharp focus under the outside lamp, his expression questioning.

Changing tack, I ask, 'Did Finty get off all right?'

'Yeah. She's fast asleep in Lauren's bed.'

'Come on then, four-eyes,' I say, as I lead him inside, past the kitchen debris and up to our shared and squeaky bed, where I surprise him by making love to him.

*

Dear Jake,

Did I ever tell you how difficult it is to laugh, to sing, to read a book, watch the telly, to just be happy, when it feels like a betrayal? Like, if you can't do this, be this, then I don't deserve to either.

Gerry says I'm wallowing in my misery and that's not what you'd want. For all I know you could be happy inside that lame brain of yours.

One of the doctors said you have problems with abstracts – I want to say you were always more a concrete type of person in any case. But I know what he means.

You used to definitely know what you liked: sunsets, singing songs with your guitar, first Star Treks with James T. Kirk, Monty Python sketches – fetch the comfy chair! – the laughter of your children, a piece of furniture well made, a class well taught – the rush of air past your face as you roar off on your fuckin' motorbike…

If anything you've been the simple to my complex, because if I ever over-thought stuff I'd give you a ring, and you'd tell me to stop being a wally. So what do I do now? It's like I've lost the other side of those scales which kept me balanced.

And so, twin brother of mine. Tell me. Is it wrong to laugh, when I can't remember the last time I saw you have a proper laugh; or to enjoy sex when Angie says she can't bear you to touch her – ever again – because you're like a stranger?

God help me but sometimes I feel like you're a stranger to me too. Like some rubbish doppelganger. And that's not a sisterly thing to think, is it? What would you do if it was the other way around? That's what I keep thinking: What would Jake do? And then I know. He'd be exactly the same as me and have no bloody idea. Ha.

I know it's not your fault, and I know you're trying your best and that somewhere, somehow you are trying to come back. But how long must I wait in limbo? We made walkie talkies once from tin cans and a long piece of string. Do you remember? Hello, is anybody there? Hello? Testing. One, two, three, testing.

That's all. Big sis, over and out.

TWENTY-FOUR

Thursday

It's morning, and it's the day I've agreed to take Jake through his exercises in the villa's dining room. Concentration hangs in the air like a whiskey fug around a drunkard attempting a straight line. We're doing Jake's walking practice.

'That's good,' I'm saying. 'Now, drop your right arm. Turn. No, to the right...'

Jake carefully corrects and turns, his right leg performing exaggerated knee bends with each step. There's no doubt he's much improved. Angie and Jake have done a good job with their exercises, I have to admit.

With my professional head on, I instruct Jake to walk across the sitting room towards me. He smiles and for the first time I can see that his dimple – the one which always indented his right cheek – has returned. I rush over – stopping him in mid-walk – to give him a kiss on the cheek, whereupon he raises one eyebrow.

'It's no good doing your Roger Moore impersonation at me,' I tease, then step back to admire him. 'You're almost looking human,' I say with a wink.

Because it really is a good sign as it means that the right-hand side of his face – smoothly undimpled since his accident

– now has dimples when he smiles. And this means the part of his brain which pulls that corner of his mouth is back in action. To see any sign of improvement is what I need.

'Right, now walk towards me.' I'm alongside a full-length mirror so he can watch his whole self as he advances. 'Keep going. Good, that's right,' I encourage until he's in front of the mirror, admiring his reflection as he flicks back his hair – much like he used to. His old friends from college joked he could never pass a shop window or a mirror without checking himself out.

'You vain sod. There's no time for admiring yourself. C'mon, chop chop, and let's try again.' Slowly he turns, but he's pivoting on his good leg, which he's not meant to do. 'Stop, stop. Now step round with that leg – yes, that's better. Now. Walk towards the opposite wall. No. The other leg. Better…'

I watch the back of his head as he retreats: his hair's sort of perching on top, a bit like it's been dropped there by a passing pterodactyl. Poor Jake. His hair forever the bane of his life, would stick up in cow licks, refusing to be flattened with water or hair gel. Weirdly it's now thicker and more greasy and sort of – yup – sort of perched. Perhaps it's because all the increased activity in his brain and the bringing of extra blood to the area, has made his hair thicker? Who knows? I'll file it under another of my theories.

We used to share our half-baked theories with each other.

'Wassup?' he says.

'Nothing.' I can't tell him how I'm imagining his white blood cells busying about in his head, munching away, like one of those *Pac-Man* arcade games. Annihilating the bad guys of scar tissue and inflammation before they do any more damage. Munch munch munch. Beep!

No, I can't tell him, what would be the point?

Jake moans and sways. 'Feel unnecessary,' he says, as I hurry to catch him and sit him gently on the jazzy sofa.

'Feeling dizzy?'

He nods.

'Okay, that's enough for today. I think you've done really well, but we'll stop now.' I plonk myself alongside him and pat his shoulder. 'Jake, though, listen.' He turns his head slowly to face me. 'Feeling dizzy is good – because...' (and here he's frowning at me) 'after a head injury your movements are abnormal, but your brain' (I point to his head) 'your stupid lame brain, tells you that abnormal is normal. See? So when you start to relearn how to do things properly – then your brain tells you you're doing it all wrong. And that's what's making you dizzy. Do you follow?' His face is blank, and he shakes his head. 'Kind of like you're seasick or something, yeah? Or like you're about to fall over?'

Jake rubs the scar on the side of his forehead. 'Yes, that's necessary.'

'Although it is important that you—'

But we're interrupted as Angie sticks her head around the door. 'Everything all right?' she says.

'Yes, fine, except Jake's feeling a bit groggy now,' I say.

'Honestly, Veronica,' says Angie as she bustles in and kneels on the floor next to Jake. 'Do you have to work him so hard?' She strokes the hair back from his eyes. 'It'll knock him out for the rest of the day.'

'S'all right,' says Jake.

I mumble sorry, and head for the door.

'Oh, and by the way,' Angie intercepts. 'I've put our extra money in the kitty. So you don't have to worry about that anymore, do you?'

Sometimes she sounds as if she hates me.

'All done and dusted?' says Gerry as I join him where he's leaning against the garage wall, watching the girls play in the yard. 'Exercising go okay?'

'Great, yes. All fine and hunky dory,' I say, sounding as if it's not. 'Except for Angie coming along and giving me a telling-off.' He comes in for a hug, but I push him away. 'Don't, I'm fine, honestly. Pretty much par for the course.'

'Right,' he says, as if he's made a decision, then claps his hands at the girls in Butlins' Redcoat fashion. 'Kids! Listen up! I've thought of a fantastic game.' They're all agog. 'Why don't we go and count stones!'

'Yay!' they chorus.

I watch, flabbergasted, as he guides them to their own little places on the gravelled yard.

'You stand here. Lauren over there. Finty?' His enthusiasm eggs them on, until they're merrily counting away, and he's able to sneak back to my side.

'Good idea, yeah?' he says. 'I have my uses.'

'That's mean, though.' But already I'm half-laughing.

Sarah is up to one hundred and something, and Lauren is pottering around the back step half-heartedly picking up stones and throwing them down again. Whereas Finty has wandered off to give the trees a good going-over. Sniffily they endure the wind's ruffling and the little person's prying.

Sarah rushes over to show me an interesting stone shot with orange stripes. I admire its tiger-ness before she runs back to her counting.

'Should keep them busy for a while,' says Gerry as he hooks his finger into the belt hook on my shorts and pulls me in for an affectionate hug. But then we turn, as one, to hear Angie shouting – loud and clear – her voice carrying to us from the open kitchen window.

'...don't you be getting angry with me unless there's something to be angry about...' She says something else which I don't catch. Her voice gets louder again: 'Is that it, then? Aren't you talking to me?'

'No!' Jake's loud response makes me jump. Good God, he's talking back. He's actually talking back. I look around, checking the kids haven't overheard. Either they haven't or they're doing a good job of pretending.

'Is it because...' Angie is saying.

Turning to the children I say, 'Right, you lot. Listen up. It's time to go and look at the tree out front, I've heard a giant lives there.' As I usher them off, Sarah slips her hot little hand into mine.

Well, didn't Angie say she wanted Jake to argue with her? Looks like she's got what she wished for.

Gerry has popped to the shop for a newspaper, and on his return, he's full of the news that there's going to be a motocross event further along the beach where the sand dunes are at their tallest. As we all know, Jake still loves motorbikes, and so we discuss whether or not to tell them because Angie now loathes them – and who can blame her?

'Don't you see, Ron? This could be the tangible thing you've been looking for? That thing to remind him of who he is? Is this a great idea or what?'

But I'm thinking of how six months after his accident police and fire engines were called to Jake's house in Cambridgeshire. Because it turned out that Angie had taken Jake's spare motorcycle – plus the small Japanese one she used on occasion – dragged them both onto their lawn, had next flung one on top of the other in some crazy sort of union and then proceeded to pour petrol over them like some mad thing, setting the bikes alight. They'd burned so fiercely (their handlebars locked in a grisly embrace) that their old cherry tree with the garden swing on it also caught fire. The tree had burned surprisingly quickly and before anyone knew it, Angie was sobbing, a neighbour holding her back as if she might well throw herself on the motorcycle funeral pyre like a Hindu widow, when blue lights and sirens announced the arrival of the emergency services, and then it was all over. Their next-door neighbour was the one who couldn't wait to tell me all about it.

At the time it had put me in mind of how Jake would say he wanted a Viking funeral – come the time – complete with a long ship set on fire and pushed out into the waters on its final voyage to Valhalla.

When we first tell Angie and Jake about the motocross, there are flickers of excitement on Jake's part and a frown from Angie. Gerry, though, is thrilled he's discovered it – you'd think he'd discovered penicillin. I personally think watching idiots race bikes in the dunes and probably fall off, is right up Jake's street.

'Isn't this the sort of thing Jake would have done before?' asks Gerry.

'I suppose,' Angie says rather grudgingly and with her arms well and truly crossed.

'See, this could help connect Jake with his old self. What do you think? Ron and I thought we'd look out for something he can do which could remind him of old times. Didn't we?'

'Yes. Although I had put it on the back burner... well done, love,' I say to my husband.

In the end when Gerry and Jake (plus a reluctant me – I'm not keen out outdoor sports) are about to leave for the event, Angie says she can't face it. 'I'll stay behind and keep an eye on the children.'

'If you're sure that's want you want?' says Gerry, then slaps Jake on the back and nearly sends him flying, but Jake merely beams a lopsided grin at him. 'Looks like it's just you and me off out on a boys' trip. Unless you wanted to come along, Ron? You'd be very welcome.' I can tell he doesn't really want me there – he knows I'd moan about being cold or bored.

'No, you two go ahead and do your male bonding thing. I'm happy to stay behind with Angie and the kids.'

'You up for it, Jake? Just the two of us out for the day, without the women? We can get a few beers in while we're there, eh? Watch the local bikers scrambling on the dunes?'

'Can we?' he says.

'You betcha!'

'Bumble snap!' announces Jake, smiling from one crooked ear to the other.

Angie looks pained. Pained that despite what a motorcycle did to him, he still likes them and still wants to see them race.

The thing is, though, Angie (I long to tell her), he doesn't – and most likely never will – remember his accident at all.

Dear Jake,

Did you know that the brain tries to repair itself? It has these brain cells which have branches called dendrites, after the Greek name for "tree". I saw a drawing of a neurone once and at one end it had root-like branches, and at the top (where there's a sort of blob) the branches are more like tendrils, or the over-reaching branches of – yes, you've guessed it – a tree. And in the middle of this blob is a single nucleus, giving it the look of a saucer-eyed alien or giant squid. How weird is that? And these cells, with their tentacle-like dendrites, spread their branches out into an arbour – an arborisation, it's called – forming clumps, tangles and clusters resembling the overhead panoply of a rain forest.

And when there's been damage to the brain, to these structures, these other cells called glial cells, come rushing in – like all the king's frickin' horses in ambulances – trying to repair and clean up the scene of the accident. But if there's too many of them, they get in the way and make matters worse, combining with the dead and dying neurons until, in the end, they go all clumpy and form plaques and blocks. Or that's how I understand it – mind you, it's been a while since I studied neurology.

Once I saw a short film of brain cells firing across their synapses in a filigree of dendrites, and it was quite beautiful. Like something in outer – instead of inner – space. These electrical impulses sparking across synaptic gaps like electricity arcing in those Victorian revivification experiments. Maybe they were onto something after all, those Victorians. The spark for the story of poor stumbling and brain-injured Frankenstein's monster. See? My own dendrites are making their own connections.

It must be tiring work – all the growing and arboring (is that even a word?), all the sweeping and clearing, repairing of damage, and constructing of detours.

Consider – while bits of you will have died, other bits of you are brand new. In that Zen equation, does this make you less or more than the sum total of your parts? Or is it now a different equation altogether? If enough of you changes will you eventually evolve into a wholly different person?

Confused? Me too.

Your sis xxx

P.S. You are the one person I can talk to about this sort of thing. Which is why it's oh so fucking annoying that I can't!

TWENTY-FIVE

Motocross

Standing braced against the wind are two men. One turns to the other and slaps him on the back as first one motocross bike – then another and another – roars up a sand bank, wheels leaving the ground as each takes to the air – and for those few seconds their wheels stop turning and they are suspended like birds hovering in flight. For one of the men standing, watching, this spectacle brings back memories of that exhilaration of speed and that sensation of flying, and for a brief moment a broad grin spreads across his face.

Sand dunes which undulate and shift slowly in their constant flux are today being churned up and assaulted by motorbikes speeding through the highs and lows of the race, but tomorrow tides and winds will take over, doing their thing of smoothing and sculpting the sandscape: swallowing cigarette butts and oil spills, obliterating footfalls and bike ruts, and the shapes made by illicit lovers.

Although they appear as if they'd be soft to the touch, the dunes' undulations belie their coarse graininess and the sharp jags of their tall grasses. Seductive, they can entice in the secretive and the clandestine, only to lure to their deaths children who tunnel into their all-too-collapsible sides – for a dune opening and closing its maw can swallow any child whole.

Perhaps the two spectators of this day's motorcycle sport would be too busy, too distracted, to hear that there are five to ten times more stars in the known universe than there are grains of sand on all the world's beaches, and how a single grain of sand has more atoms than the number of those stars. As the men stand and watch the races, gritty stardust scratches the back of their throats.

'Fancy a pint?' says one, who has noticed the other is shivering, clearly freezing in the off-shore wind in only his T-shirt and shorts.

'Ss good,' says the one with the broken head who executes a wobbly thumbs-up.

I'm enjoying the last of the evening's sun, pulling a cardigan around my shoulders as it's turned chilly, when a car pulls into our driveway and looking up, I can see it's Xavier who is driving. *Oh, fuckety fuck*, is my first thought, swiftly followed by: *What's he doing with Jake and – with Gerry – in the back?*

Xavier clambers out of his battered old white Renault, his hair all tousled as he dips his head and shakes it in the sunlight. He sure is rocking those tight black leather trousers, there (with a bulge – I can't believe I looked at his bulge!). His biker jacket is undone just enough to show a white and red T-shirt with black curly chest hair poking above... (I have a tactile memory of running my fingers through... oh God.) And, seriously, why are both Gerry and Jake in the car, now getting out of the car. Why? After Gerry punched him in the shop?

Hang on...

As Gerry dashes around from his side of the car, I can tell he needs to give Jake extra help to get out. What is wrong with Jake?

Xavier holds the door open in his louche sex-god kind of way, while Lauren and Finty stand together holding hands and watching. Sarah dodges around me to see what's occurring, as Angie thrusts herself forwards to assume charge.

'What's the matter with Jake's chin?' she demands.

I give Xavier a quick look, and then pull my husband to one side. 'What are you doing with *him*?' I hiss.

'I could hardly say no to a lift, could I? Not with Jake like this.'

'Like what?'

Gerry moves to help Jake stand upright against the car. 'You all right here a minute, mate?' He's clearly pissed.

Angie examines Jake's chin and says to Sarah, 'Run in and get the arnica, darling. Daddy's hurt himself,' and Sarah scoots off.

'There's no need to worry,' says Gerry. 'I'll take him from here.' Reluctantly Angie stands back as Gerry grabs hold of Jake's elbow and begins to steer him towards the back door.

Angie dodges in front of them, causing their progress to halt. 'What the hell happened?' she says while Sarah arrives and passes over a small bottle, from which Angie dispenses a pill and swiftly pops it into Jake's mouth. 'Why is he in such a state when you were meant to be looking after him?'

'I'm sorry, but Jake got cold, didn't you, mate? So I took him off for a couple of beers, and a brandy to warm him up, and...' Jake sways so he has to hold him up again. 'Look, can we have the post-mortem later, only we need to get him inside.'

They all make it into the kitchen, Xavier following us in too, when Gerry continues with, 'It really is no big deal – Jake didn't even have that much to drink. Not really. But then, when we were walking back to the villa Jake must have stumbled or something – didn't you, mate?'

'Yes,' Jake says, nodding his head.

'Next thing,' says Gerry, 'he's taken a tumble, and is on the pavement bleeding from his chin. But you can see how it's only a graze.'

Jake gives what may be an apologetic grin, but Angie's having none of it, as she stands, looking daggers.

'Luckily,' Gerry continues, his jaw set as he waves in Xavier's direction, 'yer man over there stopped to offer us a lift.' He glances at me. 'As there were no taxis or any other alternative, so we were lucky that he happened to come along. For which we're most grateful.'

Xavier inclines his head. 'It is a bad pavement. Full of the holes and the bumps.' He approaches Angie and looks like he may clasp her in a gallant Gallic way but, perhaps thinking better of it, lets his arms drop by their side. '*Vraiment*, it is not a catastrophe,' he says, as he squints his blue eyes against the sun angling through the kitchen window. 'He go – how you say – arse over tit, *non*? Perhaps one too many beers, I am thinking?'

Angie looks fit to burst – but she's too polite and settles for giving him a strained smile as she pulls Sarah close to her side.

'Honestly, Ange. Two drinks – plus a very small brandy. I swear that's all we had,' says Gerry.

'*Ah bien tot*,' says Xavier, as he gives a little kind of salute in my direction. 'Enjoy the rest of your stay.'

Un-buh-lievable, I think as Xavier turns his blazing smile to me, and Gerry gives him a warning look, to which Xavier merely shrugs.

'Goodbye, Xavier,' Gerry says, pointedly.

Me? I'm hoping Angie hasn't picked up on anything.

As Xavier passes Finty and Lauren, he touches each of their little heads as if bestowing a blessing on them, and then he's outside, and clambering into his car, and with much scattering of gravel, he reverses back down the drive.

Gerry has Jake by the elbow as he mutters, 'Tosser,' in the general direction of Xavier's departure.

'Yes. Tosser,' says Jake.

'How could you!' Angie starts in on Gerry. 'Don't you realise that he can't regulate his temperature? He gets cold, and too much alcohol interferes with his medicine and with his homeopathy.' She tries to get a few drops of Rescue Remedy under Jake's tongue, but he's having none of it.

'Her...' he starts, then stops and gives an unfocused grin. 'Oh fuck,' he says, then heads for the downstairs loo.

'That's the last time I let him go anywhere with you!' says Angie

'Chill out. No real harm done.'

'No real harm? You stupid, selfish bastard—'

But this time I've had enough. 'Leave it!' I say, louder than I meant. Everybody freezes like a pistol shot has rung out. 'Don't you dare speak to Gerry like that! He was only trying to do a nice thing. Giving you a rest and Jake the opportunity to feel like a regular bloke again. So what if Jake got pissed. At least that's normal!'

Angie stares at me as if I've slapped her. Of course, then she dashes from the room in tears while Sarah throws me a look which confirms what she thinks of me – a Big Mean Meanie. I make a move to go after Angie, but Gerry puts a staying hand on me.

'Best let her go. She'll calm down.' He still has hold of my arm when he says, 'You're kinda sexy when you're sticking up for me.'

'What about our plan? Getting him to do something tangible? Did it help at all?'

'I'm not sure. We were certainly enjoying ourselves as if we were just two blokes out on a jolly. At times I even forgot he had a head injury, but then when he fell over... I don't know if it did help.'

'It must have.'

TWENTY-SIX

Thursday Evening

After the earlier dramas of the day, it's nice to be away from the villa for our night out. Angie and I have made up – more like an uneasy truce – and it's mine and Gerry's turn, so we're off to this village party on the quay, and when we find the venue we discover we're amongst the first to arrive. It's early evening and a pinkish light tinges the sky and dances along the top of the sea, where it kisses the horizon. That's a good sign, isn't it? Red sky at night, shepherd's delight.

The domed ceiling of an evening sky lends cathedral-like acoustics as villagers and band members arrive to take their places for the evening's entertainment. Overhead, the light fades as if someone has turned down a dimmer switch. It promises to be a clear and starry night, as befits the end of a holiday. I give a heartfelt sigh, thinking how, for whole moments of time, I have managed to forget…

Gerry slips his arm into mine. 'Looks like this is the place,' he says as we peer into a barn-like boatshed which is already alive with people ready for their evening of festivities. It's easy to imagine how during the day this place would be busy with whistling boatmen building or carrying out repairs, scraping the bottoms or painting the hulls of boats named after girls. Tonight, it's transformed with storm lanterns and fairy lights: the inside of the building lined with long trestle tables with a space left in the middle for dancing, I'm guessing.

Excitement tingles the air; I can feel its electricity.

'C'mon,' he says, as he leads me inside.

Clearly, it's a local event. (Definitely not organised by our tour operator.) It's so French. If this was me before the accident I'd probably squeal and turn to Jake...

'You okay?' says Gerry, peering at me in that concerned way he's adopted of late. But I'm after none of that tonight, because tonight is when I let my hair down and forget all about our woes and instead have fun.

'Yes, I'm fine.' I plant a swift kiss on his cheek. 'Right, let's go get some of that lovely rustic grub, then?'

At a large oak table generous cooking pots are lined up, holding locally sourced and freshly cooked seafood dished up with large steel ladles: a bowl of lobster bisque, a plate of langoustines, hunks of warm and crusty French bread served on a tray. My mouth waters in anticipation as I receive my own tray of food, and we choose a table angled to face both the inside of the boatshed and the quayside. Around us, our fellow diners are clearly relishing the food and company, and I can't help noticing how alike their faces are. Gerry gives me a nudge.

'Notice how they all look very similar...?'

'Ssh. Yes.'

'Reminds me of the Forest,' he whispers.

And Gerry should know. We both know about the Forest of Dean, in Gloucestershire. I'm West Country, and although Gerry's father is Irish, his mother's folk hail from the Forest. Proper Dennis Potter country, it is. And full of tales.

If you go down to the woods today,
You're sure of a big surprise,

If you go down to the woods today,
You'd better go in disguise.

Mother is telling us a bedtime story. 'Once, about a hundred or so years ago, a travelling band of four Frenchmen visited the Forest, with their two Russian dancing bears. Those were the days when men in the Forest worked down the mines, their faces black with coal dust. Sometimes on a dark night you could only see the flash of their eyes or teeth as they walked home to Mitcheldean, Littledean or Ruardean.

'There wasn't much to do in those days. No television like we have now.'

Jake and I snuggle down in bed as we watch every nook and cranny of Mum's face, not wanting to squander a single precious moment of her story-telling. Our eyes widen in the gathering dark and before the expanding landscape of our imaginings, as the edges of the room recede and the light from my bedside lamp fans upwards and outwards like trees in a forest opening to the sky. And I can hear blackbirds singing in those trees, and leaves crunching underfoot, as we follow the story deep into the Forest.

'Now, the people in those parts hadn't seen dancing bears for a long while. Some hadn't seen them ever before. They came out of their cottages to stand and stare at the men and their bears. A big mummy bear and a little baby bear.

'It was a sunny spring day where pink foxgloves clanged their silent bells as the people and children of the Forest followed in pied-piper fashion through brightly greening woods to the clearings and villages where the bears, chained and muzzled, would do their act.

'When the bears stood up tall, there were "Ooohs" and "Aahs", and even some screams from faint-hearted women and little 'uns scared of their big furry power and huge swiping paws. But the bears were gentle, and at night, they would lie with their masters, keeping them warm and giving them licks – which are bear kisses –

on their noses. Anyway, just in case, the bears' teeth had been filed down so they weren't sharp, and their nails cut so they couldn't claw. They relied on the goodwill of their keepers for food, who in turn made sure the bears ate first, and who loved them as if they were their own children.'

Mum takes an ice-clunking swig from her tall glass of orange-and-something, as Jake and I draw closer to each other.

'The Frenchies played on their pipes and accordion and danced and performed tricks with their bears. It was nearing the end of the day when the troupe first came across the coal miners, who, having finished their shift, had come to see what all the fuss was about. The miners gave those Frenchies quite a fright, I can tell you, jumping out in front of them, their faces covered with coal dust like they'd been catapulted from the pits of hell. Those bears stood on their hind legs, towering over the colliers, for they'd been scared nearly out of their skins, as they were gentle bears.

'"Yer, get they bears off of us," shouted one of the men, and the bears dropped down onto all fours once again.

'One of the Frenchmen said, "Do not worry, she is as gentle as a lamb."

'The troupe moved off, but the coal miners started to follow them. Some rushed ahead to tell those in the next village that the bears were coming. Men spilled out of the pub as they passed. They had been drinking cider. The day was getting dark, and the Frenchies were growing nervous as the Foresters began to mumble, until the mumbles became more like rumbles.

'A full moon arrived early in the sky before the sun was fully down, and the Frenchies quickened their pace, leaving the village behind to head once more into the forest.

'Now, Forest folk didn't like strangers. They kept themselves to themselves and had lived in the Forest of Dean for generations, for so long they'd come to all look alike. Many were short and many had ginger hair. The Frenchies became quite jittery from looking at one of those small people, and then another, and seeing the same face looking back at them. Also, there was much whispering by then. A story started that a boy had been killed, and a woman mauled. By – yes. By bears. And once started, the story grew and grew like a big tree from a little seed. You see, in some ways it was easy for them to believe the story, because in those parts they believed that bears fed on the flesh and bones of little children. And, like I said, they didn't like foreigners. Anyone different who wasn't like them.'

I hug the blankets closer, trying to fend off an overwhelming sense of impending doom, as I travel – forced to listen and watch it all unfold in my mind's eye.

'The crowd grew uglier, and the mutterings louder. Someone picked up a stone and threw it at one of the Frenchmen. "Bloody frogs. Get back to thee own kind." Someone used a broom handle to trip another and kicked him when he fell down, and kicked him again on his bottom when he got up as if to send him on his way. Then somebody shouted, "Get them bears. The beasts. They did it! Kill the beasts!" The mob held its breath, and a jackdaw cawed overhead.

'The Frenchmen took off, running down the path, frantically pulling back branches of trees which plucked at their hair, at their coats. The bears crashed through the undergrowth at a run in front of them. But not too far ahead, mind, as they were scared and bewildered and didn't want to leave the side of their protectors. Some of the Frenchmen had tears streaking their faces as they shouted to their animals, "Run. Run, my beauties. Don't wait for us. Save yourselves." But the kind bears didn't understand.

'The people of the Forest were catching up with them, pelting them with stones, hitting them with sticks, as they drove them and their bears into a disused quarry. They jumped on the Frenchmen and pulled them back, punching and kicking, away from their bears.

'Majestically, the mummy bear stood in front of her baby and rose to her full height. The people nearly turned and ran and might have done so if one of the Frenchmen hadn't called out to the bear. She turned her head for one last look of love, and in so doing, broke the spell that had held them off. The mob howled as one, picked up stones and rocks and stoned those poor bears. The mummy bear tried to fend off the stones with her big shabby paws, but her baby soon fell and was jumped on and beaten until it lay still. Its fur matted with blood and dust.

'The mother threw back her head and roared her sorrow and pain. But one of the Foresters shouted, "Quick. Get that bear. Afore 'ee attacks thee." One stone hit her right smack between the eyes. Groggy, she dropped to her four paws and shook her head from side to side, as one, then two, then more, darted forwards to prod her with pointed sticks or hit her on the back with a club. She fell to the forest floor and, turning over onto her back, looked her final murderer in the eye as he brought the crashing blow from a huge rock down on her head, cracking her skull open and letting her spirit fly free.'

I am sobbing now. 'Oh, those poor bears.'

Jake is stunned, like he too has been knocked senseless.

Mum laughs softly. 'Don't be silly. It's only a silly story. Anyway, some say they weren't bears they killed that day, but two Americans dressed in bearskins who had murdered a little boy in his bed.'

'Was a little boy really killed?' asks Jake.

'Who knows? It's an old story. They still don't like to talk about it in the Forest.' She pulls back the bedcovers. 'Come on, Jake. It's time for you to get into your own bed. School tomorrow. Good night, Veronica.'

'Leave the landing light on, Mum.'

'All right. But no need to be silly, mind.'

About two minutes later Jake sneaks back in to my room. 'Quick. Jump in,' I say as we giggle under the dark tent of bedcovers until: 'Sssh!' He holds his breath.

I can hear it too. A scratching sound coming from outside. From the outside wall of my bedroom. We both peep from beneath the covers. The light from the landing casts large, looming shapes which loiter in corners and by the side of my wardrobe.

'What was that?'

'Ssh. There it is again.'

And with the full certainty of our child imaginings, we know – we both know for certain – that it's a bear. Climbing up the side of the house. Hanging on with its long talons and snuffling the pebble dash with its nose. Or an American. Yes, that's it. Not the nice, friendly bear but an American. The sort that dresses up in bearskins and murders little children in their beds. Without moving we cling to each other. Hairs prickle the back of my neck as I break out into a cold sweat. I'm too terrified to know whose voice – Jake or mine's – screams out, 'Dad! Dad!'

He runs in. 'Good heavens. What's wrong? What is it?'

'The b-b-bear,' I blub.

'There's a man. Man dressed as a bear. Outside the house. On a ladder.' Jake points to the wall.

'Now, don't be silly.'

Mum appears in the doorway.

'Lily. What bloody stupid ideas have you been putting in their heads?'

'Don't swear, George.'

'Now, now,' says Dad. 'What are you doing in here, my lad? You're nearly eight, and big enough to sleep in your own bed. Now come on.' He collects Jake in his arms and carries him off.

'Dad. Please. Please. Look outside. Look outside. Look outside.' I'm close to hysteria.

'All right. Okay,' Dad says. Mum moves aside to let him pass.

*

Careful! Don't step on the cracks, or the bears might get you.

TWENTY-SEVEN

At the Quayside Party

Back in the boatshed at the quayside party, Gerry and I are having a good look around, but there's nobody we recognise from the village – or from Intasun. Most appear to be locals, the women wearing crimplene frocks, whilst the men sport collarless shirts or vests with or without holes, their dark trousers kept up under overhanging bellies by thickly buckled leather belts – the kind that can easily be taken off to tether a dog or to beat a wayward wife or child.

From our table I watch our fellow diners attack their freshly boiled crayfish with a surprisingly delicate brutality, as they rip off legs, heads and skeletons, to expose soft pink carcasses which they flip into their mouths to crush between strong teeth. This is more like it. Foreign. Away.

'Wonderful food, isn't it?' says Gerry as he attacks his crayfish with apt gusto.

'Mmm.' I knock back the rest of my smooth red wine, and someone pours me a glass of cloudy cidre. '*Merci*,' I say, smiling at Gerry as I give it a good sniff, swirl it around my glass then take a sip and do that sucking between the teeth so beloved of wine experts. 'I'm getting apples, I'm getting sunny days.' A sniff and another sip. 'Sunny days with a hint of armpit and a touch of truffling pig overlay.'

'Stop it,' Gerry says into my shoulder. 'You know how much I fancy that woman off that telly wine programme.'

'Yes, I do know.' I'm feeling frisky and wondering if we're going to have sex tonight, when I see Xavier weaving his way through the party. My stomach does a backflip. God, don't let Gerry see him, please don't let Gerry see him. I turn away, but not before I notice there's a tall leggy blonde on Xavier's arm.

Xavier. Just saying his name in my head conjures up the touch and smell of him. Luckily, Gerry hasn't noticed he's here too. 'Must nip to the toilet,' he says, getting to his feet. 'Don't let anyone pinch my chair, will you?' I almost ask him not to leave me on my own, but already he's off striding towards the back of the hall.

There's then a touch on my shoulder and I know before turning just who it is going to be. 'Xavier,' I say, trying to keep my voice light.

For a moment he doesn't say anything, merely stands towering over me. I don't think I've ever met a man who oozed so much animal magnetism. He enfolds my hand, his voice low as he says, 'It is fine, Veronique.' (Honestly, the way he says my name is so magically French.) 'We had a moment of madness, *oui*? That is all. Do not worry about it.'

'But Gerry hit you.'

'Ah, bof – he show the passion, and that is good for you but sad for me.' He runs his finger up my arm, causing an involuntary shudder. Then he gives me a small bow and moves off – clearly having seen that Gerry is returning. More hungrily than I should, I watch Xavier weave seamlessly through the crowd to join his girlfriend at the bar.

'Was that that Xavier bastard?' Gerry looks sharply in his direction.

'Don't make a fuss, please.'

'Okay. Just for you.' He gives me a quizzical look. 'Is

everything all right with you, though? Are you sure he didn't annoy you or anything?'

'No,' I say. 'He was just trying to apologise. So why don't we leave it at that?'

I'm determined to not let what happened ruin the remainder of our holidays… Unlike that day when Jake and I ran into the sand dunes to fetch the ball which Dad had batted high into the air.

The gusts off the Bristol Channel are pretty strong, as I head – reluctantly – for the dunes where the cricket ball, hit by my dad, has soared out of play. My feet trudge along the sands in my Clarks school sandals as I set off to find it.

'Hurry up!' calls Dad. Glancing back, I see he's waiting by the stumps while Jake is running to catch up with me.

'All right,' I call back. 'I'm going as fast as I can!' Pulling my grey cardigan closer around me, I enter the dunes, Jake somewhere behind me. It's sheltered in here: the wind has dropped off, and I'm enjoying the warmth of the sun on my shoulders as I search for the ball. Where is it? I can't see it anywhere. But wait a minute. What's that? I can hear a soft laugh coming from the direction of that dune up ahead.

Jake has now joined me, out of puff from running, as I place my fingers to my lips – 'Ssh' – and signal for him to drop down beside me in our special Secret Seven trailing crouch. 'There's someone behind that dune,' I whisper, pointing ahead. We begin our approach with caution. It could be smugglers, for all we know. As we reach the sand dune, I stop Jake in his tracks. 'Ssh.'

'Ow! No! I've got sand in my eye!' yowls Jake, blinking.
'Ssh.'

'Can't see,' he whispers as he rubs the heels of his hands in his eye.
'Ssh. You wait here.'

Edging round the corner I see there's a woman lying on her back in a hollow; she's wearing a light-coloured coat with a black velvet collar and black buttons, but I can't see her face because there's a man on top of her – a man whose grey trousers are dropped round his ankles as his deathly pale bottom moves forwards and back. In and out. Her long shapely legs – "like ballet dancers", Mum would say – are apart and I recognise her navy pointed court shoes. 'Nnn,' she groans, her black permed hair tousled in the almost-white sands. Above the pair's heads, long coarse marram grass sways in rhythm. I can't take my eyes off her exposed stocking tops, where her full skirt has ridden up.

Jake must still be attending to his eye, because when I look behind me, he's not there.

I'm still rooted to the spot. The woman's eyes are closed and the bald patch on the top of the man's head is red. Good. He's going to have nasty sunburn, I'm thinking, when she opens her eyes and sees me.

'Stop, stop,' she's saying, pushing at his shoulders. 'Bob, stop. It's Veronica. Stop.'

I stagger back to where I find Jake at the next dune; it's clear he's not seen or heard anything.

'We'd best get back to Dad,' I say.

'Did you find the ball?'

'No.'

I stop him before we exit the dunes. 'Whatever happens,' I say, as I know this is going to be bad, 'we are going to stick together.'

'It's only a ball, Ron,' he says. Then, 'What? Did something happen? Did you see something that I missed?'

'Nothing. Now, is your eye better? Good. Come on, let's go.' And I run on ahead with him chasing behind, calling, 'Ron, Ron, wait for me!'

Dad is waiting for us, swinging his cricket bat. 'Well? Where's the ball?' He looks from one of us to the other. 'You've been gone a long time – so where is it?'

'Lost,' I mutter. 'We couldn't find it.'

'Right.'

He looks up from the two of us to see Mum come stumbling out of the dunes holding her shoes in one hand as Slimy Bob crosses the sands to his wife.

'Pack up and get in the bloody car,' we can hear him say to Beryl. 'Now!'

'Lily?' says Dad as Mum approaches and gives him a shrug, and me a pointed look.

It's been a while since I've thought of that day. Oh, there was fallout all right. There was lots of shouting which we were banned from being around. Mum moved in with her sister for what turned out to be a few months – I think – it's hard to recall. Slimy Bob put his house on the market and they soon moved away. I seem to remember that Dad bloodied Slimy Bob's nose – but there again I'm not a hundred per cent certain. Perhaps I'm imagining it from something I saw in a film. Eventually Mum returned, but things were never quite the same again. It felt like it was all my fault even then, and of course, later – when I accidentally told Jake and the two of them had words, she blamed me. She never had been good at taking responsibility.

'You okay?' says Gerry. 'Only you look a little sad.'

'I'm fine,' I say, injecting more I'm-fine-ness into my voice than I felt. Now, shaking my head and fixing on a smile, I say, 'You know how it is…' I trail off. He does indeed know how it is.

Right on cue, a jolly accordion starts up, sending its incessant jiggling beat right down to my toes.

'That sounds like fun,' says Gerry, pulling me to my feet. 'Let's go see where the action is.'

Outside, electric light spills from the boatshed to combine with the beams from two large spotlights as together they shine upwards and outwards until they fade into a darkening sky. The man with the squeeze box plays what sounds like a traditional

French song, and he is soon joined by a workman – in his fifties, I'm guessing – who rolls up his sleeves, flings his navy peaked cap up into the air and, laughing his enjoyment, sashays into the dance area. Despite his bulk and age he is amazingly agile as he clicks his fingers, jaunts around and flashes his eyes in challenge to the people starting to crowd around in a circle.

Then *she* appears. Dumpy and with a pudding complexion, she swishes her box pleated skirt as their dance begins. Together. Apart. They dip their heads then lift them up, up to the sky: the accordion music twirling faster and faster. They are flamenco dancers, aggressively tantalising; they are passionate apache dancers from the backstreets of Paris complete with berets, split skirt and striped Breton shirt. They entwine and gallop in a combination of waltz and polka until, breathless, they pull apart to stalk the crowd.

Gerry and I have been clapping away to the beat, enjoying the event. The temptress homes in on Gerry. Usually plain, she is tonight transformed into a fun-loving beauty. Putting her all into the moment. She has an incandescence which I know Gerry will find irresistible. Normally he hates dancing, is terrified of making a spectacle of himself. Yet here he is, being pulled onto the dancefloor, his glasses flashing as he matches her provocative look for look as they posture around each other, break into laughter, then chastely embrace and dance in a clinch. She tries to teach him the steps. I count along with them. One two three. One two three, when there's a touch on my shoulder. I turn, and there is the worker himself, ready to transport me too. Why not? I nod, and he clasps me to his pot belly as we spin round and around until the dance is done.

'Bravo!' cheer and clap our two partners.

'Bravo!' cheers the audience.

We bow, hug each other and then our partners before skipping off to get another bottle of cidre.

As the evening wears on, the warmth of the night and the bonhomie of the revellers start to weave their magic. Wine and cidre do their love potion stuff as couples kiss, dance and walk with their arms about each other as if skin-grafted together. I am pleasantly light-headed. Free floating.

'You do love me, don't you?' asks Gerry, giving me a playful nudge. 'Go on. Tell me you love me.'

'Might do.'

'Go on. Say it.'

'Oh, all right, then. I love you.'

'Whoopee!'

He runs up the quay, has a go at a wobbly cartwheel and lands awkwardly on his bottom, legs splayed out in front of him like a puppet whose strings have been cut.

'I love you, Veronica O'Keefe,' he shouts, his arms outstretched. 'I love yoooou!' he shouts at a moon which has emerged from behind a wispy cloud to see what all the fuss is about.

'I love her,' he says to a passing couple. 'That woman over there is the love of my life!' They smile indulgently and carry on their way.

'Gerry, will you please get up. You're acting like an idiot!'

'Okay.' He clambers to his feet, skips around and then darts off to a steel ladder attached to the side of the boatshed. *What's he doing now?* I think as he leaps onto it climbs about halfway up and then turns, swinging out one arm and one leg. 'I'm not coming down until you say you love me, like you mean it.'

'Stop being a twerp,' I say, as I reach where he's drunkenly mucking about. 'People are staring.'

'Let them! Say you love me.'

I turn away with half a grin on my face, as I'm loath to admit that I'm rather charmed by his reckless Romeo-type gesture.

But then the next thing I know is there's a shriek – 'Aargh, my shoulder!' – followed by a thud as he drops to the ground.

'Oh, for crying out loud,' I say as I dash over to his side.

He's holding his shoulder, which is at an awkward-looking angle. 'I've dislocated my fucking shoulder,' he says. 'Don't worry – aargh, ouch – it sometimes pops back in.'

A man joins us and gently edges me out of the way. 'It's okay. I am a medic,' he says, and with a swift manoeuvre, an audible click, plus some loud grimacing on Gerry's part, the shoulder is back in.

'Thank you, thank you,' I say as he backs away with a cheery wave, and someone thrusts a brandy at each of us. People smile. People laugh. They throw their hands up at the follies of *l'amour*. We laugh too as the warm winds blow around us.

'You won't ever leave me, will you?' asks Gerry.

I take a good look at his face and can see what's on offer and realise that of course I won't.

'Come on, you prize melon,' I say. 'Let's get you back to the villa. You're pissed.'

'Seriously, Ron, I'm not that pissed,' he says. 'Tell you what! Let's get married.'

That stops me in my tracks. 'But Gerry. We already are.'

TWENTY-EIGHT

The Party Continues

It was Gerry's boyish playfulness and his natural way with children which made me stay with him when I accidentally fell pregnant, a little over eight months into our on-off relationship. We weren't even living together or anything. Then after Finty arrived, and soon after Jake had his accident leaving us glaringly aware of our own mortality, we decided to cement things by getting married.

It turned out to be a sorry, sad and sober affair with two hastily acquired witnesses, and our daughter as a three-month old bridesmaid in sailor romper suit (why?) and Hitler fringe (I'd been too scared to cut it, unsure if doing so would ruin her new baby hair – funny the things you don't know/aren't sure of when you have a baby – it's not like they come with a manual, worst luck). And so there I was, still traumatised from a long and difficult birth, and from the aftermath of The Accident, without the emotional wherewithal to buy an outfit – that seemed far too frivolous and joyous a thing to do, so instead I borrowed someone's dress, which was forgiving over my still stretched-by-baby tummy, plus a weird hat I found from somewhere. One of the witnesses took our only wedding photos showing an unsmiling, dazed-looking me, a worried Gerry and a baby held in front slightly slumped forwards as she was too young to sit up unsupported. We had no party, invited no friends or family as celebrating felt too disloyal, what with Jake still in a specialist hospital receiving shedloads of rehab. Not every girl's dream wedding.

And now Gerry's down on one knee, in traditional fashion.

'Veronica – love of my life, mother of my child – will you do me the great honour of marrying me. Again.'

'Get up, idiot. We don't want you dislocating your knee as well as your shoulder.'

'Seriously. I'll do it properly with a ring and everything this time. I know you've felt I was immature, in the past—'

'Yeah, well—'

'But I've grown up, trust me. Now that there's the three of us. You, me and Finty makes three – have changed my life, for ever. And for the better. You have been the making of me, Veronica O'Keefe. I am now a bona fide grownup.' He places my palm against his heart. 'Say you'll marry me. Oh, mother of my child. Light of my life. We can have a big fuck-off wedding and do it in style this time. It will be packed full of joy, and orange blossom, and we could even have little Shetland ponies. Finty would make a gorgeous bridesmaid and wouldn't she just love it! We can have a band, and dancing, yes, lots and lots of dancing. You'll like that, won't you?'

'Let's wait until we get back home to Bristol,' I say. 'You can ask me then, if you still want to.'

'I do, Ron Ron Ron, I do, Ron Ron.'

'Yeah. Not funny even the first time round,' I say, but there's a stupid grin on my face which matches his, and we touch forehead to forehead.

We're in bed; it's 2am, or thereabouts, when I say, 'Ger? Are you awake?'

'Nnn.'

'Ger?'

'Nnnn… What time is it?'

'I need to talk to you.'

'Sleepy… Can't it wait until the morning?'

'No.'

He turns over to face me. 'What is it?'

'It's just…' Deep breath. 'Are you sure you're okay about the whole Xavier thing?'

'Oh, that.' He reaches out and pulls me towards him. 'I said I am, didn't I?' He stares into my eyes. (Or in the direction of my eyes – it's dark and womb-like in the bedroom.) 'We're going to move on from this, I promise, and we'll end up stronger, yeah?' He pauses. 'I know you've not been yourself.'

He's right there. I don't know who I've been lately.

'In any case,' he continues, 'this Xavier fella was a bloody chancer who took advantage of you—'

'But—'

'No ifs or buts. Why don't we agree to not talk about it again as it's over and done with? In any case, I shouldn't have made you feel all insecure with the whole Hilary thing, so it's partly down to me. Now, can we agree not to talk about this ever again? Okay?'

'And you're sure you won't bring it up in the future? That you won't throw this at me if we have a row or something?'

'What sort of person do you think I am? Look, you forgave me about my whole getting cold feet and sleeping with Fran at that stupid conference…'

'Yeah – well…' (I hate being reminded of that…)

'We've managed to put that behind us, haven't we? And the whole Hilary thing. It only seems fair that you're allowed this one wobble.' He kisses me on the top of my head. 'Just the one, mind.'

'So you're saying we're quits. Is that what you're saying?'

'If you like.'

He props himself up on his pillows and pulls me tighter to him. 'That's why I want us to get married, again. To show everyone that we're getting through this. I want to renew our vows, read out new ones and do it properly this time. We will invite everybody –friends, family, and have a whale of a time with flowers, dresses, doves, a fairytale coach... the whole kit and caboodle, whatever you want. Hey, Finty can even dress up as Ariel from *The Little Mermaid* – you know she'd feel as if she died and went to heaven.' He tenderly holds my face. 'We deserve a chance to be happy, and we owe it to Finnoula too, for her parents to be happy and married and all to be secure.'

I kiss him, and he kisses me back.

'I do love you,' I say.

'That's lucky.' I can hear the smile in his voice. 'Because I love you too.'

These "I love you"s are like the glue in a marriage, aren't they? Perhaps this is how we can put our own Humpty Dumpty back together again.

'So that's it, then. Time we both stopped faffing about and committed to our life together.'

'I guess so.'

'Ron,' he says, winding one of his legs round mine. 'It was an awful thing which happened to Jake, but we have to find a way forward. Me, you and Finty. Together and without Angie and Jake. Because they will find their own way, and it's about time we pulled back and let them do that, don't you agree?'

'I guess so...' I'm yawning... feeling sleepy... 'Better not tell Angie – about the wedding... Not until after the holiday.' I start to edge back under the covers... sleepy...

'Ron?' Gerry pulls me into him, and it's nice and cosy and dark and warm when he snuggles and nudges and moves on top of and into me, and we have lazy, middle of the night, comfy married sex. Both together. Like millions of couples everywhere.

TWENTY-NINE

Friday

It's proper morning now, and I can hear Finty grizzling from the girls' room, so reluctantly I realise I'd better go and fetch her before she wakes the other girls. Quickly, I fill a glass from the tap in the corner, then quietly open our door and pad across the landing to where Finty snuck into the girls' room last night. Gingerly, I push the door open. Ah, there's my little darling. Amazing to think Gerry and I actually made this unique human being who's sitting smack bang in the middle of a mattress on the floor. Curled up next to her – like the second babe in the woods – is her cousin Lauren, fast asleep. The moment Finty sees me, she stops mid-whinge and bestows such a smile that my ovaries yelp. *Maybe we* should *have another child*, flashes through my mind. We even could be – might be – as I've not been good at remembering my pill, not since, you know.

'Mummee.'

I quickly collect her up, careful not to wake Lauren or Sarah.

'Ahh.' Finty gives me one of her inexpert pats. Closing the bedroom door carefully behind us, I pause to blow raspberries in that tickly part of her neck above the collar of her pyjamas, when – 'Pwah' – mid-raspberry I say, 'What's that terrible pong, missy?' Sniff her bottom. 'Gah. That's disgusting. Ugh. We'd better change your nappy before men in decontamination suits arrive.'

Jake sits with the morning sun glinting his hair and sparkling his eyelashes as he concentrates on his toast. I want to place him in my pocket to keep him safe. But I can't and that makes me sad.

'Good morning!' I hadn't noticed Angie by the sink. Jake glances my way and gives me a nod.

'Morning,' I say to them as I lower Finty to the floor. Sarah guides both her and Lauren over to the sofa and coffee table, where there's an assortment of pencil cases, hairbrushes, hair slides, Barbies and other girlie stuff.

'Can I have two lots of selves?' Jake asks Angie.

She places down the cup she's been rinsing. 'You don't mean selve, do you?' She turns to face him. 'Selve, or self, is a person.'

'No,' he insists, pointing. 'Selves.'

'Do you mean jam?' She points to the pot by the dresser.

'Yes, Sarah,' he says with an emphatic nod. 'I do.'

'The name's Angie.' She plonks the jar in front of him, but he pushes himself to his feet and heads for the cooker.

'Want tea?' Clearly, he's forgotten the urgency of the jam.

Be a good name for a book – or a film, that: *The Forgotten Urgency of Jam*. 'Dying for a cuppa,' I say, filling Finty's breakfast bowl with cereal, then wresting a hairbrush from Finty's so I can feed her Cheerios.

'Ange,' I start. 'About yesterday.'

'Let's not talk about it, yeah?' She whips Jake's plate away.

'If you're sure,' I add. 'But I *am* sorry.'

'Yeah, well.' She turns a somewhat forced smile on me. 'Did you and Gerry have a good time at the party on the harbourside?'

'Yes, we did, it was good fun,' I say, and have second thoughts about regaling her with tales about how good. Finty is kicking her heels so I set her down from the table. 'Although Gerry played silly buggers and dislocated his shoulder.'

'Yeah?' she says. 'Well, *we* went to bed early. But the girls kept waking up, didn't they? Jake?' No response. 'Didn't they?'

He stands, waiting for the pot to boil.

'Oh, for fuck's sake!' She shoves past him to lift the pan off the hob.

'You okay, Jake?' I ask. No reply.

Angie pours hot water into two mugs. 'Jake was useless last night – and look at him this morning.'

'He's probably a bit whacked out from yesterday?'

'Hm. He just stood there in a corner practically all night.' She sets about squeezing the tea bags. 'It's no wonder the girls have nightmares – it's the way he moves around so quietly, creeping about like some ghost, and then all of a sudden he's there! It frightens the life out of you.' She leans against the sink. 'If only he'd *do* something. *Say* something.'

'I'm sure he's doing his best.'

Jake's ruminatively chewing a piece of toast, much like a cow chewing the cud.

'You don't have to live with it day in day out like I do,' says Angie.

There's an almighty crash, and we both turn as one. 'That enough!' shouts, Jake who is on his feet and has smashed a meat platter on to the tiled floor.

Gerry rushes in. 'What's up? Anyone hurt?'

'I am here. Now!' Jake shouts. His anger crackling in the air, seeming to somehow pull him more into focus as if he's a shimmering shade trying to materialise. He holds on in there long enough to say, as clear as a bell, 'You can make your own fucking tea!' And then he turns on his heel, slamming the door behind him.

'Jake, Jake? Where're you going? Wait for me!'

I stop to pull up my white knee socks. The elastic around the top went ages ago, so now I wear a pair of garters Mum made from a piece of elastic stitched together so they can grip under my – sturdy, she calls them; fat, I think – knees. I sort of do a hop and a skip to try and keep up as I pull first one, and then the other.

'Jake. Wait.' But already he's ahead of me, hurtling through the undergrowth.

Here it is, past this bush. I duck under the branches crashing through after him, following one of our regular paths.

'Jake!'

I can't see him. The dark green of rhododendrons gone wild threaten to hamper my way, but I know our secret routes like the back of my hand. (Wonder why people say that? I never have the time to look at the back of mine.) This time I don't need to track Jake. But automatically I keep my eyes on the ground, on the lookout for a fox track or even a badger's. Ah ha! A broken branch. Sign that Jake has been this way. Placing both thumbs together, I try an owl hoot by blowing between them. But my mouth is too dry, so I lick my lips. 'Who-oo-oo-oo.' My call is somewhat wobbly.

'Who-o-o-o-o-o,' answers a stronger one. Jake's better than me at hoots, but I whistle better with two fingers. Showing off, I blow a particularly loud and piercing one.

'Come on,' shouts Jake from somewhere ahead. 'Hurry up!'

I burst out of the bushes, like someone running and jumping over waves at the seaside.

'Ah-ah-ah-ah-ahhh,' I yell, Tarzan-like, and land right in front of the crumbling summer house. It looks like pictures I've seen of Roman villas in our school encyclopaedia, except it's a lot smaller. There used to be a white stone statue of some god or other on a pedestal, but that got knocked to the ground ages ago and was decapitated in the fall. The head used to lie alongside it but now I see that it's gone, along with half of the right arm. Metal wires stick up from the torso as if they're going to pump white-grey blood. The remains look like they've been left by some scavenging animal. A jackal, maybe. A demon jackal with metal teeth for crunching stone and bright yellow eyes for seeing in the dark.

'Ow-ooooh,' I howl, and do a couple of whooping leaps onto the tree-lined avenue which sweeps down from the summer house to the now-derelict mansion of Kingsweston House. The overgrown path is little more than a wide track, its gravel mostly gone or trampled into the ground. Jake and I have three dens in the bushes which creep in on either side – one on the left, and two on the right.

Suddenly a man wearing a windcheater is standing by my shoulder.

'Want to come with me and pick some mushrooms?' he's saying, in a strange, intense way. He's dishevelled with an unshaved, stubbly chin and browning teeth. My heart sinks, sensing that something is wrong.

'Nice, pretty girl like you...' he leers.

Then 'Eeeyah-ah!' comes a shriek, as Jake catapults from out of the big overhanging bush that's Den No. 2. He emits another blood-curdling shriek, this time accompanied by his version of the Red Indian Rain Dance, and the stranger scarpers.

'Ha!' Jake shouts triumphantly at the man's back, then he turns to me. 'Hurry up, slow coach.'

And I run, windmilling both arms until I'm bowling into Den No. 3 with Jake hurtling behind me, both of us so fast that I trip and fall over.

'Ouch.'

'Don't be soft,' says Jake. 'It's nothing.'

I rub my knee anyway, all the while regarding it with disgust. Both my knees are covered in old and healing scars. Big criss-cross scabs like someone's been darning my knee with bright new patches of skin. Bubbles of scab are dotted here and there, where some bits have healed faster than others – or I've picked them off. And then there's the scar on my left knee which I'm particularly proud of. I attained it one night when we were having a midnight feast of Smiths crisps and Jammie Dodgers under my bedcovers, both of us giggling away. Jake had stuffed his spud gun with match heads so it would be more realistic when he fired it, and then it accidentally went off. Stunned at first, I'd watched as the flash of sulphur flared spectacularly from where it had embedded itself in my knee. Although I tried, I couldn't stop the scream which brought Dad running and a clip around both our ears.

It was exciting, though. God. I hate my flippin' knees. They're fat and podgy. And it's not fair, because Jake has nice sharp boy's knees, and if I'm his twin then mine should be the same. Shouldn't they? And anyway, I can do everything he does. He might be a faster runner, but I'm a better climber. I mostly climb trees. I'm the one who risks getting caught when we go scrumping apples at the house on the edge of the Dark Woods. He only has to stand beneath and catch them.

'What a weird man,' I say, picking at one of my scabs.

'Yeah.' Jake is poking the ground with a stick, and then scouts around as if to check no-one is about. 'Ssh.'

We listen out for any snapping twigs which might signal a burglar, or a snooper creeping up on us, but all is quiet except for a bird twittering, and far off I can hear a woodpecker tattooing a tree. Cross-legged we huddle together like Enid Blyton's Secret Seven on a mission. Except we call ourselves the Daring Duo. Took us ages to think up that one.

'Has he gone now?'

'Yeah.'

'What did he want?'

Jake looks at me intensely. 'Don't you know? Ya ninny.'

I give him a shove. 'Know what? I'll give you a Chinese Burn if you don't tell.'

Jake regards me as if checking whether I can keep a secret. 'Okay,' he finally says, as he bends closer. 'He was one of those.'

'One of what?' I sit back so quickly that I nearly fall over and get tangled in the branches hanging down as if trying to touch their toes.

'Don't be so thick. You know.'

'Oh.' The penny drops and I realise that he'd been one of those strangers. One of those you don't take sweets from, or get into cars with, or go off with to hand-pick mushrooms.

A cloud passes overhead and the shadows are getting longer. I shiver cos I've forgotten my cardigan.

'Reckon I saved you from a fate worse than death.'

'Did you?'

'Best be going home cos it's nearly tea-time.'

I look at my Timex watch, and through the scratches I can just make out it's a quarter to four.

'Wait,' Jake says. 'Before we go, we have to swear a secret pact.'

He roots around inside his pockets, pulling out sweet wrappers, a shrivelled-up conker, Spangles with fluff attached to them – he sucks one clean and pops it in his mouth before offering me one – and finally a piece of string.

'Right then.'

I sit up straight. 'Hands up like this,' he says as he holds his up like a boxer's. Duly I obey and he winds the string around my wrists and then around his with all the symbolism of a nine-year-old. Next, he stares steadfastly into my face.

'Ready?'

I nod my head. I don't giggle.

He starts, 'With these ties...'

He nods at me. 'With these ties...'

'I swear to keep the other...'

'I swear to keep the other...'

'Safe from harm, and solemnly promise to stick together for ever and ever.'

Even the air is still now.

'Go on,' he says, 'swear.'

'I swear.'

'That's it. We are now sworn to be bound together for ever and ever.' He clambers to his feet. 'Race you to the Iron Bridge!'

Outside the back door of our house, Jake turns to me and says, 'We won't tell Mum about the stranger. Deal?'

'Deal.'

Indoors, Dad has come home early. As we enter the hallway, he's helping Mum up the stairs.

'It's a rat race, George,' she half-sobs, half-slurs. 'A bloody rat race.'

Dad turns to us. 'You'll have to get your own tea,' he says, then continues holding Mum under her arms, which flap as if they're caged birds trying to escape.

'Come on, Lily. That's it. One foot in front of the other.'

Dear Jake,

D'you remember those days when we'd camp with Mum and Dad in that field alongside the road which runs out from the beach? There was a social club in the campsite at Brean sands. We'd play outside in the dark, where sounds echoed up into a sky with stars dotted across its ceiling. Those nights felt dead mysterious, and totally different from nights spent out on our street after dark, playing tag with neighbouring kids, or knock-out ginger, or later on, kiss touch. At night, there in Brean, we'd creep between tents and caravans, to go charging through the sand dunes.

'C'mon, Ronnie,' you'd shout.

'Wait! Wait for me!' as my stupid shoe – one of those black daps Mum bought from Woolworths – would slip off, as you disappear over the brow of a dune. Sharp tall grass whips my bare legs; sand scrunches in between my toes. Cold. It's cold and damp. 'Aaargh!' you shout, jumping out at me, commando-style.

Your sis xxxx

In our teens and early twenties, Jake and I sometimes take the train down to that very same Brean site, for a weekend's camping, tent and rucksacks hoisted on our backs.

One time we're travelling back home to Bristol, me staring out of the window, when a commotion in the carriage up ahead causes me to look up to where a youth is standing, lurching, next to an aisle seat.

'Don't be like that, dahlin',' he's saying, as he leers down at a girl about the same age as me. One hand is on the back of her seat, whilst in the other he clutches a can of beer. I can see, by leaning out a little, that she's a student or something, dressed as if she's travelling home to her mum and dad.

Behind this guy another pasty-faced youth gives him a nudge. 'Aye aye,' he says. 'Ask her for a kiss.'

I can sense that it's about to kick off at any moment, and I'm alert to how the girl is going to react. I can just see her face – pretty – when she turns her head to respond to the youths. 'Look,' she says. 'Do you mind?'

'Don't mind if I do, sugar tits,' says the first young man.

He tries to push past into the seat next to her, but she's saying, 'Please!' His friend's grinning. 'Leave me alone,' she says, and with that I think, Right, and I'm up on my feet.

'Excuse me,' I call, as I proceed to walk the aisle towards them. The young man looks up, startled at first, and then adopts a more confident air, as he sees that I'm a lone woman.

'Can you not hear that she wants to be left alone?'

Yobbo One and Yobbo Two lose interest in their original prey and start to focus their attention on me.

'Oh yeah? You gonna stop us?' Yobbo One has that open-handed gesture so beloved of those walking towards someone they're getting ready to fight. 'You and whose army? Eh?' he says.

'You and whose army, did you say?' It's Jake, coming up behind them. Yobbo Two has his mouth open; Yobbo One turns to square up to him. 'I think you'll find that army is me, pal.' Jake head-butts him, and he goes down.

THIRTY

Friday at the Beach

We're sitting outside the villa without the others, and it's one of those weird mornings when a watery moon hangs in the sky, and I'm wondering about the effects of this moon on the Earth's tides, governed as they are by lunar cycles.

Jake used to have a passing interest in astrology – at university, as I recall. (Yes, that's right, astrology, not astronomy – I do know the difference.)

He'd say (in that pompous way students new to philosophising about life, often have), that because humans are made up of ninety per cent water it stands to reason that the pull of the moon and planets must have an effect on us. Ipso facto why wouldn't astrology be, at the very least, a possibility?

Might a daytime moon signify anything? Would Angie, with her new-found faith in homeopathy and the like, be finding signs and augers in its presence? I think of what she said about "proving". The diluting over and over of a substance until its presence was smaller than a grain of sand or a star in the Milky Way (or am I making this up?). She said how this extra dilution of what ails you can heal you. I don't know. Is that any stranger than the butterfly wing effect? The hummingbirds?

I imagine the tide shushing in and out, the moon and the

Earth locked in their own push-me-pull-you embrace. Like a mother's blood whooshing as two babies once turned in their own sealed and briny seas. I rub my forehead. I'll be writing poetry next if I'm not careful...

'Oi. Dolly daydream,' calls Gerry, who's stopped in front of me.

I shade my eyes and ask, 'Where's Finty?'

He looks puzzled. 'Isn't she with you?'

I sit up straight. 'No. She's not.'

He looks about the backyard, and just as I'm getting to my feet, Sarah comes charging around the side of the house, running and looking backwards, running and looking backwards. She's followed by Jake, who is holding Finty out in front of him, by the back straps of her Osh Kosh dungarees like she's some parcel he's holding by the strings.

Sarah points at them as she shouts, 'Finty was going to run into the road! Finty nearly got knocked down!' She's jiggling from one foot to the other. 'Daddy saved her!'

Gerry steps forwards to take Finty off Jake. 'Thanks, mate.'

As if a switch has been flipped Finty bursts into tears as she clings, limpet-like, to her father's neck.

'Daddy catched her before the bus squished her dead!'

Oh my God! I took my eye off my daughter – too bloody absorbed in my own stuff – and she nearly died. Am I so wrapped up in myself that I can't even see that Jake is more present than I think? Maybe my idea to focus on a tangible thing like the motocross has helped after all.

Angie, hearing all the commotion, arrives. 'Well done, darling,' she says, and then sets about flapping out laundry for hanging on the washing line as if Finty nearly getting run over was a daily occurrence.

'You really ought to keep a closer eye on Finty,' she says to me over her shoulder. 'Jake and I *always* make sure the other one knows exactly who is minding which child.'

I could cheerfully throttle her.

'Can't thank you enough, Jake,' says Gerry, who's clearly shaken too.

Jake gives him a thumbs-up.

Finally, our little family have made our escape and are walking down the slipway to the small beach. 'Shall we try the sands on the left?' suggests Gerry.

'Might as well, I suppose.' I'm still smarting from what Angie said.

An early mist creeps in from the sea, giving the sky above the appearance of a not-quite-finished picture being coloured in by a child. It matches my mood: wispy and unclear around the edges.

'This fog will burn off soon,' he says, as he scans about him. 'This beach is pretty cute, don't you think so?' He gives me a smile. 'Shall we find a patch of clean sand? Over there looks good.'

I'm not in the mood for chit chat.

Together, we pick our way across the high tide mark's tangle of plastic non-biodegradables and organic matter. We're the only ones on this small beach as it's still early. It's situated next to the harbourside where last night we partied and Gerry asked me to marry him. Was that really only last night?

'This'll do,' he announces, as he cheerfully sets about unpacking our rucksack while I undo Finty's buggy straps. No way is she escaping from us again.

Gerry settles on a blanket shaking out his newspaper, ready for a read, when he peers across at me. 'We are all right, aren't we?' I do wish he'd stop asking.

'Of course we are. I'm a little pissed off with Angie, that's all.'

'Remember we agreed to having a proper wedding? You're not going to change your mind, are you?'

I'm not saying anything.

'What with all that business about Finty not being with me this morning, I thought you might have had a change of heart?' He gives me a rather pleading look.

'Don't be daft,' I say, sitting beside him. 'What did you make of all that in the kitchen? There was no need for Angie to be such a cow about Fints wandering off, don't you agree?' I sigh. 'In many ways I'll be glad when this holiday is over, especially as I'm finding her rather draining with her holier-than-thou attitude.'

'I'm sure she doesn't mean it.'

'Could have fooled me.' I wipe some sand off Finty's fingers, then take off my shirt. Underneath I've shorts and a bikini top. 'I'll take Finty off to explore while you read your paper. Want to come with Mummy?'

Finty's upturned face is so sweet and open. The fright of earlier all forgotten about, I hold her adorable cheeks in my hand and kiss her, much to her delight.

'Let's you and me take your bucket and go find crabs!'

'Mabs!' she says with her gorgeous baby-toothed grin.

'Don't go getting lost, or run over by buses,' teases Gerry.

'Oh, ha ha,' I say, giving him a shove.

'Oi,' as he topples over.

Off we set – mother and daughter – ambling over to the rocky part of the shore to hunt for a suitable spot where we can peer into a rock pool, scouring its shallow depths.

'Look. There.' I point. Clumsily Finty gets down on all fours for a better look while I lift up a rock, taking the roof off a tiny crab's home. Little and almost transparent, it scuttles beneath a neighbouring rock from where it'll probably shelter, trembling away and hoping that the God-like faces (of Finty and me) – which suddenly and inexplicably appeared in its sky – will just as mysteriously pass on by. Finty reaches for the crab but I pull her away. 'No, Finty. Let's leave the crab alone. Poor little thing's terrified. Anyway, it might nip you.' She looks at me with surprise. 'Nippy nip nip,' I say, pretending to nip at her so that she squeals and nearly loses her footing on the slippery rocks. Accidently she steps into a neighbouring rock pool, and for a split second she stares at first me, then at her foot, then lets out a surprised wail.

'Ssssh. Sssshhh,' I say, gathering her to me.

She quietens down.

'Nasty mab bite me,' she says, her sobs little hiccuppy ones now.

'I don't think it did, sweetie.'

She screams, 'Did! Did! It did!'

To distract her, I run around with her in my arms, then swing her up in the air and pretend to threaten to throw her into the sea. 'No, Mummy! No!' she squeals, delightedly, as I kiss then cuddle then hug her, until she's giggling fit to burst. When I stop she's all sunny-faced and smiling once more.

Returning to our place on the beach, Gerry takes over with our daughter whilst I idly watch fishermen loading and unloading their boats on the jetty, wood and metal making clunk- and clanking noises as they thump onto planks. Male voices boom across, and a crocodile of schoolchildren – their teacher snapping orders from its head – file along the walkway to board a boat for some trip around the harbour.

Gerry places his cool palm on my bare skin. 'Why don't I take Finty for a stroll? Maybe grab an ice cream while we're about it. You fancy one?'

'Uh oh!' I say as Finty shoots a look at the mention of ice cream; hilariously her mouth is full of sand. 'Typical,' cries Gerry as he starts clearing the sand from her mouth, while she spits and protests – 'Dabbee' – then clambers to her feet. 'Dabbee!'

I'm unable to resist her chubby leg so close that I grab hold and give it a kiss, loving how she squeals with delight. 'Mubbee!'

She double-hand-pats my bottom, nearly falling over in the process, and Gerry leans over us both, snuffling into my neck.

'Mm. I love your smell,' he says.

'Pervert,' I say, but I'm smiling.

'We'd better go,' he says, as he stretches himself. 'But first, let's give Mummy a family hug?'

'Oh no!' Too late as he sandwiches Finty in between, and he rolls us over and over, as one. Backwards and forwards. Laughing and cuddling.

'Aaah,' says Finty once he's done.

'Push off, moron. Oof. You're squashing me.'

'You heard Mummy,' he's now saying. 'We'd better give Mummy a squash.' And they both lie on top of me until I heave them both off.

'Hilarious. Now, go! Leave me in peace.'

'Mummy in peas?'

'Okay, okay. We're going. We're going.' And with a final wave the two of them set off for more rock pools plus a promise of ice cream. From the back they resemble Pooh and Piglet, I think, as I lay back, the sun so bright it makes the space behind my lids bright red, complete with Finty and Gerry reflected like negatives on a screen as they walk together, Finty swinging her bucket in time with each of her overly high steps.

'How long have you had her?' asks Jake, visiting inside my head. He smiles that handsome smile of his: dimples cheekily dimpling.

'Three weeks before your accident. Don't you remember? You came to visit us when she was one week old. I took a photograph of you holding her. Curiously, part of your head was cut off when the picture came back from Boots.'

'You've gone on without me,' he says, as his smile wavers and disappears.

When I open my eyes Gerry and Finty have disappeared among the rocks, so I watch this large Pyrennean Mountain dog amble into the waves and then strike out towards the horizon. He then turns and swims sideways to the shore, transformed into a huge sleek otter with ears laid back flat against his head.

Now it's coming ashore; hauling itself out of the sea, freed from its watery grip, the dog sets off at a lumbering trot, weaving to right and left as smells distract. All the while it's heading towards me – oh no. Yep, that's right, it's headed for you. Great.

Sitting up, I manage to grab my towel as he stops right in front and gives himself a massive shake. Gah! Droplets of water fling outwards as his fur fans like the ruffles of a triceratops – spattering my warm bare bits with cold. Talk about a rude awakening.

'Thanks a bunch!' I mutter as it stands, regarding me with his mouth open like he's grinning or something. Then without further ado, he turns to head back to the ocean. Why do they always pick on me? And gingerly I lower myself back down on to the blanket, where I'm soon nearly back into my doze when water is flicked on me again. But this time not by that bloody dog – this time it's Gerry and Finty grinning down at me.

'You've caught the sun,' says Gerry. 'Show Mummy what we caught in the rock pools.'

Gerry is humming a tune.

'It's a shame Jake can't sing in folk clubs anymore,' I say.

'Why not?' says Gerry as he slips on his garish Hawaiian shirt.

'Because he can't play his guitar anymore, can he? Silly.'

'Can't he find somebody else to accompany him?'

'I don't know. I don't think so. Their friends have all but deserted them.' I watch Finty dig with her spade in the sand. 'He taught himself to play a twelve-string guitar, did I tell you?'

Of course I must have told him this hundreds of times, but it's considerate of him not to say so. 'His voice sweeter than Sweet Baby James.'

'Hm.'

'I used to sing with him sometimes.'

'God help us all,' says Gerry, so I give him a playful shove.

'Oi.' I hug my knees. 'I was very good, so there.' I poke my tongue out at him. 'When we were kids we used to record ourselves on this big tape-recording machine with these saucer-sized spools of tape.' I'm miming the huge spools with my hands. 'We dreamt we'd be the next James Taylor and Carole King. And when we used to go camping at Brean we'd sing around a campfire on the beach, like a right couple of hippies.'

'Very Woodstock.'

'I'll have you know I do excellent harmonies.'

'I can vouch for that,' says Gerry with a filthy glint in his eyes.

'Ssh.' I glance across at Finty but needn't have worried as she's engrossed in her own little world.

'I'm glad we're more on track,' he says, giving my thigh a bit of a stroke. 'Speaking of which, you smell divine…' He leans across to give me a full-on snog.

'Not now!' I say, good-naturedly pushing him away. 'Child present!'

Finty, though, is absorbed in trying to shove a small shell into her mouth. 'Fints!' I reach her first, stretching across and hooking it out. She makes a face, thwarted – 'Bah!' – slaps the sand and then attempts to use her dad as a human climbing frame. 'Dabbee, Dabbee.'

'Off you get, young lady.'

She pulls at his shirt. 'Come, Dabbee.'

Gerry shrugs. 'Clearly madam has had enough of the beach.' Clambering to his feet, he dusts sand off his legs. 'Shall we go?'

he says as he pulls me upright, and the three of us (well, two really as Finty takes more out of bags than she packs into them) set about gathering up our stuff for the off.

In no particular hurry, we mooch about the harbourside, where fishermen are now selling their early-morning catches from the backs of Renault 4 vans, their trestle tables set up with scales for weighing and large plastic bowls for displaying. Gerry lifts Finty onto his shoulders, from where she waves at crustaceans of varying size and crustiness; they, in turn, wave their antennae and claws back at her.

'Look at that big one, Fints. That's a lobster,' says Gerry. 'See? They're blue, not red.' He whispers to me, 'As we know, they're only red because—'

'Not now!' I nod at our daughter. 'No need for all the grisly details.'

'Ahh, yes, you're right, of course. Sorry.'

I peer into a bowl where mackerels' mouths are gulping, their gills panting as they slowly expire in the sun. I'm feeling a bit queasy and instinctively go to cup my belly.

'Are you feeling all right, Ron? Only you're looking a tad green around the gills.'

'Yes, I'm sure I'm fine. It's probably all that red wine and cidre we drank last night. I expect that's it.' I suddenly have an overwhelming urge to sit down. 'Look, why don't you guys go ahead, and I'll catch you up in a minute? It feels like I've a small stone or something in my shoe.'

'If you're sure,' he says, as I pretend-hobble towards a capstan.

'Yes, yes. You go on.'

'If you're sure.'

'Don't fuss. I won't be long...'

They go on ahead as I make a show of removing and shaking out my shoe. A teenage boy with a guitar slung across his back, passes by. He reminds me of Jake – from before – Jake who was always playing his guitar, or fiddling with his bike, or making toys or furniture from wood, or working on the garden. Never able to sit still. Always on the go.

'That boy's got ants in his pants,' Mum would say.

Not for him the reading of books or the watching of telly (he was useless on who's who and what's what television-wise). To him, those were idle tasks. He was far more a human doing than a human being, as I used to say on numerous occasions. Well, he was like that once, but not now.

I wipe a tear. For fuck's sake, Ron. Enough with the crying already.

Idly watching clouds float by, I think of how my life with Gerry and with Finty is all that matters – truly, Ron. All that matters. The "us" in the aftermath, in the now and going forwards. Before has gone – it's dead and buried.

Up ahead I watch my husband and child saunter along the quayside with Gerry pushing our daughter ahead of him, in her buggy. He stops, peers over the side, moves on, then stops again to point at a sailboat making its leisurely way into harbour and then up at a tern wheeling in the sky. I wish I had on my sunglasses, as the bright sun distorts my vision.

When I squint back to where they were, I see they're right at the end of the jetty where the water is deeper. Gerry is leaning over to look at something on the left-hand side – and I can see that – wait! He's left the buggy unattended. I can't see if Finty's in there or not because its back is to me. What if he hasn't put the brake on? What if she isn't strapped in? What if?

'Gerry!'

He turns, smiles and waves at me. 'Coming!' he calls as he turns the buggy around and Finty waves at me too.

I hurry to meet them. 'What on Earth's the matter with you?' he says, clearly noting my anxiety.

'Sorry,' I say, first giving him a kiss, then Finty. 'Too much sun... I thought... I guess it's the shock of earlier. You know. Her nearly wandering into the road.' And then I burst into big sobbing tears.

Gerry has finally stopped peering at me in that strange way and we are now strolling arm in arm along the main street, about to pass the Hotel Bretagne.

'It was bloody lucky that Jake spotted Finty, wasn't it?' says Gerry. 'Before she ran into the road, I mean.'

'Don't remind me. I still don't think I'm over the shock of it.' I turn to face him, and he stops in his tracks. 'Let's promise to always, always make sure we know *exactly* where Finty is.'

'Might be a bit tricky as she gets older,' he says, clearly trying to inject some lightness into the conversation. 'It's scary being a parent, isn't it?'

'Yes, it is,' I say, thinking of how – with all my feeling sick and not being able to stand the smell of coffee – there is a definite possibility that I may be pregnant.

'Who knew that Jake could move that fast?' says Gerry.

'Hmm?'

'Jake. Thank fuck he was there in the right place, to save our Finty right in the nick of time.'

'Yes... um... Oh! Hang on a minute...'

We're drawing level with the hotel's noticeboard, when my eye is caught by a flyer advertising "Karaoke Fun in the Sun!".

'Look at this,' I say, dragging Gerry across. 'It's for tonight, see?' I point excitedly at it. 'This has given me a great idea.'

The rest of the way back to the villa, Gerry and I hatch our plan. Because the motocross didn't work out as well as we hoped, then perhaps Plan B, our singing in public, might prove to be the way to remind him who he is and who he needs to get back to.

THIRTY-ONE

Friday Night – The Plan

I won't lie – I'm nervous and excited about tonight. This could be a big moment in Jake's recovery, or that's what I'm hoping. That doing something we used to do back when, something might unlock and take him back to the Jake who loves performing. I know he won't be able to play the guitar again, but still. Right when I'm putting the finishing touches to my makeup, Angie knocks on my bedroom door and without waiting for an answer, comes right in and plonks herself down next to me on my bed. (I'll bet Carol would have a field day about boundaries.)

'I've come to wish you good luck, and to say that I do hope you have a good time tonight. You and Jake – the Dynamic Duo.' She gives me a deep look. 'I know he's not Jake – not my Jake – not your Jake either for that matter.' I'm holding my breath. 'You know what I'm saying, don't you? Don't expect too much, because he's somebody else now.'

I'm not sure where all this is going. 'He's a different yet still very nice man,' she continues. 'It's really important you hear what I'm saying before you put too high expectations on him. I'm trying my very best to fall in love with this new Jake, and I think you should too – well, not fall in love, but you know what I mean.' She wipes her nose with a tissue. 'It's not that I've given up on him, because I haven't. We both took our vows seriously when we promised for richer or poorer, in sickness and in health. We meant and plan to keep those vows, even though it might not be fashionable, and some people might not.' Is she having a dig at me?

'And... well... me and Jake, we have to find our own way, is what I'm saying.' She looks down at a crumpled tissue nestled in her lap. 'We have to find our own way through this, and you have to let him go – let go of the old Jake. If anything, this holiday has shown me that you're not ready to let him be the person he's going to be, but you must, even if that means you lose what it means to be twins.'

'Right.' I'm not quite sure what else to say. She's rather taken the wind out of my sails with this new bluntness, and I'm thinking how she can do what she wants, but I know Jake and I'm not as ready as she is to give up on him. 'Right you are,' is all I can manage.

'Well,' she says, getting to her feet, 'I'm glad we've had this chat. And I do hope that you two have a lovely time tonight. I'm sure it'll be good for Jake – and for you – to spend some quality time on your own, before we all return back to our lives. Do remember what I said, okay? Don't expect too much of him, or you'll be setting him up to fail, and that won't be good for his confidence at all, will it?'

A not very nice part of me is thinking who is she to tell me what to do? I'm his twin. Doesn't that count for anything? I'm planning on boosting his confidence by getting him singing. Does she even know my brother at all? Is she perhaps enjoying having the upper hand on Jake? He was always the more dominant one in their relationship. Or was he? Perhaps it was always her? I shake my head, tousle my hair, and am ready to go out and spend the evening with my brother.

'You ready, Jake?' I call, as I stand waiting for him at the bottom of the stairs, nervously shifting from one foot to the other. I'm glad I had this brilliant idea of me and Jake going on our own to this karaoke night without Angie, who would pour cold water on things. Just me and Jake, the two of us. Twins singing together on stage like we used to before she came along. The leaflet says there's prize money – which would be a bonus.

'Daddy's nearly ready,' says Sarah as she sticks her head around the corner of her bedroom door. 'He won't be long,' she adds, with that exasperated sigh she's adopted of late when addressing me. Sudden squeals announce Lauren tearing across the landing, dragging Finty along, followed by Gerry and Angie in hot pursuit.

'C'mere, you little monsters,' says Gerry, as he bundles them both into his arms, one either side, and then stops, on noticing me. 'You look nice,' he says, looking down the stairs at me, and I'm glad to be wearing my new floaty Jigsaw dress which I brought along especially for a night out. Topped with my black leather biker's jacket (no irony intended).

'Ta da!' announces Angie. 'Here he is!'

And there he is indeed. My brother Jake. Wearing a floppy white shirt open at the neck. (Setting off the nut-brown colour he's nicely gone in the sun. He always could tan better than me.) Somehow he's squeezed into a pair of slim jeans which I've not seen him wear before, and on his feet are a new pair of brown brogues. *Stylish*, I think. His hair's suitably zhooshed with gel, and he's looking like a not bad, if slightly wonky, version of himself. Holding on to the bannister, he jerkily negotiates his way down the stairs.

'Looking good, bruv,' I say.

'Are you ready, Ronica?' he says, carefully enunciating each word and offering me his arm.

'Sure am,' looping mine through his.

Angie calls, 'You two have a good time.' And when I glance up, it's quite the tableau: Gerry with Finty on his hip, his other hand resting on the top of Lauren's head while Sarah holds her mother's hand as they stand alongside him, both Angie and Gerry looking for all the world like parents waving their big kids off for a big night out.

I've guessed that Angie may well have designs on Gerry, yet – oh, what the hell. *They either will, or they won't,* I mentally shrug to myself.

'We'll try not to be late, Mummy and Daddy,' I call – jokily – up the stairs.

Jake and I step into the darkened bar of the Hotel Bretagne, then pause to get our bearings. The back room is all brown wood and swirly carpet. Tired red leatherette chairs are teamed with small round rickety-looking tables on which scattered beermats advertise French beer, Pernod, Remy Martin and Carling Black Label. It's easy to spot the British holidaymakers: the women with their sunburnt shoulders and clearly defined white strap marks, their ruddy made-up faces shining as if internally afire with radioactivity, white sunglasses marks giving the impression of nuked racoons; the men fiery-faced with sun and beer, most in shorts and sandals – their legs of varying hues from white to pink through to brown, depending on skin tone and exposure to rays. *There's an air of a rugby club night about it,* I think, remembering ones I've been to in the past with Jake, and then later with Jake and Angie.

One of the men – forty-something, buttons of white shirt straining to contain his beer belly – detaches himself from a group to make a beeline for us.

'Y'all right, Jake.' He slaps him on the back, nearly sending him flying, and is rewarded with a dazzling grin from my brother.

'This your bit on the side, is it?' he says, giving Jake a dig in the ribs. 'Only she's not your wife, is she?' He's all bluff and warm smiles. 'Don't worry lass. I met young laddo here at the Intasun barbecue. My name's Martin.'

'Pleased to meet you,' I say. 'I'm Veronica, Jake's twin sister.'

'Fancy that – you don't look alike!'

I smile politely as Martin calls over his wife for introductions.

'You remember Jake, don't you, love?'

Jake pulls himself up straighter and smooths his hair.

'My wife Pam,' Martin introduces her. 'This here's Jake's twin sister Veronica.'

'Lovely to meet you,' says Pam as she kisses me on one cheek. 'And yes, Martin,' she says, giving her husband a playful shove. 'Of course I remember Jake.' Pam has the leathery skin of someone who regularly travels to sunny climes and lathers themselves in Johnson's Baby Oil. 'How are you, lovey?' she asks Jake, who's absorbed in his pint.

'Dis beer not bad,' he manages. 'Is dat whassaname.' He vaguely gesticulates towards the pint – I guess he's trying to say it's some English beer or other.

'Veronica.' Martin turns to me. 'That's a big name for such a small girl, isn't it? Shall we call you Vee? Or how about Vera? We thought you were his fancy woman when you first came in – good-looking lad like him.'

Jake's positively preening at the compliment.

'Stop embarrassing the lad,' says Pam giving her husband a slap on the arm. 'Don't mind him, Jake, he's only teasing. Sorry,' she adds, looking at me. 'I didn't quite catch your name.'

'It's Ronnie,' I say. (No-one's going to call me Vera.) 'Short for Veronica.'

'That's an unusual name.' She's giving me an up and down appraisal. 'Well then, Ronnie, don't you take no notice of Martin. He means no harm.' She turns to her husband. 'Get another round in, love. Mine's a vodka tonic. How about you two?'

I try to demur, but she's having none of it, and after she places our orders with her husband, he heads off to the bar with Jake in tow. Pam leads me across to her group – 'Budge up,' she orders, as they make way. Someone fetches two extra seats. 'Sit down, love, sit down. This is nice, isn't it?'

I smile and nod. Don't be such a snob. They seem really nice and friendly people.

Pam leans forward. 'Must be hard for his wife, mustn't it?'

'Sorry?'

'Jake's wife. Must be dreadful for her.'

My mouth goes dry. Here we go. Glancing over at the bar, I will the men to return quickly with the drinks. I could do with a strong slug of vodka myself. I try willing Jake to hurry and return and… well… let's just say our connection these days suffers too many short-outs. Any case, Jake's whole attention appears to be taken up by Martin as he focuses on him and his anecdotes, face all open and eager.

Angie's right: I should not expect too much of Jake. Look at him, it's good to see him enjoying himself. But Pam is still rattling on. About… 'I can't imagine how horrible it must be for her,' Pam is continuing. 'One day she – you know, Jake's wife – has this this handsome – well, I can see that he was handsome… once…' Inside I flinch, but she's not noticing any change in me, and carries on: '…then the next thing – wham! And everything's changed in an instant.' She clicks her fingers together. 'Poor woman. I don't know how she copes…'

'She loves him very much is how,' I mutter.

'Yes, but…' Pam glances over at the bar, where the men are now preparing to return. 'For how long, though, hm? I mean, it's a lot to ask, isn't it, to stay with someone when they're like that? You don't expect, when you pledge in sickness and in health, that it's ever going to be this bad, do you?' She tapped her head. 'Seems to have made him a bit of a retard. This motorbike accident.'

I'm dying inside.

'I understand he used to be a teacher.' She drops her voice in a conspiratorial way. How I wish she'd shut up. 'Such a shame,' she continues. 'Your poor parents an' all. They still alive, are they?'

'Yes.' I'm barely whispering now. I'm not going to divulge that Mum has all but disappeared into an alcoholic haze, or that Dad frequently drives up to visit Jake and family – desperate to be near but generally getting in the way, trying to secure a connection to his son with the bits of DIY which Jake can no longer manage, or trying to be helpful by taking Jake to the pub to give Angie some respite. I'm not going to tell this woman – who I'm sure is well meaning – but still... Now she's prattling on about not being sure she could handle it – if Martin was to become an invalid.

Sometimes Mum accompanies Dad on his visits, but more often than not, her poodle gives her an excuse not to go and face the wreck which is now her son. Her beautiful, broken son. The jury's still out on whether its best she doesn't go, get maudlin and sozzled in some corner (because Jake and her weren't talking prior to the accident) or whether it's best she stays away until she can find the strength to see him without wallowing in her own grief and guilt. Frankly, it's hard to tell which is best.

Pam has said something and is clearly waiting for some kind of answer from me.

'Sorry? I didn't catch that.'

'I said – and not being funny or cruel here – but perhaps it would have been better all-round if he'd died. Don't you think?' She stares hard at me. 'For him too,' she adds. 'I know I wouldn't like to end up like that.'

'Bloody Nora, Pam!' says Martin, who's arrived a little ahead of Jake and has clearly overheard. Carefully he places their drinks on the table. 'Bit harsh, love. They are twins, you know.'

He nods in my direction and then at Jake, as I manage a weak smile.

'No offence,' she says, beaming at Jake, who stands by the table as if seeking permission to sit. 'You all right, Jake, love? Park your bum here, why don't you?'

I do my best to be phlegmatic, even upbeat, about it all (it's mere ignorance on their part; they mean no ill). As the night continues with its drunken revelry Martin and Pam get up – about three karaoke numbers in – to sing "Islands in the Sun" to each other. She's no Dolly Parton and is woefully out of tune, but he has a pleasant-enough voice. I've already looked at the song menu with Jake, and it's a no-brainer what to choose.

The compere is on her feet. 'Next up,' she says, 'we have a brother and sister act. In fact, they're *twins*.'

'Yay!' The audience cheer as if we've done something amazing.

'Give it up for Jake and Ronnie! The Jackson twins!'

Booze has loosened up the audience, and the applause is warming – it gets louder and even involves a whoop or two – as Jake rises shakily to his feet and begins his lopsided, juddering walk to the stage. Eyes straight ahead in his man-on-a-mission mode. Pam is giving me a thumbs-up then pulls me aside so she can stage-whisper in my ear, 'Hope he doesn't muck up any of the words.'

'Don't worry,' I say. Because I know what she clearly doesn't, that even though he has limited word retrieval, song lyrics remain embedded – pretty much intact – in his memory banks. Something to do with songs involving the whole brain. Well, that's the latest theory. I suspect that song lyrics are stored in a some separate, more accessible part of the brain. Whatever.

It confuses people that, although he can recall and sing clearly the words of a song, this does not mean his speech is improving or will improve if he keeps on singing. Sadly, we know this. Because we've tried.

The indisputable fact that Jake can, and does, fish the right nouns from his own skittering-about-noun-fishpond-of-a-brain is neither here nor there. Singing songs will not improve his speech – a concept that our father still can't grasp, as each time Jake sings, it brings a tear to Dad's eye and a conviction that this must be evidence of Jake being "on the road to recovery". Cue metaphors of journeys, struggles, battles, we'll-win-in-the-end, etc., etc., heard them all – been there, come back with the T-shirt. "Veronica went to the hospital and all she brought back were these lousy platitudes" emblazoned on my chest.

Ahhh, brain injuries – full of false starts and blind alleys, and blips.

On stage, I take one of the two mikes then mouth, 'Ready?' to Jake and, once satisfied, nod to the organiser, who switches on our track.

The chords of an acoustic guitar ring out clear and sharp as a bright April day, and Jake lifts his head. Once he starts to sing, the bar is preternaturally quiet. You could hear a pin or plectrum drop, as his softly seductive, even-better-than-sweet-baby-James-Taylor's voice fills the air as he begins the opening line of "You've Got a Friend". I stand, waiting for my Carole King entrance. I'm not bad either.

Shoulder to shoulder we perform in the spotlight, the rest of the room retreating into the brown haze of any folk club or music bar in the world. The audience, the now, the sorrow, slip away…

The first time we sing this together is in the downstairs bar of the Hawthorn Hotel in Bristol. It has a small or "intimate" bar with a small stage, which every Wednesday has a folk club night.

Jake and I spent the afternoon practising in his bedroom.

'Shut that noise up!' Mum calls up the stairs. 'You're giving me one of my headaches.' So we shut the bedroom door, wait until we hear she's gone back into the lounge and then begin all over again. This time quieter. Over and over we work the harmonies – Jake playing his acoustic guitar – until we're sure we're spot on.

That night at the Hawthorn there are many dreamy-eyed girls when Jake sings, and he's discovered the power of the guitar to seduce. He cops off with a gorgeous willowy blonde in bare feet, a see-through cheesecloth top and flowers woven into her hair. 'See you later, sis.' He grins as they roar off into the night on the back of his BSA motorbike, leaving a strong whiff of her patchouli oil in their wake. She's going to freeze, *I think,* even in that Afghan goat-smelling coat of hers.

I don't do too badly either by getting right and royally fucked in the hotel gardens – up against a big old tree – by Paul Wolf (one of the hottest and wolfish boys in Bristol). He has a chunky cock and is quick and hard. He doesn't take my number, and I don't expect him to. Hey, that's show-business.

Now, up on stage singing, I can make out Xavier moving near to the front of the stage. I nearly falter as I think of my sexual shenanigans with him. But I lift my head to sing out, and Jake and I finish the song. The crowd erupt – 'More! More!' – as I glance across at Jake, and he gives me a thumbs-up.

'More!' The throng are still insisting. Xavier is clapping and giving me a Gallic shrug in his very French way. I look over to the organiser as she walks across to us. 'Yes, please do another.'

'Thank you. You okay with that, Jake?'

He smiles and nods. 'Yes,' he manages.

'Do you have "Will You Still Love Me Tomorrow"?'

The organiser's forehead crinkles in a look of concern. 'Um… no… we don't… um.'

'Do not worry,' calls out Xavier, who is holding a guitar case.

He climbs onto the stage and gives Jake a nod. 'I hope you will allow me to play this song for you, *mon ami*?'

Jake looks at me, and I shrug: why not? The organiser seems flustered, so Xavier takes charge and says something in French to her. Dressed in jeans and a leather jacket he moves about the stage, light as a jaguar, and sets about his business, plugging his guitar lead into the PA system and checking the levels. Pretty soon he is tuning up, and before anyone can step in and say enough's enough or what the frick are you doing with your would-be seducer, Ron, the organiser has moved back to the wings and Xavier gestures that he's ready when we are. A cheer goes up from the people crowded around the stage as Xav smiles his enigmatic yet sexy smile at me, and a thrill hits my stomach. 'You're sure you're okay with this?' I say, at the same time deciding to forgive and forget. It's that kind of forgiving night, and with a quick stride I give him a fleeting embrace (I don't want him to get the wrong idea).

'Thank you,' I whisper in his ear. 'It means a lot to Jake.'

He nods and starts up the first chord.

As Jake and I harmonise, I catch Xavier's eye – the words of "Will You Still Love Me Tomorrow" not entirely lost on him. *Ah, life*, I think, *so full of woes – you have to take your joy where you can.* I sing of moment's treasures and pleasures, words unspoken, hearts broken – and how it's kind of all right. Standing tall, singing out and letting the words flow, it's almost like the old days when Jake and I sang in folk clubs and bars. Together, in harmony, like we're any normal duo. When we're done and come off stage, I say, 'That was great, bro.' And he says, 'Yes. It was, sis.' He's not called me sis since the accident. I'm following him back to our seats when Xavier catches up to us.

'Veronique. Ssh. Come with me – *maintenant.*'

Jake gestures that he'll be okay, and Xavier pulls me into a corridor where people are coming and going, squeezing past.

He takes me round a corner and outside into the alley out back, where he kisses me. Deep, passionate, hungry kisses. For a moment I kiss him back – high on adrenaline which makes me want to fuck him. His caress sneaks up my thigh when someone bursts through the back door, drunkenly staggers, and calls out, 'Sorry. Sorry, mate. Didn't mean to disturb,' then lumbers back in again.

I pull away. The moment well and truly lost, thank goodness.

THIRTY-TWO

Friday Night, Continued

Back at the villa, Gerry is gently peeling Angie from around his neck. She has surprised him by launching herself at him as they were relaxing over a bottle of wine, and now she pulls back to stare challengingly at him.

'We can all see what's going on between Ron and that French bloke, so why shouldn't we get comfort from one another? I fancy you, and I'm pretty sure that's mutual, the amount of time you spend with me. I've seen you looking.'

Gerry pushes her away. 'Whether I do or not, Angie, I am not going to act on it. Besides, you're married to Jake, and in any case,' he looks at her so she can see the sincerity in his face, 'Veronica and I may have had our wobbles – but that's all in the past, now. And that includes her flirting with Xavier. We're back on track now and solid, stronger than ever, even. And, although I am very flattered...'

'Yes, well.' Angie sets about lighting a cigarette. 'I'm sorry if I made an idiot of myself. It won't happen again.'

'You're feeling vulnerable, that's all,' he says as he moves to reassure her. 'We'll say no more about it.'

But she launches herself at him again.

*

'Your husband. He is a very lucky man,' says Xavier as he offers me a cigarette which I take, and we light both light up as we lean side by side against the wall, then inhale and blow smoke up into the night air. I say nothing to that. There's nothing much to say.

'You have a beautiful voice,' he adds, throwing his cigarette to the ground. '*Ma chere*, I am sorry about your brother. The life, *oui*? Sometimes she is not fair.' He rests his back against the wall. Turning to face me, I'm aware of his height towering over me. 'I shall think of you with fond memories.'

I groan. 'Oh, Xavier...' Part of me is thinking, *If only*. But my life is too full of if onlys already. Indeed, I am squashed under the weight of them, of the missed opportunities, the possibilities lost, the if only I'd done this, gone there – been free... But I'm not.

'Veronique. You are ze very sexy lady.'

No. No more with the French clichés, Ron. He's a slightly ageing lothario, isn't he? On the lookout for a holiday bunk-up. Why pretend it's anything else? Why do you have to over-glamorise everything? Right now your twin is back in the bar, probably wondering where you've disappeared to; your husband is back at the villa keeping an eye on your child and hoping we can patch things up. Whilst you? Just what are you doing?

With fresh eyes I notice how we're standing next to the hotel's bins. Next to where the waste food is dumped, to where rats rummage for scraps and where – if this was television – some prostitute would be getting murdered, or some jack-the-lad knifed by a gang member.

'I must go,' I say. 'And truly, Xavier. Thank you for coming to our rescue. With your guitar, this time.' He says nothing, the light from an open back door highlighting those high cheekbones. 'You know, I am sorry that Gerry punched you.'

He rubs his jaw as if at the memory, then he gives me a wry smile plus a salute. '*Au revoir*, Veronique,' he says, and I'm grateful there's some regret in his voice.

I make my way back to the door back of the hotel only to walk smack bang straight into bedlam!

Martin is standing in between Jake and another man up at the bar – a small clutch of men gathered around them. There's an overturned stool, and the man is pointing at Jake and shouting, 'Fuckin' mong,' at him. I push through until I'm at my brother's side.

'What's going on?'

'It's all right,' Martin addresses me. 'Take a step back, mate,' he says to the man.

'Tell that twat here to apologise to my bird – or so help me – spastic or not, I'll lamp him!' snarls the man.

'Fuck's sake – he didn't mean nuffin,' says Martin. 'Look at him! He's bleedin' harmless!'

'Could be a nonce for all we know! Fuckin' spaz!'

Jake appears beyond confused. Without thinking I step in and give the man a hard slap across his angry face. 'Don't you ever – ever! – say anything like that to my brother!'

He looks as if he's going to leap at me when Martin – quick as a flash – has the man pinned by the arms. 'Leave it. Bloody fuckin' calm down. Right?'

And now Pam is wading in. She has Jake by the shoulder, ushering him out of harm's way. 'Ought to be ashamed of yourself,' she calls back at the man. Then, turning to me, she adds, 'Good for you, Vera. I'd have slapped him myself if I'd been any closer. Fuckin' muppet.'

Jake, now safely ensconced at our table, is supping from his beer and happily looking about him as if the scene had never happened.

'What was all that about?' I demand as Martin returns to his seat, having defused the situation by buying a pint for the disgruntled man (who turns out to be his cousin). I never did see the girlfriend in question.

'Oh, somethin' and nothin'.' Martin looks shifty, though.

'Go on,' I say. 'You can tell me. It's best I know.'

Jake isn't paying any attention and is now fiddling with the buttons on his shirt – this can fully occupy him for minutes if not a whole hour.

'Well,' begins Martin as he glances uncertainly at Jake. Pam takes a sip of her vodka tonic, looking as if what her husband will have to say will not be news to her.

From what I can gather Jake was standing at the bar, surrounded by well-wishers congratulating him on his turn, when one of the women was telling anyone who'd listen that her husband had bought her a pair of boobs for their fifteenth wedding anniversary. She'd been flashing them about, inviting the other women to cop a feel, saying that they felt "dead natural". This was all happening in front of Jake when – 'Clearly egged on by that stupid cow,' Pam says – he decided to have a feel for himself. That was when it all kicked off.

'Honestly,' says Pam, 'if she didn't want the attention then she shouldn't have shown them off like that.' She must have seen my crestfallen face. 'Oh, don't you worry, dear. It's perfectly clear that your brother meant no harm. Look at him, poor thing.'

Soon after, we make our excuses – even though we were probably in the running for the prize money – and head back for the villa. There's still some light left in the sky as I lead the way down to the beach and we decide to walk back along the shore. (When I say we decide – it's me, really, because Jake still seems incapable of initiating anything much.) Overhead the darkening sky is a photographic negative of the day as if washed with teal: large clouds clumped near the horizon like humpbacked beasts crouched by a watering hole. On the air there's a whiff of rotting sea creatures and seaweed, whilst the sky has an open acoustic feel as if its dome has been raised causing sound to have a minor reverb. I'm aware of the bustling noise of bars, cafes, restaurants, floating in sound bubbles beneath the top note of a whistling breeze blowing in off an inky sea. All slightly changed and other-worldly.

'Was good fun,' says Jake. We're strolling side by side, me wondering whether he remembers the fight in the bar at all, and whether tonight has reminded him at all of who he used to be.

'Except for that woman whose breasts you felt,' I remind him, and then can't help grinning as it was pretty comical.

'Yeah?' His eyebrows shoot up in clear surprise and he shakes his head.

'Oh, never mind.' I give him what I hope is a reassuring smile. 'The karaoke was fun, though, wasn't it? You and me. Singing away like the old days.' I can't see him clearly as a cloud has passed over the face of a weakly glowing moon.

'Veb the dingle brush,' he says, shaking his head as if trying to remove a wasp from his hair.

'Don't you remember our singing?' I stop, and he stops too – not looking at me but out to sea.

'Where's Angie?' It's almost a whisper.

I swallow hard as there's a lump in my throat, because I'm reminded how much I don't know who this person is that he's become. I blink hard. *It's as if...* I think, as I turn to view his silhouette in the dark... *No, it is.* It really is as if some mischievous fairies stole my twin away and replaced him with this muddle-headed version. There, I've said it. (Well, thought it.)

He turns to face me as if I've interrupted his thoughts – whatever they might be. Does he think in the same way he used to? Just how can you articulate even internally, whatever it is you are feeling, if you can't find the right nouns?

'It's late,' I say. 'We'd better get a move on.'

And so we trudge along sand chilled by the night air – side by side – until: 'Did you know,' I say, plonking myself down on the slope of a sand dune and turning my gaze up to a star-studded sky. 'That a single grain of sand contains more atoms than there are stars in the known universe?'

'No.' Jake stands alongside, in his stiff and awkward way. 'I didn't know that.'

'Yes, you did. You told me that fact, you plonker.' In the dark when light plays tricks he still seems like my brother. I peer out to sea, wondering and waiting.

'I did?'

'Yes, you did. And you also said that all of our atoms – yours and mine – everyone and everything, everywhere – were originally created in the centre of a star.'

He starts to sing Joni Mitchell's "Woodstock", about us being stardust. As he sings up, I try and join in.

'No. Dat wrong – it golden.'

I try again.

'Wubbish,' he says.

'Fuck off.'

'No, you fuck off.'

We're more at ease with each other, smiling affectionately in an echo of our old selves. Maybe his atoms only need realigning, and that's all. Maybe he's somehow got himself configured into a different universe with his own changed stars and solar systems. Maybe he just needs to find his way back home.

What? Like he's lost in space, Ron? You idiot.

'Danger, danger, Will Robinson,' I say out loud, doing the robot arm actions. Jake turns slowly, taking care not to overbalance. A glimmer of recognition on his face. We used to love that TV programme when we were kids. I hold both arms out for him to pull me to my feet, which he manages without any toppling.

'You fuck man with guitar?' he says when I'm finally up.

'No,' I say, brushing down my skirt. 'Well, almost. But, no.'

'Good.' He stands still, and I wait. 'We go home?' he says, a weary tone to his voice.

'Home,' I say, wondering what and where that is. I let out a big sigh. 'I guess for now, back to the villa will have to do.'

Jake puts his arm out as a barrier to stop me.

'What is it, bruv?'

'It's not your fault,' he says.

'What isn't?'

'Nuffing.'

Arm in arm once more, we set off like two lost children, or like Dorothy and the Scarecrow who doesn't have a brain. On past a couple of youngsters huddled around a campfire, where we pause. The boy starts to strum his guitar, the girl starts dancing, and me and Jake stand gazing into the warm night.

THIRTY-THREE

Friday Night Still

*G*rowing up, we did everything together: me and Jake, Jake and
*me. We'd hide under the stairs with our secret pretend radio
and be members of British Intelligence working with the French
Resistance sending brave messages back to Blighty in Morse code
(which we'd learned via Dad's* Pears' Cyclopaedia*); we'd listen out
for the tread of jack-booted Nazis intent on discovering our hiding
place. Or the two of us would take shelter in the attic where Mum
kept her costumes and ball gowns from the days when she "could
have been someone" in Rep, if only she hadn't fallen pregnant with
twins and "had" to marry Dad. Or else we'd snuggle under the
blankets in my bed which was slightly bigger and had a softer
mattress, and we'd read comics and munch Jammie Dodgers by
the light of Jake's small torch (bought specially for a cub scout trip
to Simmonds Yat), and we'd giggle and tell stupid jokes: 'Why did
the elephant paint his toenails yellow?' 'Why?' 'So he could hide
in a bowl of custard!' 'Ha ha' – poke in the ribs. 'What do you
call a scared biscuit?' 'A cowardy custard cream.' 'Doh!' Chinese
Burn. 'What's black and white and red all over.' 'That's easy – a
newspaper.' 'No! A penguin in a liquidiser!' Thump.*

*Yes, we did most things together – back when we were children.
And that day when the marram grass was wafting in a stiff sea*

breeze off the Bristol Channel as Slimy Bob adjusted his trousers, and Mum pulled her dress down and clambered to her feet, I did my best to keep Jake out of it.

'It's not what you think,' Mum said to me, later. But of course, it was.

I blamed myself when our parents split – in the way that kids do, and I tried my best to protect Jake. 'Where's Mum?' he asked, after she'd left for her sister's to "sort things out".

'Don't worry,' I said. 'It'll be all right.' And that appeared to be enough for him.

The time she was away were our limbo months, when Dad cried and cried – I'd never seen him cry before and it scared me – and I tried to keep Jake busy. If I think back it's rather sketchy, but I can recall standing at the sink with the help of a low stool, trying to get on with the washing up, doing my best to make beans on toast or boiled eggs and soldiers for tea, helping Dad change the bedclothes (a job he normally did with Mum). Somehow the absence of Mum's cottage pie, homemade chips and Sunday roast were more keenly felt than her not physically being there. I can see now that it was too much for a girl of ten to take on. But what else could I do? Dad insisted that if anyone ask, we say Mum has gone to visit her sick sister – he was too ashamed to tell anyone she'd walked out on him – on us.

I did my best to comfort Jake, who'd always been Mum's favourite, by telling him she'd be home soon when I didn't know if this was so, and by snuggling under the bedcovers with him and sleeping in his bed so we could hold each other tight as we drifted off to sleep. I'd make up stories to keep the nothingness at bay, because we'd abandoned our childish talks of what it was like before we existed, and what would it be like when we're dead, and whether there are such things as ghosts, and everything else that small children with big imaginations talk about to scare each other and delight in their own feelings of being safe at home in their own beds. Now, the harsh, bleak reality of a universe which didn't care, one which was random and governed by numbers and equations, was no longer a delicious conundrum to explore. Instead we consoled ourselves with reading Pan Book of Horror Stories *collections, and Dennis Wheatley novels, and the newly discovered, slightly racy* James Bond *ones with their rather thrilling and racy dot-dot-dots... Squee! We'd both squeal together. 'Dot dot dot!'*

Then two days before Christmas – when it seemed as if Christmas was going to have to be cancelled due to the absence of Mum – she was back. As if nothing had happened. That is, if you didn't notice that slightly brittle edge to her voice, and Dad's puppy-dog eyes which followed her around the room. She arrived with her arms full of shopping bags which we weren't allowed to look in (clearly full of our presents), and with a basket bursting with new Christmas decorations – all sparkles, spangles and glitz. 'Where's the tree?' she asked. Then, seeing how Dad hadn't bought one yet, she ushered us all into his Ford Zodiac and Dad – now a little lighter of spirit after some hugging and shy kissing of his returned wife – drove us all to Old Market for late-night shopping and the buying of the tree. It was very nearly like every Christmas before, except for that wariness, and for Jake surreptitiously glancing up every now and then to check that Lily was still there. She laughed like tinkly tinsel as she pulled us in for a hug. 'Oh, I've missed you twins,' she said in a jolly voice and then propelled us towards our special Christmas-shopping treat. The man selling chestnuts roasted on a big old rusting brazier. The sweet, pungent smell of chestnuts would mingle with a dark, clear sky, signalling Christmas. Or had done. I was in a sulk – not ready to fully let her off the hook yet.

'Here,' she said, passing me the cone-shaped white paper bag. 'They're hot, mind.' I took them without meeting her eyes. 'Thanks.' Keeping my own gaze firmly on the ground.

She scooched down next to me and said in a low voice, 'Don't spoil it, Veronica. There's a good girl.'

Of course, we paper over those cracks don't we, until one day, one glorious April day, it all comes tumbling down and no-one can put it back together again. She blames me. I know Gerry thinks I'm being stupid and she's my mother so she can't possibly blame me – but I know for a fact she does. She told me one day when we were all at the hospital, a few days after Jake's accident. Mum already distraught because she'd fallen out with Jake – she was for ever falling out with one or other of us over some trivial thing or such. Drinking made her paranoid. Invariably Jake and I would team up and one of us would apologise for some imagined slight. Her social drinking – once a source of parties and fun – had got out of hand. She was fond of schooners of sherry and tall glasses of supposed orange squash which in reality contained a stiff amount of vodka. Dad singing "Lily of Laguna", and of how she was his lily and his love.

So, Mum and Jake had a falling-out the Christmas before his accident, and she'd decided it was my fault. And it kind of had been because I'd let slip what happened on that day in the dunes at Brean, and Jake had telephoned Mum to remonstrate with her and – well… words were said, until they were no longer speaking.

Back to that day in the hospital, when there was only me and her in the relatives' room, she said in a low voice, 'I blame you, you know. It's your fault Jake and I aren't speaking, and now look what's happened. Your fault.' Then, quick as a flash, she painted her smile back on as a nurse entered the room. 'Cup of tea, Mrs Johnson?' she said.

'Thank you, dear. Oh, don't mind my daughter,' she said, nodding over to where I was now crying. 'She's only just had a baby.' She lowered her voice. 'Hormones.'

Once the nurse left, Mum came over to sit next to me and enveloped me in a hug. 'I'm sorry, Ron,' she said. 'It's the shock. I don't mean it. There, there.'

But we both knew she did mean it.

THIRTY-FOUR

End of Friday

The downstairs of the villa is in darkness as we enter through the back door and I fumble around for the light switch.

Jake overtakes me. 'Night night,' he says as he heads towards the stairs.

'Hm? Oh, yes. Good night,' I call after him as I fill the kettle from the tap. 'Don't let the bed bugs bite!' I call, but already he's gone. No hanging about, no chatting over the evening. I wish he'd stay because I miss post-mortems after a night out. I'm left feeling rather deflated as the earlier excitement of singing on stage with Jake is fading away.

Well, there we are then, I think, as I fill the kettle and allow my gaze to wander out the kitchen window. Tonight was hardly the triumphant return to form I'd foolishly been hoping for, was it?

Behind me there's a noise, and turning I see Gerry in his boxer shorts with his hair all tousled. 'Ahhh,' he yawns. 'Must have nodded off before I heard you come in.' He crosses the floor to hold me – he smells all cosy and sleepy. 'Mm, I've missed you,' he mumbles into my shoulder. His voice is kinda sexy. 'Good night, was it?'

I give a non-committal hm as I allow myself to relax into him, savouring the salty smell of his body, feeling the heat of sunburn radiating off him. He begins to caress me, his touch smooth on my skin and his semi-arousal pressed up against me.

'Whoah, not so fast,' I say, easing away from him. 'Sorry, but... can we talk a bit before going upstairs? Only tonight's been *really* weird.'

'Sure,' he says as the kettle switches itself off with a click, sounding extra loud in the night-time kitchen.

Fetching his jumper from where he left it on the back of a chair, he pulls open the fridge. 'I'm guessing our plan backfired, did it?' he says, reaching for a chilled bottle of beer. 'So, come on then,' he says as he expertly knocks the top off his Budweiser on the corner of the worksurface. 'What happened at the karaoke?' Swig. 'Did our grand plan not work? The one of giving Jake something tangible to do? To help remind him of who he used to be?' Rubbing his bare belly before pulling on the sweater, I notice how tanned he is, and how toned. He's almost got a six-pack. Now concentrate.

'The karaoke started off well.' I go to make myself tea. 'But then... No, it's fair to say it didn't work out – not really.'

'Oh dear. But how about the prize money? Did you win, or not, is that it?'

'No, it wasn't about the competition,' I say, flopping down on a kitchen chair, and spilling my newly brewed tea, which I then wipe with a cloth. 'In fact, we ended up leaving before they announced the winners. Bit like leaving Dodge in a hurry, kind of thing.' He's looking puzzled. 'Oh, do sit down, Ger. You're making the place look untidy.'

He takes the seat opposite and glugs some beer.

'I've also been thinking...' I start, 'that it might be time we paid Mum and Dad a visit?'

'What, seriously? I'm not so sure.' He wiped his mouth with the back of his hand. 'Of course, it's entirely up to you, and I will go along with whatever you decide, but I can't say I'm overly keen. Not after the way your mother treated you when she lashed out at the hospital. Blaming you for Jake's accident was a new low for her. Even before that she could hardly be bothered with us, could she? Remember when they came to meet our new baby? She didn't even want to pick her up. Huh? What sort of grandmother is that?'

'I hear what you're saying' (*Carol's tutelage is not entirely lost on me*) 'but somebody has to start building bridges and I don't see anyone else volunteering.' I rub my left foot, which is aching something chronic, and slip it back in its shoe. 'God only knows what I'd be like if anything happened to Fints or any of our future children. None of us do.'

Gerry narrows his eyes. 'All I'm saying is, there's no way you'd be anywhere near as cruel as she has. No matter what. It's just not in you.'

'But what if it is? I worry about the whole mother passing on traumas to daughter scenario, and I'd like to break that chain, and be forgiving, not only about Mum leaving us when we were kids, but also for her affair – if it was an affair...' I'm thinking of what happened with Xavier and wonder if Gerry is, too. 'Bottom line is that she's Finty's grandmother and the only mum I've got.'

'And what about your father? Where does he fit in all of this? He's not once tried to intervene when he could have, and I'd say when he should have! Shall we forgive him, too?'

I sigh. 'He only ever follows Mum's lead, you know that. But he'll definitely want us to get along.' Gerry waits for me to continue. 'I see it more now that I'm a mother. How they think of Jake as their baby – the whole youngest child thing. I guess whatever their age, our kids remain our babies...'

'Okay, okay. If you're sure this is what you want, then we'll contact them once we're home.' His voice is kind, and I peer up at him under my eyelashes.

'It wasn't only Jake who got broken that day,' I say.

'I know, I know, but remember what Carol said? It's still early days, and both you and Angie are currently stuck somewhere between the denial and anger stages? And that acceptance is a while off yet.' He gives me an apologetic shrug. 'I read a book on it.'

It's such a Gerry thing to do, I think, fondly.

'I tell you what, though, for what it's worth,' he continues, giving a little cough and straightening up. 'I think it will help no end if you and me talk to each other far more – pretty much like we're doing now?'

A faint memory is surfacing – isn't that more or less what Jake once said? *The trouble with you two is you don't talk?*

'You might be surprised to discover,' Gerry is saying, 'that I'm a pretty good listener – for a bloke.' He gives me a wry smile. 'But, hey, we're doing okay, aren't we? Look at how far we've come in just this week.' He starts ticking them off on his fingers. 'We've agreed to be more open and honest with each other. I've told you about Hilary, and you let me know about being pounced on by that French bloke—'

'What a couple of numpties we've been,' I mumble as I search for a tissue.

Gerry is giving me an inscrutable look as he places his beer on the table. 'Now don't go mad,' he starts. 'But seeing as we're getting things out in the open...'

'Go on.'

'Angie made a pass at me this evening.' He spread his hands in a "wasn't-me" pose.

I examine my feelings – am I angry? No, not really. I'm too worn out to be bothered with Angie's shenanigans anymore. 'Funnily enough,' I finally say, while outside the dark is gathering to a deep black velvet, and the possibility of a thunderstorm slicks the air with its fizz of electricity. 'I'm not cross with her, or with you. Although…' I pause. 'I must say it's a bit rich of her to be such a cow when I'd been worrying about being *bitchy* to her… Ha! Oh, and see? I was right when I said she fancies you.' I rub my forehead as there's a headache brewing – must be a drop in air pressure, or something? Or perhaps… 'Can you get me a glass of water, please? Only I'm feeling nauseous…'

'Sure.' He goes to fill a glass. 'By the way, I didn't encourage Angie. I promise I did not.'

My gaze falls on his ringless hand as he passes me the water. 'Do you think these "problems" you've had with Fran, and with Hilary, and now Angie… could it possibly be that you've been giving off an I'm-available vibe by choosing not to wear a wedding ring?' (*I may well be on to something here.*) 'You never did want to wear one, did you?'

'To be fair,' he parries, 'neither did you.'

We both let that sink in.

'I'm serious about us getting married again,' he says into a kitchen whose acoustics appear far too echoey and loud. 'We could have a blessing ceremony or a second wedding – and then we can *both* get rings, and wear them, and show the world how committed we are to each other.'

'Maybe—'

'Just think,' he says, his face lit with enthusiasm. 'Finty would make a gorgeous bridesmaid – she could even dress as a fairy, or ride a rainbow unicorn, I don't mind.' I'm smiling myself, now. 'And we both know how much your mother would love showing off in a swish mother of the bride outfit, don't we? And your father could walk you down the aisle… That would really mend bridges if we can tell them about our wedding plans when we get back. Because, come on, who doesn't love a wedding?' He removes his glasses and pinches his nose. 'Can't we be allowed some happiness? Hasn't enough time passed so we celebrate a joyful occasion, for a change? You could wear white, and we could do the whole thing properly, with a big party, lots of friends, and pork pies – you love pork pies… oh, and vol au vents… and we could really celebrate being alive and being together. What do you say?'

'What would Angie think?'

He puts his glasses back on. 'Stop with the whole Angie thing. I'm marrying *you*, not her.' He leans across the table to kiss me on the lips. 'You haven't answered my question? What do you say?'

'All right, yes. Yes, I do!'

In my mind's eye I imagine myself choosing a dress, and next Gerry has me on my feet, and we're dancing away to imagined tunes, carried away with the romance of it all when yet again, like a spectre at a feast, I'm brought up short. 'Wait,' I say, calling a halt to our imaginary carousing. 'I still won't be comfortable in telling the others right now. Not yet. Is that okay? And then once we're home we can really have fun planning it all ourselves. Just us. And we'll decide when it's be time to share, but for now, please Gerry, can we keep it as our own lovely secret?'

'If you insist,' he says as he moves to the small sofa in the corner, patting the seat next to him for me to come join him, which I do, tucking my leg beneath me. His demeanour becomes all solemn. 'It's not only been you who's felt lost,' he says, so quietly that I have to lean in closer. 'I've been out of my depth right from the start, trying and failing to comfort you… Sometimes,' he says, even quieter, 'it's like I'm right at the bottom of the pile.' It breaks my heart, but in seeing the truth on his face I realise how much I've been focused on myself.

'Not that I've minded,' he continues. 'No, really I haven't, because I've known that yours and Jake's family needs come first, and my role has been more trying to contain things and to keep this holiday on track. But there have been times when I've felt shut out because you, Jake and Angie, are so tight-knit that it's made me feel like an outsider.'

Of course, why haven't I seen this before? It's Gerry who's been holding us together. Gerry who's been the glue, striving to keep everyone happy, and Gerry who's been keeping this holiday on course.

'You've had a lot to put up with, haven't you?'

'Isn't that what love is?'

We both add nothing more, and it's like the whole room, the outside, the sky, the universe, *everything* is holding its breath – finally listening – as if the trees and the stars and the clouds are assembling like woodland creatures venturing into the world after a bad storm.

There comes a knock at the back door, and Gerry flicks me a silent "Who's that?". I answer with a shrug and go to find Martin standing on the doorstep. 'All right?' he says in a cheery yet apologetic way. 'I hope I'm not disturbing, like. Only I saw the lights out back so thought it best *not* to knock on the front door an' wake the whole house.' He shuffles from one foot to the other. 'I'm glad I caught you still up.'

'But how did you know where we were staying?'

'I remembered from when we dropped you off from the Intasun coach, yeah? On the first day? Beside, we all know where you live. Wait – that sounds bad, don't it?' he quickly adds. 'Like we been keeping tags, or stalking you, but we've not. What I mean to say is that me an' Pam know how difficult it must be for you, what with the lad. His wife, Angie, isn't it, she told us all about his motorbike accident and head injury. Sounds bloody awful. Mind you, I say she told us but it's more like Pam got it out of 'er. She'd give the Gestapo a run for their money, would my Pam, but she don't mean nuffin' by it—'

'Sorry, I'm forgetting my manners,' I say, shaking my head and stepping back a little. 'Would you like to come inside, Martin? Both me and my husband are awake.'

'Nah, you're all right. I don't want to disturb you. We just wanted to check you were all right – after leaving the karaoke so sharpish.'

Gerry has now joined me and looks quizzically at Martin who says, 'Sorry, mate, I'd better introduce myself, I'm Martin.' He holds out his hand.

'Gerry. Why don't you come in? I've a couple of beers in the fridge.'

'Like I was saying to your wife, I don't want to intrude – and any case, my Pam'll be wondering where I am. I was about to say to your wife Veronica here, how much we all enjoyed her singing with Jake. Quite the double act, they were.' He grinned and nodded. 'You missed out on a good night there.'

Gerry places a proprietary arm around the small of my back, and Martin is now holding an envelope out to me.

'Oh yeah, afore I forget – I come round,' continues Martin, 'to give you your winnings. Here.' He presses an envelope into my hand. 'Take it. It's five hundred francs for you and your brother. No need to look so surprised, love. Unanimous, it were – oh, and don't you be thinking it was a pity vote or anythin'. You won the competition fair and square. Two of you were the best act by a country mile. Oh, an' afore I forget, I've also got instructions to apologise on behalf of my cousin. He should never 'ave said what he did – I had a good mind to bring him round to apologise himself, but his wife took him back to their holiday place where I'm sure she'll be givin 'im a right old ear-bashin' – serves the bleeder right.' I stare down at the envelope in my hand. 'I'll be off now,' he says and on impulse I reach out to give him a hug and a kiss on the cheek.

'Thank you. For everything.'

'It was nothing. You enjoy the rest of your holiday, or what little is left of it, cos we go back tomorrow, don't we?'

'Yes.'

'See you all on the coach. Now you go back on inside,' he says, 'or you'll catch yer death.'

Side by side, Gerry and I stand and wave goodbye to Martin as he disappears into the night.

'Restores one's faith, doesn't it?' Gerry says as he follows me back into the kitchen. He eyes the envelope. 'Let's have a look?' He watches as we both sit at the kitchen table, and I count the money.

'Five hundred francs,' he says. 'That's not to be sniffed at.'

'It was never about the money,' I say.

'Fair enough. But good of him to take the trouble of delivering your winnings?'

'Gerry?' I say, placing the cash in my handbag.

'Yes?'

'You know what we said about no more secrets?' He's examining my face, expectantly (*which turns out to be quite apt*). 'Only, right... what I'm trying to say is... I might be... that is, I'm I could be...' (deep breath) 'pregnant.' I wait for my statement to sink in – for both of us. 'I'm not sure. But I could be.'

He puts both hands on the table. 'Pregnant? Did you say *pregnant*?' He pushes himself up, nearly knocking the chair over in the process. 'A baby. Hello, baby.' Next, he's kissing my bump and then peering back up at me. 'Wait, but... you've been drinking.' He gives my belly one last kiss and gets back to his feet, although (thankfully) doesn't look cross.

'I'm sure the odd drink won't have hurt,' I say. 'In any case, I've not confirmed it or done the test yet, so I could be wrong. But I have been feeling sick – on and off – and not wanting to drink coffee, and I'd totally forgotten that I missed a period, and I'd forgotten my pill so many times because I couldn't be bothered... Sorry.'

'No, don't be sorry. Wow. I can hardly take this in... If it is true, and you are up the duff, then it's the most fantastic news ever.' He's beaming away at me, and I'm happy at his response. 'Oh, and if you're not preggers then we shall have to start trying for a baby straight away.' He stops, another thought clearly barging in. 'But when did you get pregnant? And how?' It's hardly surprising he's wondering because lately we've hardly been at it like rabbits... not since...

We might not have been having much sex, but there was that date night we treated ourselves to? Last month when Jenny babysat? Do you remember?'

He's staring at me, working out the dates in his head, and then as the penny drops, he appears gobsmacked as if he can't believe I've done something so miraculous. Because it is miraculous, isn't it? Growing a whole other human being inside you?

'I hope you are pregnant!' Gerry does a spin of the kitchen. 'Imagine, a baby. And imagine how excited Finty will be having a baby sister – or a baby brother – to play with, or more like boss around.'

'Our next baby could be a boy, couldn't it? And I don't know how I'll feel about that because it'll be weird if it is a boy. Because what if he looks like Jake did, when he was a baby? What if he's *exactly* like Jake? I don't know if I'm strong enough to cope.'

He holds me away so he can hold my full attention. 'You are the strongest person I know. Ever. So don't go thinking you're not. And don't you ever forget that you are *not* alone and that whatever is worrying you we can face together because we've got each other, right?' He pulls me to him and holds me as I have a little cry. 'Sssh,' he says, drying my eyes and my nose with a tissue he's produced from his pocket.

'You still haven't told me the full story of what happened tonight? Is that what's causing this wobble about expecting a baby?'

I move away from him a little. 'I know we've said we should take no notice of her – but what about Angie? If – or when – I am pregnant? It'll be bad enough when she finds out about the second wedding, but a baby?'

'Ssh. You worry way too much about Angie. Seriously. What I say is, fuck her! That's right, so don't cry. This is about you and me.'

'It's not just that,' I say, brushing him aside and getting to my feet. 'Most of the time it's like I'm dying inside, like my life force is ebbing away, and this wound,' I say, grabbing at my middle, 'won't ever scab over because Jake is a constant reminder of what I've lost.'

'Ron, I know it must be hard—'

'But you don't know!' I snap, turning with a ferocity he doesn't deserve. 'You can't ever know! To think I harboured a stupid thought that this holiday could fix things and that some miracle might happen – fat chance? It's not going to, is it!' I grab the front of my dress and twist it. 'How can I bring a baby into the world when I feel like *this*?'

'We've managed to keep Finty on an even keel, haven't we? Through these difficult months?' Gerry says, but I push him away.

'Have we? Have we got her on an even keel? Don't you think all this atmosphere must be having an effect on her?'

'I guess we've got years of therapy to look forward to, then.' He's clearly trying to lighten the mood. 'Look, you've had a tough night and tomorrow we go home. I promise you that once we're back, we shall concentrate on sorting things; we'll go to the doctor if necessary, book more sessions with Carol and really get things in place.' He goes to touch my shoulder, but I'm still high on adrenaline and there are things I must say, that he must listen to.

'I know Martin was kind coming round to apologise, but you weren't there – ha! The night of our great plan. Oh, it was fine at first,' I say, picturing it all, 'but then it went to shit. A whole bar full of people watching, judging, pitying Jake; it was awful. When I think of how courageous he's been – just staying alive when nobody expected him to live. Only Jake could have survived his injuries because he is special… But these people – people who will never be half the person he was – they called him a "spaz", or a "mong", or a "poor thing", when they aren't half the person he used to be!'

'Ssh, I know. And he still is a good person.'

Tears are streaming down my face. 'Then, just when I think everything's going to be all right – that *he's* going to be all right, that there might be the faintest glimmer of hope that the old Jake is in there somewhere, trying to find a way back to us – he goes and does something so fuckin' *not* Jake.' My hands are balled into fists. 'He only went and *felt up* some woman's tits!'

Gerry almost smiles. 'He didn't, did he?' Then thinking better of it, adds, 'It must have been a mistake on his part, because that doesn't sound like Jake at all, not even as he is now.'

'I wish…' I lift my head and look straight at Gerry. 'In my darkest hours, I do, I really do wish that he *had died*. I know that's a dreadful thing to say.' I'm shaking my head. 'All the doctors expected him to die, you see. Which would of course would have been bloody awful – beyond awful. But then we all could have mourned him, couldn't we? At least we'd have got some sort of closure.' I'm clenching and unclenching my fists now. 'But he didn't die, did he? He didn't die and there is no closure. Instead, we have to carry on tending our wounds, trying to be cheerful, trying to be optimistic. With him serving as a constant reminder of what he once was and what we've lost.'

'You don't mean that,' he's gently saying.

'I never thought I'd say this but – yes – right at this very moment, right now, I do feel it would have been better for *us*, and better for Jake too, if he'd just *died*!'

There it is – out in the open – with me half-expecting the skies to crack and for thunder and lightning to announce the arrival of the wicked fairy, here to claim her prize of the baby I'm carrying.

But nothing. Silence. As if the world is holding its breath. The Earth spins at 600mph so that in that one moment, I've shifted from where I was to a different place. I can feel it. *It's like a judder*, I'm thinking, when I notice Jake standing in the kitchen doorway, having heard most of what I said by the stricken look on his face. I go to step forwards, but he shakes his head, turns steadily on his heel and strides out – not stumbling: not shaking.

'Jake!' I call after him.

Angie wanders into the room, bleary-eyed, as Gerry grabs my arm, trying to stop me running after my brother. 'What the hell's going on?' Angie says. 'I heard raised voices...' She rubs her eyes and scans the room. 'Where's Jake?' As one, we turn in the direction of the villa door as it closes shut, followed by footsteps on the gravel, leading away.

'Jake? Is that Jake? Has Jake gone out?' Angie gives me an enquiring look. 'Where's he going – at this time of night?'

She's in her nightdress, while I've grabbed my coat and bag.

'Gerry?' Angie says, looking from him to me. 'Was that Jake? Where's he going to, do you know?'

'Angie, I'm so sorry,' I say.

'Sorry about what? About what?' She looks to my husband for an explanation.

'It'll be some silliness,' he says.

'I'd better go find him,' Angie says, although she makes no move to leave.

But I know what is to be done, and so does Gerry. He gestures for me to follow my brother.

'Ronnie is going to go find him,' he says slowly to Angie, as if to a child.

'You go,' he mouths to me.

'But…?' Angie looks from me to Gerry, but I'm already half out the door.

'Take the torch,' says my husband. 'Here. Take this blanket too, just in case.'

'Thanks,' I mouth back at him.

As I close the door, I can hear him saying, 'Don't you worry, Ronnie will find him. She'll find him and fetch him back safe.'

I pause at the head of the drive, letting my eyes adjust to the dark as I get my bearings. Jake has a head start on me, but I have a pretty good idea of where he's going.

THIRTY-FIVE

The Aftermath

The streets are full of evening revellers. Seemingly the whole town is out and about on the streets, as I push against a stream of people to-ing and fro-ing back to their holiday homes or staggering on to the next bar.

'Watch out.'

'Oi, darling.'

'Excuse me… sorry… sorry…' I say, over and over. All the while, there's a fluttering in my chest. It reminds me of another time. Another time when I was lost. Lost.

*

Jake and I are six, maybe seven, and we're sitting on the sands of a sunny seaside beach – yes, there we are – our heads craned upwards as we watch a Punch and Judy show – enthralled. Mum and Dad have dropped us off with strict instructions to wait for their return, when they'll buy us both a 99 ice cream for being good.

This time it isn't Brean or even Weston; this time we've travelled further afield down the A39 past the champagne-perry factory at Shepton Mallet (where its Bambi-like and enormous statue of the

Babycham fawn stands proud on top of its building), and driving onwards to our seaside destination, excited, bored, until the first shouts of, 'The sea! I can see the sea!' 'No, I saw it first!' 'No, me!' as we arrive at Weymouth: Jake and I sitting in the back of Dad's Ford Zephyr.

The Punch and Judy show is the seaside attraction we love the best – especially the crocodile and the sausages. Jake and I glance at each other, giggling and fizzing with excitement as we hug our knees. 'Behind you!' we shout, with the rest of the kids. 'Behind you!' as the crocodile creeps up on Mr Punch and steals his sausages. Now the puppet is banging the crocodile on the head with his stick, and we're fully in the moment squealing along with Mr Punch. 'That's the way to do it! That's the way to do it!'

I'm filled with an urge to return to where Mum and Dad have set up camp on the beach. (I can't now remember why we're on our own.) 'That's the way to do it!' shouts Punch again.

As I clamber to my feet, Jake peers up at me. He's wearing navy blue swimming shorts from Woolworths, in some sort of heavy knitted fabric, whilst I have on a one-piece swimming costume – blue with little white flowers – covered in shearing stitching, making it both rumpled and fitting at the same time.

'Wait here!' I order Jake, and he nods his affirmation – I was always the twin in charge (as if you haven't guessed by now). He returns his attention to the show and soon he's laughing away as I set off, barefoot, with the harsh white sand sharp on the soles of my feet. Somehow I find the pathway at the top of the sands furthermost from the sea. It's not really a path, or maybe it was once, but the sand now covers it. It's worn by many feet, much like a trail is trodden through woodland earth and undergrowth. Marram grass snags at my toes, and I wish I'd worn my flipflops. A big dog stops to snarl at me, causing me to jump and then squeal. His owner tugs on the lead as I sidle past. 'Down, Caesar,' the man says.

I'm trying to remember where my parents are as I push through the holidaymakers who seem to be busily going in the opposite direction. It's just past this ice-cream stall, I'm sure of it, but on the other side all I can see is the expanse of flat white sands, covered with beach umbrellas, wind breaks, families in varying stages of sunbathing, picnics being eaten, children squealing and running about, fathers playing cricket with their children on the hard damp sands, kids hand in hand dapping back on their long walk from the sea which is a long way out, and I can't get my bearings.

My stomach feels hollow and I'm scared, and a crashing feeling of being alone and lost in a crowd overwhelms so that soon I'm not the confident young girl striking out on her own anymore, but someone very small and standing on a path alone, unsure which way to go as she's buffeted by the press of people passing by. Eventually, a lady bends down so that her face is level with mine. 'Hello,' she says.

All I can do is look up and try to be brave, but my blubbing has now turned into uncontrollable sobs. Somehow, I nod my head.

'Where's your mummy and daddy?' she asks, beckoning over her husband. I turn my by-now-probably-large-and-certainly-tear-filled eyes towards him. He's stripped to the waist and lobster-red with sunburn, but he has a kind face.

'Poor little mite's lost,' his wife informs him.

'Here,' he says. 'You'd better come along with us, little lady.' And although I've been told not to speak to, or go anywhere near strangers, all I can feel is the kindness of this couple, and I must have trusted them because I took his hand, and the next thing I remember is that I'm inside some sort of large tent with an enclosure, within which various children of differing ages run around. Someone is wiping away my tears. (Later, when this becomes a family story to be trotted out, I discover this is called the Lost Children's Area.)

Suddenly, there's a booming cry. 'Veronica! There you are!' And my big strong daddy has arrived! He lifts me up on to his shoulders and carries me back to the others, the holiday crowd parting to make way as if he's some conquering hero returned from a far-off land.

*

That lost feeling. I used to have nightmares about it. It's back now.

As I stand in the middle of the pavement, I take stock. I know I ought to check that Jake's not sitting in some bar or loitering on the street – but these are cursory checks because I remain convinced that I know where he's gone.

Pushing on through people spilling out on to the walkways, pushing on through the ghosts of two children running on ahead: 'C'mon, you can't catch me...' Playing chase out in our street after dark and before bedtime, camping in the back garden in the summer, eating Jammie Dodgers on the sofa in front of *Doctor Who*, reading under the bedcovers with a torch... and then the two children are teens, strolling again, giving the other a shove as they walk inside Stoke Bishop Youth Club, where friends beckon them over to play pool or dance to singles turned on a Dansette record player. A Mini passes me in the street: 'C'mon, get in,' I shout as there I am, in my own white Mini Cooper, skirt high up my thighs, pulling up alongside Jake. I lean through the open door: 'C'mon, get in,' and... there we are, dancing to Jimmy Mack on the floor of Bristol's Locarno Disco.

Tears streak my face as I stride faster, on to my twenty-first birthday party thrown in my flat in Bristol, not expecting Jake as he's at uni in Bognor, and then there he is – surprise! – roaring up on his motorbike, and I have far too much to drink and pass out, and Jake carries me up the stairs to my bed where he places a drink of water by my side and a kiss on my forehead: 'You muppet!'

I've reached the turning for the beach now, and I'm hurrying along the path like I once hurried along the sands at Bognor where Jake was at college – and Angie stood on the prom, waiting, watching, and I'm running away from her, after Jake who's at the shoreline and who turns at my approach and says, 'I'm always here. You know that.' He smiles, dimples deepening. And there he is, holding my newborn baby in those big hands which I know will never drop her. Because once we kicked and stretched and turned together in our own briny seas until expelled out into the world.

Jake! Where the fuck are you?

I'm on the beach. Sand dunes.

Jake! Jake! I call in my head, running my fingers through my hair as I cast about, seeing if I can spot him. No. The moon glows its dim wattage, barely helping to light my approach to the bank of dunes. It's sheltered here as I begin to scrabble up the side of the closest dune, finally gaining purchase on sand not fully cooled by the deepening chill of the night.

Once I reach the top, I may be able to see him. Brushing the sand from my palms I stand slightly unsteady on the crest, feet sinking into the dune. A brisk breeze reaches my nostrils carrying smells of deep unknowable oceans, shipwrecks and clammy weeds. Where is he?

Over that hump, there, I'm sure will be the remnants of that small campfire where those teens had earlier gathered to sing and to snog and to dance and drink beer. More from instinct, I let myself be pulled in that direction, heading sideways to the beach as I clamber up and down – blowing hard now – he must be here – my open-toed sandals burying in the damp sand: every now and then I wince as a blade of marram grass catches in between my toes. Using my body for balance I lean backwards as I stride down into a dip, feet gaining purchase to halt the slide, calves working, and then up and over another dune, and another, all the time headed for the fire which I've glimpsed up ahead which has not fully gone out.

He's in the lee of one of the dunes, facing the ocean and the campfire. He's sitting so still that any passing walker would surely miss him. He looks up to where I'm silhouetted against the sky at the apex of the dune: I go to wave, but already he's turned his head back to resume his staring out to sea. I slither down the dune in *Ice Cold in Alex* style. How we once loved that film. What a shame I don't have a couple of cold beers with me now, and we could drink a toast to... what?

'There you are,' I say unnecessarily as I make the base of the dune.

'Here I am,' he answers but doesn't look my way.

'I'm...' I start.

Finally, he turns his head.

'I didn't mean what I said earlier... You know, about the whole wishing you had died. I was only mouthing off. You mean more to me than—'

'I know,' he says, fixing me with his cock-eyed stare.

Did we even say those words out loud? I'm not sure. The cool sands give slightly to mould around my seat as I take my place beside him and lower the rucksack to the ground. I reach my arm about his shoulders: they're surprisingly thin and bony and as unyielding as the white cuttlefish Mum would buy for her budgie. Poor Billy who escaped when she left the window open. Through Jake's thin shirt I can feel his wing-like scapulae, reminding me of the young Icarus who flew too high to the sun. Foolish boy. 'Here.' I open my rucksack and pull out the blanket Gerry gave me. 'You're freezing.' I huddle close to him and place it around the two of us.

'Snug as a bug in a rug,' he says, smiling at me now. I can't fully see his face, but I can feel him. He's my Jake. Oh, he may be changed or damaged or what-have-you, and we may not be together for ever as we once pledged as kids, but for now this will do. The two of us, sitting side by side, huddled up against whatever might come.

'Life, Ron,' he says. 'Life.'

Overhead, the sky is high like the glass of a snow dome, not studded with snow but with tiny specks of stars struggling to shine their pinpricks of sharp light through clumps of cloud. The sounds of laughter and carousing from the town whip past our ears, making no impact as what I can hear is the rush of the wind, the shushing of the seas, the whispers of planets turning and of solar systems suspended up high. We sit inside this domed theatre, the sand a darker orange at night, spreading towards an inky blue sea with its white washes of waves leisurely creeping to shore. The sand under my fingers, as light as that of an egg-timer. Sands of time, the pulverised debris of pods of whales, of dragons and sea monsters, Spanish galleons and Viking longboats, and whole civilisations devoured by waters which don't care. I wonder if some of Atlantis may wash up on this shore? Or Mount Olympus, where the gods once tormented mortals here on Earth?

Next to me, Jake sighs, and it's as if we can see his breath float away as together we lift our heads to track its progress as it's caught by a soft summer breeze which will carry it off to who knows where. Perhaps, if it's South America, a butterfly will flap its wings in response?

There's something about a beach. Even in the lee of this dune there's the feel of the sea's chill breath as it sweeps across the shore, as the winds and tides cleanse all before them, making the world anew as each day, each moment, seas and sands shift, and nothing ever stays the same. Even the dunes, which look the same, are constantly on the move with their own rhythmic flows synchronised to the tides and winds and the pull of stars and planets. Permanent and impermanent: the perfect conundrum.

Because we are nothing, are we?

'No,' he says, and leans his head on my shoulder.

Sitting side by side are two children – they're people now. Once they turned together to their own rhythms in their own briny seas, until one of them threatened to beach too soon. The planet turns and holds them both. It is not yet time.

Author's Note

I hope you enjoyed Jake and his sister's story. In common with Ronnie, my own brother suffered brain damage following a freak motorbike accident. Over the years I've had several goes at writing this story as memoir but felt constrained by what family members might say. Eventually I gained enough distance to turn our story into fiction, and although my lived experiences may have breathed life into Ronnie's tale, this is her story and not mine, any similarities are purely co-incidental. All characters in *Only Hummingbirds* are fictional, as is the French town, and what happened during Ronnie and Jake's family holiday.

I hope I've shown Jake's disability in an authentic and relatable way plus highlighting the fact that disabilities disable whole families. My own overriding emotions, after the initial shock, were bafflement and discombobulation. I'd like to say the novel was cathartic, but only in parts. I remain mostly baffled. This story of twins is a mix of Ronnie and Jake, of Brittany and Britain, of reality and fantasy.

There's a wonderful Japanese art form called *Kintsugi,* where the cracks of a treasured broken artefact are filled with gold, re-transforming it into a thing of beauty. Some talk of how it's the very cracks and the breaks we suffer in life which allow the light in. Those who've suffered loss of a loved one via brain damage may agree, some may not, I suspect it's a mixture and dependant on how our day is going.

I've not offered up any answers, if anything this novel posits questions on the nature of love, of guilt, on what makes us human, and how a split second can fracture one's universe. My Ronnie and Jake exist somewhere separate from me, living their own lives, experiencing their own different and difficult choices. I tip my hat to them, aware of the privilege it has been to walk alongside the two of them, if only for a while.

Acknowledgments

I owe many thanks to my first agent Maggie Noach (sadly no longer with us), who believed in this novel and with whom I shared many a laugh over enormous glasses of wine, as we swapped tales of our disastrous love lives. On publication day, I shall raise a glass in honour of her memory.

Thank you to my daughters who have put up with my frustrations, my moaning, and my rubbish mothering – particularly on bringing this story to the page.

Thanks are due to the anonymous reader from the New Writers Scheme at the Romantic Novelists' Association, who inspired me by voicing her certainty that this novel will find a publisher – soon. A few years later and – look – it has!

Finally, thanks to all my writer friends, especially Lola Jaye, Julie Cohen, and Jane Purcell.

If my brother could read this novel, I'm certain he'd enjoy it and not mind the liberties I've taken. He'd stop to admire himself in a mirror first and run a comb through his hair. Love you always bruv.